# College life 301;

## Junior Seminar

J.B. Vample

Book Five

The College life series

COLLEGE LIFE 301-JUNIOR SEMINAR

Copyright © 2017 by Jessyca B. Vample

Printed in the United States of America

First Printing, 2017

ISBN-10: 0-9969817-9-9 (eBook edition)
ISBN-13: 978-0-9969817-9-8 (eBook edition)

ISBN-10: 0-9969817-8-0 (Paperback edition)
ISBN-13: 978-0-9969817-8-1 (Paperback edition)

For information contact; email: JBVample@yahoo.com

Website: www.jbvample.com

Book cover design by: Najla Qamber Designs

This is a work of fiction. Names, characters, places and incidents are either the product of the author's imagination or are used fictitiously, and any resemblance to actual persons, living or dead, business establishments, events or locales is entirely coincidental.

Thank you to the readers who continue to not only follow my characters' journey, but my journey as well.

My readers' rock!

# Chapter 1

"Daddy, how many more bags do I have in the car?" Emily Harris asked, placing a suitcase in the entry way of her new living quarters.

"Just two more, and I still have to grab your TV," Mr. Harris answered from the front step. Emily smiled; it had been three weeks since she moved out of her mother's home in New Jersey to go live with her father in North Carolina. For the first time since she'd begun college, Emily returned to school to start her junior year of Paradise Valley University feeling like a huge weight had been lifted off her shoulders.

Emily looked around as her father brought the remainder of her things in. *This is ten times better than that lonely apartment*, she thought, pushing her straight, sandy brown hair, which almost fell to her shoulders, behind her ears.

The clusters was a housing complex that Emily knew well. She'd visited a few times her first two years, and now, she was living in them. The three bedroom, two bath mini home, equipped with living room, kitchen, and dining area was a huge step up from her drab, small apartment that she was forced to live in her sophomore year.

Running upstairs with her roommate assignment card in hand, Emily eagerly knocked on the door to room number three. The door opened and Emily smiled a bright smile. "Hi," she beamed to her new roommate.

"Emily, I love you, but I can't do this with you. I can't be your roommate," Malajia Simmons rudely retuned as Emily moved in for a hug.

"Malajia, that's so mean," Emily giggled.

"I'm sorry, you already knew this shit wasn't gonna fly," Malajia replied, fanning herself with her room assignment card.

Misplacing her room assignment mail that had arrived at her home over summer break, Malajia went straight to the housing office upon returning to school earlier that morning. Her mood went from happiness to learn that she was assigned to a cluster, to horror when she learned that her new roommate was none other than Emily Harris.

Pushing her straight, burgundy-streaked, long tresses over her shoulder, Malajia darted across the hall to room number two and kicked open the door, which was easy since the door was already cracked.

"Girl! Are you out of your damn mind?" Sidra Howard hollered, spinning around as the door slammed against the wall.

"Shut up. Listen, one of y'all trade me rooms," Malajia demanded. "I'm not living with Emily."

"Girl, nobody is trading you. Stop being rude." Sidra waved her hand dismissively at Malajia before greeting Emily, who had walked into the room, with a hug.

"Look here damn it, I'm not playing," Malajia grunted. "Either *you* or your *roommate* is getting out of this room, Sidra."

"Malajia, I'm standing right *here*," Emily reminded.

Malajia shot her a confused look. "*And?*" she barked. "I mean, you're my girl and all, but you know you're boring." Malajia's blunt response made Emily shake her head.

Before Sidra could scold Malajia, she saw her roommate heading up the steps. "Why is your friend over here trying to get us to trade rooms with her?" she asked.

"Because she's a fool," Alex Chisolm answered, plunking a large plastic container on the floor. "Malajia, stop being rude."

"That's what *I* just said to her," Sidra giggled, adjusting the collar on her blouse.

Malajia sucked her teeth, then grabbed Alex's container. "Y'all think I'm playing," she muttered, dragging it across the hall. "I'm not rooming with no damn Emily." She gave the container a kick into her room.

"What the hell are you doing?!" Alex exclaimed, hands on her voluptuous hips.

Malajia walked back across the hall, dragging one of her suitcases. "I'm moving your dusty crap into your new room," she informed, nonchalant. "Y'all got me chopped."

Alex shook her head then put her hands up. "You know what, *fine* Malajia, damn." Grabbing the remainder of her bags, she headed for the door. "Come on Em, *I'll* be your roommate... She's messy *anyway.*"

Emily followed Alex out of the room, as Malajia did a dance in a circle.

Sidra stared at the scene for several seconds. "So now you're going to be getting on *my* damn nerves," she fussed, slamming a shirt on her bed.

"Nah, I'm a fun roommate," Malajia boasted, pulling her mini skirt down. She looked across the room. "Why does *this* room have bunkbeds?" she ground out.

"You're *just* noticing them?" Sidra asked, tone smart.

"Don't ask me no damn questions, just figure out how we're gonna pull them things apart," Malajia threw back, shaking her hand in Sidra's direction. "I'm not sleeping on another top bunk. I had enough of that shit freshman year."

Sidra sighed. *This is going to be a long semester.* "Fine," she said. "I'll call Josh and David over to do it for us. They're back already."

Malajia flung her hair over her shoulder and skipped across the hall to grab more of her things. She was greeted by a coat hitting her chest. "Real mature, Alex."

"Yeah? Hurry up and get *your* dusty crap out of *my* room," Alex shot back.

"Shut up and give me my damn makeup that I left in there," Malajia demanded. "I don't need you tryna use up my shit."

Alex grabbed Malajia's makeup case from the dresser. "Even if I *wanted* to use that mess, I *can't*," Alex ground out, pushing the case in Malajia's hands. "I'm like two shades *darker* than you."

Ignoring Alex, Malajia tossed the coat into her room. Then slid the makeup case in after it.

"Hey, come put this stuff up!" Sidra yelled.

"I'll do it later! Don't start that neat-freak bullshit," Malajia yelled back, heading down the stairs. Crossing the kitchen floor, she reached room number one and gave the door a loud bang.

"Open up, open, open, open!" she hollered, banging repeatedly. The door snatched open and Malajia threw her arms out.

"I was hoping that my being quiet would make you think that I wasn't here," Chasity Parker sneered.

"Your car is outside, fool," Malajia ground out as Chasity walked over to her desk.

"That doesn't mean that I couldn't still be *out*, *dumbass*," Chasity threw back. "I just talked to you earlier, what do you want?"

Malajia waved her hand dismissively. "What I *always* want, cranky. To bug you." she jeered. Sitting on Chasity's bed, she looked at the suitcases and bags on the floor. "Damn, I almost forgot about how much shit you have," she chuckled. "Where is your new roommate gonna put *her* stuff? ...I bet you the heffa won't be as fun as *me*."

Chasity smirked at Malajia's sour face. "Still mad you got Emily, huh?"

"*I* ain't got no damn Emily. I threw *Alex's* big ass right in that room with her," Malajia boasted, examining her manicured nails. She liked the way the burgundy polish complemented her brown skin. "*Princess Ponytail* is my roommate now... I would've kicked *your* roommate out, but I don't know the chick, so I can't threaten her just yet."

Chasity placed a jewelry box on her dresser. "I don't have a roommate this year," she revealed, much to Malajia's surprise.

"Bullshit," Malajia countered. "There're *no* single rooms in the clusters unless you're an RA and your evil ass ain't *nobody's* resident advisor."

Chasity was unfazed by Malajia's attitude. "According to the office, the girl that was supposed to be in here decided not to come back at the last minute," she revealed. "So, I have my own room."

Malajia stomped her foot on the floor. "That is *so* not fair!"

"Oh yes the hell it *is*," Chasity argued. "I've been cheated out of my own room for *two* years. Shit, it's about damn time."

Malajia sucked her teeth as she stood from the bed. She stuck her hand through an open door and turned the light on. "And you got your own *bathroom*?" she observed. "Fuck Sidra, I'mma go get my stuff and bring it in here."

"Malajia, I just got back, please don't make me drop kick you already," Chasity warned, as Malajia ran for the door.

Malajia stopped and spun around. "Sooo, I *can't* move in here with you is what you're saying?" she asked.

Her hazel eyes flashing, Chasity pointed to the door.

Malajia sucked her teeth. "Oh come on, I can keep you warm when Jason's not here," she joked.

"Get out!" Chasity yelled, inciting laughter from Malajia.

Malajia walked out of the room, then immediately darted back in. "Hey—"

"Girl, I said get out!" Chasity barked.

"Calm your light ass down," Malajia hissed, referencing Chasity's light brown complexion. "Who's that man bringing stuff in?" she pointed to the man in question.

Curious, Chasity walked out along with Malajia. They watched the tall, brown skin, distinguished man carry bags up the steps. "Hell if *I* know," Chasity shrugged.

"He's cute, with his old self," Malajia mused, prompting a side-glance from Chasity.

Emily ran down the steps, followed by the other girls. Emily skipped over and gave Chasity a hug.

"Yay, we're all living together," Emily gushed.

Chasity shrugged Emily off of her. "Don't start your corny shit."

Emily chuckled, then signaled for her father, who came back downstairs, to come over. "Daddy, I want to introduce you to my friends."

A warm smile on his face, Mr. Harris walked over and shook each girl's hand. "It's nice to finally meet you ladies. I've heard great things about you."

"Thank you, you fine a—"

Malajia's inappropriate compliment was halted by Alex nudging her. "Nice to finally meet you too, Mr. Harris," Alex put in.

"Well, I'm going to run to the campus diner to grab something to eat, do you ladies want anything?" he offered.

"No thanks," they collectively answered.

"Uh, Miss Harris, how does your mother feel about your father dropping you off and not *her*?" Sidra asked once Mr. Harris was out of the door. She, like the other girls, knew how possessive Emily's mother was when it came to her. Not only did she drop Emily off herself each semester, she even unpacked for her and stayed the night.

Emily pushed some hair behind her ear. "I'm sure she's not happy about it...especially since I moved out of her house a few weeks ago."

The look on the girls' faces were of complete shock.

"Say *what* now?" Chasity charged.

"Wait, you moved out?" Malajia followed up.

Emily nodded. "Yes. I live in North Carolina with my

dad now."

"Why didn't you say anything *before*?" Alex asked. She had spoken to Emily several times over the past weeks before returning to school, and Emily had neglected to mention that.

"Well, I don't know. I guess I was still trying to come to terms with everything," Emily admitted. "My mom is really mad. She hasn't spoken to me at all."

"Count your blessings," Chasity mumbled, causing Alex to shoot her a glare.

"We're proud of you sweetie," Sidra slid in, giving Emily's shoulder a slight rub. "You finally took a stand and you'll be better for it,"

Emily smiled. She knew that Sidra was right. Maybe her mother would come around one day or maybe she wouldn't. Either way, Emily knew that she couldn't focus on that, especially if she wanted to pull her grades up far enough to be removed from academic probation.

"So, wait a minute," Malajia began, grabbing everyone's attention. "Emily, your mom won't be bringing her miserable ass around here this semester?"

"Seriously Malajia?!" Alex exclaimed. It never ceased to amaze her how inappropriate Malajia could be at times.

"What? I'm just asking," Malajia explained, defensive.

Emily sighed. "Yes, that's correct Malajia."

Malajia let out a squeal of delight as she jumped up and down. "Yeeeesssss! Time to celebrate. Let's go get some drinks," she bellowed. "Chaz, drive me to the liquor store."

Without responding, Chasity shook her head and walked into her room, shutting the door on everyone standing there.

"First you stingy with your room, and now you stingy with your car?!" Malajia shouted through the door. "Forget you bitch!" Malajia then took off running for the steps when Chasity snatched the door back open, chasing her.

"Malajia, stop messing with her!" Alex yelled after them, laughter in her voice.

Sidra shook her head when she heard Malajia scream from upstairs. "God, why does her voice have to carry so damn far?" she griped.

Plopping down on an accent chair in the living room, Mark Johnson reached for the TV remote. "Shit, now that y'all have this kitchen, I'm coming off the meal plan," he declared.

Later that evening, after unpacking their belongings, and heading to the grocery store, the girls decided to call the guys over and make dinner.

Sidra frowned. "What do you mean *y'all?*" she questioned, voiced laced with disdain. "You guys have a kitchen in *your* cluster too."

"Sid, you know none of us guys know how to cook," Mark stated, flipping through channels.

"*Jason* does," Chasity slid in from the kitchen.

*Damn it*, Jason Adams thought, shooting his girlfriend a glare. His look was met by a sly smile from Chasity.

"Yes! My roommate can cook!" Mark boasted, holding his hand up to give Jason a high five. "High five for home-cooked meals."

Jason stared at the silly look on Mark's face for several seconds before turning his attention to David Summers and Josh Hampton. "One of y'all *please* switch rooms with me," he begged. "Please, I'll throw in my stereo."

"Sorry Jase. I've already been through that. It's *your* turn," David teased, opening a can of soda.

"Damn it," Jason groaned, grabbing his drink from the floor.

Alex approached Chasity, who was standing over the stove stirring beef strips, green peppers and onions in a pan. She waved a ten-dollar bill in Chasity's face.

"Alex, I already told you to go head with that raggedy ten dollars," Chasity snapped.

"What's wrong with you?" Alex frowned. "I'm just trying to contribute to some of the food that was bought today," she explained.

Chasity frowned at her. "What, you think I spent twenty dollars?" she sneered. "You forgot that fast that I spent *a hundred and fifty* dollars on food for this house. What is *ten* dollars gonna do? Nothing but piss me the hell off... Put it away."

"Hey, Miss take-all-the-damn-credit, *you're* not the only one who spent money on stuff for this house," Malajia put in from the couch in the living room. "*I* bought all these wine coolers."

"Girl, stop lying," Alex snarled. "You bought *one* wine cooler. Sidra gave you the money for the *rest* of them."

Malajia opened her drink, sucking her teeth in the process. "Stay out my goddamn business, Alex."

"I don't even know *why* I offered to pay for those drinks," Sidra said, running her hand over her long, straight ponytail. "I'm just going to pay for it later. Her drunk behind will be getting on my nerves all night."

Malajia titled her bottle in Sidra's direction. "You know me *so* well, ponytail," she teased.

Alex shook her head, then turned her attention back to Chasity. Still holding up the bill. "Anyway, here."

Chasity slammed her spoon on the edge of the pan. "Alexandra, I will fuckin' shred that ten-dollar bill and put it in your damn fajita," she warned. "Get the hell away from me."

Alex sighed. "Fine. Don't say I didn't offer." She shoved the money into the back pocket of her jeans.

"All you offer is ten bucks? You could've kept that to yourself," Malajia quipped. "You see me? I never offer *anything*. Chaz's rich ass is just gonna pay for it *anyway*."

Annoyed both by Malajia's comment and by the laughter resonated around the room, Chasity grabbed the plate of food that Malajia sat aside earlier. "Mark, here," she said.

"Bet!" Mark bellowed, running for the plate.

"That's mine!" Malajia exclaimed. "That has the chicken. He was supposed to wait for the *beef* ones."

"Now he's eating *yours*," Chasity hissed.

Mark started dancing while taking a big bite out of Malajia's food. "Ahhh, you gotta wait now."

Malajia stared daggers at Mark. "That's why I dug in my nose before I made it, you dusty roach," she jeered.

Sidra busted out laughing so hard at Malajia's insult that her brown face turned red. "Oh my God Malajia, that's terrible."

Mark glanced at Sidra as she continued to laugh. "It's so terrible, but your ass is laughing real hard over there," he bit out.

"I didn't say it wasn't *funny*," Sidra threw back, wiping a tear from her eye.

Mark rolled his eyes, then focused his attention on Malajia, who was frowning at him. "I *still* got your food," he boasted, eating.

Angry, Malajia turned back around in her seat. "She gonna make me another one," she grunted of Chasity, taking a sip from her bottle.

"Bet money I *don't*," Chasity challenged.

Emily stood up, giggling. "Aww Malajia, I'll fix you another one."

"Emily, if you come over here I'm gonna throw *yours* in the trash," Chasity sneered, halting Emily's progress to the kitchen. "Go sit your happy ass back down."

Not wanting her food to suffer a worse fate than Malajia's, Emily quickly turned and made a beeline back to her seat at the dining room table. "Sorry Malajia, but I'm hungry," she teased.

"Don't worry about it Emily." Malajia waved her hand. "I'mma feed *hers* to those frogs that be outside in the grass."

"Ooh, we have frogs in our grass?" Alex beamed, running for the door.

"Whatchu' gonna do, *eat* em?" Malajia ground out. Laughter erupted around her. Alex was not amused. "Sit your big ass down and leave them damn amphibians alone."

Fed up with Malajia's mouth, Alex tossed a throw pillow at her.

# Chapter 2

"No not the weave, not the weave," Malajia pleaded, quickly opening the door and darting in the house to escape the pouring rain. She had hoped that she could run to pick up her class schedule from the registrar office before the rain started, but she wasn't that lucky.

Snatching off her wet, high heeled sandals, she hurried up the steps to the bathroom. "Damn rain is disrespectful."

Reaching in the cabinet under the sink for her hair dryer, Malajia caught a glimpse of herself in the mirror. "Oh shit!" she exclaimed, noticing that her red and black bra was visible through her soaked white tank top. She shrugged after a moment. "Well, at least it's a cute bra," she mused to herself.

Cutting on the blow dryer, she began the process of blow drying her sewn in extensions. If having to use her half-broken hair dryer wasn't annoying enough, hearing a knock on the door nearly made her curse. Groaning, she hurried down the stairs.

"Which one of y'all heffa's forgot your key?" Her agitation changed to nervousness once she saw who was standing on the other side of the door. "Ty—Tyrone?"

"What's up Malajia?" Tyrone Edmonds replied. Not bothering to wait for an invitation, he walked into the house, a flat package in his hand.

Moving towards the steps, Malajia folded her arms to her chest. "What are you doing here?" she asked, voice not hiding her disdain. "How did you find out where I live?"

"Come on Malajia, damn near everyone on this campus knows who you are," Tyrone grunted. "All I had to do was ask."

"Well, you might as well forget that you know, because you're not welcome here," she hissed, then backed up slightly when he took a step towards her.

"What the hell is wrong with you? I haven't seen you or spoken to you in *weeks*." Seeing her back up, Tyrone stopped his approach towards her. "I go through all of this trouble to come see you and you act like *this*?"

Malajia's eyes widened. "Do you *blame* me after what you did?"

Tyrone rolled his eyes. "Malajia, come on. That was weeks ago and I already said that I was sorry."

"Tyrone, you *hit* me!" she yelled. "You slapped me like I was some bitch that owed you money. And now you expect me to just accept your apology?"

Tyrone ran his hand over his low-cut hair. "Okay, I shouldn't have hit you," he admitted. "But you knew you were wrong for letting that damn Mark take your phone."

Malajia stared at him in disbelief. She couldn't believe how nonchalant he was acting over what he had done to her. "He only took my phone and argued with you because he heard me tell you not to call me a bitch."

"I *told* you I didn't want you hanging out with him!" his loud voice boomed throughout the empty house.

"It was my damn birthday and he's my *friend*!" she yelled back. "I didn't know he was even *going* to New York. Hell, *I* didn't know that I was going for a party for me. If I *did*, then I would've invited you. I wasn't trying to hide anything from you."

Malajia spent days after her and Alex's surprise birthday celebration in New York dreading the face to face conversation that she and Tyrone would eventually have.

After several harsh text messages and bitter phone calls, she finally saw him when he requested that she take the train to Virginia to meet him. His initial cheerful reaction changed to jealous rage when he brought up her birthday. Angry that he wasn't invited and even more angry that Mark was there celebrating *with* her, he lost his temper and slapped her across the face when she accused him of being jealous. Completely shocked and terrified, Malajia fled his apartment and hopped on the next train back to Baltimore. She hadn't seen or spoken to him since.

"Okay babe… Maybe I overreacted."

Malajia was baffled, and it showed on her face. "*Maybe? Maybe* you overreacted?" she snapped. She stepped further back when he took more steps towards her. Her back was now touching the wall; Malajia shut her eyes tight as he came within inches of her face.

Staring at her intensely, Tyrone stroked her cheek with the back of his hand. She resisted the urge to smack his hand away. On one hand, she was furious at him. But on the other, she missed his touch.

"Listen, I know that I hurt you and for that, I'm sorry," he apologized. "I should've *never* hit this beautiful face and I promise I will *never* do that again."

A few tears fell from Malajia's eyes as Tyrone pulled her to him, wrapping his muscular arms around her. Malajia was still and silent. Both when he hugged her and when he finally released her.

"Can I take you out to lunch or something? You know, as a peace offering?" Tyrone asked, wiping the tears from her face.

"I—I can't. I have a bunch of stuff to do before I start classes on Monday," she quietly replied, pushing hair behind her ear.

"Okay… Can I see you later this week then?" he pressed.

She could do nothing but nod.

Tyrone breathed a sigh of relief. "Oh, I brought you a

late birthday gift," he said, handing her the package.

Malajia couldn't get any words out, she just stared at it.

"Here, let me show you," he persisted, opening the box.

Malajia stared at the hand mirror that he pulled from the box. The silver rectangular mirror with a stem, looked a little like an antique, and looked a bit heavy.

Tyrone smiled, holding it in front of her. "When I saw it, I thought of you," he said. "You know how you're always in your mirror." His attempt at a joke received no reaction from Malajia. He cleared his throat. "Anyway... I hope that you like it."

Malajia finally took the mirror from Tyrone's hands. He gave her a quick kiss on the cheek then walked out.

Malajia let out a long sigh, as if she had been holding her breath the entire time. Not knowing what to think or how to feel, she could do nothing but put a hand over her face and sob quietly. Hearing chatter outside of the door, followed by a key jiggling, snapped her out of her tears. She quickly rubbed her eyes and hurried up the steps.

"Mark, you're so greedy, go home!" Sidra yelled with amusement, opening the front door.

"Come on, I know y'all got food!" Mark shouted back from across the pathway.

"Sidra, shut the door, because if he comes in here we'll never get his ass out," Chasity chimed in, walking through the door.

"I heard that," Mark said as Sidra shut the door, giggling.

"He's such a moron," Chasity scoffed, snapping her umbrella shut.

"Yeah I know. That's my brother though," Sidra mused, heading for the steps. "Hey, are you taking any calculus classes this semester?"

"Don't ever say calculus to me again," Chasity jeered, remembering all the trouble she went through just to pass those three calculus classes.

Sidra giggled. "Sorry. If you were, I just thought that

you could help me pass," she replied, adjusting her purse on her shoulder. "I already know that I'm going to need help,"
"Which one do you have?"
"Calc 1," Sidra answered.
Opening her room door, Chasity shook her head. "I don't even know why I asked you, as if I could actually help you," she said. "I don't remember any of that shit. You better ask Jason to help you."
Sidra sighed. "Very well. See you later." She headed up the steps and stopped short of entering her bedroom, to see Malajia blow drying her hair in the bathroom. "Got caught out there without an umbrella huh?"
"Yeah," Malajia answered, turning the dryer off. "My dryer is acting stupid; can I use yours?"
"Sure, it should be under the sink in the back." As Malajia reached for the other dryer, Sidra raised an eyebrow, something with Malajia was off. "I'm surprised you actually *asked* me to use it. You normally just *take* stuff."
"Just trying to be respectful," Malajia's tone was dry, even.
"Okay, now I *know* something is up with you," Sidra concluded, folding her arms. "Is everything okay?"
Combing her hair, Malajia held a blank expression. *No, I'm not.* "Yeah, I'm good," she lied. "Just salty because I got caught in the rain. Don't want my dye to run."
Sidra stared at Malajia for seconds, not sure whether to believe her or not. "Oh, okay," she finally answered before heading for their room. Leaving Malajia alone.
Leaning over the sink, Malajia gripped the sides and let out a long sigh.


Alex folded her class schedule and placed it in the back pocket of her jeans. "What did they say about your academic probation?" she asked Emily, who was walking along side of her.
Sighing, Emily adjusted her pocketbook on her shoulder.

"I have to bring my grade point average up to a 2.0 by the end of this semester," she informed.

Emily and Alex meandered through groups of students after leaving the registrar's office. The rain had finally stopped and the sun began to peak through the clouds, which was a relief for the girls as the walk back to their little house was a long one.

"Well that doesn't sound too bad," Alex placated. "As long as you focus, you'll be able to do it."

"Yeah, I know. But I shouldn't have allowed myself to be put in this situation in the *first* place," Emily sulked. "I'm so mad at myself."

"Em, *everyone* falls at one point in time," Alex consoled. "The good thing is that you're willing to pick yourself up and start over. You'll do fine."

Looking down at her cell phone, Emily gave a slight smile.

Alex glanced at her. "As nice as your new phone is, you've looked at it three times before we even stepped *foot* in the office," Alex observed. "Now you're checking *again*... You waiting for your mom to call?"

"Yeah," Emily replied, tone sullen. "Don't get me wrong, I know that I made the right decision in leaving her house, but..." Emily searched for the words. "I guess I didn't think that she would *actually* not talk to me because of it."

Hopping over a puddle, Alex tried to think of something encouraging to say to Emily. She herself wasn't surprised at Ms. Harris's reaction. The woman was known for throwing a temper tantrum when her daughter didn't do what she wanted her to do. However, Alex didn't want to upset Emily more by telling her that. "Why don't you try calling her again," she suggested finally.

Emily shrugged, then dialed. *Here goes nothing.* Both girls waited in silence as the phone rang several times before going to voicemail, "Well, that's that," she muttered, hanging up.

Alex watched Emily toss her phone in her purse. "You

not going to leave a message?"

"I left a bunch of messages over the past few days," Emily admitted, agitated. "I'm not leaving another one."

Alex put her arm around Emily. "Don't worry sis, she'll come around."

"Yeah maybe," Emily sighed.


"Damn Jason, your place seems to be the *popular* one," Sidra mused, stepping foot into his cluster house.

"Yeah, I know right," Jason agreed, opening a can of soda. "We haven't been here a whole week yet, and *already* everyone knows where I live."

A party in the clusters on the Saturday before classes were to begin was an upperclassmen tradition at Paradise Valley University. Having the houses placed at the end of the campus made it easy for students to drink and throw parties outside, without campus security hovering.

Even though numerous students were piled into several of the houses in Jason's cluster, *his* house seemed to be the most popular. Being the school's star football player, it wasn't surprising.

"It's going to be rowdy in here all the time," Alex put in, amused. "David isn't going to like this *at all*. You know how much he likes the quiet, *especially* when he has to study."

"There is *never* any quiet with Mark around," Jason jeered, taking a sip of his beverage.

Sidra giggled, "Still annoyed that you got him as your roommate this year, huh?"

"Sid, I tell you, every damn day I'm trying not to kill that dude," Jason complained. "He's loud for no freakin' reason *and* he keeps bugging me to cook all the time. I'm not his damn mom."

Placing her arm around Jason, Sidra looked at him sympathetically. "Tough break, sweetie."

"Yeah, well Josh and David don't have it any better," Jason stated. "They may live upstairs, but Mark doesn't hesitate to run up there bugging them all the time."

Alex laughed, "What do your other housemates say about him?"

"They don't pay him any mind," Jason laughed back.

Alex and Sidra made their way back outside to mingle with other people in the commons area. Jason leaned against the wall, taking another sip of his drink while he bobbed his head to the music that was blaring through the stereo. Hearing Mark's loud voice over the music, Jason rolled his eyes.

"Jase!" Mark bellowed.

"What?" Jason hissed.

"Yo, you gonna make this taco salad?" Mark asked, holding up a pack of ground beef.

Jason shot him a glare. "Dawg I'm not making that. I told you, I'm not cooking anything," he bit out, annoyed. "You better eat those chips and leave me alone."

"I'll just ask you later," Mark resolved after a few seconds of staring at Jason with a dumb expression, completely ignoring his protest.

Jason threw his hands up in the air in frustration as a female guest approached him.

"Hey Jason, where are the cups?" the curvy, dark skinned girl asked him.

"In the kitchen, where you just came from," Jason stated, pointing in that direction.

Flicking her long faux dreadlocks over her shoulder, she giggled. "How about you come over and show me exactly where they are?" she proposed, striking a seductive pose.

Jason shook his head. *Just go away*, he thought. Being a tall, handsome man, Jason was used to being flirted with. That didn't mean that he liked that type of attention all the time. "How about no, and you go find them yourself," he replied.

The girl was about to say something else, when Jason looked behind her and smiled. *And there she is*, he thought, seeing Chasity approach. "You may wanna go get that cup," he warned.

"Come on Jason—"

"Little girl, you might wanna step off," Chasity snapped. Startled, the girl spun around. "Excuse me?" the girl scoffed, shooting Chasity a challenging look. "Who the hell are *you*?"

Chasity held a piercing gaze on her. If the whole school knew who Jason was, they surely knew who his *girlfriend* was. "Bitch, you already know who I am. Don't fuckin' play yourself," Chasity bit back, as Jason wrapped his arm around her small waist.

The girl rolled her eyes and walked away, not saying another word. Flinging her hair in the process.

"Ho ass bitch," Chasity sneered, turning to face Jason.

Jason hugged her and laughed. "Alright, calm down," he soothed. "She knew she had no chance."

"That didn't stop her ugly ass from *trying*," Chasity muttered.

"Forget her," Jason chortled. "No fights this year, okay?"

"I can't make any promises," she threw back.

"Aye Jase, you change your mind about making this taco salad?!" Mark hollered over the chatter from the kitchen.

"Man, I already told you I'm not making no goddamn taco salad!" Jason erupted, inciting a laugh from Chasity.


"God, that smoke is killing my nose," Sidra complained, waving the cigarette smoke from her face.

"Yeah, I hear you," Alex agreed. Sitting outside had its disadvantages. Students were having their cigarettes and cigars, sending smoke in all directions. "But it's either deal with it, or move."

Sidra shifted in her seat. The benches in the cluster commons area were far from comfortable, but it beat standing. "I'm not moving from this spot," she refused. "I'd rather go back to our house and get in my bed, than stand around all night."

Alex looked up as Malajia and Emily approached. "Mel, you're *just* getting here?" Alex teased. "I figured you would've been one of the *first* people over here. You know how you get when a party is going on."

Malajia, still reeling from the earlier encounter with her boyfriend, was in no mood to party. Despite her disinterest, she figured she would come anyway to avoid people asking her what was wrong. "I had stuff to do," she stated flatly.

Alex and Sidra gave slight frowns. Malajia's low, tart tone was unexpected. "What is *your* problem?" Alex sneered.

Malajia tossed some hair over her shoulder. "Nothing. Where's everyone else?" she hoped that her quick reply would change the subject.

"In the guys' house, I think," Alex answered, taking a sip of her soda.

"Thanks," Malajia huffed, walking away, leaving the girls dumbfounded.

"Emily, did she say anything to you on your way over here?" Sidra asked, still unsettled by Malajia's tone.

"No, not a word…which is weird," Emily replied, shoving her hands in her jeans pocket.


Malajia made her way through the crowded house. Normally, the loud music and flowing drinks were her cup of tea, but not today. She regretted leaving her room.

"Mel, my drinking buddy," Mark called, noticing her.

Malajia sighed, approaching. Seeing him hold up a bottle of brandy, she shook her head. "Mark, nobody wants that nasty dark liquor," she spat, folding her arms.

He sucked his teeth. "Stop bitchin'," he shot back, pouring a small amount into two plastic cups. "Come on big head. Take a shot with me."

"I just don't want that," she refused.

Mark tossed his head back in frustration, letting out a groan. "Fine Mel. You don't have to drink the brown. We have *vodka* too," he offered, pointing to the clear bottle under the sink.

He poured a shot of the clear liquid and handed it to her. "I don't want that *either*," Malajia spat, pushing his hand away.

"Whatchu' *mean*?" He frowned. "You not gonna have any drinks?"

"No. I'm not in the mood."

"But...you're my drinking buddy," he implored. "You know the *rest* of them can't hang."

Malajia rolled her eyes. She knew that Mark was right. Normally they would party and drink together. He may have gotten on her last nerves, but he was always a good party partner. Her mood just wouldn't allow it. "Dawg, I said I'm not in the mood!" she snapped. "You drink that nasty shit by *yourself.*"

"Forget you, then," he grunted when Malajia walked away. "I don't need your whining ass to drink with me... Jase, come take this shot while you make this taco salad!"

"Mark, I'm about to punch you in the fuckin' face!" Jason yelled back, earning a snicker from Mark.

Josh jogged over to Alex, Sidra, and Emily, holding a few bottles of wine coolers. "Anybody want one?" he offered.

"No, I'm cool," Alex declined, leaning back on the bench.

Sidra reached for one. "You know what, yeah I'll take one," she grumbled. "Maybe it'll calm me down."

"What's the matter Sid?" Josh asked, concerned.

Alex chuckled. "She's mad because some guy keeps blowing his blunt smoke over here," she said. "She's about to go off."

"I swear to God, I'm about to shove that damn thing up his black ass if he don't get away from here with all that," Sidra fussed, twisting open the top. "Stupid, smoking bastard."

Josh successfully suppressed a laugh. It had been a while since Sidra went from zero to one hundred on the snap meter. Although he thought she was overreacting a tad bit, seeing her upset never sat right with him. He tapped the culprit, which happened to be his housemate, on the shoulder.

"Westley, do you mind moving to another spot with your smoking?" Josh kindly asked.

Westley looked at him. "My bad man," he apologized, then turned to the girls. "Sorry ladies."

Alex waved her hand dismissively. "It's fine." The smoke didn't bother Alex. Most of her cousins smoked, so she was used to it.

"Yeah well, just move or put it out," Sidra snarled.

Westley stared at Sidra, watching her take a sip from her bottle. "If I put this thing out, can I come back over here and holler at you, sexy?" he proposed, smiling.

Josh's tall body stiffened as Sidra returned Westley's look with a venomous one of her own. "Um, that would be a *no*," she replied, haughty. "I don't talk to men who smoke."

"Well, maybe I can change your mind," he persisted.

"Wes, back off," Josh fumed, clenching his fist. "She's not interested."

His housemate caught Josh's glare and registered the stern tone in his voice. "Sorry, I didn't know she was yours, man," he relented.

*I wish she was*, Josh thought. "It's cool," he said to his retreating housemate.

"Thank you, Josh," Sidra smiled. "You're always around when I need you."

Josh smiled shyly, looking down at the ground. Alex and Emily exchanged knowing glances. "Um, anyway, Emily do you want a cooler?" Josh stammered.

Emily thought for a second before reaching for the bottle.

"Emily, are you sure that's a good idea?" Alex charged.

Emily let out a sigh. "Don't worry Alex, I'm not going

to start abusing alcohol again," she declared. Emily knew Alex was just concerned; after all she did develop a drinking problem her sophomore year.

"I really *hope* not," Alex said, tone caring. "I know you're stressed about getting off academic probation—"

Emily resisted the urge to roll her eyes. "I *get* it," she cut in. "Never mind, Josh, I don't want any."

"Okay," Josh shrugged.


Mark hopped on top of a picnic table with a drink in one hand and a plate of food in the other. "Yoooo this party was wack bee," he said between crunches.

The crowd had dwindled down about a half hour ago, leaving the stragglers outside enjoying the summer evening.

Malajia rolled her eyes. "You're just mad because nobody wanted to drink that nasty concoction you made," she jeered, leaning back in her seat.

"It wasn't *that* bad," Mark protested. "It would've gotten people to have more fun."

Malajia looked at him, shocked. "Boy, you mixed, brandy, vodka, tequila *and* rum together!" she exclaimed. "Then had the nerve to put a splash of fruit punch in there. Like that was gonna cut the taste."

David frowned, pushing his glasses up his nose. "Damn Mark, were you trying to kill people?"

"Y'all are exaggerating," Mark dismissed. "Always talking shit."

"Then why aren't *you* drinking it?" Alex asked, pointing to the can of beer in his hand.

"'Cause that shit was nasty bee," Mark admitted, putting another forkful of food in his mouth.

His quick response caused eye rolls and snickers from the group.

"Where were *you* two?" Alex asked Jason and Chasity when they walked up, hand in hand.

"I know, right?" Mark added. "Y'all disappeared like an

hour ago."

"We were minding our damn business," Chasity sneered, pushing some of her long, black hair behind her ears.

The group stared at them silently before realization hit.

"Eww, *really*?" Sidra scoffed. "Y'all snuck off and did *that*?"

"Y'all some horny bastards," Malajia slid in evenly.

"Way to go Jase," Mark cheered, holding his drink up.

Jason narrowed his eyes at him. "Shut up," he hissed. Mark worked his nerves all night. If Jason didn't hear another word from him, he would be happy.

Alex spun around at the sound of Mark crunching loudly. "What are you crunching all loud in my ear?"

"Taco salad," he answered, wiping his mouth with his hand.

Jason frowned. "Where did you get *that* from?"

"Oh *now*, you want me to talk?" Mark hurled at Jason. Catching Jason's glare, Mark cleared his throat. "Sidra made it."

Jason shook his head. "He talked you in to it, huh Sid?"

Sidra let out a loud sigh. "Yeah man," she mumbled. "He was in my face looking all pitiful while he held up that thawed pack of ground beef."

"Beggin' ass," Malajia joked. She leaned over to him, reaching for his fork. "Let me get some."

"Fuck outta here bee," Mark snapped, moving his plate out of her reach.

# Chapter 3

Sidra curled her legs up on her bed. "I wonder how many cups of coffee it would take for me to become a jittery mess?" she wondered, flipping through the pages in her folder.

Josh looked at her. "How many cups did you have this morning?"

"Three," Sidra shrugged.

"Then three," Josh joked, earning a playful backhand from Sidra.

Sidra made a face at him. "Funny, Joshua," Having gotten through their first few classes of the day, Josh stopped by Sidra's room for some one on one hangout time. However, he became more of a bystander while she was going over syllabuses from her morning classes.

"How bad are your classes this semester?" Josh asked, adjusting his position on her bed. Sidra shot him a knowing look and he let out a chuckle. "*That* bad, huh?"

"I mean—" Sidra looked up when Malajia barged through the door. "Do you *have* to come in that hype?" Sidra snarled.

Malajia turned her lip up. "I'll slam this door against the wall and dance in here *butt naked* if I want to," she threw back. "It's *my* room too."

"Can you at least *knock* if you see the door closed?" Sidra argued, closing her folder.

Malajia let out a loud huff. "Oh my God! You act like I walked in on you sucking Josh off or something," she exclaimed.

Sidra put her hand over her face in embarrassment, while Josh, feeling a wave of heat fall over him, pretended to read a piece of paper that was on the bed.

"Now, where's the pack of cookies that you bought yesterday?" Malajia asked, folding her arms.

Sidra too folded her arms. "I hid them."

"Why would you do that?" Malajia frowned. "We *share* shit in this house. How you gonna hide shit from everybody?"

"Not *everybody*, just *you*," Sidra clarified, defiant. "Your greedy behind is the reason why the *last* pack had to be replaced so soon. You sat there and ate two rows of cookies in one sitting."

"I like to crumble cookies in my cereal!" Malajia snapped, clapping her hands with each word. "I don't say nothin' when you drink all the coffee."

"Because I *don't*!" Sidra yelled back. "And even if I *did*, I'd replace it before anybody *asked* me to."

Josh laughed. "Mel, I'm amazed that you're still so skinny," he mused of Malajia's slim figure.

"Yeah, me too," Malajia chuckled. "Look Sidra, my cereal is getting soggy, just tell me where the cookies are."

"No," Sidra refused.

Malajia stared at Sidra, eyes flashing. Seeing that her stare wasn't making Sidra budge, Malajia nodded slowly. "Okay then."

Before Sidra knew what was happening, Malajia ran over and jumped on Sidra's bed. Josh jumped up and stood by the door, watching in amusement as Malajia rolled over Sidra's bed, crushing her papers in the process.

"What the hell is wrong with you?" Sidra shrieked, trying to push Malajia off the bed. "You're wrinkling my papers!"

"Tell me where the cookie are," Malajia ordered, continuing her rolling. She rolled on Sidra's legs.

Sidra slapped Malajia on the arm. "Ow, girl!" She tried to get up from the bed, but Malajia pulled her back down and rolled on her. "I swear to God."

"Tell me where the cookies are!"

Tired, hot and irritated, Sidra gave Malajia a hard nudge. "In my freakin' closet, on the top shelf."

Malajia stood up from the bed. Smoothing her disheveled hair with her hands, she went to the closet and retrieved the cookies. "Carry on," she said, skipping out the room.

Snatching her crumbled papers up, Sidra started mumbling cuss words. Hearing Josh's laughter from the corner, she glanced at him; her grey eyes blazing. "Don't laugh at her, she's such a weirdo."

"It's hard *not* to," Josh teased, sitting back on Sidra's bed. He watched Sidra straighten out her clothes and smooth her hair back up into her ponytail. "You okay now?"

"I'm *hot* now," she grumbled.

Josh stared at her. *You sure are.* Even in loose fitting dress pants and a blouse, Sidra's slim figure was noticeable. He quickly shook the thoughts from his head.

"I swear, I'm two seconds from trading places with David and moving in with *you*," she jeered.

Josh swallowed hard at the thought of Sidra living in the same room as he. He gave a nervous laugh. "Yeah, this campus hasn't joined the co-ed living arrangements team yet," he joked.

Sidra sighed, once again studying her papers.

"Hey, it's about twelve, you want to go grab some lunch before your next class?" Josh asked.

"You wanna go this early?" Sidra asked, not bothering to look up at him.

Josh shrugged. "Might as well go now and get the fresh food," he chortled.

Sidra looked at her watch. "Good point, let's go—" The rest of her reply was interrupted by the sound of her cell phone ringing. She grabbed her phone from her nightstand and smiled at the name on the caller ID.

"Umm, sweetie, I'm sorry," she said, pushing the talk button. "I'm going to have to take a rain check on lunch. It's James and I haven't talked to him in a few days so I want to catch up before I go to my next class."

Josh rolled his eyes as he quickly gathered his books from the floor. "Fine Sidra," he grunted.

Months later, and he detested the name James. He hated the fact that her eyes always lit up when he called. Or the fact that she blew him off for a conversation. *Why is she wasting her time with some guy who is hardly ever around? What does she see in him? Why won't he just disappear?* Josh thought, as Sidra rambled on the phone.

Although she spoke to James, Sidra was focusing on Josh's sudden change in mood. His facial expression, paired with the way that he jerked his book bag onto his arm and jumped up from the bed, she could tell that he was annoyed.

She asked James to hold, then pulled the phone away from her ear. "Joshua?" she called.

Josh paused on his way to the door and turned around, not saying a word.

"Is something wrong?" she asked.

"Nope, nothing," Josh spat, walking out of the room, leaving Sidra astonished.

*What's his problem?* she thought before putting the phone back to her ear.


Josh was still fuming when he stormed through his room door. He slammed his book bag on the floor and flopped down on his bed. Luckily, David wasn't in their room, or Josh would have been embarrassed by his temper tantrum.

"Punk ass James," he mumbled to himself. "Ooh I'm a fancy lawyer. I have a nice car and fancy clothes," he mocked. "He probably gets manicures and shit, bitch."

His tantrum was interrupted by Mark barging in his room. "Joshua," he called.

Josh rolled his eyes. First Sidra and now Mark; everyone knew that he hated being called by his full name. "Dude, you still haven't learned to fuckin' knock?"

"No," Mark answered bluntly. "Never. Shit ain't changed just because we in a different spot."

"What do you want, Mark?" Josh hissed.

"Me and the fellas are trying to get a game of spades going. You want in?"

"No, I don't want to play no damn spades with your cheatin' ass," Josh spat.

Mark frowned. "The fuck is your problem man?"

"Nothing," Josh lied. "Now get out. I'm trying to chill before my next class."

Mark sucked his teeth. "You always girlin'," he scoffed, walking out the door. "Aye guys, bitch ass Josh is on his period so we gotta get another person!" Mark hollered on his way down the steps.

Shaking his head at his loud friend, Josh propped his pillow under his head and closed his eyes.


"I hate all these baggy clothes," Emily grumbled, tossing a shirt on the floor. She had been going through her closet and drawers for nearly forty-five minutes, trying to find something to wear. The warm September weather called for some stylish attire. Only, her wardrobe was far from stylish.

Kicking her pile of strewn clothing items out of her way, she headed down the steps. Hearing voices come from Chasity's room, she knocked on the door.

"Alex, I'm not going to the gym with you," Chasity argued, opening the door. "What's up, Emily?"

"Can I come in?" Emily asked. Without a word, Chasity stepped aside to let Emily in the room.

"Don't you have your Early Childhood Education

class?" Alex asked, frowning.

Emily looked at her, *no Mom,* she thought. "Not until later," she answered. "What are you two up to?"

"Nothing," Chasity answered, sitting at her desk.

"I'm trying to get this icebox to come to the gym with me," Alex contradicted. "But she's being stubborn."

"*I* don't *need* to work out," Chasity snarled, pointing to herself.

Alex's eyes became slits. *Just rub your slim, toned body in my face, why don't you?* "Usually I hate to use this word, but I'm not fat, you bitch," she ground out.

Chasity laughed. "I never *called* you fat," she pointed out. "I just said that I didn't need to work out."

Flagging Chasity with her hand, Alex turned her attention to Emily. "What's up, Em?"

"Well…" Emily looked down at the drab, oversized faded grey t-shirt and baggy pink sweatpants that she had on. One wouldn't be able to tell that she had a nice figure under all that fabric. "I need to go shopping for new clothes. And I was hoping that you would go with me…Chasity."

Chasity gave a slight frown. "Say *what* now?"

Emily smiled. "I like your style," she complimented. "All the clothes in my closet are…in the words of Malajia, 'mommy approved.' I think it's time for a change."

As Chasity pondered Emily's revelation, Alex held her hand up. "Wait a minute. You don't like *my* style?" she pouted.

"No, I'm not saying that at *all*, Alex," Emily amended, shaking her head.

"Don't lie to her Emily," Chasity teased, looking at Alex. "She don't like your baggy ass, off the shoulder, shirts."

Alex playfully tossed a pillow at Chasity in retaliation. "Smart ass."

Chasity stared at the pillow as it landed on the floor in front of her. "Your non-aiming ass is mad 'cause I'm right," she jeered.

Alex sucked her teeth at Chasity, then turned her focus back on Emily. "I'm just messing with you Emily. I don't take offense," she assured.

Emily leaned her back against the door. "I mean, I admire *all* of your individual styles, it's just that Malajia's style is a bit too much for me and Sidra…"

"Dresses like she's going to work every-damn-day," Chasity cut in.

Emily giggled. "Yeah, *exactly*."

Alex looked at the clock on Chasity's desk. "Well, we all have time *now*, why don't we go to the mall?" She stood from her seat.

Chasity rolled her eyes. Her idea of relaxing did not include going to the mall with Alex and Emily. "Don't you have to go sling pizzas, Alex?" she asked, exasperated.

Alex smiled. "Nope. I don't start working at the Pizza Shack for another two days." She was glad that the manager held a waitressing spot for her. She was looking forward to the extra money.

Chasity let out a loud sigh. "Come on, man," she whined, standing up.

"Hush up," Alex demanded, shuffling both girls out the room.


Sidra stared at Josh while he slowly ate his BLT sandwich. "How is it?" she asked him.

Josh finished chewing, then took a sip of his cola. "Not bad," he shrugged. "The ones *I* make taste better though."

Sidra nodded, before scooping up a piece of grilled shrimp and some seasoned rice with her spoon. Feeling bad that she skipped out on lunch with Josh, Sidra agreed to go to dinner with him later that day. Though she was quiet through most of their dinner, something was bothering her and she felt the need to get it out.

"So…are you going to tell me what that was all about earlier today?" Sidra questioned after some silence.

Josh looked up from his food. "Huh? What are you talking about?"

She squinted at him. "Don't play with me, Josh," she chided. "You know *exactly* what I'm talking about. You caught an attitude with me." Josh's behavior when she declined lunch with him, didn't sit right with her. "Now, I'm sorry that I cancelled, but you don't think that your response was a little uncalled for?"

Running his hand over his head, he sighed. *Crap, I thought she forgot.* "I apologize," he said. "I was just…irritated."

"Irritated about *what*?"

Josh sat silently while pondering what to say. Truth was, he was jealous. Jealous of the fact that Sidra was talking to James Grant. A successful man, who was seven years her senior. "I…was just thinking about all the homework that I have to do later," he answered, finally.

She raised an arched eyebrow at him. "Is that so?"

"Yeah… That's so."

Sidra watched him take another sip of soda. "So, this had *nothing* to do with the fact that I answered James's phone call?" she asked.

Josh nearly choked on his drink. His eyes widened. "What? *No* that wasn't it," he lied, patting his chest.

Sidra looked concerned as Josh continued coughing. "You okay?" she asked. "You need me to pat your back?"

Josh put his hand up. "No, I'm fine," he assured, coughing now subsiding. "Like I said, James had nothing to do with anything."

Sidra folded her arms on the table top. "Josh… It may take me a minute to figure things out sometimes, but… I *do* eventually figure them out." After ending her hour-long conversation with James, Sidra began reflecting on what could have set Josh off. Thinking back on not only that situation, but others in the past, when Josh's mood changed instantly, she came to the 'James' conclusion.

Although he appeared calm, Josh was nervous on the

inside. *Oh God, did she figure out that I'm in love with her?*
"And *what* do you think that you have figured out?" Josh
carefully asked.

"I figured that you feel some kind of way about James
because you, like my *father,* feel like he's too old for me,"
she replied. "And the fact that he lives in a different state..."

*The fact that he's talking to you period.* "Sidra, I
promise you that I couldn't care less about James." Josh's
tone had some bite. "He's just your friend, so it shouldn't
matter how old he is, right?"

Sidra frowned. "There's that attitude again."

Josh put his hands on his face and pulled down in
exasperation. The last thing that he wanted to talk about
while having one on one time with Sidra, was James. "I don't
*have* an attitude. I just want to finish my dinner without being
interrogated about my opinion on a guy that I barely even
*know*. Hell, that *you* barely even know," he spat. "Can we
please talk about something else? Class, maybe?"

Sidra sat back in her seat and let out a huff. "Okay,
whatever you want," she relented.

Josh sat back in his seat as Sidra went back to eating her
food. Plucking a piece of bacon across his plate, he let out a
sigh. *Way to throw a temper tantrum, stupid,* he chided
himself.


Sidra kicked a pebble across the path as she slowly made
her way back to her house. Upon finishing her tense dinner
with Josh, she parted ways from him when he journeyed to
the library. She was enjoying her early evening stroll through
campus. That, paired with her pebble kicking, was easing her
mind a bit.

Before reaching the door, she gave the pebble one last
kick, sending it rolling into the grass. "Well, it's the frogs'
pebble now," she mused to herself, opening the front door.
The sound of bickering both concerned her and made her
curious.

"How the hell are y'all gonna take Emily shopping for new clothes without *me*?" Malajia barked.

Chasity frowned at her. "What the hell is your dramatic ass so *mad* for?" she bit back.

"What is going on?" Sidra cut in, setting her purse on the couch.

"Malajia has an attitude because Chaz and I went shopping with Emily earlier today," Alex informed. "She feels that we should've waited for her to get back from class, so she could have gone."

"I'm not even mad at Emily. I'm mad at *you* Chaz," Malajia fumed, pointing. "*You* already know not to go to the mall without me."

"No the fuck I *don't*," Chasity snapped. "You don't give me no damn orders about where I go without you. You must've lost your goddamn mind."

Emily tried to stifle a laugh. "Malajia, I just wanted to go before my class. It was nothing personal."

"Whatever, Emily," Malajia huffed, waving her hand dismissively. "I just hope you got some dark colors. 'Cause all that ashy, pastel shit washes your bright ass out."

"Oh wow." Emily couldn't help but chuckle. She knew that Malajia was right, the worn fabric didn't complement her light complexion.

"This *whole* argument was so uncalled for," Alex laughed. "Malajia, you always take things overboard."

Malajia stared daggers at Alex. "I wonder what ugly fashion advice *you* gave the girl," she snarled. "All *your* shit has cheap fabric and ugly colors. Be having snags and runs in 'em and shit."

"Hey! My clothes do not have snags and runs!" Alex yelled, slapping the coffee table with her hand.

"What are you even *talking* about?" Malajia threw back, clapping her hands. "That shirt you got on *now* has a hole in it."

Alex quickly glanced down at her shirt as Chasity busted

out laughing. Alex sucked her teeth. "It does *not*," she muttered.

Sidra giggled. "Emily, did you get everything that you wanted?" she asked, hoping to diffuse the tension.

Emily nodded and smiled, then ran up the steps. Returning moments later with bags in her hand. Sitting back on the couch. "I got as much as the money that my dad gave me would allow."

Malajia watched as Emily pulled several trendy tops, jeans, and accessories out of her bags. Her eyes fixed on a black and silver top. "Ooh let me see," she said, walking over. Before Emily could hand her the shirt, Malajia snatched it. "I'm borrowing this," she declared, running up the steps.

"No! Wait Malajia, I didn't get to wear it," Emily exclaimed, taking off after her.

"Just let me hold it!" Malajia shouted from upstairs.

"What just happened?" Chasity asked, confused after a moment of silence.

Sidra laughed. "Emily just joined the 'Malajia wants to borrow stuff' club."

# Chapter 4

"This course is an introduction to the management function. It will focus on the theory and fundamental concepts of management, including planning, organization, leadership, and control," the professor droned, pointing to the course syllabus. "Be prepared to partner up on several projects."

Malajia let out a long sigh. *God will he shut the hell up?* she thought. Principles of Management was not what she wanted to be thinking about at that moment. The only thing that was on her mind was her dinner date with Tyrone. She last saw him a week ago, when he showed up at her house unexpectedly. But she'd had a phone conversation with him since. During it, she agreed to have dinner with him after much pleading on his part.

Her stomach was in knots. Sneaking to check her phone for text messages, Malajia jerked her head up when the professor moved near her desk.

"Your first project will be due next week. You might want to get a head start by reading up on—"

Malajia pinched the bridge of her nose as the professor continued to speak. The heavy smell of collard greens wafted in her nose. *What the fuck? Was he eating greens for breakfast?* she wondered of her burly professor.

Annoyed both by the smell and at the fact that he had yet to move from near her desk, Malajia let out a loud huff. "Why does it smell like greens?" she blurted out. She immediately looked at her professor, who was glaring down at her. Her eyes became wide and a nervousness fell over her. It didn't help that her classmates were laughing.

"I swear on everything, I did *not* mean to say that out loud," Malajia sputtered.

"Guess whose group will be going first next week?" he ground out, folding his arms.

Malajia smacked her hand against her forehead.


Malajia was relieved when the hour was up. Her homework assignment had her reeling.

"How he gonna assign five chapters of reading?" she grumbled to herself, walking. "Ol' funky ass… I'm not reading that shit."

Malajia was startled when she walked up to her house to see Tyrone sitting on the front step.

"Hey sexy," he smiled, standing up.

Malajia looked skeptical as Tyrone hugged her. "What are you doing here so early?"

"Yeah, I know I said dinner, but I figured lunch would be better," he proposed.

"How so?" Malajia questioned.

"I didn't want to wait anymore to see you," he answered, grabbing her hand and holding it. "I knew your class was letting out about now, so I figured I'd just wait for you."

Removing her hand from his, Malajia opened the door. "You should have called and told me that plans were changing. I still have one more class this afternoon," she spat, walking inside the house with him following. "You can't just do things like that and not tell me."

"Just blow the class off," Tyrone shrugged.

Malajia was taken back. "Why would I do *that*?"

"Come on, you used to skip class because your *hair* wasn't right," Tyrone threw back, at an attempt to make light of the situation. Malajia wasn't amused. Tyrone shoved his hands in his pockets. "So, you're upset that I'm here early?"

Malajia let out a quick sigh. "I'm not upset, I just—" she quickly shook her head. He was right, she had no problem skipping class from time to time for less important reasons. She figured she could use one of her passes for him. "Never mind. Just wait here while I grab a quick shower and change," she said, heading for the stairs. "It's extra hot outside for no reason."

He walked up to her and wrapped his arms around her waist. "How about I wait in your room?" he licked his lips, holding a lustful gaze.

Malajia narrowed her eyes at him. She knew exactly what that look meant, and she was in no mood for it. "I'm not sleeping with you," she hissed, removing his arm from her. "Wait down here."

Not saying a word, Tyrone put his hands up in surrender and backed away.

*The damn nerve of him*, she thought, heading into the bathroom. Just because she'd had sex with Tyrone several times, Malajia didn't feel the need to give into him. Especially after what he did. There were many moments, such as this, where she regretted losing her virginity to him.


Malajia sat at the table, picking at her crab cakes. Although they were pretty good, she didn't have much of an appetite. A shower, new clothes, and a fifteen-minute car ride later, Malajia was sitting in a small seafood restaurant in downtown Paradise Valley.

"What's wrong with your food?" Tyrone asked, noticing her hesitation.

Sitting her fork back on the plate, she leaned back in her seat. "Nothing is wrong with it," she muttered. "I'm just not hungry."

Tyrone watched her fidget in her seat. "You still mad at me?" he asked. He figured there was no need in avoiding the elephant in the room.

"Yep," she ground out. "What, you thought I *wouldn't* be?"

Tyrone wiped his mouth with a napkin and placed it on the table. "No, I figured that you would be," he replied. "Malajia, I don't know how many times I can say that I'm sorry for hitting you."

"Keep saying it and I'll let you know," she spat. Tyrone sighed. "Granted," she continued, folding her arms. "You slapping me was the most disrespectful thing that you could have *ever* done to me. But it's not *only* that. You are insanely jealous, Tyrone."

"What? Because I don't want other guys hanging around you?" he frowned.

"If it was just *random* guys, then I would understand," Malajia argued. "But you're telling me that you don't want guys that I have known since I was a *child* to be around me. We have some of the same classes together, we live within feet of each other, and we all hang out in the same circle. What you're asking of me is ridiculous... We've had this same damn conversation over and over. And I'm fuckin' tired of it."

He rubbed his face with his hands, trying to keep his temper in check. *She's not getting it*, he thought. "Malajia, is it too much to ask for you to just honor my wishes?" his tone was low and slow.

"You're trying to control me," Malajia spat. "*Nobody* controls me. Not even my *parents*."

"Ain't nobody tryna control you," Tyrone hissed. "I don't think I'm being unreasonable... *Especially* with that damn Mark."

Malajia slowly shook her head at him. "I'm not going to keep arguing with you about Mark. I *don't* want him, never *did*, so stop getting on my damn nerves about it."

Tyrone's jaw tightened.

"I swear yo, these past weeks when I wasn't speaking to you, have been stress free," she admitted. He fixed his gaze on her. "I didn't have to worry about constantly explaining myself or arguing over the same shit... So, if you plan on continuing with your nonsense...then maybe we—"

Tyrone held his hand out for her hand. "Malajia, don't even say it," he cut in. "I couldn't handle it if you left me."

Malajia's hardened expression softened a bit. "Ty—"

"I promise, I'll try to see things your way... I'm sorry okay?"

Malajia put her hand in his. "You'll trust me?" she asked.

Tyrone smiled a deceptive smile. *You better keep your ass away from him, like I said.* "Yes," he lied.

Malajia too smiled. "Thank you," she said, giving his hand a slight shake. *I hope that I finally got through to him.* "I might have been mad but... I missed you."

"Enough to let me back in your bed?" Tyrone joked.

Malajia rolled her eyes.


"You can't beat me in basketball," Mark declared, tossing a ball up in the air repeatedly. "No way in hell."

"You always think you can beat everybody at every-damn-thing," Josh hissed, flagging him.

"That's because it's *true*," Mark boasted.

Following dinner, most of the gang decided to work off the calories by playing a game of basketball at the outdoor court behind the clusters.

"Oh *really*?" Josh challenged. "Everything you play us in, you *lose*... Let's see, there's spades."

Mark narrowed his eyes at Josh.

"And bowling," Jason chimed in.

"And rock climbing," Chasity added.

"And everything *else* that requires some skill," Alex joined in, laughing.

Mark slammed the ball on the ground. "First off,

dickhead Josh and big nose Alex," he snapped, pointing at them both. "I beat *both* of y'all teams in spades freshman year."

"Yeah, yeah." Alex waved a dismissive hand at him.

"And I already *told* y'all I was tired when we did the rock climbing last semester," Mark reminded.

"Is *that* why you fell off?" Chasity questioned smartly.

Mark glared at her. "Jase, check your girl man," he sneered.

Watching Mark grab the ball from the ground and begin dribbling between his legs, David shook his head. "Since you think you're so great Mark, why don't you try out for the school team?" he suggested.

Mark shot the ball at the basket and made it. "Yes," he rejoiced, running to retrieve it. "I *thought* about trying out, but uh, I'm not into organized sports."

Jason frowned slightly. "What's *that* supposed to mean?"

"Nothing against you being on the football team, Jase," Mark amended. "But I hate sport rules. I just wanna *play*."

"In other words, you want to cheat without being penalized," Sidra pointed out, tying the laces on her sneakers.

Mark laughed. "Exactly." He looked over and saw Malajia heading over to them. "Hey, y'all smell that?" he joked.

"Yeah, it smells like you didn't wash your ass today," Malajia quickly bit out.

"Touché," Mark chuckled. He always relished a good insult from Malajia.

"Hey girl," Alex said, stretching. "You saw the note I left, I assume?"

"Yes Alex, I *did*," Malajia confirmed. "Only *you* would leave a note on the door telling me where to meet you, instead of just texting me." Having returned from her lunch date with Tyrone, she arrived at the house and was greeted by a sticky note on her door from Alex, telling her where the rest of them had gone.

"I figured you were still in class. Didn't want to get you in trouble for your phone going off," Alex defended. "You *know* you're always forgetting to silence it...*that* and I like to use my sticky notes."

Malajia suppressed a laugh. "No, it's because that ancient flip phone you got don't have text capabilities."

Alex halted her stretching to stare daggers at Malajia. "I knew it was only a matter of time before you started in on my damn cell phone," she ground out.

Malajia giggled, holding both of her hands out for Mark to pass her the ball. "Gimme," she demanded.

"No, I ain't giving you shit," Mark jeered of his ball. Malajia sucked her teeth. Mark sat the ball down and removed his shirt.

"Boy, put your damn shirt back on," Malajia scoffed.

"I'm hot," Mark explained, slinging the red shirt over his shoulder.

"So *our* eyes gotta suffer, staring at your black ass chest all day?" Malajia threw back, disgusted.

Mark smirked at her. "You can *touch* my chest if you want," he teased. "This chocolate won't melt."

"Grooosss," Chasity complained as Malajia exclaimed, "Ewww!"

"Mark, stop talking nasty and put your clothes back on," Alex condemned.

Mark sucked his teeth as he reluctantly complied. "Hatin' asses," he muttered.

"Malajia, where *were* you anyway?" Sidra asked, changing the subject. "You're usually out of class by the time I get back from my last one."

Malajia pulled her hair to the side and began braiding it. "Um, I was out on a lunch date...with Tyrone," she answered hesitantly.

Chasity rolled her eyes and Mark let out a groan. "Don't nobody wanna hear about your raggedy date with that jackass," Mark complained.

Malajia shot him a glower before turning her attention to

Chasity. "Don't say a word, Parker."

"Wouldn't *dream* of breaking that promise," Chasity hissed, tightening her ponytail. She couldn't believe that Malajia was still giving him the time of day.

"Really? Wow, this is the first time that I've heard you mention him in a *while*," Alex pointed out. "Didn't know you were still dating."

"Can y'all stop?" Malajia spat out. She regretted even mentioning her date.

Emily put her hands up. "Okay guys, now that we're all here, let's split into teams," she suggested, changing the subject. She could see that Malajia was getting agitated by the comments.

"Girls against the guys," Mark put out, tossing the ball behind his back.

Sidra tossed her hands in the air. "Damn, we don't get a choice?" she scoffed. "You men play ball *all the time*. You already *know* you're going to beat us."

"That's the point," Mark joked.

"Forget him Sid, we got this," Alex assured. "How hard can this game be?"

The teams spread out and got into their positions. "Why did I agree to do this?" Sidra complained.

Josh grabbed the ball and dribbled as Sidra tried to take it from him.

"I'm open, pass it!" Mark yelled, waving his hands wildly in the air, while Malajia tried to guard him. Once Josh tossed him the ball, Mark made a run for the basket with Malajia running after him in hopes of preventing him from making it.

Mark ran up and dunked the ball over her head, much to Malajia's dismay. He bumped her out the way with his chest in the process. Then, to add insult to injury, he started screaming in her face.

"Yeeeaaaahhhhhh! You got dunked on. You mad as shit cuz," Mark boasted, clapping his hands together repeatedly. "I'm a beast!"

"You spittin' all in my damn face!" Malajia hollered, shoving him away from her.

"Mark, you play too much," Sidra chided. "She could have fallen."

"You shut your mouth, Princess," Mark warned.

Josh sucked his teeth. "Why are you so damn hype?"

"You shut your mouth too, *Mr.* Princess," Mark teased, pointing at Josh. Sidra might not have had a clue that Josh liked her, but Mark sure did and never missed an opportunity to tease him about it.

"You get on my damn nerves," Malajia grumbled at Mark, adjusting the straps on her tank top.

Mark passed the ball to David, who began dribbling. David went to pass it, but turned around to see Alex behind him trying to guard him. He went to run, but tripped and fell, causing the ball to roll away.

"David, what the hell?!" Mark erupted.

"Stop yelling at me, my glasses fell off," David snapped, picking the silver wire frames up from the ground and wiping them off.

"You always bitchin' about those glasses!" Mark yelled.

Sidra grabbed the rolling ball and began running around in circles, trying to avoid Josh.

"You have to *dribble* it," Jason informed with a little laugh.

"Leave me alone," Sidra spat, passing the ball to Chasity who began to dribble. Chasity tried to maneuver around Jason, who was steadily blocking her way, taunting her in the process.

Annoyed that she couldn't get around him, Chasity delivered an elbow to Jason's ribs, sending him to the ground in a heap.

"My girl," Alex cheered, clapping. Chasity ran up to the basket and shot the ball through. "Good defense, Chaz."

"Defense my *ass*," Mark loudly contradicted. He turned his attention to Jason, who was struggling to get up, holding his side. "Damn Jase, how you let her get past you? I *know* you play better than *that*," he mocked. "What? You scared she won't give you none later?"

Annoyed by Mark's taunting, Jason scowled at him, while smoothing his t-shirt down. "At least *I'm getting* some, bitch," he bit back.

Mark stood there with a stupid look as laughter erupted around him. "Fuck you, football boy," he spat. Jason flipped him off.

Chasity was not amused. "Jason! Seriously?" she exclaimed.

"I'm sorry babe, but you *know* he gets the fuck on my nerves," Jason complained.

"Yeah well, insult him *without* including me in it," she reprimanded.

Jason shot Chasity a knowing look, smiling. "I *do* get it though," he teased, earning an eye roll from her.

"Eww, come on," Malajia grumbled. "Nobody cares about your sex life."

"Says the person who don't *have* one," Mark jeered.

*That goes to show how much you know*, Malajia thought. "Whatever pencil dick, let's just finish playing," she ground out.

Mark made a face at Malajia, dribbling the ball. "Ain't *nothing* pencil about mine," he boasted.

"Oh my God, shut up," Chasity groaned, tossing her hands up. "Just do something with the damn ball."

"Pass me the ball," David urged, while Mark ran around the court. He waved his hands in the air. "I'm open."

"I'm not passing you *shit*, goggle eyes," Mark sneered, passing the ball to Josh.

"I got it!" Josh bellowed, reaching for the ball. "Damn it," he complained when the ball rolled through his hands.

"Oh come on Josh!" Mark hollered, watching Sidra grab the ball. "Y'all suck. I'm about to trade both you *and* David for two of the girls."

"You passed it all hype," Josh shot back, pointing at him.

"Sidra, for the love of God, dribble the damn ball," Jason griped, putting his hand on his head when Sidra ran with the ball.

Watching Sidra head for the basket, Alex clapped loudly. Her claps ceased when Mark jumped up and slapped the ball out of the air before Sidra's shot made it in the basket.

"Get that bullshit outta here," Mark mocked.

Sidra delivered a piercing gaze before walking away from the basket.

"Ah ha, you mad your ball got smacked out the air," Mark laughed.

Josh shook his head at Mark. "Mark, just play the damn game," he grumbled. "It's too hot for all this grandstanding."

"Man, grandstand these *nuts* and get the damn ball," Mark shot back, pointing to the ball lying in the nearby grass.

Alex, tired of the back and forth just ran and grabbed the ball. "Y'all are on my nerves, it's our ball," she declared, dribbling.

"No the hell it's *not*," Mark scoffed.

"Sure the hell *is*," Alex countered, passing the ball to Emily.

Emily looked around for an open teammate, but most were being blocked by the guys.

"Em, pass it, I got it!" Malajia exclaimed, running away from Mark.

Emily tossed the ball to Malajia, who hurried towards the basket. Malajia had a big smile on her face as she tossed the ball up. Mark, who was right behind her, jumped up, slapping the ball from her hand, bumping her yet again, sending her stumbling forward.

Furious and embarrassed, Malajia spun around and slapped him twice on the arm. "That's it, I quit!" she fumed, storming off.

Unfazed by Malajia's stinging slaps, Mark started laughing at her. "No basket for you," he taunted. "Mad as shit your ball didn't go in."

"Mel, come back," Alex laughed.

"No fuck him, I'm done," Malajia threw over her shoulder, her quick pace continuing.

"Well, that does it for me too," Sidra slid in, grabbing her water bottle off the ground. "This game just irritated my entire life."

Mark sucked his teeth. "Really? First big head quits, now you *too* Princess?" he complained, watching Sidra walk off the court. He turned his attention to Chasity, Alex, and Emily who were gathering their belongings. "What, y'all quitting *too*, thickums, witch, and little bits?"

Without saying a word, Chasity flipped him off before walking off the court.

Alex slapped her behind. "Yup, *all* this thickness is tired," she chuckled.

Mark held his hand out. "Ooh, can I slap it next?" he joked.

"Boy please," Alex grimaced, walking away. The guys laughed.

"You stupid as shit," Jason laughed, taking a sip of water.

"Yeah, I know," Mark agreed.

# Chapter 5

"Why is it so damn hot?" Malajia complained, fanning herself with her hand. "It's been like this for over a week."

"I don't know, but running your damn mouth isn't helping," Chasity snapped, moving away from Malajia. "Your hot ass breath is all near my damn face."

Not only were both girls irritated about having to go to their respective classes at ten in the morning, but the excruciating heat so early wasn't helping the situation. The heat wave was abnormal for early September, and that alone had most of the student body on edge.

Malajia sucked her teeth and sat down on a bench along the path, halting their progress.

"Malajia, no, don't sit down. Come on," Chasity urged, stomping her foot on the ground. "I'm not trying to stand around out here."

"Please, I need a minute," Malajia panted, putting her head in her hands. "My whole weave is sweating."

"I will fuckin' leave you and you *know* it," Chasity warned, adjusting the strap on her black tank top.

Malajia frantically fanned herself. "Yes, I know." She tried to get comfortable. "Why is this goddamn bench so hot!" she yelled, jumping up from the heat on her bare legs.

Chasity tried not to laugh as she smoothed her hair up

into her ponytail.

Catching Chasity's smirk, Malajia made a face at her. "Shut the hell up, Chasity," she barked. "Let's just go."

"Don't snap at *me* because your ass got singed," Chasity teased, walking off with Malajia following close behind.

"Wait, let me stop in the cafeteria and get an ice cream cone," Malajia suggested.

Chasity tossed her head back and groaned loudly. "Mel I'm fuckin' *hot!*" she fumed. "I don't feel like walking your slow ass around campus. I'm about to turn my ass around and go back to my damn room."

Malajia sucked her teeth. "*First* of all, you're a border line computer nerd, so you're not about to miss your Web Design class because of no heat," Malajia pointed out.

She was right; if it were any other class besides computers, Chasity would have had no issues with skipping a day.

"Second, there's air conditioning in the cafeteria. So stop whining and come on."

Chasity sighed loudly, she did not have the energy to argue with Malajia. "What-the-fuck-ever, Malajia," she spat out, before storming in the direction of the cafeteria.

Malajia's mood lifted once she got her cone. She smiled brightly while she and Chasity walked out of the building towards their destination. She licked the ice cream cone. "This is soooo good," she cooed, doing a dance.

Opening her bottle of water, Chasity rolled her eyes. Luckily, they were approaching the steps to the Science building, so she wouldn't have to hear Malajia's commentary on her ice cream much longer.

"Yo Chaz, you should've gotten one," Malajia said.

"I didn't want that wack ass soft serve," Chasity groused.

Before Malajia could brag anymore about her treat, a hand reached from behind and slapped it out of her hand.

"You don't want that," Mark, the culprit, teased.

Malajia watched in shock as her cone went falling to the ground. Between Chasity's loud laughter and the way Mark was staring at her, sticking his tongue out, Malajia snapped.

"You son of a bitch!" Malajia screamed, trying to grab at him. She missed when Mark darted behind Josh and David, who were walking with him.

"She's tryna kill me over ice cream!" Mark exclaimed, voice full of amusement, ducking and dodging Malajia's swings.

"Y'all are stupid," Chasity laughed, heading inside the building.

Malajia stopped trying to attack Mark. "You lucky I'm not trying to be late for class," she seethed. She flung her hair over her shoulder. "I promise, I'm gonna fuck you up later, for that...punk."

"You mad as shit your cone is on the ground," Mark taunted as Malajia stomped off.

Josh was unsuccessful at concealing his laugh. "You need to stop messing with her," he advised.

"Naw, I think I'll continue," Mark stated, wiping his face with his hand, ambling along.

"It's like a hundred degrees out here," Josh groaned.

"Look on the bright side, we get another week or so of girls wearing those short shorts and skirts," Mark pointed out, lifting his sunglasses on to his head.

"True," David laughed. Shifting his book bag from one arm to the other, he felt a blast of cold hit him on his back. "What the hell?!" Reaching his arm around to feel his back, he felt wetness. "Why am I wet?"

Mark laughed. "David, why you piss on yourself man?"

David frowned at Mark; he was in no mood for his teasing. "I peed on my *back*?" he snapped, sarcastic. "On the middle of my damn *back*? How the hell would that even *happen*?"

While Mark stood there with a dumb look on his face, Josh examined David's wet shirt, then noticed something on the ground. "Uh, I think you just got hit by a water balloon," he informed, pointing to the bright red balloon remains.

David let out a long sigh. "Come on man," he growled, pushing his glasses up his nose. "I can't go to class with wet clothes. I have a science presentation to make."

Mark sucked his teeth. "Man, stop bitchin'. You act like you got hit with shit or something," he mocked. "It's fuckin' water, it'll dry."

David's jaw tightened. He was about to fire off an insult when a blue water balloon flew past him and hit Mark on the side of his head, knocking his sunglasses off his face.

"Oh shit," Josh reacted, seeing the glasses tumble to the ground.

"Yo, who threw that?!" Mark shouted, spinning around in every direction.

"Chill Mark," Josh laughed. There was nothing funnier than seeing Mark get his just desserts.

Mark stomped his foot on the ground, while frantically rubbing his eyes. "Come on man! Water splashed all in my eye and shit."

"Stop bitchin', you act like you got hit with shit or something," David mocked.

Hearing his words thrown back at him, Mark made a face as David headed off for class. Picking his sunglasses up, Mark let out a frustrated sigh. "Oh, I am fucking somebody up with a water balloon *today*," he declared. "It's on."


Towel around his neck and water bottle in hand, Jason left the football field after a long practice later that afternoon. *Fuckin' idiot, we could have all passed out*, he thought, continuing his steady pace back to his house.

He was annoyed that the coach didn't cancel the practice because of the heat. His temper only amplified when a water balloon hit him on his shoulder. Frowning, Jason spun around to see Mark running pass him, laughing loudly. "What the?—Are you serious dawg?!" Jason shouted after him.

"Water balloon fight!" Mark yelled over his shoulder.

"I'm not even *playing*!" Jason fumed.

"No exemptions!"

Jason shook his head. "Fuckin' idiot," he mumbled, continuing his walk.

Mark, approaching the landscaped grounds in the middle of the campus quad, halted his sprint. He removed the book bag from his back and sat it on the ground. Unzipping the bag, he removed several water-filled balloons. "Yeah buddy," he mused to himself.

Determined to get in on the water balloon attacks that were going around on campus all day, Mark had headed straight to the Mega Mart earlier and bought a bag of balloons. "Somebody is gonna get it."

Smiling, he began tossing balloons at unsuspecting students. He laughed as people screamed, ducked, and ran. He didn't even get mad when he was hit with a balloon, thrown by another student.

"Oh, it's on *now*," he goaded, engaging the thrower and another student in a water balloon fight. "You about to get a balloon to the face, dickhead," Mark laughed, tossing one with force. His laughing ceased immediately when his balloon hit a Professor on his chest, causing him to stumble back, dropping his papers in the process.

"Aww crap, he just hit Mr. Bradley!" one of the balloon throwing students exclaimed.

Seeing the angered face of his former Sociology professor, Mark froze. "Oh shi—shucks," he stammered. "I apologize profusely, Mr. Bradley."

"Still acting a fool huh, Mr. Johnson?" Mr. Bradley fumed, storming towards him. "Maybe a trip to the Dean's office will—"

"Wait, no it was an accident," Mark panicked, quickly grabbing his bag from the ground.

Mr. Bradley's anger intensified when Mark took off running. "If I see you throw *one* more balloon!"

"I was only trying to have fun!" Mark yelled back, continuing his hurried departure.


"I hope this weather gets its act together soon," Sidra commented to Alex, fanning herself with her hand.

The weather was still sweltering later that evening. But it didn't stop Sidra and Alex from sitting outside of the house.

"I know, I was sweating so bad. I had to come home and wash my hair," Alex replied, taking a sip of orange juice from her cup.

"Don't even *talk* to me about washing hair," Sidra scoffed, pulling a bottle of water out of an ice-filled bucket. "I'm not looking forward to washing mine at *all*. Having long hair is great until you have to blow dry and straighten the mess."

Alex chuckled. "Do you really have a makeshift cooler full of bottled water sitting out here?"

"Are *you* going to feel like running back to the fridge for more water?" Sidra threw back.

"Absolutely not," Alex chortled. She looked up and saw Chasity walk out of the house. "Hey Mama," Alex smiled. "Did you get hit by one of those water balloons that were being thrown around today?"

Chasity shook her head.

Sidra laughed, "I heard that Mark hit Mr. Bradley with one," she said. "Was it in the face?"

"No, the chest," Alex corrected. "Mark plays too damn much."

"Yeah, well—" Chasity's train of thought was interrupted when she felt cold water splash her; soaking her from her hair to her t-shit. Startled, she let out a scream, then spun around to see Malajia standing there holding a bucket. "Malajia, what the fuck is your problem?!" Chasity screamed.

"That's what the hell you get for laughing when Mark smacked my ice cream out of my hand," Malajia shot back, pointing at her.

Chasity's face held a shocked expression for several seconds. "Are you fuckin' *serious*?" she fumed, wiping her face with her hand. "That was like six hours ago!"

"So the hell what, you know I hold grudges, bitch," Malajia retorted.

Sidra, who darted out of the way when the water splashed, was stunned. "Mel, that was terrible," she chastised.

"*And*?" Malajia sneered. "Serves her right… That water did her ass some good, being in hell all damn day… Lucifer."

Chasity could have spit fire. Better yet, she could have strangled Malajia right then and there. "Come here," she demanded, signaling Malajia with her finger.

"Why? So you can hit me? You wish I *would* come over there," Malajia refused. "I'm not stupid."

"Are you *sure*?" Chasity hissed, voice dripping with sarcasm.

Malajia narrowed her eyes. "That's why people can see your bra now," she mocked.

Chasity quickly looked down and noticed that her black bra was completely visible through her wet white shirt. "I don't give a shit," she fumed. "It cost more than every cheap ass thing you have on."

Malajia and Chasity both grabbed a bottle of water from Sidra's bucket.

"Oh, you want some *more*?" Malajia taunted, opening her bottle.

Alex, having had enough of the nonsense, jumped in between the girls. "Come on you two, chill out," she urged. "You're acting juvenile. It's not that serious. It's only water, it'll dry."

Chasity snatched the top off her bottle. Then she and Malajia both stared at Alex with the same look. The "mind your own business for once" look.

"I don't care about those faces," Alex shot back, folding her arms. "You know I'm right… As *usual*."

Shooting each other a quick glance, both girls squirted Alex with water from their bottles.

Alex let out a scream. "Seriously?!" she exclaimed, putting her hands on her hair. Sidra was doubling over with laughter. "What the hell was *that* about?"

"You looked hot," Chasity replied evenly, earning a laugh from Malajia.

Alex stomped her foot on the ground, she was furious. "You wet my damn hair! Do you know how long it took me to tackle this mess earlier? Do you have *any* idea what it's like to deal with wet, natural hair? This shit takes *forever* to dry!"

"Sucks for *you*, mop," Malajia jeered.

Alex's jaw tightened. She stared daggers at Malajia and Chasity. "I swear, I *hate* when you two team the hell up," she fumed, stomping in the house. "You both make me sick," she threw over her shoulder.

Chasity turned her attention to Malajia, who was busy laughing and poking fun at Alex. Still angry over the sneak attack, Chasity splashed the remaining water from her bottle on the startled Malajia's face. Then tossed the empty plastic bottle at her head; hitting her with it.

"Fuck you, you two-middle-name-having ass bitch!" Malajia hurled, grabbing her head.

"Yeah, *that* hurt my feelings," Chasity threw back, sarcastic.

"Stupid heffa play too much," Malajia muttered at Chasity's departing back. She ran her hand over her hair. "She always gotta go overboard."

Sidra looked puzzled. "Did you *not* throw a bucket of water on the girl?" she reminded. "What? You thought she wasn't going to get you back?"

Angry, Malajia went to raise her half empty water bottle in Sidra's direction.

Sidra put her hand up. "Wet me if you *want* to. You have

to go to sleep *sometime*," she threatened.

Not wanting to run the risk of Sidra messing with her while she slept, Malajia put the bottle to her lips and began drinking the water. "I wasn't even gonna do nothing," she lied.

"Yeah okay," Sidra replied skeptically, folding her arms.

# Chapter 6

Josh shoved his folder, along with his notebooks, into his book bag. "One ten-page paper down, a million to go," he sighed to himself. Grabbing the bag, he headed out of his room. He trotted down the staircase to the kitchen. Setting the book bag on the counter, he opened the refrigerator in search of the previous evening's leftovers.

"Please let there be more chicken parm in here," he said aloud. Moving several Tupperware containers aside, he came across what he was searching for. "Yes," he rejoiced, popping the container into the microwave.

Jason made the chicken parmesan meal the night before, making enough to feed the guys and girls. Josh was focused on finishing his paper for his Political Science class, he couldn't tear himself away long enough to eat.

Mark opened his room door, which was located near the kitchen, "What's up, Hampton?" he greeted, stretching.

"Nothing much. About to tear up this food before going to class," Josh replied, removing the warm container from the microwave. Just as he was about to dig in with his fork, Mark lunged forward, smacking the container from his hand.

"You don't want that," Mark declared as the food fell in the sink.

"What the hell was *that* for, man?!" Josh erupted, taking a missed swing at Mark. He could have pushed him through a wall at that moment.

"You salty your chicken parm is in the sink," Mark taunted, pointing to it.

"Damn it Mark, something is *seriously* wrong with you. You play *entirely* too much," Josh fussed, snatching his book bag off the counter. "I didn't even get any from last night."

"You didn't?" Mark asked, feigning concern.

"No, you jackass, I *didn't*," Josh confirmed. "I was writing my paper all night, remember?"

"Damn that's a shame, it was good too," Mark teased, rubbing his toned stomach. "Chaz was right, Jase *can* cook."

Josh's jaw clenched. "Somebody is gonna punch you in the fuckin' face one of these days," he predicted, reaching for an open pack of cookies sitting on the counter. He was starving; he was determined to eat something for breakfast, even if it *was* junk food.

"Man, don't touch my cookies," Mark barked, trying to snatch the pack from Josh's hand.

Josh shoved him away with his free hand. "Back the hell off, or I swear I will shove these cookies right up your black ass nose," he warned.

Mark folded his arms. "Yeah well… You better not eat 'em all," he mumbled as Josh headed out the door shoving a cookie into his mouth.


Josh finished off the cookies quickly. He tossed the empty pack in the trash can next to the girls' house before knocking on the door. He smiled when Emily opened the door.

"Hey Josh," she smiled.

"Hey, you finish that paper for your education class?" he asked. Both of them having papers due that week, Emily and Josh had been practically living in the library together for the past few days.

Emily sighed. "No. But I *need* to, it's due in like two days," she admitted. "I'm late, so I'll see you later."

Josh waved as Emily scurried off. He walked in and headed up the steps to Sidra's room. He knocked. "Sid, you ready?" he called through the closed door. "We only have a few minutes before class starts."

He and Sidra walking to their nine o'clock class several times a week had been a routine that he had gotten accustomed to. He enjoyed their morning conversations and relished the fact that, even for a few moments during the day, he had her all to himself.

As Josh switched his weight from one foot to the other, Sidra opened the door. Noticing her pajama clad body and the pained look on her face, he frowned.

"Josh you're going to have to go without me today, I don't feel good," she groaned, heading back to her bed.

He headed over and sat down next to her. "What's wrong?" he asked, not hiding his concern. "You *never* miss class."

"Yeah well, these freakin' cramps say *otherwise*," she sneered, curling into the fetal position.

*Oh, that time huh?* "Oh… Sorry," he commiserated, rubbing her shoulder. "Um, do you want me to bring you anything on my way back from class?"

"No," she spat.

Josh stood up silently. He'd been around Sidra and the rest of his female friends long enough to know their tempers that could erupt during their monthly cycles. "Okay, I'll see you later then," he said, walking out the door. "Feel better." *Well so much for our morning one on one time,* he thought, shaking his head.


"I'm so glad it's finally starting to feel like fall," Alex said, taking a bite out of her chicken wing ding, enjoying the cool fall breeze. "September finally got it together…even if it *is* almost the end of the month."

Chasity, who was sitting next to her on the bench in front of the library, shot her a side-glance. "You greedy as shit, eating them hard ass wings outside," she jeered.

After leaving their afternoon classes and not wanting to sit in the cafeteria, Chasity and Alex walked to the campus take-out diner to grab a quick bite while waiting for their next classes. Alex, who had barely eaten breakfast that morning, grabbed a container of fried chicken wing dings, Chasity opted for a slice of pizza.

Alex nearly choked from laughing. "Hush up," she said. "You're no better, eating that pizza out here."

"Yeah well…those things look like they been sitting for a while," Chasity mocked.

Alex nudged her. "Silly," she said, taking another bite.

As Chasity was about to take a bite of her already half-eaten pizza slice, a hand reached over her shoulder and slapped it out her hand.

"You don't want that," Malajia laughed.

Chasity watched the pizza fall to the ground. "Damn it Malajia. I *did* actually," she said evenly, moving her high heeled boot out of the way to avoid the pizza hitting it.

Malajia adjusted her book bag on her shoulder. "You mad your pizza's on the ground."

Chasity shook her head, pushing some of her hair behind her ears. "I'm not picking that shit up, either."

"*I* don't give a damn," Malajia replied, folding her arms. "Those damn birds can eat it, for all I care."

Alex shook her head. "What is up with this damn 'you don't want that', crap that y'all are doing?" she scoffed. "*Obviously* people *want* their food, which is why they *have* it. Smacking it out of their hands is ignorant and bound to get *you* smacked."

Malajia rolled her eyes at Alex. "It's *funny*."

"It wasn't funny when Mark smacked that ice cream out your hand that time," Chasity reminded.

Malajia thought for a moment, looking off into space. "I almost forgot about that," she stated. "I still owe him payback." Malajia logged the thought away in her mind for later, then turned her attention back to Chasity. "I'm surprised you didn't try to fight me when I smacked your pizza on the ground," she chuckled.

"Do you *want* me to?" Chasity questioned, raising an arched eyebrow at her.

"Hell no ninja hands, I *don't*," Malajia threw back. "Are you *actually* in a good mood?"

"Yeah bitch, I *was*," Chasity hissed, frowning at her. "I found out I got an A on a Numerical Analysis test that I took last week."

Malajia scrunched her face up. "The hell is Numerical Analysis?"

"Some algorithm bullshit," Chasity answered, tone dry.

"Well, that's good Chaz," Alex slid in, grabbing another piece of chicken from her container. "Now maybe you can stop complaining about how much you hate math stuff. You seem to be getting better at it."

"No, I still hate it," Chasity jeered.

Malajia was staring at Alex with disgust. Catching her stare, Alex frowned. "Why are you looking at me like that?"

"Why you eatin' them old ass wings from the caf, outside?" Malajia barked. Chasity snickered.

Alex sucked her teeth. "I keep *telling* y'all behinds, these are *not* the same wings from the cafeteria," she fussed. "The joke is getting old now." She took another bite of her wing.

Malajia shook her head as Chasity stood up from her seat, adjusting her book bag on her shoulder. Smiling slyly, Chasity smacked the chicken wing out of Alex's hand, much to Alex's astonishment.

"You don't want that," Chasity teased.

Alex jumped up. "Damn it Chasity!"

"You don't want that *either*," Chasity laughed, smacking the container holding the last few wings to the ground. She then took off running.

"Shit! Girl I'm gonna slap you," Alex hollered at Chasity's departing back. Running over, Malajia stomped her foot repeatedly on the fallen wings, crushing them. "Y'all play too much!" Alex yelled when Malajia took off running to catch up with Chasity.

Sidra sat a large mug filled with tea on the coffee table. "I'm feeling much better now, Mama," she said into her cell phone.

"I'm glad, sweetie," Mrs. Howard replied. "I know how bad your cramps can get."

Sidra adjusted her position on the couch and picked up the TV remote. After sleeping for what felt like forever, Sidra finally felt well enough to attend her last class of the day. Upon returning to the house after class was over, she returned her mother's call.

Sidra sighed. "Yeah I know. I'm about to pull a Malajia move and get on birth control pills to help with this cramping."

"That *may* help…along with keeping you from coming home with any babies," Mrs. Howard advised, tone stern.

Although her mother couldn't see her, Sidra rolled her eyes. *Again with this baby mess.* "Mama, how many times do I have to tell you that I'm not having sex?" she hissed. "Don't worry, I won't make you a grandmother anytime soon."

"Sweetie, you'll be turning twenty-one in two days. So, although you're still a virgin *now*, I know that will eventually change. *Especially* with you dating James and all. I just want you to protect yourself."

"Exactly Mama, we're just *dating*," Sidra stressed, reaching for her cup. "We haven't established that we are a full-on couple. He's working all the time and I'm here at school. I don't think a relationship will be ideal right now."

"Who are you trying to convince? Me or yourself?" Mrs. Howard asked.

Sidra sighed again. Leave it to her mother to call her on her crap. "I guess *me*," she admitted. She glanced over at her books sitting at the other end of the couch. "Anyway, I'd love to talk more, but my homework is practically staring me in the face... I have to go."

"You don't have to make up an excuse to get me off the phone."

Sidra giggled. "I promise that's not what I'm doing," she assured. "If I could avoid this work, I *would*."

"I'm just kidding sweetie, I'll talk to you later. Love you."

"Love you too." Sidra tossed the phone on the couch once she disconnected the call.

She stared at the contents in her cup while her mind wandered. The conversation with her mother struck up some feelings. She'd been thinking a lot about James lately. Wondering what it would be like to be in a relationship with him...in a relationship *period*.

"I need chocolate," she muttered to herself.

Rising from her seat, she headed into the kitchen, then began searching through cabinets. Finding a box of brownies, Sidra grabbed one. The front door opened just as she opened it.

"Hey crampy. You feeling better?" Malajia teased, tossing her book bag on the couch.

Sidra rolled her eyes. "Just because *you* don't have to deal with bad cramps doesn't mean you can make fun of *me*," she chided.

"I'm not making fun of you," Malajia assured, walking in the kitchen.

Sidra put her hand on her hip. "You *just* called me 'crampy'."

Malajia laughed. "My bad."

"Anyway, yeah I'm better thanks," Sidra said.

Malajia hopped up and sat on the counter. "So 'almost birthday' girl, how does it feel to know you're about to be twenty-one?"

Sidra took a bite of her brownie. "The same way it felt when I turned *twenty*...it's another year."

"Oh, come on, Sid. You can't tell me you're not excited." Malajia couldn't believe Sidra's nonchalance. She herself, was beyond excited to finally turn twenty-one. "You'll finally be a full-fledged adult."

"I was a full-fledged adult at *eighteen*," Sidra replied evenly.

Malajia shook her head. "It must be your period talking," she conceded. "I was *hype* to turn twenty-one."

Sidra chuckled. "That's because *your* drunk ass just wanted to be able to buy *liquor* on your own."

"You damn skippy," Malajia admitted. "Do you know how tired I was of asking them damn burnt out, upperclassmen fools to buy my drinks? They always came back with the wrong shit."

Sidra shook her head, then proceeded to take another bite of her treat. Before she knew it, her brownie had been slapped out of her hand by Malajia.

"You don't want that," Malajia teased, jumping off the counter.

"You stupid, stank heffa!" Sidra yelled at Malajia's retreating back.

"You mad as shit your brownie on the floor!" Malajia hollered from upstairs.

Furious, Sidra sighed loudly as she retrieved another one from the cabinet.

# Chapter 7

"I hope Sidra likes this cake," Emily said, lighting the number two and one candles on top of a chocolate-iced, black forest cake.

"Sidra is a chocolate fanatic. Trust me, she'll *love* it," Alex mused, sitting blue plastic plates and spoons on the dining room table. The girls made it to the bakery and back before Sidra was set to return from her afternoon class.

"I want some of that cake *now*," Malajia groaned, reaching for the cherry on top of the cake.

Alex quickly slapped her hand away. "Move your greedy behind," she warned. "And don't try to sneak any, like you do everyone *else's* birthday cake."

"I'll do it and you'll *like* it," Malajia shot back, pointing at Alex, who in turn flagged Malajia with her hand.

Chasity grabbed her bowl of cereal that she just poured off the counter when Malajia darted over to her.

"You don't—"

Spinning around, Chasity pointed at her, halting her mission. "Malajia, I swear to God, if you try to smack my damn cereal out of my hand, you're gonna have to fight me," she barked.

Deciding to call Chasity's bluff, Malajia reached for the bowl in Chasity's hand. Slamming the bowl on the counter,

Chasity grabbed Malajia's arm, and would have succeeded in punching her if Malajia hadn't started screaming like somebody was killing her.

Alex slammed her hand on the counter. "Malajia, come on!" she hollered at the unnecessary noise. "Chasity, let her go before I go deaf. *Please!*"

Chasity let go and shoved Malajia away from her. "Keep your fuckin' hands away from my food."

"You were about to fight me over *cereal?*" Malajia scoffed, rubbing her arm. "Childish."

Chasity stared at her, annoyed. She was unable to fathom why she was even friends with this silly girl in the first place. Chasity then looked at Alex. "Get her away from me," she demanded, pointing to Malajia.

"You mad you can't get rid of me," Malajia laughed.

"Malajia, you were supposed to be tying those balloons to the chairs," Alex barked, pointing to the cluster of blue balloons sitting near the couch.

Malajia sucked her teeth as she made her way over. "Why did you buy all this blue shit?" she grumbled, untying the helium balloons from the small weight on the floor.

"Blue is her favorite color," Alex huffed. "You already *know* that, stop being difficult and do your part."

Malajia mumbled something incoherently while untangling the balloon strings.

"I think I hear the door," Emily slid in, hearing the doorknob giggle.

"Not enough time to tie these," Malajia said, letting the balloons go, sending them flying up to the ceiling.

Alex smacked her face with her palm. *Never again am I trusting her with a task*, she thought of Malajia.

Sidra opened the door and was greeted by a loud, collective, "Happy birthday!"

"Awww you guys," Sidra gushed, looking around. "That's so sweet."

"We got you a cake," Alex said, hugging her.

"Thank you," Sidra cooed, eyeing the cake before

blowing out her candles.

"We're going to take you to dinner later and we can go party for *real* this weekend," Malajia informed. "Sucks that your birthday is on a Wednesday."

Sidra placed a piece of cake on a plate. "Eh, it's fine. And thanks, I'm happy to be spending my day with you girls." She took a bite, relishing the rich flavor. "My parents are coming down here on Sunday for the day. They want to take me out."

"That's nice," Emily commented, slicing a piece of cake with her fork.

Chasity grabbed a piece of cake, then stared at Sidra as she ate hers. Sidra's eyes were closed and she was breathing heavy. "Why do you look like you're borderline orgasmic?" Chasity chortled.

"'Cause I probably *am*," Sidra laughed. "This damn cake is so good."

Malajia put her hand up. "Hold up, the cake is like *that*?" she quipped. "Shit, the rest of that is coming in the bed with me later."

"Eww!" Alex yelped.

A knock at the door interrupted the girls' conversation. "It's open," Sidra called. Surprise resonated on her face as she saw James open the door and walk in, holding what had to be about two dozen blue and white assorted flowers in one hand and a gift bag in another. "James!" she shrieked, running over to hug him.

"Happy birthday beautiful," James smiled.

"Oh my God, that is *so* sweet," Emily gushed, holding her hand to her chest.

"What are you doing here? I thought you had a case to work on," Sidra asked, still in shock.

James handed her the flowers and bag. "I finished my work yesterday, so I figured that I would surprise you," he replied. "I thought that maybe I could take you to dinner, if you're free."

*Hell yes you can take me to dinner!* she thought. "Oh,

um…" She looked at the girls, who were standing near the table, smiling. "I would *love* to go, but the girls were already going to—"

"She's free," they cut in, in unison.

Sidra smiled at them gratefully. "Okay then. You mind waiting while I freshen up?" she asked him.

"Of *course* I don't mind. Take all the time you need," James smiled, sending Sidra skipping up the steps.

James unbuttoned his suit jacket. "How have you ladies been?" he asked, sitting on the couch.

"About as fine as *you* are," Malajia mumbled, earning a stiff backhand to the arm from Alex. Malajia snickered.

"We've been great," Alex answered, handing James a piece of cake. "You really put a big smile on my friend's face today."

James smiled, taking the plate. "I'm glad. I was determined not to miss her birthday."

"Mmm hmm. I'm sure you *was*, you sexy black bastard," Malajia slid in. Chasity nearly choked on the piece of cake that she was eating. Emily frantically patted her back.

If it wasn't for James's dark skin, the redness on his face would have been noticeable.

"Malajia, I swear to God, you really need help," Alex scolded.

Malajia looked around shocked. "What? What did I *do*?"

"Just go away," Alex commanded through clenched teeth, pointing to the kitchen. "So damn inappropriate."

Emily giggled as Malajia stomped away.

"Where's the birthday girl?!" Mark hollered, busting through the unlocked door with Josh and Jason in tow.

"Upstairs getting ready to go on her date," Emily informed.

The guys looked at James, who waved to them. "Oh, hey man, how's it going?" Mark greeted, shaking his hand.

"Everything is great," James replied.

Josh was far from excited to see him. *What the hell is he doing here?* "So, when did you get into town?" Josh asked, voice laced with disdain.

Ignoring Josh's curt tone, James shrugged. "Not too long ago. I came to see Sidra for her birthday."

Josh slowly folded his arms. "And when will you be *leaving?*"

James frowned up at Josh slightly. "Umm, I might drive back in the morning," he answered.

"You might as well roll *tonight*," Josh grunted. "You know...rush hour traffic in the morning and all." His friends were stunned.

James slowly stood up from the couch, straightening his jacket. Josh's tone couldn't be ignored any longer. "Have I done something to you Josh?" he charged.

"Aww shit," Chasity mumbled. Alex, hearing the comment, nudged her.

Malajia craned her neck from the kitchen. "Can I come back in now?" she asked.

Alex sucked her teeth. "Girl, come on."

Jason, sensing that Josh's temper was rising, decided to cut in. "Uh James, so what's it like being a lawyer?" he asked, stepping in front of Josh. "Do you try a lot of high profile cases?"

"Um, it's great. Very busy, *challenging* even...but great," James answered. He saw what Jason was trying to do and was grateful for the interruption. The last thing James wanted to do was argue with a college student, especially a friend of the woman he liked. "*Some* of the cases are high profile."

"Oh, that's cool," Mark added. "Do you deal with traffic cases? 'Cause I have these parking tickets and I was hoping—"

"Hush boy," Alex interrupted. "Just pay your tickets, and stop parking where you aren't *supposed* to."

Sidra trotted down the steps moments later. "I'm ready," she smiled.

"Great. I saw this place downtown on my way to campus that I think you'll like," James replied, taking her hand.

"I'm sure I will," she blushed. "Bye everybody."

"Have fun Sid," Emily said, waving to them as they headed out the door.

Jason laughed once the door closed. "Josh, you need to chill man," he said.

Josh's eyes widened. "What are you talking about?"

"Oh, come on Josh," Chasity jeered. "You had a whole attitude with that man. You looked like you wanted to punch him in the face."

"No, I didn't," Josh declared defensively. "Just because I wasn't smiling all in his face like the *rest* of you, doesn't mean that I was about to do anything *to* him."

"You told the man to drive home *tonight*," Malajia reminded.

"I was just a *suggestion*," Josh huffed, tossing his hands up.

"Josh's jealous ass was about to get his ass beat by James and shit," Mark teased.

Josh sucked his teeth. "Yeah whatever," he grumbled.

"You *know,* James is gonna tell her what you said to him. And she's gonna cuss you a new ass," Malajia pointed out, putting a slice of cake to her mouth. She flinched when the cake was slapped out her hand, falling, icing side down, on the table.

"You don't want that," Mark laughed.

"Shit!" Malajia yelled, stomping her foot on the floor. "Mark, come the fuck *on!*"

"Boy, you better wipe our damn table off," Alex demanded.

"I'm not wiping *shit,* cuz," Mark taunted, sticking his tongue out. Alex narrowed her eyes at him as he started doing a silly dance. His teasing was interrupted by cake being smashed in his face from both sides by Chasity and Malajia. "What the hell?!" he yelled. Before he could react any further, Jason smashed a piece on top of his head. "Oh, for real, roommate?"

"You damn right," Jason replied. "*That's* for smacking

my orange out of my hand earlier."

"That serves your childish ass right," Alex ground out, grabbing paper towel from the kitchen. "*You* started this mess."

"I didn't smash nothing in nobody's damn *face*," Mark argued, wiping cake from his face with his t-shirt. "Y'all always gotta take stuff overboard." He sucked his teeth when a piece of cake hit him on his chest. "*Really* Emily?"

Emily giggled. "Sorry Mark…You slapped my chips out of my hand in the cafeteria the other day."

Josh, deep in thought and not in the mood to participate, just sat on the arm of the couch.

# Chapter 8

Sitting at a table, a light breeze blew past Sidra's face, moving her hair in the process. She pushed her ponytail back over her shoulder while taking in the scenery in front of her. "You *would* find a place with a roof top restaurant," she mused.

Sidra didn't know what to think when she and James walked into the upscale building, down town. She was pleasantly surprised when James gently took her by the hand, and led her to an elevator which stopped at the top floor of the four-story building. She had a full view of the Paradise Valley skyline. The lighting and soft music, paired with the autumn breeze, had Sidra relaxed and smiling.

"Yeah, I figured we'd try some place a bit different," James said. "It's too beautiful out to sit indoors."

Sidra reached for her glass of wine. "Yeah, that's the lucky thing about having a birthday in September; not too hot, not too cold." She took a quick sip and bobbed her head slightly to the R&B song that was playing. "This music is so good," she beamed. "I heard about five of my favorite slow songs so far."

James nodded in agreement. "I like a woman who can appreciate good music," he said, taking a bite of his fried calamari.

"You're lucky it's not faster music, or I'd be forced to get up and show some moves," she chortled.

"Ah, you dance?"

"Define *dancing*," she giggled with a wave of her delicate hand. "No, I'm more of a swayer."

"Swaying can be good," James chuckled.

"Not when reggae starts playing and some of your friends begin dancing like they're straight from the islands…and I'm just standing there stiffly swaying."

James broke into laughter when Sidra demonstrated her movement with her shoulders. "Oh come on, I'm sure you're exaggerating. You look like you have some good moves."

Sidra pinched her fingers together. "A little," she admitted.

James held his gaze on Sidra as he watched her take another sip of her wine. The more he talked to her, the more time that he spent in her presence, the further he found himself drawn to her. Not just to her beauty, but to her personality, her spirit. *This casual talking thing isn't working for me anymore,* he thought.

"So umm, how are you liking your shrimp cocktail?" he asked, after a moment of silence.

Sidra gave a nod while she finished chewing her food. "It's really good," she answered, reaching for another piece of the chilled seafood. "I need to stop eating it before I get too full. I need to reserve some of this appetite for the entrée."

Not more than a few moments after Sidra spoke those words, the server showed up with their entrees. Between eating and being engrossed in conversation, both Sidra and James had lost track of the time and the other patrons surrounding them.

James sat back in his seat, as the waiter took their empty plates. "Man, that was good," he breathed, satisfied.

Sidra wiped her mouth with her napkin. "I know, probably one of the best meals that I've had in a while." She took a sip of water then leaned in. "James, I know I said this already, but I really appreciate you coming down here for my birthday." She smiled. "The flowers, the dinner, this *bracelet*—" She lifted her wrist, gesturing to the sterling silver bracelet, with the crystal heart shaped charm that he gifted to her. "Everything...I'm enjoying myself."

"It's *my* pleasure, Sidra," James replied. "I didn't want to miss your special day... Besides, I missed you and this was a perfect opportunity to see you."

Sidra glanced down at the table, blushing. "I missed you too," she replied, coyly.

James straightened his tie. "To be honest, I hate the fact that we don't live closer to each other," he said. "With me living in Washington DC, you living in Delaware and going to college in *Virginia*—"

"Yeah, I know," Sidra solemnly replied.

"But, both Delaware and Virginia are no more than a few hours from me, so it's not bad," James said. "You're worth the miles."

Sidra sighed. Sure, James talked a good game, but she knew that they were only dating casually. How much traveling would he really do for someone who wasn't technically his girlfriend? Would he even consider being with someone on a serious level who wasn't close by?

"The distance thing can be hard, I know," she shrugged. "...I guess that's why most long-distance relationships don't work." *Stupid! Why even put that in his mind?*

James held an intense gaze on Sidra. "*Any* type of relationship can work if both people are willing to *make* it work," he pointed out. He took a brief pause. "...Is this something that you want to make work?"

Sidra raised a curious eyebrow. *Wait, did he just ask what I think he did?* "Um...is this something that *you* want to make work?" she countered.

He chuckled, "I asked you first?"

"I asked you second," she returned, humor in her voice. "And it's my birthday, so you *have* to answer first."

James shook his head in amusement. "Is that a rule?"

"*Tonight* it is," she threw back.

James's smile was bright. "Yes, it *is*," he confirmed. "If *you* want to."

Sidra sat in stunned silence for a few seconds. She put her hand up. "Wait, are you asking me to be in a relationship with you?" she asked. "I just want to make sure this wine isn't making me hear things." She felt butterflies in her stomach when James gently took her hand and held it.

"Yes Sidra, I'm asking you to be in a relationship with me," James cooed.

She put her hand on her chest. *Play it cool Sidra, don't you jump out this seat like a starry-eyed teenager.* "I'd love to be in a relationship with you," she replied, trying to tone down her inner excitement.

"That settles it... I *finally* get to call you my girlfriend," James beamed.

"How long have you been thinking about this?" she wondered.

"A while," he admitted.

Sidra was smiling so much that her cheeks were starting to hurt. This was turning out to be one of the best birthdays. "My friends are probably going to scream when I tell them," she giggled.

James's smile faded, as a thought came back to him. He didn't know if he should address what he wanted to tell her at that moment, but he wasn't one for holding things in. "*Speaking* of friends...I feel that I should address something with you about one of them."

Sidra snapped out of her happy thoughts. "Huh? One of what?"

"One of your friends...Josh," he clarified.

Sidra frowned. "What *about* Josh?"

"I don't want to sound like I'm nitpicking but, I pride myself on presenting myself in a good way and... I don't know what I ever did to Josh, but...he seems to have something against me."

The frown never left Sidra's face. "Why would you say

that?" she asked, confused. "Did he say something to you?"

"It's not what he says, it's *how* he says it," James answered. "When I was waiting for you back at the house, his disdain for me was very...*noticeable.*"

Sidra rubbed the bridge of her nose with two fingers. She thought back to her conversation with Josh about James weeks ago. "I'm sorry, James," she apologized. "He's just protective of me...I'll talk to him."

"Sidra, I'm all for your friends being protective of you. Good friends *should* be. But...it's something different with him," he cautioned. "I know he's your best friend and I would never tell you to stay away from him—"

"I hope you *wouldn't*," Sidra interrupted, bite in her voice.

"No, I wouldn't," James assured. "I'm a secure man and you're a grown woman. I'm not going to tell you who you can and cannot hang out with. But in my opinion, his attitude... I don't think it stems from him just being *protective*...I'll just leave it at that."

Sidra was taken back. "What are you insinuating? That he doesn't like you because he likes *me*?" When James just looked at her, she quickly shook her head. "That's crazy, I'm like a sister to him."

"In *your* eyes, yeah. In *his*..." James let out a quick sigh. "Look, I'm sure you'll handle it," he resolved, signaling for the waiter. "I didn't mean to ruin the evening. I just thought that I should bring that to your attention."

Sidra folded her arms on the table. "You didn't ruin anything," she assured. *Oh, I'm surely going to have a conversation with Josh's ass tonight.*


Although James dropped her off at her door, Sidra couldn't go inside just yet. She couldn't let the rest of the day pass without talking to Josh. What James had said was still plaguing her.

Once James's car pulled off, Sidra made her way to the

guys' cluster. She knocked on the door and waited. Just as she hoped, Josh opened the door.

"Hey you, happy birthday," he smiled, hugging her.

"Thanks Josh," Sidra replied. "Are you busy?" she asked, once they parted from their embrace.

"No, not really." Josh moved aside. "You want to come in?"

Sidra shook her head. "Take a walk with me?" she suggested.

"Of course," he beamed.

Sidra ambled out of the cluster gates with Josh. Their journey took them through the quad. Her mind was trying to figure out how to start the conversation.

"I know I owe you a birthday present," Josh said, breaking through the silence as they continued to walk. "When I get my paycheck from the Pizza Shack on Friday, I'll get you something."

"Josh, you don't have to get me a present," Sidra said. "Use your money for something important."

"But, I *want* to," Josh insisted. "And *you* are important... You deserve a gift."

Sidra let out a sigh. "That's sweet Josh, thank you." Josh *was* being sweet, but she was still annoyed by his behavior. "Josh—" she looked at him. "I need to talk to you about something."

"Okay...what is it?"

She took a deep breath. "James told me that you had an attitude towards him earlier," she said.

Josh stopped dead in his tracks. The last thing that he wanted to talk about during their walk was James. "Oh, he *did* huh?" he hissed.

Sidra stopped walking and stood in front of him. "Yes Josh, he *did*," she affirmed. "Why did you do that?"

Josh rolled his eyes. "Sidra, it was nothing," he dismissed. "Let's just keep walking."

Sidra grabbed his arm, halting his departure. "Don't brush this off," she argued. "That was uncalled for. You may have your reservations about him, but he never did anything to you and didn't deserve your damn attitude."

Josh frowned. "What exactly did he tell you that I *said*, Sidra?"

"It doesn't matter what you said, it's how you *said* it," she bit back. "I think you should apologize."

Josh let out a laugh. "Yeah, okay," he dismissed. Then let out a sigh. This wasn't the conversation that he saw them having. "Look Sid...I don't want to argue with you and I especially don't want to talk about *James.*"

"But we *need* to Josh," Sidra insisted, tone calm. "You can't be acting like that towards him. Especially since...."

Josh looked perplexed when she trailed off. "Especially since what?"

"Especially since...he's my boyfriend now."

Shock and disappointment registered on Josh's face. "He's your what? ...He's *what*?"

"James is my boyfriend."

Distraught, Josh put his hands on his head. "Well when the hell did *that* happen?" he snapped.

"Tonight."

"Did you sleep with him or something?" he barked.

Sidra's eyes widened. "What? No!" she exclaimed. "What, you think the only way that he would agree to be my boyfriend is if he *slept* with me?"

"No—"

"I can't believe you don't think *more* of me, Joshua," Sidra fumed.

"I think the *world* of you Sidra. It's *him* I don't like," Josh argued. "What does some stuffy ass, damn near thirty-year-old want with you? Why isn't he with someone his *own* damn age?"

Sidra rolled her eyes. "God, Josh you're really being ridiculous," she bit out. "I can handle myself and I can handle James. You don't have to protect me from him. He's not going to hurt me."

"I don't want to talk about this bullshit anymore," Josh

ground out. "I can't believe that you actually allowed that arrogant bastard to persuade you to be in a relationship with him."

Sidra shook her head. She didn't recognize the person standing before her. She'd never seen Josh be this spiteful and jealous before. "What the hell is *wrong* with you?" she sneered. "You're acting crazy. I don't like this side of you."

"Forget it Sidra," Josh grumbled, kicking a rock with his sneaker.

"No, I *won't* forget it," she persisted. "You're acting jealous and you need to stop."

"I can't!" Josh yelled, startling her.

"Why *can't* you?!" she hollered back.

"What do you want from me?" Josh asked, desperate for Sidra to drop this disagreement.

"I want you to respect my feelings, my *decisions*," she pressed, stomping her foot on the ground. "Can't you just put aside your dislike for him, for *me*? I don't want things to be awkward for *any one* of us."

"It's because of you that I *can't*, Sidra," he vaguely replied. "I can't...accept your relationship. I can't support it."

Sidra was both confused and hurt, and managed to show both emotions on her face. "Why not?"

Josh hesitated. He had every intention of lying to just end the conversation. He even thought about apologizing to her for his behavior, but knew that it wouldn't be sincere. Looking into her questioning eyes, he couldn't hold it in any longer. "Because...I love you," he answered, finally.

"I love you *too* Josh," she replied.

Josh's heart jumped. "Really?"

"Yes, we're best friends; of *course* we love each other."

Josh shook his head. "No, no... I mean I'm *in* love with you... I have been for a long time."

Those words took Sidra by surprise. *Oh my God...James was right.* She tried to find the words to say, but nothing would come out.

Josh waited in agony as Sidra stood there in silence. The feelings that he had been hiding for years were finally out, and he couldn't take them back. "Please say something," he begged.

"Josh I…I don't know what to say," she stammered. She was reeling, how could she not have seen this coming?

Josh put his hands in his jacket pockets. "Well…You can say that you feel the same way about *me*," he said, hopeful.

Sidra tried to hold her tears in, but couldn't. "But…I *don't*," she carefully replied as the tears fell from her eyes. The hurt on Josh's face was hard for Sidra to bear. She knew at that moment their relationship would never be the same.

"You don't?" he asked, voice barely audible.

"I'm sorry…I don't love you like that," she reiterated, voice trembling. "You mean the world to me Josh…You're my best friend, always *have* been. I just…I don't see you in that way."

Josh's jaw tightened. He couldn't believe what he was hearing. The emotion on his face turned from sadness to anger. "You mean to tell me that this has *nothing* to do with the fact that I don't have any of the money, clothes, or cars that James has, huh?" he hissed.

"Josh, what he has doesn't have *anything* to do with it," she cried. "I'm not shallow, you *know* that."

"Yeah, I *thought* I did," he hissed. "I thought I knew a lot of things." The more Josh spoke, the angrier he became. "You know, I'm starting to think that you knew all this time how I felt and pretended not to, just so I would continue doing whatever the fuck you wanted."

"What?!"

"Yeah," Josh snapped. "Those tears are bullshit."

"Josh, I promise you, I didn't know how you felt." Sidra found it hard to breathe. Not only was he accusing her of liking James for his money, but now he was accusing her of playing with his emotions. Something that she would never do.

"Whatever yo," Josh barked.

Sidra reached out and tried to touch his arm again, but he jerked away from her. "I'm sorry, I don't know what to say to you," she sniffled.

"You don't have to say shit *else*," he fumed, turning to walk away. "I hope you're happy with your *boyfriend*. When he hurts you, don't come crawling to me."

"Josh, please don't leave like this!" Sidra yelled after him. When he ignored her, she put her hands over her face and sobbed.

# Chapter 9

Josh stomped up the step to his front door and pushed it open with so much force that it slammed against the wall. Startled, Mark, Jason and David looked up from their game of cards at the dining room table.

"Damn, you breaking doors and shit bro?" Mark jeered.

"Fuck this door," Josh barked, slamming it shut.

"The fuck is wrong with *you*?" Mark threw back.

Josh stood there seething. "Leave me alone."

Mark looked at David and Jason as he pointed to Josh. "Sid didn't like his bullshit excuse about not having no money for her gift and shit," he joked.

Josh breathed heavily as Mark began to laugh. "Mark, I'm not in the fuckin' mood for your commentary, alright?!" his voice boomed through the house.

Mark thought about continuing his taunting banter, but the pure rage on his friends' face let him know it was something serious. "Yo Josh, my bad, what's going on man?" he asked.

Josh flopped down on the couch in a huff. "Nothing."

"Naw, it's *something*," Mark insisted, slamming his cards on the table and jumping up from his seat. "Who we gotta jump man?"

Jason studied the pained look on Josh's face. It looked familiar. "Mark, calm down. I don't think we have to fight anybody," he said, putting his hand up.

"Naw, fuck that shit," Mark fumed, pacing back and forth. "*Nobody* pisses my brother off but *me*. We are whopping somebody's ass *tonight!*" he hollered, knocking his chair over.

Shaking his head at Mark, Jason turned his attention back to Josh. "What happened bro?" he asked.

"I don't want to talk about it," Josh mumbled.

"I don't understand," David put in. "You only went for a walk with Sidra. What could have *possibly* happened between then and *now*?"

"Nobody mention that name to me ever again!" Josh erupted, slamming his hand on the arm of the couch. His three friends stared at him. "What?!" he yelled, noticing their stares.

Mark and Jason gestured for David to say something to him. David cautiously walked over to Josh and sat down next to him on the couch. "Um…you want to tell us what happened?" he drew out slowly.

Josh threw his hands up in the air. "Might as well. For all I know she's probably laughing about it with the girls as we speak," he ground out. Playing with the zipper on his sweat jacket, he let out a sigh. "I told her."

"Told her *what*?" Jason asked.

"I told her how I felt…that I was in love with her," Josh admitted, voice low.

The guys sighed collectively. Jason looked at Mark, who in turn put his hands up, silently saying that he was staying out of it. "I'm guessing by your anger that she didn't return your feelings?" Jason assumed.

"Bingo," Josh grunted.

Jason understood how Josh felt. He himself went through the same thing when he first declared his love for Chasity and she shot him down after they'd slept together their sophomore year. "Look man, I get how you feel right now. I really do," Jason sympathized. "But trust me when I say that being angry at her won't make you feel any better. *I* should know. I went through that with Chaz."

"Yeah well, this isn't going to turn *out* like you and Chaz," Josh sneered. "Sidra is with James…apparently they're in a full-fledged *relationship* now."

Mark shook his head as he tried to avoid eye contact with Josh. Sensitive issues weren't his forte.

"That may be *so*, but you can't let your disappointment ruin your friendship," Jason stated bluntly. "You've been friends' *way* too long."

"Screw that friendship and screw *her*," Josh spat, standing from his seat. "I'm over it," he threw over his shoulder as he walked up the steps.

Hearing his room door slam shut, Jason let out a heavy sigh. "Damn man, that's tough," he commented, rubbing the back of his neck.

"It's gonna be tough for *David*, 'cause *he* gotta sleep in the same room with crying ass Josh, and shit," Mark joked. He then looked around at David and Jason, who shot him stern looks. "What?"

"That's not funny," Jason chided.

"Jase is right, Mark," David added. "*Clearly* Josh's feelings are hurt. It's not time for your jokes."

"Oh come on. We all know that Josh can't stay mad at Sidra," Mark argued. "He'll be calling her first thing in the morning. You'll see."


"Damn it Chasity! Do you *have* to keep making your player kick mine over and over like that?" Malajia hollered, tossing a game controller down on the floor.

"Bitch, you better not break my shit!" Chasity hollered back.

Malajia pointed to the black controller on the floor. "Fuck *you and* that controller," she fussed.

"Yeah a'ight," Chasity dismissed, reaching for her cup

of juice.

Alex laughed. She knew when Chasity purchased the game system earlier that evening, that Malajia would want to get her hands on it. Popcorn in hand, Alex watched in amusement while the girls played round after round for the past few hours. "Malajia, how are you mad at her because *you* lost? ...Again," she teased.

"Alex, shut up, that's why you ain't get a turn yet," Malajia hurled back.

"I don't *want* to play," Alex returned, voice calm.

"Then you don't need to be in the damn living room with us," Malajia barked, still upset over her frequent losses. "Sucking up our air and shit. Take your ass to the library with Emily."

Unfazed by Malajia's attitude, Alex simply waved a dismissive hand at her. Hearing the door open, she turned around to see Sidra walking in. "Hey Sid, how was your date?" Alex charged, enthused.

When Sidra just stood there, not answering, Chasity and Malajia turned around and looked at her as well.

Alex's smile faded once she took notice of the distraught look on Sidra's face. "Sweetie, what's wrong?"

Noticing Sidra's glistening eyes, Chasity frowned. "Are you crying?" she asked, concerned.

Tears streaming down her face again, Sidra nodded. After her blow up with Josh, Sidra just sat on a bench, crying. If it wasn't for the chilly air forcing her inside, she would have stayed out all night.

"What happened?" Malajia exclaimed, jumping up. "Whose ass I gotta kick? I need sneakers. Chaz, give me some sneakers!" she yelled, running towards Chasity's room.

"Girl, stay your ass out my room," Chasity called after her.

"Sidra, come here, sit down," Alex ordered, making room on the couch. "What happened?" she asked once Sidra settled in.

Unable to speak, Sidra just wiped her face with her

jacket sleeve.

"Do we need to beat James's ass?" Chasity assumed.

Sidra shook her head. "James didn't do anything to me," she assured, sniffing. "It's Josh."

Malajia looked bewildered as she sat on the arm of the couch. "Soooo, we need to beat *Josh's* ass?" she slowly drew out

"No Malajia, nobody needs to beat anybody's ass," Sidra snapped.

"Then what's the matter?" Alex asked, moving some of Sidra's hair behind her shoulder. "You're obviously upset over *something*."

"Josh is in love with me," Sidra blurted out. When she didn't hear any response from the girls for seconds, she looked around at them. They all looked as if they weren't surprised, avoiding eye contact with her. She frowned when realization set in. "Wait a minute," she spat, putting her hand up. "You all *knew*?"

"Uh *yeah*," Malajia confirmed, smartly. "Duh."

Sidra was shocked. "Seriously?"

"Honey, I think *everyone* had an idea," Alex added, rubbing Sidra's shoulder.

"And nobody told *me*?" Sidra fumed, pointing to herself.

"You *seriously* didn't know?" Chasity wondered. "He was as transparent as Malajia's clothes."

"Exactly...wait, what?" Malajia replied, picking up on Chasity's subtle dig.

"No damn it, I *didn't* know," Sidra assured. "He told me he was in love with me after we argued about James being my boyfriend and *now* he's pissed at me because I don't feel the same way about *him*."

"You told him that?" Chasity asked.

"I *had* to. I couldn't lie to him," Sidra said, wiping her eyes. "I just can't get the look on his face out of my head. He looked like I stabbed him in the heart."

Chasity shook her head. "Yeah, I know that look," she said, remembering her own encounter with Jason not even a

J.B. Vample

year ago. "All you *can* do is be honest with him. If you don't
feel for him what he feels for you then you did him a favor
by letting him know." She tilted her head at Sidra, fixing her
gaze. "...You *don't* feel the same way, *do* you?"

Sidra shot a piercing look Chasity's way. "What exactly
are you trying to imply Chasity? Huh?" she bit out.

"I'm just asking a question," Chasity returned, folding
her arms.

"Okay, let's not—"

"No, it seems that you're insinuating that I'm *lying*,"
Sidra hurled back to Chasity, cutting off Alex's words. "Like
*you* did to *Jason.*"

Chasity narrowed her eyes slightly. "That was uncalled
for," she replied with a forced calm. She resisted the urge to
lose her temper with Sidra, for Chasity knew that she was
upset, "And I would hope that you *wouldn't* put Josh through
what I put Jason through."

"I don't run from my feelings like *you* do, Chasity,"
Sidra hissed. "*I* didn't screw Josh and shoot him down after
he poured his heart out to me."

Chasity's jaw tightened. Now Sidra was hitting below
the belt, throwing a situation that Chasity regretted in her
face. Feeling like her temper was about to hit the ceiling;
Chasity rose from her seat.

"Let me remove myself before I punch this bitch in her
face," Chasity seethed.

Alex watched Chasity walk into her bedroom. "Chaz,
she didn't mean it, come back," she called after her.

"Nope!" Chasity threw over her shoulder, slamming the
door.

Malajia looked at Sidra who had put her head in her
hands. "Damn Sid, that was pretty rude," she admonished.

"I know," Sidra admitted. She knew that what she said
was uncalled for, but she couldn't take the words back.

"She'll be okay, Sid," Alex assured. "But back to *you.*
Chaz *is* right, you did the right thing by letting Josh down."

Sidra shook her head. "I don't know Alex... He's so

angry with me," she sulked. "I think he hates me."

"Josh could never hate you, Sidra," Malajia said, folding her arms. "That man would walk through fire for you."

"Not anymore," Sidra realized. "I don't know what I'm going to do if he doesn't want to be my friend anymore."

"That's not going to happen," Alex promised.

Sidra leaned back against the couch cushions, sighing in the process. "Some birthday *this* was," she grumbled.

"Um, it's not *all* bad. What did I hear about James being your *boyfriend*?" Malajia pointed out.

Sidra let a smile come through. "Yeah…we decided to give a relationship a try," she said, looking at her bracelet. "I really like him girls, and I hope this works out."

"I'm sure it will," Alex declared. "He seems like a great guy."

"He really *is*," Sidra agreed.

Malajia smiled as she twirled some of her hair with her finger. "His chocolate self looks like he can lay some pipe too."

Alex slapped her hand on the arm of the couch. "My God," she huffed, inciting a chuckle from Malajia.

Sidra, grateful for Malajia's silliness at that moment, giggled. "I wouldn't know. I haven't slept with him…or *anybody* for that matter," she admitted.

"And there is no *rush* to," Alex said, swatting at Malajia. "Sex is overrated anyway."

"Says *you*," Malajia laughed. Alex just shook her head.

# Chapter 10

Sidra awoke the next morning feeling groggy. Having tossed and turned all night, that wasn't surprising to her. She also wasn't surprised when Josh didn't call or come by for their morning walk to class.

Walking down the stairs, Sidra came face to face with Chasity, who was heading out for her class.

Sidra hadn't seen her since Chasity retreated to her room for the night. After Sidra had lashed out at her. Both girls paused and stared at each other for several seconds.

"I'm sorry," Sidra said sincerely.

"I know," Chasity replied evenly.

Sidra adjusted the silk scarf on her neck. "I was just upset last night. I didn't mean to throw that in your face."

"I know," Chasity repeated. She'd realized as she fell asleep that Sidra was feeling hurt by Josh's behavior. The same hurt that *she* felt when Jason told her that he couldn't be friends with her anymore after she admitted that she didn't want to be in a relationship. Chasity had reacted in a similar fashion. "Are you okay?"

Sidra sighed, relieved that the issue was squashed between them. The last thing she needed was another strained friendship. "I'm okay, I guess" she answered. "Well...not really. Chaz...what if he never talks to me again?"

"That may be a possibility," Chasity stated bluntly. "His pride is hurt. Guys react without thinking when that happens."

Sidra looked at the floor.

"But either way it goes, you'll be fine," Chasity declared. "And once he gets over not being able to get his way, *he'll* be fine too."

"I hope so," Sidra mumbled. "I just hate this conflict between us."

"Yeah well, conflict is a part of life, trust me," Chasity said, grabbing a bottle of juice from the counter.

"Yeah," Sidra moped.

Chasity shot Sidra a sympathetic look. "Look, I gotta get to class. You going in my direction?" she asked.

Sidra nodded.

"I may not be Josh, but you can walk with me," Chasity offered.

Sidra smiled. "Thank you."

"Sure," Chasity nodded.


Josh's focus was hardly on his professor, who was going over math problems in his calculus class. He hadn't spoken to Sidra since their falling out two days ago; it was an eternity. *Just forget her*, he thought. Staring out the window at the fall-colored leaves blowing across the manicured lawn, he didn't hear his name being called.

"Mr. Hampton," Professor Turner repeated, stern.

"Huh, did you call me?" Josh asked, snapping out of his trance. Much to the humor of some of his classmates.

Professor Turner pointed to a problem on the board. "Maybe whatever is out that window that you've been looking at, can help you solve this problem on the board."

Josh stared at the board, before looking down at his scrambled notes. "No ma'am, I don't think it will," he mumbled.

Handing him a piece of chalk, Professor Turner frowned.

"Please go up and solve the problem," she demanded, much to Josh's dismay.

Josh hesitantly grabbed the chalk and slowly approached the board. "Use the limit definition to compute the derivative F(x)," he read aloud.

"Thank you, Mr. Hampton, for the reading lesson." Several classmates snickered. "Quiet please," Professor Turner scolded. "Please solve," she directed to Josh.

Josh swallowed hard then began scribbling on the board. Realizing that he had no idea what the answer was, he sat the chalk down and faced his teacher. "I'm sorry, I don't know the answer," he admitted.

Professor Turner shook her head. "It pays to pay attention, Mr. Hampton," she chided. "Take your seat."

Embarrassed, Josh quickly headed back to his seat and plopped down. As the professor called another student to the board, he put his hand over his face, wishing that he could disappear.


Josh was still kicking himself once the hour was up and he walked out of class. It didn't help that he came face to face with Sidra, who was heading to one of her classes in the same building. They stopped short of bumping into one another.

Josh stared at her, face void of any emotion.

"Hi Josh," Sidra stammered, clutching her books to her chest. She wondered if today would be any different. Would he smile? Would he *speak*? She got her answer when Josh moved around her and walked away.

She closed her eyes and let out a long sigh. *Nope, no different,* she thought, continuing on her way.


Josh's pace quickened as he headed towards the gates of the clusters. *I need a damn nap.*

His eyes shifted when he saw Malajia and Emily heading

in his direction. Hoping that they wouldn't notice him, Josh lowered his head and walked past.

"For real Josh? You gonna act like you don't see us?" Malajia sneered, turning around to face him.

Josh looked up. *Shit!* "Sorry ladies, I'm in a rush," he lied.

"Is your *mouth* in a rush too?" Malajia jeered. "You act like you can't say 'hi'. I mean, I know your man pride is still hurt, but you don't have to act like you don't know us."

Josh rubbed the back of his neck and sighed. "You're right, I'm sorry," he said. "Hi."

"It's too late now," Malajia scoffed, waving her hand at him dismissively.

Emily titled her head. "Josh umm…we're taking Sidra out tomorrow night… *You* should come *too*," she proposed. "It's for her birthday."

"No, I'll pass, thank you," Josh hissed, walking away.

Malajia turned to Emily and sucked her teeth. "Good job, Emily," she sarcastically spat.

Emily's eyes widened. "What did I do?" she exclaimed.

"You know *damn* well he's still mad at Sidra," Malajia chastised, poking Emily's shoulder. "Why would he want to party with her?"

Emily shrugged. "I just thought he would want to go out," she defended. "I mean, they're still friends…right?"

Malajia shook her head. "Just come on," she commanded, giving her a playful shove towards the gate.


"Oh, this place seems nice," Emily mused, craning her neck out of the car window.

"It *better* be, as hard as it was to get a damn reservation," Malajia muttered, adjusting an earring in her ear.

Chasity pulled her black Lexus into the parking lot of their chosen restaurant around nine o'clock Saturday evening. The girls jumped out the car and made their way to the front of the restaurant.

"I'm starving," Alex complained, adjusting her blouse on her shoulder. "I haven't eaten all day."

"I don't know *why*," Malajia said, pushing some of her curled hair over her shoulder. "You worked around pizza all damn day; you should've eaten *that*...and brought some home for *us*."

Alex rolled her eyes; the last thing she wanted after working her shift at the Pizza Shack all morning, was pizza. "I didn't *want* pizza," she admonished.

Sidra solemnly walked alongside the girls as they approached the entrance. Although she was appreciative of the girls making good on their promise to take her out that weekend, she would have much rather spent the night curled up in bed.

"You girls didn't have to bring me to dinner," Sidra said. "I appreciate it but...I'm not really hungry."

"Oh chick, you better *get* hungry," Malajia demanded, shooting her a glance. "Ain't nobody fuckin' around with you tonight, Sidra."

Chasity snickered at Malajia's reaction.

Sidra sighed, shoving her hands into the pockets of her dark blue knee-length jacket. "Okay," she resolved.

Alex put her hand on Sidra's shoulder. "Try to cheer up, sweetie," she smiled. "Tonight is about *you* and we're going to have fun."

"These shots that she's about to take will get her ass to have fun *real* quick," Chasity commented, glancing at her watch.

Sidra rubbed her forehead. "One drink couldn't hurt," she agreed.

"Nah, we said *shots*, as in *plural*," Malajia pointed out. "Oh and we're going to a club afterwards."

Sidra's eyes widened. Clubs were not her scene. "A *club*?... Seriously?"

Chasity shot Sidra a stern look. "Sidra, stop acting twelve," she ground out, earning snickers from Malajia and

Alex. Sidra rolled her eyes.

"I wonder where the guys are," Emily said, looking around. "It's chilly out here."

Emily's question was answered when Mark, Jason, and David headed straight for them.

"Let's hurry up and get this table, so we can hit the club," Mark said, bobbing his head as he walked.

"Why you bobbing that big ass head of yours?" Malajia scoffed, folding her arms. "There ain't no music on out here."

Mark smirked at her. "I can bob my *other* head for you if that'll make you feel better," he joked, much to Malajia's disgust.

"I swear to God, I'm about to throw up," Malajia complained.

"Mark, come on," Alex grimaced. "Nobody wants to hear about your damn penis before we go eat."

Mark opened his mouth to fire off a vulgar retort, but was halted when Chasity pointed at him. "Shut up," she said to him. Mark chuckled.

Sidra craned her neck to peer past the crowd gathering on the sidewalk. She was hoping that one more figure would approach. "Josh isn't coming, *is* he?" she asked after a few moments.

The guys glanced at one another, almost as if they didn't want to answer. "Uh, sorry Sid. But, no he isn't," Jason answered carefully.

Sidra looked at the ground as she pushed some of her straight hair behind her ear. She decided to wear it down that evening.

"He sends his regards though," David added, hoping that would make her feel better.

"No, he *doesn't*," Mark ground out, much to the dismay of the girls. They didn't want Sidra to feel any worse than she already did. "He sends his *bitch assness* though," he added.

"Mark, chill out," Jason scolded.

"Naw Jase," Mark snapped, shaking his hand in Jason's direction. "He was all yelling in my face and shit. Talking about he was gonna slap somebody if they mentioned Sidra's name again. He can slap me if he *want* to," he fussed. "I'll punch his hairline back."

David just shook his head. Although he wished Mark would have a little more tact, he understood Mark's aggravation. They had to endure Josh's snapping and ranting before leaving the house, at the suggestion of him coming along.

"Talking about, 'why don't y'all call James to go out with y'all since you seem to think he's so damn cool'," Mark ranted.

Jason pinched the bridge of his nose with two fingers, as Sidra held her solemn gaze down on her black pumps.

"Talking about—"

"Shut up!" Chasity, Malajia and Alex collectively snapped.

"*Thank* you," Jason seethed, shooting Mark a glare.

"Oh, now y'all wanna snap at *me* when *Josh* is acting like the asshole, huh?" Mark shot back full of sarcasm.

"Naw man, we *told* you on the way here, not to repeat what he said," Jason chided. "You run your mouth too much… Always talking shit."

Mark pointed at Jason. "You know what, I don't like how you've been treating me lately," he barked.

"Do you *want* to get punched in the face tonight?" Jason fumed.

Trying not to laugh, Chasity stepped in between Jason and Mark. "It's not about y'all right now," she pointed out, putting her hand on Jason's chest, moving him away.

"*Exactly*," Alex scolded. "Drop the nonsense and let's go celebrate for Sid." She walked into the restaurant with most of the gang following her.

"What's gotten in to you?" Chasity whispered to Jason, voice full of amusement. "You've been cussing Mark out all day."

"He keeps using my fuckin' deodorant, babe," Jason huffed. Chasity busted out laughing.


"I feel so much better now," Sidra smiled.

"Yeah, I *bet*," Chasity agreed. "Those three margaritas that you had probably have something to do with it."

Dinner now over, the gang made their way to the night club. Sidra barely touched her dinner, but didn't skimp on the drinks, which explained why she didn't put up anymore fight about going to the club.

"Yes, I'm sure they did," Sidra giggled, standing at the bar with the girls. "They were good, too."

"*I* wouldn't know," Chasity sneered.

Sidra playfully poked Chasity's cheek. "Aww, is baby Chasity mad because she couldn't order any drinks?" she teased.

Malajia laughed. "She mad she's not twenty-one yet." She took a sip of her rum and cola. "This is gooooood."

Chasity glanced down at her bright pink, 'under twenty-one' wristband that was put on her by the bouncer at the door. "Y'all heffas are real funny," Chasity huffed, sipping her ginger ale.

"You know you don't want that bullshit," Malajia taunted, pointing to Chasity's glass.

Chasity nearly spat her soda out. "I *don't*," she laughed.

Emily giggled. "It's okay Chaz, *I'm* not twenty-one yet either," she said. "We can *not* drink together."

"*You* don't count alchi," Malajia joked.

Noticing the slight frown on Emily's face at Malajia's joke about Emily's previous ordeal with alcohol, Alex nudged Malajia. "Shut the hell up, Mel," she fumed.

Malajia looked up from her drink. "What?" she asked, looking around; then noticed Emily's glare. "Oh too far, huh?"

"A little," Emily admitted, before putting her hands up. "But it's fine. I guess I'm not immune to jokes."

Malajia let out a sigh of relief. "Good, 'cause I have a *lot* of them."

Mark darted up and tried to snatch the drink from Malajia's hand but she resisted by keeping it out of his reach. "Mel, just let me take it," Mark demanded through clenched teeth.

"Cut it out before I make you *wear* it," Malajia threatened, nudging him away from her. "Get your broke ass away from me."

"Fine," Mark huffed. "I don't need your watered-down drink anyway." He tapped on the bar counter, signaling the bartender. "My man, let me get two shots of vodka. One regular, one melon flavored."

"Eww, who's drinking that nasty melon flavored shit?" Chasity scoffed.

"Not *you*, pink wristband," Mark threw back, earning laughter from his friends. "You sober as shit right now."

Chasity nodded, amused. "It's fine, you got it," she resolved. She drank the rest of the ginger ale. "Fuck y'all."

Once the bartender handed Mark his shots, he handed the melon flavored one to Sidra. "Here ya go, Princess."

Sidra put her hand up. "Oh no, I don't like shots," she protested.

"Girl you better *take* that shit," Malajia urged. "It's not every day or *ever* that Mark pays for shit."

Mark made a face at Malajia in retaliation for her dig.

"Sidra, if you don't want the shot, you don't have to take it," Alex said, amused.

"Yes, she *does*," Malajia insisted, slamming her hand on the bar counter. "Those are the birthday rules."

Alex frowned in confusion. "What rules—"

"The rules that tell you to shut the fuck up and mind your damn business!" Chasity snapped. "I'm too fuckin' sober to listen to your ass ruin shit all night."

"Oh my God, *thank you*," Malajia agreed, tipping her glass to Chasity.

Emily spat out her soda, laughing at the annoyed look on

Alex's face.

Ignoring the bickering around her, Sidra gave a long look at the shot in Mark's hand. "What the hell," she shrugged, taking the shot. She then put her hand over her mouth and coughed. "Ugh!"

Mark downed his shot, then gently grabbed Sidra's hand. "Come on birthday girl, come dance with me," he smiled.

Patting her chest at an attempt to relieve the burning, Sidra returned his smile. She allowed herself with the girls in tow to be led to the dance floor to party.

"I can't believe he hates me. My best friend hates me," Sidra sobbed on Chasity's shoulder.

"He doesn't hate you Sidra, he's just mad," Chasity placated, holding onto an intoxicated Sidra.

Throughout the two hours that the group was in the club, Sidra took several more shots of straight liquor, accompanied by a few mixed drinks. As the alcohol took effect, it brought Sidra's emotions to a head. Now outside of the club, she was pouring those emotions out.

"Chaz, give me the keys, I'll grab the car," Alex urged, reaching for Chasity's purse. "There is *no* way she can walk." Keys in hand, Alex and Emily took off jogging towards the parking lot.

Sidra's arms went limp around Chasity. "I swear I didn't mean to hurt him," she slurred through her tears.

Chasity tightened her grip around Sidra. "We know that," she sympathized, then gestured for Malajia to stop laughing.

"Oh, I'm gonna throw this up in her face *so* hard tomorrow," Malajia assured. "She's always getting on *me* about being drunk."

Chasity shook her head as she tried to keep Sidra's limp body from sliding. "Goddamn it Sid, you're heavier than you *look*," she complained.

"It's that drunk, dead weight," Malajia joked, helping to hold Sidra up.

When Sidra began heaving, Chasity shoved Sidra's body into Malajia. "Shit."

"Chasity! What the hell?" Malajia exclaimed, holding Sidra around her waist. "Don't make her throw up on *me!*"

With Malajia steadying her and Chasity holding her hair behind her back, Sidra leaned forward and threw up on the sidewalk.

Malajia frowned in disgust. "Ugh, we probably shoulda' forced her to eat more, first," she realized as Chasity grabbed some tissue from her purse.

"Don't think that would've helped," Chasity muttered, wiping Sidra's face.

"Damn, she's gonna feel like shit tomorrow," Jason said, walking up to the girls.

"Fuck tomorrow, she's heavy *now*," Malajia jeered, keeping Sidra steady.

Jason grabbed the limp Sidra and picked her up in his arms.

"She just threw up. She might do it again," Chasity said, when Sidra's head rested on Jason's shoulder.

"It's okay," he stated. "David went with Mark to get his car."

"Yeah, Alex and Emily went to get mine," Chasity said. She looked over at Sidra who started slurring incoherently. "Yeah, nobody can understand you, sweetie."

Jason chuckled.

Alex pulled the car to the curb and Jason carefully placed Sidra in the backseat. "Y'all get home safe," he said as Chasity and Malajia hopped in the back to tend to Sidra.

He waited until the car was out of sight before heading to the parking lot in search of the guys.

# Chapter 11

Sidra forced open her eyes. Finding the room spinning, she shut them again. Turning over, she clutched her stomach and groaned in pain.

*God, let me die, please.*

Sidra didn't remember how she got into bed, let alone how she ended up in just her panties and bra. Forcing herself to sit up, she felt her head pound.

Malajia skipped into the room. "Hey drunkie," she teased, holding a glass of orange juice.

"Very funny," Sidra croaked, running her hands through her disheveled hair.

Malajia giggled. "You look like death."

"Yeah well, I *feel* like it," Sidra agreed. "God, my head hurts so bad," she moaned, putting her head in her hands.

"Welcome to your first hangover, Princess," Malajia said, handing Sidra the glass of juice and two aspirin.

"It'll be my *last*."

Malajia waved her hand dismissively. "Yeah, I said that before *myself*," she laughed.

Sidra took the aspirin and sipped her juice. "What *happened* last night?"

"How much do you remember?"

Sidra slowly shook her head. "I was dancing…I think." She squinted.

"You were *dancin'* alright," Malajia chortled. "Didn't know you knew how to shake your ass so much."

Sidra put her hand over her face in embarrassment.

"Well after you danced, you went back to the bar and started downing those melon vodka shots like *crazy.*"

Sidra cringed. "Please don't mention shots," she moaned.

"*Then* your emotional ass started crying about Josh," Malajia continued. "You was crying all on Chaz's shoulder and shit. Getting lipstick all on her dress—" Sidra sat there listening to the recap, she was completely embarrassed. "Then you threw up on the curb outside the club…and in the grass on the way in the house…and on Jason."

"Are you serious? I threw up on Jason?!" Sidra exclaimed, mortified. Malajia nodded. "Oh my God, that's horrible."

"He wasn't mad... He was *salty*, but not mad," Malajia chortled. "It happened when he carried you up here to your bed…Alex took your dress off, because it was just gross and we were *gonna* put your night gown on, but your limp ass wasn't having it."

Sidra had her hands over her face, shaking her head. "I cannot believe that I showed my *entire* ass last night."

"Well, it was bound to happen," Malajia laughed, much to Sidra's annoyance. "You better get yourself together. Your parents are downstairs."

Sidra gasped. "Shit, I forgot they were coming to take me out today," she panicked, struggling to stand up. "Do they know I got drunk last night?"

"Yup. Your mom was up here touching your nose to make sure you were still breathing," Malajia laughed. "They're downstairs chillin'. They're cool."

The thought of doing anything besides sleeping was not on Sidra's to do list, but she knew that she had to get herself together since her parents made the trip down. "Ow, my stomach hurts," she groaned, slowly walking to the door.

"Yep, that sounds about right," Malajia teased. "Hurry up and don't breathe on me."

"Shut up," Sidra hissed, passing her on her way out the door.

After staying in the bathroom for what felt like an eternity, showering and primping, Sidra slowly and painstakingly, got dressed and headed downstairs to meet her parents.

"Well, well look who's finally awake," Mrs. Howard mused, giving her daughter a hug.

Sidra shook her head. "Mama, Daddy, sorry I kept you waiting," she said, rubbing her head with her hand.

"It's fine sweetie," Mrs. Howard assured. "Are you sure you want to go out? I know how those hangovers can be."

"I'm okay. Just don't put any drinks in my face," Sidra stipulated, grabbing her stomach. "Just thinking about it is making me nauseas."

"You know what they say. The best way to get over a hangover is to have another drink," Mr. Howard teased.

Sidra shot her father a warning look. "Daddy, not funny."

Sidra spent the ten-minute ride to a local restaurant laying down in the back seat of her parents' van, while filling them in on what was going on between Josh and herself. She wasn't the least bit surprised that the topic of discussion continued through lunch.

"I'm sorry that you two are going through this," Mrs. Howard sympathized. "You and Josh have always been the closest."

Sidra poked at her pan seared chicken breast. "I know, which is what's making this so hard," she said. She closed her eyes when she felt her head pound. "Ugh, I am *never* drinking again," she whined.

Mr. Howard chuckled. "I remember those days from college," he reminisced. "I'm just glad that you were around people who looked out for you."

"Me too," Sidra mumbled, leaning back against her seat. "Wouldn't have drank if I *wasn't*."

Mrs. Howard took a sip of her juice. "So, how was your date with James on your birthday?" she asked. "You were supposed to call me and tell me about it."

"I know, I'm sorry. I just had a lot on my mind," Sidra replied. "But it was really nice. And…we've established that we are in a relationship."

Mr. Howard looked up from his steak. "A relationship? With you living in different states?"

Sidra glanced at her father. "Daddy, please don't start this."

"I'm just curious as to how that will work," her father persisted. "And I *still* think he's a bit old for you."

"Seven years older isn't that drastic," Sidra sneered. "And with all due respect, I'm not a child. I can date who I *want*."

Mrs. Howard saw the tension rise between her husband and daughter. She understood her husband's concern. But having met James and knowing how Sidra felt about him, she was fine with Sidra's decision. "Okay, calm down you two," she cut in, touching her husband's arm. "Sidra is a smart girl and you know she doesn't make any major decisions without thinking them through."

Mr. Howard sighed. "Fine, I'll stay out of it," he relented, putting his hands up in surrender. "I'm just looking out for you."

"I know that Daddy," Sidra realized. "And I'm sorry for being a smart ass."

He chuckled as he sipped his juice. "It's okay, I should be used to it from your mother." Mrs. Howard playfully backhanded him on the arm as Sidra giggled.


"Why do I keep putting off homework until the last
minute?" Malajia huffed, tossing her pencil across the living
room.

"And now you have to go get it," Alex stated evenly, not
removing her eyes from her textbook. Both she and Malajia
were assembled at the dining room table later that evening,
doing hŏmework.

"If I have to write *one* more fake ass proposal for this
business class, I'm gonna scream," Malajia complained,
snatching open her notebook.

"Whining isn't going to write it *for* you," Alex jeered,
jotting down notes in her notebook.

Malajia frowned at Alex, preparing to fire off a smart
comeback, when Sidra walked through the door.

"God, I forgot about my homework," Sidra groaned,
seeing the girls' books sprawled across the dining room table.

"You still feeling like trash?" Malajia asked.

"Um…a little," Sidra admitted, sitting a bag down on the
table. "I brought some leftovers."

"Ooh, mine!" Malajia exclaimed, snatching the bag and
running to the kitchen, digging through it.

Sidra shook her head, flopping down on the couch. "This
has been a long week," she sighed. "Where's Chaz?"

"At Jason's getting her freak on," Malajia joked,
opening Sidra's food container.

"She's helping him with his coding assignment," Alex
corrected, shooting Malajia a warning look.

"Oh," Sidra replied. "I meant to ask, has anybody seen
my cell phone? I can't find it."

"Yeah, Chaz took it from you last night," Malajia
informed, sitting back at the table

Sidra frowned. "Why?"

"Because you woke up last night and tried to drunk dial
James," Malajia giggled.

Sidra's eyes widened. "Seriously?!"

"Girl yes," Alex put in, voice full of amusement. "You were saying that you wanted to call him so he can come have sex with you."

Sidra slammed her face into the couch cushions. "Oh my God," she groaned. "I am *such* a sloppy drunk."

"That you are," Malajia laughed. "*And* you shoved the phone down your panties and took a picture of your vag."

Sidra was horrified. "I *what*?!"

"Yeah, you tried to text it to James," Malajia added. Sidra looked like she wanted to cry, then Malajia busted out laughing. "Sike naw, you didn't do that."

Alex shook her head as Sidra breathed a sigh of relief.

"I hate you sometimes," Sidra hurled at Malajia, pointing at her.


"Y'all want to head to the caf?" Mark asked David and Sidra as they moseyed out of the English building.

"Yeah," David answered, rubbing his stomach. "Now that my presentation is over, I'm suddenly starving."

"I still don't know *why* you get nervous before doing any of your school work, David," Sidra quipped. "You know you're going to get an A anyway."

"Well, my nervousness pushes me to do the best that I can," David stated, adjusting his glasses.

"You're such a nerd," Mark teased.

"Yeah well—" David nearly dropped his books when Mark punched him on the arm. "Ouch! What the hell?!"

"Punch buggy no punch back," Mark taunted, pointing at David, who grabbed his struck arm with his free hand.

"*Where* do you see a damn buggy?!" David erupted. Mark stood there, looking stupid. "There're no *cars* out here, we're in the middle of the fuckin' campus!"

"My bad…I thought I saw one," Mark calmly replied. "But that's for a future bug—"

"Just shut up and get away from me," David barked. He

turned around and saw Sidra clutching her stomach, doubling over with laughter. He held an annoyed gaze on her.

Sidra wiped a tear from her eye when she caught David's glare. "I'm sorry David, but he's so *stupid*," she laughed, giving Mark's arm a light tap. "You have no sense."

Mark too laughed. "I know," he agreed. He held his hand out for David to give him a high-five. "Up top."

"I said get away from me," David hissed, making Sidra laugh louder. She hadn't laughed that hard in weeks.

Looking around, Mark adjusted the book bag on his shoulder. Noticing Josh across the yard, he waved his arm. "Yo Josh!"

"You guys go catch up to him, I'll see you later," Sidra said, turning to walk off.

"No, you're coming with us," Mark demanded, clutching her arm. Sidra reluctantly allowed herself to be pulled along as they met up with Josh.

"Guys, I have to study," Josh hissed, shifting his books from one arm to the other.

Mark frowned. "At two in the afternoon?" he sneered. "Naw, come to the caf with us for lunch," he insisted.

Josh glanced at Sidra, who was trying to avoid eye contact with him. "I'm not hungry," he spat.

Sidra shook her head. Over the past two weeks, her feelings about Josh's treatment of her went from sad to annoyed. "Mark, David, you guys go on without me. I have food at the house."

Mark stomped his foot on the ground when Sidra walked away.

"Sid, don't go," David pleaded at her departing back.

"See you later," she threw over her shoulder.

Mark and David both glared at Josh, who was looking at his watch. They'd had enough. Mark pointed to the bench off the path. "Josh, sit down," he demanded.

"Look, I don't have time for this," Josh huffed.

"I said sit your bitch ass down!" Mark snapped, voice carrying.

Josh thought about just ignoring the request and walking away, but figured he would just have to hear whatever they were going to say back at the house later anyway. He let out a loud, frustrated sigh and flopped down on the bench.

"Josh, it's been two weeks. This has got to stop," David began, sitting next to him. "You are being completely rude to Sidra and to the *rest* of us."

"So?" Josh bit out, examining his knuckles.

"*So*, you're pissing us off," Mark fussed, sitting down on the other side of him. "You're about to get jumped."

"Yeah, whatever," Josh challenged.

"You're not Jason, dawg," Mark fumed. "You're not *going* to get the girl in the end, so you're wasting your time pulling this bullshit."

"Who said I was trying to be like *Jason*?" Josh spat. "I'm reacting how I *want*, so leave me the fuck alone."

Mark rubbed his face furiously as he searched for the words to say. "Okay look, all joking aside; you need to check this attitude," he bluntly stated. "You didn't get the response that you wanted when you told her how you felt. So what? Are you *really* gonna throw years of friendship out the damn window because you can't get what you want?" Mark shook his head. "And people say *I'm* the immature one."

Josh was silent.

"Mark is right," David added. "You're mad at her for being honest with you. But I think the person you're *really* mad at is your*self*."

"Guys come on. Just let me deal with this my own way," Josh pleaded.

"*Your* way is hurting our sister," Mark chided.

Josh let out a sigh. "Are y'all finished?" he asked after several moments of silence.

Mark and David looked at each other. "For *now*," David replied, grabbing his books from the bench. "But if you don't fix this soon, I'm going to beat you in your sleep with a pillow."

Mark laughed as he stood up. "That's what *I'm* talking

about," he approved. "Come on David, let's hit the caf before people start digging all in the food and shit."

Josh watched his friends walk off, leaving him sitting there alone with his own thoughts.


If it wasn't for his stomach growling, Josh could have possibly sat in the same spot all day. Not wanting to deal with the crowd at the cafeteria, he decided to grab a burger and fries from the campus diner and head back to his room.

Upon entering the house, he saw Jason walk out of his room, holding a gym bag. Hearing the opinions of everyone else over the past weeks wasn't helping; Josh needed the opinion of someone who knew what he was going through. "Jason, do you have a minute?" he asked.

Jason grabbed his water bottle from the refrigerator. "Uh, I'm on my way to practice right now," he stated. "Can this wait?"

Josh sighed, placing his food container on the kitchen counter. "Sure," he replied, tone sullen.

Jason thought for a moment. Josh's sad demeanor he was used to at this point, but the fact that Josh actually wanted to talk to him, Jason couldn't just brush the request aside. "Hey, you know what, why don't you walk with me to the field?" he offered.

Josh nodded, smiling slightly.

"What's on your mind?" Jason asked, adjusting his bag on his shoulder as they walked the path towards the football field.

Josh hesitated momentarily. "When did you get to the point after you and Chasity had your falling out where you decided that you couldn't stay mad at her anymore?" he blurted out.

That question took Jason by surprise. "Wow," he pondered. "Well, I realized as time passed, that I missed being her friend."

Josh looked at him.

"I'm not saying that I was over the feelings that I had for her, because I definitely *wasn't*," Jason added. "It was a struggle for me, but I just felt I'd rather keep our friendship, than lose her entirely."

"Yeah?" Josh replied.

"Yeah man," Jason confirmed. "See, being angry at her wasn't doing anything but driving us further apart." When Josh didn't respond, Jason looked at him. "Is that what you want to happen between you and Sidra?"

"Of *course* it's not what I want," Josh assured. "I don't *want* to stay mad at Sidra. I do miss her. I'm just...salty."

Jason chuckled. "I get that, but you have to man up and decide what's more important... your pride, or your friendship."

Josh stopped walking as they approached the field. "I hear you," he said. "I guess I have some serious thinking to do."

"Yeah, I'd say that you *do*."

"Thanks for the time man," Josh replied, grateful.

"Anytime bro," Jason smiled, before walking off.

Josh stared at the blank page in his notebook. He rubbed his eyes, then picked up his half-eaten burger to take another bite. He'd been holed up in his room, trying to work on an assignment for his Fundamentals of Contemporary Speech class, for the past few hours. But no matter how hard he tried, how many words he scribbled, how many papers he tore out of his notebook, Josh's thoughts and ideas just weren't materializing.

He leaned back in his seat and put his face in his hands. "This is torture," he sighed to himself. Taking a deep breath, he rose from his seat. Grabbing his jacket off the back of his chair, he headed out the door.

Josh's short journey took him across the path towards the girls' house. He raised his hand to knock, but hesitated. *Just do it. You can't focus on anything else.* Listening to his heart, Josh finally knocked on the door.

He was both relieved and nervous when Sidra answered the door.

"Josh," she blurted out, shocked. He was the last person that she expected to see.

"Hey... Can I talk to you?" he asked, shoving his hands in his jacket pockets.

She held a skeptical gaze. "Uh, yeah sure... You want to come in?"

"I'd rather sit outside, if that's okay with you."

"That's fine," Sidra agreed. "Let me grab my jacket."

Josh waited on the step while Sidra hurried to her room to retrieve her jacket. When she returned, he led her to the seating area behind their cluster.

Sitting on top of one of the wooden tables, Josh gathered his thoughts. "Sidra...I know it's been a while—"

"Two weeks," Sidra cut in, playing with the zipper on her jacket. "The longest that we've ever gone without talking."

"I know," Josh sighed. He paused for a moment. "Look, I'm sorry for how I've been acting."

She glanced at him. "You are?"

"Yes," he admitted. "I know that I have been acting like a jerk."

"You figured that out before or *after* everybody told you about yourself?" Sidra sneered.

Josh rolled his eyes. Then ran his hand over the top of his head. "Sidra—"

Sidra closed her eyes and put her hand on Josh's arm. "Okay, I don't want this to turn into another argument," she interrupted.

"Me either," Josh agreed. "I shouldn't have said what I said about you... I know you're not shallow, or materialistic...and I know that you wouldn't purposely hurt me."

"*Never*," Sidra said. "Josh...it killed me to see you hurt... I wish I could take that day back."

"I wish I could take my *confession* back," he admitted, fixing his gaze on her. "I wish I could forget these feelings that I have for you, but I can't....so I just have to deal."

Sidra looked down at her hands. "Do...do you think things will ever be the same between us?"

Josh sighed. "You're still my best friend Sidra. That won't change," he assured. "But...I need to try to get over the idea of us being together."

"So, the answer is no." Sidra's words were more of a statement than a question.

"That's not what I'm saying," he replied, sensing her sadness. "I'm not mad at you. I'm ready to hang out and talk again—just...not too much one on one time, if that makes sense."

"It does, I guess," Sidra sulked.

"I'm done acting like an asshole," Josh promised. "That was completely out of character."

Sidra nodded in agreement. "We all get out of character at times," she consoled.

"Yeah." Josh started to feel lighter. "I have to ask...did you tell James about—"

"No, I didn't," she answered. "He doesn't need to know... Don't worry."

Josh managed a smile.

Sidra looked at him, tears filling her eyes. "Can I just...give you a hug?"

Josh chuckled. "Sure." He closed his eyes when Sidra wrapped her arms around him. The hug was brief, but he appreciated it. "Don't cry," he said when Sidra sniffled.

"I can't help it." She wiped her eyes with the sleeve of her jacket. "I missed you."

"Missed you too," he returned.

# Chapter 12

"Homecoming is going to be so much fun this year," Emily mused, reading a flyer on the bulletin board outside of her classroom.

"I know! There's cookouts, games, a concert and the big football game," Alex gushed, running her finger down the list written on the flyer. She laughed. "Are they *really* having a tricycle race?"

"Yep, and paintballing." Emily nodded. "I finally get to enjoy stuff without having to be dragged home or having to entertain my mom all week."

Alex chuckled. "Yeah, she did a good job at keeping you away from us," she reminisced. "Is she still not talking to you?"

Emily pushed some of her hair behind her ear. "Nope, still nothing," she mumbled. "I'm starting to get angry now," she vented. "I mean, she acts like I went off to get married without telling her. I just moved in with my dad."

Alex shrugged. "I know Em. Her feelings are just hurt, I guess," she stated. "But you're right. That's no excuse for her not to talk to you."

Emily shook her head in an effort to remove her negative thoughts. "Anyway, I have to go study. I'll see you later."

"Oh, wait," Alex blurted out, grabbing Emily's arm.

"What's wrong?" Emily asked, concerned.

"I've been meaning to ask you, how your classes are going?" Alex said. "With you working to get off of academic probation and all."

Emily shrugged. "I'm doing pretty well. So far so good," she replied. "It's amazing what actual *studying* can do," she joked.

"Yeah, imagine *that*," Alex laughed as Emily walked off. "See ya girl."

Turning on her heel to head out the building, Alex was nearly knocked off her feet when she collided with someone. "Ooh, sorry" she blurted out, grabbing her chest.

"No problem," the man replied, holding his arms out. "Are you okay?"

Alex smoothed her sweatshirt down, looking up at the tall, dark-skinned, handsome man in front of her. She stared, mouth practically hanging open.

He waved his hand in front of her face, chuckling. "Hello?"

Snapping out of her trance, Alex frowned. "What did you say?"

"I asked if you were okay?" he repeated.

"Oh, yeah I'm fine," she assured, slightly embarrassed. "I better get going."

Intrigued, he spun around as she walked pass him. "Listen, um... I just transferred here, can you show me where the registrar's office is?" he asked.

Alex turned around and glanced at the door next to her. "Right here where it says 'registrar'," she pointed to the sign above the door.

The man looked down at the ground and laughed in embarrassment. "Nice, that umm…didn't seem obvious at all."

Clutching her books to her chest, Alex smiled. "Well hey, since you go here now, I guess I'll see you around."

"I guess you *will*," he crooned. He extended his hand. "I'm Eric, by the way."

"Alex," she replied, shaking his hand. "Later." Alex continued her departure out of the building. She blushed as the sunlight hit her face. A guy hadn't caught her eye since her ex-boyfriend. Although she wasn't interested in a relationship, she didn't rule out the possibility of having a friend. *Maybe, just maybe,* she thought.


Jason flopped down on his bed, letting his water bottle and towel hit the floor. He'd been at practice for hours. Homecoming football games were probably the most important games of the college football season. He was beginning to feel the pressure, just as he did every year.

As soon as his eyes closed, he heard his cell phone ring. "Hello," he answered tiredly, not looking at the caller ID.

"Hi son," Mr. Adams answered.

Jason bolted up. "Dad, is everything okay?" he asked, slightly panicked. Ever since his father's heart attack last semester, Jason secretly dreaded every phone call, thinking that something bad has happened.

A deep laugh came through the phone. "Everything's good son," he assured. Jason breathed a sigh of relief. "I was calling to check on you. How is practice going? I know that the big game is this weekend."

Jason ran a hand over his hair. "Practice is good. It's been really intense lately because of this game…because of the whole *season* actually," he responded.

"Well, you just make sure you try to relax in between. I know your classes are getting tougher as well, so you make sure you take care of yourself," Mr. Adams urged.

"I will… Are you, Mom, and Kyle still coming down for the game?"

"We wouldn't miss it," his father mused, proudly.

"Cool," Jason smiled. "Oh and Dad, can you talk to

Mom and make sure she doesn't come down here tripping on Chasity? ...I'm not going to allow her to do what she did the *last* time."

Mr. Adams cleared his throat. He was aware of his wife's feelings towards Chasity; she had been vocal about them. "I promise, I'll talk to her. Don't worry yourself."

"Okay, talk to you later."

"Bye son."

Jason set his phone on his nightstand. Hearing a knock on his door, he rubbed his tired eyes. "Come in." He smiled as Chasity entered the room.

"Hey, I'm on my way to the store to get something to make for dinner," she informed. "Want anything in particular?"

"No. Whatever you make, I'll eat."

She looked at him as he yawned. "Long practice, huh?" she assumed, sitting on the bed next to him.

"That's an understatement."

"Well, hopefully after this week your coach will lay off you," Chasity said, not hiding her frustration. "He's been killing you out there."

"I know, but I have to do what I have to do," he replied. "The football scholarship is putting me through school. So I have to just deal with it."

"I understand that, but you're not trying to go to the pros after you graduate. All that isn't necessary," she argued. "Your coach is an asshole."

Jason chuckled; he knew she was just being protective. But she didn't understand; pros, or no pros, he was playing for the school and he had to do his job. "Don't worry about me, I'm fine."

"If you say so," she muttered.

He stared at her intensely. "You know what would make me feel better right now?" he asked.

"What's that?" she wondered, looking at him. He smiled a knowing smile at her. She rolled her eyes. "Go to sleep," she jeered, pushing him down on the bed, inciting a laugh from him.


"Well, I signed us all up for paintballing," Alex informed her friends as she twirled some spaghetti around with her fork.

"Seriously? You know I hate playing sports," Sidra jeered, breaking a roll in half.

Not feeling like cooking dinner as they had done the past few nights, the gang decided to eat in the cafeteria.

"Stop whining. It'll be fun," Alex chortled. "For the past two homecomings, we didn't participate in any of the games. I think it'll be fun to do it this year."

"I agree," Mark put in, breaking his biscuit in half. "Paintballing will be fun. Our team is gonna kick everyone's ass."

"That's the school spirit," Alex beamed, setting her fork back on her plate. "You guys want to go to the alumni basketball game later?"

"Man, ain't nobody going to that bullshit," Mark answered instantaneously, causing Josh to nearly spit out his juice from laughing.

"What happened to you being on my side?" Alex laughed.

"I'm not tryna watch a bunch of old ass former students break hips and shit while playing basketball," Mark replied, taking a sip of his juice.

"That's terrible," Emily giggled. "*You'll* be an alumni one day, you know."

"That's if he actually *graduates*," Malajia ground out, checking her reflection in her butter knife.

Mark made a face at her as he continued to eat his food.

Alex shook her head. "So nobody wants to go?" she persisted.

"Hell and no," Chasity spat. "I'm not sitting through that game… I'd rather do math problems."

Malajia laughed. "I know right?" she put in. "I'd rather talk to Emily's mother for an hour."

Emily looked up from her bowl of soup. "Malajia," she warned.

Malajia glanced at her. "Is *that* one too soon too?" she asked, Emily nodded. "Damn it. I don't think I like this tougher Emily," she jeered, slamming her hand on the table. "I want to say what I want."

"You still *do*," Emily laughed, picking up her glass of water.

"So, what about the talent show? Y'all want to go to *that*?" Alex slid in.

"What? Are you on the homecoming committee or something?" Jason asked, full of amusement.

"No, I'm *not*," Alex declared. "But it'll be nice to get out and mingle with some of the other students."

"Why would I want to do that?" Chasity sneered. "I barely want to hang with *y'all*."

"Oh wow," David chuckled, wiping his mouth with a napkin.

As her friends chatted around her, Alex continued to eat her food while letting her mind wander. Truth was, she was hoping to run into Eric at one of the events. It had been a few days since she bumped into him, and she was hoping it wouldn't be the last time.

"Let's get out of here," Josh suggested. "You guys want to catch a movie?"

"Yeah, why not," Mark said, rising from his seat. "It's better than *Alex's* suggestion."


Making their way back to the cluster parking lot for their cars, the group noticed several tricycles being stored behind the gym. "What the hell are these doing here?" Malajia asked, face frowned.

"I think these are for that tricycle race tomorrow," Emily

informed.

"They're *really* going to do that bullshit?" Chasity scoffed. "A bunch of grown ass people on baby bikes."

Malajia looked at Chasity. "Come on Chaz, we should sign up and race," she proposed.

"I wish I *would* get my tall ass on a damn tricycle," Chasity refused.

Jason laughed. "I bet you that race is going to be hilarious," he predicted.

"Man, *damn* a race, I'm taking one of these bikes *now*," Mark said, walking over to the tricycle.

"Mark, what are you doing?" David asked, confused.

"Yo, cover me," Mark demanded, grabbing a handle bar.

"Boy get away from those!" Alex urged. "You're always doing something."

"Shut the hell up," Mark hissed. "You all loud and shit. I said cover me."

"I don't want any part of this," Alex said, putting her hand up.

Mark sucked his teeth. "Forget it. I don't need y'all." He picked up the small cycle and placed it on the path. The others watched as he began riding the tricycle like a scooter, holding onto the handle bars. "Come on y'all," he called to them.

Chasity stared at the scene in confusion. "Is he freakin' serious?" she asked, pointing at him.

Jason laughed, "I'm afraid so babe."

"So stupid," Malajia grunted, watching him ride ahead. She busted out laughing when he tripped and fell.

"Damn it!" Mark yelled, holding his knee.

Alex shook her head when Mark began to yell as if he was in excruciating pain. "I can't deal with him," she stated, walking off.

Sidra put her hand over her face from embarrassment. "Mark, come on, get off the ground," she sucked her teeth. "Boy, don't roll. You act like you broke a bone."

Josh sighed. "Come on, let's pick this fool up," he said, making his way over to his exaggerating friend.

Head down, earbuds in her ears, Alex sat in the library, focused on writing her paper. Critical reading and writing was beginning to be one of her favorite classes. Studying and writing about literature was something that she always had an interest in.

Clicking through her MP3 player playlist, she didn't notice when someone tapped on her table. When the person didn't get a response, they tapped her shoulder, startling her.

"Sorry, I didn't hear you," she said. Recognizing the person standing in front of her, she smiled. "Hi…Eric right?"

"That's me," he replied, returning her smile with a bright one of his own. "Your name is Alex, right?"

"Sure *is*," she replied, gesturing for him to sit in the seat across from her. *He's even more handsome than I remember.* Even through his sweatshirt and jeans, she could see that he had a great body. "You said you transferred here?" she recalled. He nodded. "What school did you come from?"

"I used to go to Monroe College in Maryland," he replied. "It was too damn small. Besides, Paradise Valley University has a better marketing program, so here I am."

"Oh okay." She was intrigued.

Eric was equally intrigued. He stared at Alex; the wavy haired, curvy, dark skinned beauty was someone who he really wanted to get to know. *She's stunning.* "So, what's fun to do around here?" he asked after seconds of comfortable silence.

"Well, you're probably aware that it's homecoming week, so there are some activities to do for that," she said, pushing some hair out of her face. "But usually my friends and I just hang out. We sometimes find our own stuff to do."

"Sounds cool," he said.

Alex smiled. Her paper would have to wait; this

conversation was much more interesting.


Alex let out a happy sigh as she walked through her front
door a few hours later. She'd had a great conversation with
Eric and she even got some of her paper finished once he left
to do research on his own assignment.

Her thoughts were interrupted by bickering. "What's
going on in here?" she asked, setting her books on one of the
accent chairs.

"We're trying to decide on what movie to watch," Sidra
answered, grabbing a bag of popcorn from the microwave.

"That doesn't explain the arguing," Alex chuckled.

"Because Chasity wants to be a bitch and not let us
watch the movie that I bought earlier," Malajia snarled,
reaching for the remote.

"Because I already *know* what kind of movie your freak
ass picked," Chasity shot back, holding the remote out of her
reach.

"And just what kind is *that*?" Alex asked.

"Probably porn," Sidra laughed, sitting down in the other
accent chair. "She's done it before."

"That last time was an *accident*," Malajia defended. "I
had no idea that move was gonna turn out to be a porno."

Chasity narrowed her eyes at Malajia. "Really?" she
sarcastically asked. "So, you thought that a movie with the
title 'Do me long dick daddy', was what? A love story?"

Malajia tried to conceal her laugh as she shrugged.
"*This* is not porn, just push play."

Alex joined the girls in front of the television. "Go
ahead and push play Chaz," she urged. "I'm sure it can't be
that bad."

Alex couldn't have been more wrong. A half hour into
the movie and there had been five explicit sex scenes,
including the one they were currently watching.

"I *told* y'all," Chasity said, shaking her head. "Nobody
wanted to listen to me."

Emily tilted her head. "How do they get into those positions?" she asked, the sound of awe in her voice.

"I don't know, but…I wanna try that," Malajia replied, studying the activity on the televising screen intensely. She then looked over at Chasity. "Have you ever done that, Chaz?"

Chasity looked at Malajia with disgust. "Get your horny ass away from me," she barked, nudging her away.

Sidra stared at the screen, shoving popcorn in her mouth. "Mel, you are banned from picking out movies—Look at the *size* of it though," she mused.

Chasity tried to fast-forward the scene, but Malajia snatched the remote. "Yo, they are getting it *in*," Malajia chuckled, leaning on Chasity. "I think I need to make a phone call to my man."

Chasity once again nudged her. "Girl, go rub one out and get off me."

Grabbing popcorn from a bag, Alex was silent. Normally she could sit through explicit movies and not be affected, but much to her surprise, she was beginning to get hot and bothered by what was taking place on the forty-two inch television screen. "You know what. That's a good idea Chaz," Alex said, standing from her seat.

"*What* is?" Malajia asked, not taking her eyes off the TV.

"Handling my business," Alex threw over her shoulder as she walked up the steps.

"Seriously Alex? *Now*?!" Sidra exclaimed, realizing what Alex was implying.

"What is she talking about?" Emily asked.

Malajia laughed. "Alex is about to play with herself under your sheets, Emily," she teased, much to Emily's dismay.

"Ewww," Emily whined, picking up her cup of soda.

"Shut up Malajia!" Alex yelled from up the steps.

Malajia continued laughing. "Nasty ass," she teased. The remaining girls watched the scene go on for not even a minute.

Chasity jumped off the couch and grabbed her keys off the table as Malajia picked up her cell phone and dialed a number. "I'll be back," Chasity said, hurrying to the door.

"Where are you going?" Emily asked, following her progress to the door.

"To Jason's," Chasity replied, closing the front door behind her.

Holding her phone to her ear, Malajia flicked her hair over her shoulder as she darted for the steps. "Tyrone, come pick me up…Yeah now…like *right* now."

Sidra jumped up from her seat. She grabbed her phone and went to hit James's number on the speed dial. "Shit," she huffed. "Damn my stupid virginity." She let out a loud sigh. "I guess my imagination will have to do," she concluded, running up the steps past Malajia.

"Sidra, wait! Let me get my stuff first," Malajia hollered, running up the steps after her.

"Too late, I already started," Sidra joked.

"Sid, don't be gross!" Malajia yelled.

Emily shrugged as she grabbed a bag of popcorn off the coffee table and returned her attention back to the movie.

# Chapter 13

"Em, can you hand me that fork over there?" Alex asked, pointing to the utensil in the dish rack.

"Here you go," Emily replied, handing it to Alex.

The smell of eggs, bacon, and biscuits filled the house. Waking up earlier than normal, Alex and Emily decided to make breakfast for the rest of the girls before morning classes.

"Oh man, I have to finish those last two math problems for homework," Emily remembered, stirring the eggs in a large skillet.

"Go finish them, I'll finish *this*," Alex insisted, taking the spoon from Emily. Emily hurried up the stairs as Alex simultaneously flipped the bacon with her fork in one hand and stirred the scrambled eggs with another.

After turning the stove burners off and pulling the biscuits from the oven, Alex began to grab plates from the cabinet. She looked over at the front door as Chasity opened it.

"Well, well, look who it is," Alex teased as Chasity shut the door behind her. "Doing the walk of shame huh?"

"Shut up Alex," Chasity hissed, slowly and carefully walking towards her room. Chasity hadn't been back to her room since she ran out to Jason's after watching the explicit movie the night before.

Noticing the way that Chasity was walking, Alex laughed. "That's what you get. Your hot ass got yourself tore up last night, huh?"

"I hurt my back," Chasity shot back, opening her door.

Alex shot Chasity a knowing look. "Oh, I just bet you *did*," she mocked, laughter in her voice.

"Mind your fuckin' business."

"Very well," Alex relented, handing Chasity a plate of food. "Here, Em and I made breakfast."

"Thanks," Chasity mumbled, taking the plate.

"Don't forget, we're going to the park behind Court Terrace for paintballing at five," Alex reminded.

Chasity rolled her eyes. "Oh God," she groaned, walking into her room and shutting the door.

"Get over it," Alex ground out, spooning food onto the remaining plates.

Malajia hurried through the front door. "Damn it, I forgot I have a finance quiz today," she complained, slamming her purse on the couch. "I'm gonna fail the *shit* outta that quiz."

"Walk of shame number two," Alex teased, laughing.

"You damn skippy," Malajia chuckled.

"Here, breakfast is ready," Alex said, handing Malajia a plate.

Malajia eyed it skeptically. "Did you wash your hands?" she jeered. Alex narrowed her eyes.

"Girl, shut the hell up and eat this damn food," Alex fussed, shoving the plate into the laughing Malajia's hands. "So stupid."


Mark, clad in black jeans, black hoodie and black boots, entered the tree-filled field behind the male dorm Court Terrace. He stood with his hands on his hips and looked around. The massive field, normally desolate, had been transformed into a battle field. Barrels, sniper towers, haystacks, fog machines, and bunkers littered the field. Mark rubbed his hands together in anticipation of the afternoon's events that were about to take place.

"They really transformed this place," Alex mused, adjusting her wild ponytail. "The school went all out."

"This is gonna be crazy," Mark anticipated, looking at his friends' attire. "Looking good, team."

Jason adjusted the sleeve on his black, long sleeved t-shirt. "Did we really have to wear all black, though?" he asked.

Mark nodded. He stipulated earlier that day that their entire group must dress in all black for the battle. "We gotta look badass, dawg," he declared. "Plus, it goes with the team name that I picked out."

"Which *is*?" Chasity asked, unenthused.

"Team Ninja Strike," Mark answered proudly, inciting chuckles from some of the group.

"Team Ninja Strike?" Malajia repeated, frowning. "What the hell does that have to do with us wearing all black?"

"Don't ninja's wear black?" Mark sneered, pointing to his head. "Think Mel, think."

"Not *all* of them do," Chasity contradicted.

Mark flagged her with his hand. "Whatever, Team Ninja Strike it is," he affirmed. "Now stop complaining and come on."

"He's so hype," Josh laughed, following Mark's lead.

The three teams assembled on the grass in front of a row of three tables. One held the paint-filled rifles, another held black vests with numbers spray painted on the back, and the last held goggles.

The announcer; Mr. Bradley, held a microphone to his mouth. "Here we go. Team Battle Ready—"

"Battle Ready?" Mark scoffed at the team name. "That shit corny, cuz."

Mr. Bradley shot Mark a warning glance, then

continued. "Team Science Project—"

"Booooo," Mark jeered.

Trying to ignore Mark's outburst, Mr. Bradley continued. "...And Team Ninja Strike."

Mark clapped his hands loudly. "Yes!" he exclaimed, much to the embarrassment of his friends.

"Will you shut up?" Jason barked.

Mr. Bradley cleared his throat. "Each team member will put on a vest and goggles. You may take one paint-filled gun. Each gun is loaded with a different color; this makes it easy to know who shot you. If you get shot, you're out and must leave the field. You can wait in the refreshment section for the rest of your team mates," he informed. "We have scouts in the towers watching, so once you are declared hit, your number, which is on the back of your vest, will be called and you will need to leave. The team with the most un-hit people at the end wins." His eyes scanned the faces in front of him. "Does everyone have it?"

"So, we only get one gun?" Mark asked, raising his hand.

Mr. Bradley rubbed his head. "Yes Mark. There are plenty of pellets in the guns, so you won't run out any time soon...except for *yours* because I will make sure that you have no pellets," he replied.

Mark sucked his teeth loudly. "There better be some paint in my gun," he mumbled.

"Why did I let you all talk me into this?" Sidra asked, putting her vest on. "I've never shot anything in my life."

David chuckled. "I don't think *any* of us have," he said. Examining the weapon, he scratched his head. "It shouldn't be too complicated." He was startled when two orange paint pellets splashed on his chest. He looked down, shocked. "What the—"

"Number ten, you're out," the tower announcer called over the loud speaker.

David looked at the tower. "I didn't even get to *start!*" he exclaimed. "That's not fair."

Mark, being the one who shot David, winced. "My bad man, I was trying to see how this thing works," he apologized.

Furious, David slammed his gun on the ground and stomped off the field.

"You play too fuckin' much," Malajia scolded, smacking Mark on the back of his head.

"It was an *accident*," Mark defended, rubbing his head.

The teams scattered and split up throughout the field. Sidra ran and hid behind a tree. Peeking her head out to see if anyone was coming, she raised her gun and shot several of her blue pellets at the approaching figure. "Yes," she rejoiced, taking off running.

Mark started shooting wildly at the opposing team members who were running in all directions. "Yeeeaahhh!" he yelled. "I'm a beast, you can't catch me." He took out several people, before bumping into Josh. "Damn man, you almost got shot. Move," he snapped.

"What? You mean like *you* shot *David*?" Josh mocked, adjusting his gun in his hand.

"Man, I said that was an accident," Mark insisted, annoyed.

Josh rolled his eyes and shot another opponent.


Half an hour into the battle, Team Ninja Strike had taken out most of the opposing teams. They had suffered a few casualties of their own. Alex was hit trying to cover Emily, and Josh was taken out by a female opponent who climbed one of the trees and sniper shot him.

Seeing two rival players approaching, Jason dove behind a haystack. Lying on the ground, he pointed his weapon and shot a player who was searching the haystacks in front of him.

Just as Jason turned around, he saw another opponent standing over him. The guy was about to fire at Jason, but was hit in the chest with four purple pellets. "Damn," the guy huffed, hearing his number announced over the loud speaker. Grateful for the backup, Jason stood up and ran off.

Chasity, watching from behind a tree in the distance, saw that Jason had gotten away safely. *Nice aim girl*, she mused of herself. Watching as another opponent stalked Sidra off in the distance, with his back towards her; Chasity fired a purple pellet, hitting her target.

As the guy walked off the field, Chasity adjusted the gun in her hand. She let out a scream when several pellets hit her; striking her ribs and back. Looking down, she saw the red paint on her vest. Spinning around, she saw Malajia standing there holding her hand to her mouth, stunned.

"Malajia, what the hell?!" Chasity yelled, snatching her goggles off.

"Number twenty-one, you're out," the announcer called. Chasity sucked her teeth and let out a frustrated sigh.

"I'm sorry Chaz, I thought you were the other girl," Malajia apologized.

"Do I *look* like the other damn girl?" Chasity snapped, jerking out of her vest.

Malajia shrugged. "All you light-skinned; light-eyed people look alike," she joked, trying not to laugh.

Chasity narrowed her eyes at Malajia. Before Malajia could react, Chasity raised her gun and began firing off pellet after pellet at her chest.

Malajia screamed as she stumbled back. "Are you crazy?!" she hollered as Chasity shot her last pellet at her.

"Number eight, you're out," the announcer called.

Malajia slammed her gun on the ground. "You are so damn *petty!*" she fumed "What is *wrong* with you?"

Lowering her weapon, Chasity shrugged. "Sorry, all you dickheads look alike," she jeered, before walking away.

"You play too much," Malajia huffed, following her.

Another fifteen minutes passed, and Sidra was ready for the game to be over. She'd hid behind tress, crawled through barrels and broke several of her painted nails trying to take opponents out.

Tired, she raised her weapon at a female opponent who had her weapon raised at her. After having a staring match for moments, both girls shot at and hit each other.

"Number twenty-five and number twenty-eight, you're out."

"Thank God," Sidra breathed, moving her ponytail off her shoulder. She and her opponent walked off side by side.

Jason and Mark ran for cover as pellets went flying. "Shit!" Mark yelled when one hit a tree right by his head. "This is getting real."

"I know," Jason agreed, looking around. "I took out another one of them a few minutes ago."

"Good job." Mark signaled for Jason to walk with him. "There can't be but a few of them left," Mark whispered as they slowly crept through the grass.

His back facing Mark, Jason heard what sounded like someone stepping on a branch nearby. He quickly raised his gun. "They're close," Jason said, voice low.

"Naw, that was me," Mark confessed, dusting himself off.

Jason frowned at the dirt on Mark's clothes. "What happened?"

"I went to roll and I landed on those branches."

Jason looked at the broken branches that Mark had pointed to. He then shot him a confused look. "What were you rolling on the ground for?" he snapped.

"I was trying to be stealth," Mark shrugged.

Jason was so busy looking at Mark like he was crazy, that he didn't see the shooter in front of him. Several pellets hit Jason's chest, startling him. He dropped his gun and put his hands up in surrender.

"Number twenty-seven you're out."

Removing his vest, Jason looked at Mark, who was being shot by another opponent in front of him. He shook his head as he watched Mark drop his gun, roll on the ground and start yelling, while clutching his chest.

"Oh my God, I'm hit. I'm hit!" Mark shouted, lying on his back.

"Number twenty, you're out."

Still lying on the ground, Mark unzipped his vest. "It's going dark. Tell my mom I love her," he croaked.

Jason sucked his teeth and without a word, stepped over Mark and walked off the field.

"Oh, you can't help your teammate up?" Mark yelled at Jason's retreating back.


"Damn, I could have sworn that one of you would be the last man standing," Alex laughed, seeing the two guys approach the refreshment table.

"Yeah well, I got stuck with an idiot," Jason jeered, grabbing a bottle of water.

"Who's left?" Mark asked, tossing his paint covered vest on the ground. "It was three people out there, last I heard."

Before anyone could answer, they heard the announcer announce two more numbers. The group watched as the last two standing opponents from Team Science Project emerged with their vests soiled with bright pink paint.

Alex put her finger to her chin. "Did she really..."

Emily emerged from the field, her gun held high, smiling from ear to ear. "I got them, I got them!" Emily bellowed, jumping up and down.

"Number three from Team Ninja Strike is the last survivor. Your team wins," the announcer declared, inciting cheers from the group.

"Yes!" Mark hollered, picking Emily up and spinning her around. "My little sniper buddy," he praised.

"I knew those pink pellets were yours," Alex mused, hugging her.

"Where were you all this time?" David asked, taking a bite out of his sandwich.

Emily wiped the sweat from her forehead, then removed

her vest. "After Alex got hit, I hid in one of those barrels and just waited," she chortled. "I tried to get that guy before he hit Jason, but my gun jammed."

"Don't even worry about it. You redeemed yourself," Mark boasted, rubbing Emily's head with his hand. "I'm hype. Come on, we gotta pose for this picture that they're going to put in the school paper." he said, pointing to the camera man in front of them.

"I have paint all in my hair," Sidra complained, smoothing some loose strands back up into her ponytail.

"Less complaining, more posing," Mark smiled, putting his arm around her. Once the picture was taken of the group, Mark clapped his hands together. "Let's go get some ice cream."

"How about frozen yogurt instead?" Alex suggested, letting her ponytail down.

"We're getting *ice cream!*" Mark hollered in her face.

# Chapter 14

Relieved that she had gotten through another week of classes, Alex moseyed through the campus courtyard, listening to the music blaring through her earphones. *This MP3 player purchase was a great idea*, she thought. It had been a while since she'd treated herself to something that had nothing to do with school.

Coming face to face with her new friend, Alex smiled. "Hey stranger," she said, removing her headphones.

As Eric enveloped Alex in a strong hug, Alex closed her eyes, relishing the smell of his cologne. *There goes that hot and bothered feeling again*, she thought.

"Hey your*self*," Eric replied, parting. "I'm about to go to the cafeteria, you want to come with me?"

She stared at him. Food was the last thing on her mind at that moment. "Uh, I'm not really hungry," she answered honestly.

Eric nodded. "Okay, no problem. Maybe another time then?"

Alex glanced at the ground, before turning her attention back to him. "You know what, if you want some *home-cooked* food, I have some back at *my* house," she offered. "Me and my girls usually cook too much, so we always end up with leftovers."

"If it's not too much trouble," he smiled. "Truth is, I miss a home-cooked meal."

"I hear you," she chuckled. "Well, I hope it tides you over."

"If *you* cooked it, I'm sure it will," Eric crooned, gesturing for her to lead the way.


"Sorry girls, I forgot my student ID," Emily stated, entering the house.

"I don't know why you don't carry it in your purse," Malajia chided, closing the door behind Sidra and Chasity.

"I usually *do*, but when I got in from the library last night I just dropped it on my desk," Emily replied.

"Just hurry up and get it," Chasity slid in, examining her nails. "I don't even want to *go* to this talent show. The first one was dry as shit, and they have the nerve to have another one in the same week."

"Because people keep signing up for it," Sidra giggled.

"Has anybody seen Alex?" Emily asked, heading up the stairs.

"Not since this morning," Sidra replied. "But I'm sure she'll meet us there later. This was *her* idea to go anyway."

"I'm glad we came back. I wanted to change my shirt anyway," Malajia stated, following Emily up the steps. "This thing is too tight."

"That never stopped you *before*," Chasity jeered.

Malajia sucked her teeth. "Shut up and come help me decide which one to put on...smart ass."

Emily stuck her key in her room door, while the other girls headed for Sidra and Malajia's room. Pushing the door and finding it stuck, Emily frowned. "Huh?" she said, confused.

"What's wrong?" Sidra asked, turning around.

"I can't get the door open," Emily informed, giving it another push. She stuck her hand through the small crack and felt around. "How did the bolt lock get on here?"

The others rushed to the room and tried to peek inside.

"Wait, shut up. I hear something," Malajia said, squinting through the crack. The room was dark. Hearing loud whispering and seeing figures move, Malajia started banging on the door. "Hold up, Alex is in there!" she exclaimed. "With a *man*."

Chasity and Sidra gasped as they tried to look. "Ooooh," Sidra laughed.

"Wait, he just jumped out the bed," Chasity called out, pushing Malajia's head down to see better.

"I see a penis, I see a penis!" Malajia yelped, sticking her hand through the opening.

As the girls screamed and laughed, the door slammed shut. They heard a lock jiggle and the door jerked open slightly, Alex poked her head out. "Will you stop all that damn noise?" she snapped.

The girls smiled knowing smiles at her. "Whatcha' doin' in there, Alex?" Chasity teased.

Alex let out a loud sigh. "I'm studying," she hissed.

"*Sure* you are," Malajia jeered.

"Uh huh. You were studying that dick we just saw in there," Chasity mocked.

Malajia busted out laughing while Emily and Sidra snickered.

Alex glowered. "Just go wait for me downstairs," she fussed.

"Can I see it?" Malajia asked, trying to push the door open.

"No. Take your ass downstairs," Alex demanded, teeth clenched.

"Wait, I need my ID," Emily laughed.

"I'll bring it to you, just go." Alex slammed the door in their faces.

The girls looked at each other. "Oooohhh," Sidra repeated.

"Oh, I want to hear *all* about this," Malajia declared, walking down the stairs. "Alex is getting her freak on!"

The four girls sat at the dining room table, patiently waiting for Alex to come down. They stared at Eric when he hurried downstairs. Embarrassed, Eric quickly waved and hurried out the door.

Hesitantly, Alex walked down the steps. She faced the girls, folding her arms. "Okay, let's hear it," she challenged.

"Mmm, mmm, mmm," Malajia charged. "Alexandra Broomhelga Chisolm."

Alex frowned at her. "My middle name is *Danielle*, Malajia," she sneered. "You already knew that."

"Don't try to change the subject," Sidra slid in, pointing at her. "Your hot-tailed behind was having sex."

Chasity looked confused. "*Tail*?" she mocked.

"Hey, no time to tease *me*, we need to focus," Sidra ground out, putting her hand up at Chasity.

"You're right, I'll save it for later," Chasity agreed, causing Malajia to snicker.

Sidra focused her attention back on Alex. "Well Alex. Is that what you were doing?"

Alex sighed, "Yes, I *was*," she admitted, shameful.

"Why didn't you tell us that you had a boyfriend?" Sidra asked, confused.

"Because he's not my *boyfriend*," Alex corrected. "He's just…"

"A fuck buddy?" Chasity asked smartly.

Alex sucked her teeth. "Don't call him that," she hissed.

"Call him what? A fuck buddy?" Chasity taunted.

"Chasity," Alex warned. "Stop."

Chasity put her hands up. "Fine, I won't talk about your fuck buddy."

Sidra giggled as she playfully tapped Chasity's arm.

"So, the moral lecture queen is screwing a man that isn't her boyfriend," Malajia condemned. She knew how much flack one of the other girls would have gotten from Alex, had the shoe been on the other foot. "My how the tables have turned."

"I'm not *screwing* him," Alex amended. "This was the

first time. And will probably be the *last*."

"You don't have to lie Alex," Chasity commented. "If you want to screw somebody, that's your business. You're grown."

Alex ran her hands through her hair as she sat down. "God, I don't know what happened," she whined. "I invited him back here to get something to eat—"

"I bet you *did*," Malajia teased.

"Anyway." Alex rolled her eyes. "We were having a deep conversation, then next thing I knew we were..." She buried her face in the couch cushions. "He's so gorgeous and I was so horny," she admitted.

"Yeah well, we've all been there," Malajia said; she looked at Sidra and Emily. "Well, *me* and *Chaz* have been there."

"Leave me out of this," Chasity sneered.

"Not gonna happen, horny," Malajia teased, earning a middle finger from Chasity.

"Wait a minute," Sidra cut in, grabbing the girls' attention. "Malajia, when did you start sleeping with Tyrone?" she asked, picking up on Malajia's previous comment.

Malajia's eyes widened. "Huh?"

"Don't 'huh' me," Sidra barked. "You didn't tell *any* of us that you lost your virginity, you secret keeping hussy."

"I used to spend the night at his place *all the time* last semester," Malajia reminded.

"Yes, I *know* that but you never actually came out and said that you had sex with him," Sidra pointed out. "You ran your mouth about *Chasity's* first time, but you didn't spill about *yours*?"

Malajia's eyes darted as she tried to search for the words to say. Malajia glanced at Chasity, who looked away. Sure Chasity knew about it, but she wasn't about to tell the other girls that.

"Um...well..." Malajia hesitated. "Look this isn't about me. This is about *Alex*," she deflected, pointing to Alex.

"Miss hypocrite."

Putting her hand over her face, Alex closed her eyes. "I *am*," she agreed. "This is just…*crazy*."

"Well, I hope you used protection," Sidra said.

"Hell *yes*, I did," Alex assured. "I may have been fast, but I'm not stupid."

"Do you *want* him to be your boyfriend?" Emily asked. "How long have you known him?"

"Well, I only met him this past Monday—"

"Five days?! You knew him for only five days?" Chasity exclaimed. "Do you even know the boys *last name*?"

"Yes, I do, smart ass. It's Wendell. Eric Wendell," Alex shot back. "God, you make it seem like I'm a whore."

"*You* said it, not me," Chasity teased.

"Damn girl, even *I* waited to sleep with Tyrone," Malajia added.

Sidra slapped her hand on the table. "When did that *happen*?" she snapped at Malajia, not over the fact that she wasn't told about the milestone. "I don't appreciate being kept in the dark about stuff like that."

"I'm sorry Sid," Malajia chuckled. *It wasn't that great of an experience to talk about anyway*, she thought, recalling her first time.

Malajia wasn't happy with the circumstances surrounding her first sexual experience. After arguing with Tyrone constantly, she felt pressured to finally sleep with him in an effort to make their relationship better. Although she later developed a better sexual relationship with Tyrone, she still wasn't over the disappointment of her first time and it wasn't something that she wanted to be reminded of or celebrate.

Alex shook her head. "Look, I wasn't a *virgin*, so it's not like he was my first," she said. "I haven't had any since I was with Paul…." She waved her hand. "Forget it. To answer your question Emily, no, I don't want him to be my boyfriend."

"Is that so?" Malajia pressed.

"Yes, that's so," Alex swore. "I'm not interested in a relationship right now. I'm cool with being single. I just needed—"

"To get your back scratched?" Malajia joked.

Alex couldn't help but chuckle. "Yeah, exactly."


"Yo Alex, we heard you got banged yesterday," Mark blurted out as he squirted ketchup on his french fries.

Alex nearly choked on her drink. She turned and looked at him with shock. "Where did you hear *that*?!"

Mark smiled and pointed to Malajia, who was vigorously shaking her head at him.

Alex's head snapped towards Malajia. She was fuming. "Malajia!" she yelled.

Malajia put her hands up. "It just came out," she defended, backing up. "I didn't even *want* to tell them anything."

Mark frowned. "What are you talking about?" he asked her, confused. "You came to our house all hype and shit last night, talking about you saw some guy come out of—"

"Shut up," Malajia snapped through clenched teeth, delivering a punch to Mark's arm.

"Thanks a lot, big mouth," Alex ground out, rolling her eyes at Malajia.

"Oh, calm down. It's not like they know who the guy is or anything," Malajia threw back, flicking her hair over her shoulder.

"It's that new guy Eric, right?" Mark asked.

Alex held a piercing gaze on Malajia, slowly folding her arms in the process.

Malajia laughed nervously. "Oops."

Without saying another word, Alex walked towards the bleachers on the football field.

"I can't tell you *nothin'*," Malajia hissed at Mark, who just shrugged while eating his fries.

The football field was packed that Sunday. Current

students, alumni, teachers, and family members filled the space in anticipation for the big game.

"Did you talk to Jason this morning?" Emily asked Chasity, opening a pack of candy.

"Yeah, he's nervous," Chasity replied, looking at her phone.

"Nervous?" Mark repeated. "Naw, Jase *never* gets nervous. He's gonna kill it in this game like he does *every* game," he boasted.

Chasity ignored him as she continued staring at her phone. Malajia walked over, snatched the phone out of Chasity's hand, and looked at the text message.

"'I love you baby. Thanks for your support'," Malajia read aloud, then giggled. "Awww Jason loves Chasity."

"Give me my damn phone," Chasity fumed, snatching it back.

"Aren't those Jason's parents and his brother?" Sidra slid in, pointing to the familiar people in front of her.

Chasity looked ahead. "Yeah," she confirmed. She smiled when they approached.

"How are you, Chasity?" Mr. Adams smiled, giving her a hug.

"I'm good, thanks," she replied, parting from their embrace. After waving to Jason's smiling, fifteen-year-old brother Kyle, she looked over at his mother, who was shooting daggers at her with her eyes. "Hi Ms. Nancy," Chasity said, forcing a smile.

"Chasity," Mrs. Adams spat, then walked off.

Mr. Adams shook his head at his wife's departing figure, then turned to the visibly irritated Chasity. "Don't worry about her," he soothed.

Chasity just nodded as Mr. Adams and Kyle walked off.

Sidra and Malajia stood beside Chasity. "Eww, Ms. Nancy's attitude sucks," Sidra concluded.

"Yep," Chasity agreed.

"To hell with her," Malajia sneered. "If she *still* got a damn attitude because Jason chooses to be with you, that's *her* old ass problem." She adjusted her purse strap on her arm. "You want me to trip her for you?"

Chasity sucked her teeth at Malajia's silly offer, then walked off without a word.

"Malajia—never mind," Sidra shook her head, then followed Chasity.

"What? I was just trying to be helpful!" Malajia shouted after them.


Jason held his breath as the ball that he threw reached the hands of his teammate, who stood at the goal line. Hearing that the Paradise Valley Panthers were the homecoming winners for yet another year was like music to his ears. He had done his job.

After briefly celebrating with his team members and coach, Jason took the long walk off the field. All he could hear was the loud cheering from the crowd as he departed. He ended up outside the gates. Leaning against the gate, he enjoyed a few quiet moments to himself.

"Another game down, seven more to go," he said to himself, rubbing the back of his neck.

The sound of clapping broke into his thoughts. Turning around, he smiled seeing his father clapping loudly. "Good job Jase," Mr. Adams gushed, embracing his eldest son. "I'm proud of you."

"Thanks Dad," Jason smiled.

"Jase, that was so cool the way you made that first touchdown." Kyle was in awe of his big brother. "I can't wait to make a touchdown like that from the other end of the field when I play football at *my* school."

Jason patted Kyle atop his curly hair, smiling. "The game didn't bore you too much, did it Mom?" he chuckled, knowing how much his mother detested sports.

Mrs. Adams waved her hand at him. "I could *never* get bored watching you play sweetie," she assured, hugging him. "You are amazing."

"Thanks," Jason humbly replied.

"We'll let you celebrate with your friends. I know they're on their way out here," Mr. Adams stated. "If you're not too busy, we can take you out to celebrate later."

"Sounds good. I'll see you later," Jason replied.

"We'll call you from the hotel," Mrs. Adams said, waving.

Jason watched his family walk off, then heard the loud mouth of Mark approaching. Jason laughed.

"Wooooooo!" Mark yelled. "We beat those fools. We won, we won," he chanted, doing a dance, embarrassing the rest of the gang as they walked up. "My roommate is better than yours," he taunted passersby, who shot him warning glances.

Jason embraced and kissed a visibly proud Chasity. "You're simple Mark," Jason concluded. "You have these people looking at you like you lost your mind."

"What *else* is new?" Mark shrugged.

"I have never enjoyed a football game *this* much," Sidra grinned, excited. "That was awesome."

Jason frowned. "So, you never enjoyed any of my *other* games, Sidra?" he asked, with feigned hurt.

Sidra's eyes widened. "Huh? No, that's not what I meant," she stammered.

"Liar," her friends teased.

"I'm *not* lying!" she exclaimed.

Jason smiled. "I'm just messing with you Sid."

Sidra gave Jason a playful poke to his arm.

"So, what do you want to do to celebrate?" Josh asked. "There's a party later, at the gym. You guys want to go?"

"I'm sure Jason's family wants to spend time with him," Alex slid in. "We can celebrate with him another time."

Jason shook his head. "They only want to take me to dinner," he informed. "That won't take but so long. We can still go out later." He looked at Chasity. "You want to come to dinner?"

"Nope," Chasity answered instantaneously.

Jason sighed, though he understood why she didn't want to go. Last time Chasity went out to eat with Jason's family, she endured snide comments and a lecture from his mother.

"Then it's settled, we'll meet up later to go to the party," Alex concluded. "I might even have a drink tonight. I'm in a good mood."

"Yeah, sex will do that to you," Mark teased.

"Oh yeah, I *did* hear that you got some last night, Alex," Jason said, pointing at Alex.

Alex glared at Malajia, who laughed nervously. "Um, I'm gonna practice not running my mouth back at the house," Malajia sputtered, then took off running.

"You get back here so I can tape your damn mouth shut!" Alex yelled after her, chasing her.

# Chapter 15

"Are we still on for dinner tonight?" Malajia asked into her cell phone. "Okay great…I'll see you later." She was beaming when she put her cell phone back into her purse. "I'm going to eat dinner with my man while y'all eat that leftover food from the cafeteria," she joked to Chasity, who was silently walking beside her.

"Good for you, Malajia," Chasity grunted, scrolling through the messages on her cell phone.

Malajia shot her a sideway glance. "No need to be snide," Malajia chided. "Can you just be happy that things are good between me and Tyrone?"

"Malajia, I promise I don't care," Chasity hissed.

Malajia sucked her teeth. "Still got that attitude, huh?"

"Yup," Chasity responded instantaneously. "And you're not supposed to talk to me about him, remember?"

Malajia shook her head. She couldn't believe that Chasity was still holding to her promise not to allow her to talk about Tyrone. Ever since their falling out last semester, they decided that Chasity's issues with Tyrone was causing tension in their friendship and made an agreement not to talk about him anymore. Malajia kept her promise ever since; she never told Chasity, or *anybody* for that matter that he'd hit her.

"Well…I figured that was when things weren't good between us," Malajia replied. "We're good now."

Chasity rolled her eyes. *Why is she still with his raggedy ass?!* "Happy for you," she spat, voice dripping with disdain.

Malajia narrowed her eyes. "Thank you for that sarcastic well-wish," she hissed.

"Anytime. I've got *plenty* of them," Chasity shot back, walking away.

Malajia frowned at Chasity's departing back. "Whatever," she grumbled.


Malajia skipped up the steps after returning from class. "Slow talking ass professor, taking us over the time limit and shit," she griped, darting for her closet. Malajia was in a hurry; she only had a few moments to freshen up before Tyrone was due to pick her up.

She was excited to see him. After the long week that she had, she couldn't think of a better way to unwind than to spend time with her boyfriend.

Sidra entered the room as Malajia was searching in her closet for a different shirt.

"Mel, can you do me a favor?" Sidra asked, sitting her books on her desk.

"What's that?" Malajia's eyes were still focused on the contents of the closet.

"Well, I know you've done a few business proposals for your marketing class and I was wondering if you could help me with *mine*," she asked, hopeful.

"I don't know if you want my help. I'm only making a C in that class…*maybe*," Malajia joked. "Hell, it *could* be a *D*,"

Sidra let out a sigh. "Fine, can I see your textbook?" she asked. "I can try to figure it out myself."

"Knock yourself out," Malajia said, pointing to the textbook on her dresser. "Isn't Josh a business major? I'm sure he's done plenty of proposals *too*."

Sidra grabbed the book and started thumbing through it.

"He *is*, but I don't really want to bug him," she muttered.

"Things still awkward between you two?" Malajia wondered, scratching her head.

Sidra gave a quick shrug, but didn't answer. Noticing Malajia tossing several tops out of her closet, Sidra frowned. "Girl, why are you making it look like a tornado hit our room?"

"I'm trying to find something to wear," Malajia informed. "Tyrone is taking me to dinner so I have to get ready."

"Oh," Sidra nodded. She turned to leave the room but a thought stopped her. "Can I ask you something? And don't get mad."

Facing Sidra, Malajia gave a slight frown. "Why would I get mad at a question?"

"Because it's about your boyfriend," Sidra stated bluntly.

Malajia let out a sigh and folded her arms in anticipation of the question. "Go ahead."

"Why don't you ever bring him around us?"

"What do you mean?" Malajia removed the shirt that she had on.

"Well, he's your man and everything and our group is really close...so why doesn't he ever come around to hang out with us when we do group stuff?" Sidra asked. "I'm not saying he has to hang around *all* the time, but if this is someone that you care about, we should at *least* be able to get to know him...don't you think so?"

"Why would I bring him around?" Malajia asked defensively. "Nobody likes him."

Sidra pointed to herself. "*I* never said I didn't like him," she argued.

"You said that he was 'questionable'," Malajia reminded, giving air quotes.

Sidra looked at the ceiling for a second, while trying to recall her comment. "Oh, you mean when we were arguing last semester?"

Malajia gave a vigorous nod.

Sidra rolled her eyes; she did remember the comment that she had made at Malajia in the heat of the moment during a nasty fight. "Okay look, I'm sorry. I formed an opinion based off meeting him *one* time," she admitted. "But this is my *point*. I don't know much about him to form a *real* opinion."

*Damn, she's right*, Malajia thought. "Like that's ever stopped you before," Malajia attempted to joke. "Your little uppity, judgmental ass."

Sidra made a face. "Whatever," she hissed. "Anyway, if some of the people in our group seem to not like him, maybe it's just because they don't know him like that."

Before Malajia could open her mouth to respond, she saw Tyrone heading up the stairs through her open door. "Hey baby," she smiled.

"Why aren't you ready?" Tyrone barked, seeing Malajia standing there with her bra on and holding a shirt in her hand. "You already know that I hate to wait."

Sidra shot him a glare. Not only did he walk into their room and not even speak to her, but he had the nerve to snap at Malajia. *How freakin' rude! "First* off, *hi* Tyrone," she sneered, waving her hand at him.

Tyrone just looked at her, face void of any pleasantries.

"*Second*, her not being ready is *my* fault. I started talking to her when she was trying to get dressed."

"Malajia *knows* that I hate waiting," he reiterated, tone stern.

Sidra turned to Malajia to see if she was going to say anything to defend herself. When she didn't, Sidra mouthed the words 'cuss his ass out.'

Malajia shook her head. "Sid, it's okay. I *was* supposed to be ready," she replied. "We *do* have reservations."

Sidra, not believing what had just happened, rolled her eyes and walked out.

Malajia sighed; no longer having an audience, she tossed her top on her chair and put her hands on her hips. "Why did you have to be rude to her?" she snapped. "And why did you have to talk to me like that? You act like I was butt naked when you came in."

"Did I *not* tell you to be ready when I got here?" Tyrone asked, tone nasty. "I don't have time to play with you."

"What the hell—" Malajia's retort was interrupted by the sound of her cell phone receiving a message. She picked it up and seeing that she had a text message from Sidra, frowned. *'Now I really don't like him'*, it read. Rolling her eyes, Malajia deleted the message just as Tyrone went to grab the phone from her.

"Who are you texting?" he fumed.

"Boy, don't touch my phone," she bit back, moving her hand out of the way.

Tyrone's jaw clenched as Malajia stared back at him defiantly. "Just come the hell on before I change my mind," he hissed, storming out the door.

"Yeah whatever," Malajia muttered.

"I'll be waiting in the car. You have five minutes," he threw over his shoulder.

Malajia, embarrassed and annoyed, ran her hand along the back of her neck. "Nice to see you too," she mumbled to herself. *So much for being on good terms.*

Tyrone opened the front door to walk out, just as Chasity was walking in. Seeing him stand there staring at her made her frown. He completely disgusted her, and Chasity hoped he knew it. Without a word, she moved pass him and headed to her room door.

"Not going to say hi?" he spat, following her progress.

"Don't fuckin' talk to me," Chasity snarled, shutting her door.

Without saying another word, he walked outside. Malajia hurried down the stairs just as the front door shut. Having overheard what Chasity said, she knocked on her door.

"What?" Chasity scoffed, opening the door.

"Yo, chill with the ignorant ass comments," Malajia

charged, angry. Even though she herself was annoyed with Tyrone, she still didn't like other people to disrespect him.

Chasity raised an eyebrow. "You sure you wanna do this with me right now?" she challenged. "Isn't your boss outside?"

Malajia's eyes widened in fury. "Screw you, bitch."

"You *can't,*" Chasity threw back, before slamming the door in Malajia's face.

Shocked, Malajia raised her hand to bang on the door but decided against it; Tyrone was waiting for her. Gritting her teeth, she walked away.

Malajia leaned her head on the passenger side window, glancing at the street lights passing by. "So, we're really going to spend this car ride in silence?" she grunted to Tyrone whose eyes were fixed on the road. When he didn't answer her, she sucked her teeth and folded her arms.

"What do you want me to tell you, Malajia?" Tyrone bit out.

"How about '*I'm sorry*' for starters?" Malajia bit back. "You embarrassed me in front of my friend, you acted like a complete ass at dinner, and you ignored me for half this damn ride."

Malajia's excitement for a nice outing with Tyrone decreased when he first came into the house. Nevertheless, she still had hope that the evening could be salvaged. That hope went out the window when Tyrone failed to keep his attitude in check during their evening out. Now riding in his car on the way back to campus, Malajia decided to finally address the issue.

"How the fuck am I ignoring you when I'm *talking* to you?" Tyrone spat. "You sound stupid."

Malajia rolled her eyes. "And *now* you're insulting me. Nice." She reached into her purse and pulled out her phone. "I could have stayed my ass home."

"I wish you *would've.*"

Malajia let out a loud sigh. "There must be some other shit going on with you because you can't be *this* damn angry over having to wait a few extra minutes for me, earlier," she argued.

"Malajia, shut your annoying ass up for five seconds," Tyrone demanded.

Not feeling like arguing any longer, Malajia began playing with her phone in silence.

Tyrone glanced over at her as her fingers moved along the screen. "What are you doing?" he barked.

Concentrating on her game, Malajia refused to answer. *Let's see how you like being ignored.*

"Malajia, I asked you a question, what are you doing?" Tyrone persisted, his voice becoming louder. "Who are you texting?" When she remained silent, Tyrone pulled the car up to a curb and put it in park. "You better not be talking to your nosey ass friends about me."

Malajia sighed. "Boy, ain't nobody thinking about you," she mumbled, still eyeing her phone.

"What?" Tyrone challenged. Reaching his breaking point at Malajia's defiant behavior, Tyrone grabbed Malajia's wrist, startling her. "You just gonna keep texting on your damn phone while I'm talking to you?" he snapped.

"Get off me, are you crazy?!" Malajia yelled, trying to pry his firm grip from her tiny wrist.

"Don't fuckin' disrespect me!"

Tears built up in Malajia's eyes, when Tyrone twisted her wrist. "You're hurting me!" Malajia's tears didn't affect Tyrone; he just squeezed tighter and twisted harder.

Fearing that he might break her wrist, Malajia leaned forward and bit him on his arm.

"Ouch!" he yelled, releasing his grip, to grab his own arm.

Seizing the opportunity, Malajia grabbed her purse and jumped out of the car, slamming the door in the process.

Tyrone too got out the car. "Malajia, get back in the car," he ordered. When she didn't listen, he started to approach. Malajia spun around, face streaked with tears. "Leave me the fuck alone," she panted. She felt like she could barely breathe, she was so angry. "I can't deal with this."

Knowing that there was nothing he could say to justify his actions, Tyrone just stood there, watching Malajia storm away. He put his hand on his head and let out a heavy sigh before getting back into his car and driving off.

"Thanks for staying and waiting for me to get off," Alex said, sitting down next to Chasity in a booth. "I'm too tired to walk back to campus."

"No problem," Sidra replied, breaking off a piece of a breadstick. "I'm not in a rush to get back anyway. There's a business proposal waiting for me," she chuckled.

Alex removed her apron and sat it down on the table, letting out a long sigh. She'd been on her feet at the Pizza Shack for hours and dreaded the walk back to campus. She was relieved to see Sidra and Chasity walk into the parlor a half hour earlier to order food and to wait for her.

"Yeah, I have a paper draft waiting for *me*," Alex stated. "I just have to wipe off those last few tables over there and we can go."

Sidra took a sip of her water. "Do you think we should take a pizza back to the house?"

"Yeah, I'll put one in the oven," Alex offered. "The last thing I want to hear is Malajia complain that we didn't bring anything back for her."

Sidra adjusted the bracelet on her wrist. "*Speaking* of Malajia," she began. "Tyrone came to pick her up earlier and...I don't like him."

Alex chuckled. "Join the club."

Sidra shook her head. "No seriously. Not only was he rude to *me*, but the way that he talked to her today was just uncalled for. Like she was a child or something," she informed. "I didn't like it."

"Yeah well, I've already expressed my dislike for him when they started dating again... It's something about him," Alex said, rubbing her neck. "And I didn't like how Mel acted when they first started talking... I don't know exactly what happened between them, but she would get depressed quite often."

"Well, I had only met him the one time, so I had no *real* reason to dislike him, but today changed that," Sidra declared. "He's a jerk and she deserves better."

Leaning her head on the wall, Chasity just sat there silently, listening to Sidra and Alex express their concerns about Malajia's boyfriend. She had them herself and had already expressed them to Malajia; she knew far more about their relationship than the other girls did.

"Well, I'm staying out of it," Alex proclaimed, putting her hands up.

Sidra glanced at Alex. "*You're* staying out of something?" she teased.

Alex made a face at her. "That's funny," she ground out. "I'm *trying* to anyway," she amended. "Mel is a grown woman and it's her decision. As long as he doesn't put his hands on her, I'm fine."

"He just better *not*," Sidra hissed.

Noticing Chasity's silence, Alex looked at her. "You're awfully quiet tonight," she observed. "No comments?"

"Nope," Chasity mumbled.

Alex frowned, noticing Chasity's low voice and half lidded eyes. "Are you okay?"

"I have a headache," Chasity replied, tone even.

"Probably because you haven't eaten anything," Alex implored. "You haven't touched any of your pizza."

"That's because I don't *want* it," Chasity snapped. "I just *said* I have a headache. So can you hurry the fuck up and wipe those nasty ass tables off so we can go?"

Alex stared at her, unfazed. "Are you taking your iron pills?"

"*Why?*" Chasity asked, exasperated.

Alex sucked her teeth. "Look, don't get all snappy with *me* because I care about your ignorant ass," she chided. "Does the word *anemia* ring any bells? You passed out from it last semester, remember?"

"I remember, I was *there*," Chasity sneered.

"*Exactly*. Scaring us half to death," Alex threw back, folding her arms on the table top. "You looked *then*, like you look *now*, so I'm concerned. Get the hell over it."

Chasity rolled her eyes. She remembered the symptoms she had felt leading up to her collapsing. Being diagnosed with anemia due to iron deficiency wasn't what she was expecting to hear upon leaving the hospital. *Nosey heffa got a point.* "I've been taking my damn pills. Just come the fuck *on*."

Alex grabbed her apron and rose from her seat. "So freakin' difficult," she scoffed, walking off. "Still love you though."

"The feeling ain't mutual," Chasity snarled, folding her arms.

"Yes, it is," Alex threw back, continuing her departure.

Gathering her coat, Sidra giggled. "Come on cranky, let's get you home so you can go to sleep," she said to Chasity, gesturing for her to get up.


The desk lamp illuminated the room; Malajia tapped her pencil at a rapid pace on her notebook. *Stupid accounting. I don't give a shit about credits and debits.* Tossing the pencil on the desk, she ran her hands through her hair and sighed. "Come on Malajia, get it together," she coaxed herself.

She rubbed her wrist, wincing. The soreness had yet to subside. She blinked back tears as she recalled the incident in Tyrone's car two nights ago. *I can't believe he put his hands on me again.*

Her troubled thoughts were interrupted by her phone ringing. Seeing Tyrone's name pop up on the caller ID, she sucked her teeth and clicked the decline button. Before she could pick her pencil back up, the phone rang again.

"God, leave me alone," she fumed to the empty room. After the third call, she snatched the phone up and put it to her ear. "What do you want?" she snapped.

"Can you meet me outside?" Tyrone asked, tone calm.

"I'm not meeting you no-damn-where," she barked. "I told you the other night to leave me alone."

"I *can't* leave you alone," he replied. "Can you *please* come outside? I have something that I want to give to you."

She let out a loud, quick sigh. "Look, I have homework to finish and it's taking me a long time to do since my damn wrist hurts."

"Malajia, I'm sor—"

"Save that shit," she scoffed, interrupting his apology.

"*Please* Malajia," he begged. "Just come outside."

Malajia gritted her teeth and kicked the side of the desk. She was mad at herself for answering the phone in the first place. "Fine, I'm coming," she said.

Hanging up, Malajia made her way out of the room. She folded her arms to keep her black cardigan closed as she walked outside and stood on the step.

"Can you make it quick? I need to get back to work," she snarled.

Tyrone held out a bouquet of red roses. "I'm sorry that I lost my temper."

She sucked her teeth, not bothering to take them. "Whatever Tyrone, go home," she ground out, turning around to return inside. She froze when Tyrone lurched forward and grabbed her arm. Even though it was a gentle hold, Malajia still stiffened. "Please don't touch me," she pleaded softly, back towards him.

He let go and backed up. "I don't want you to be afraid of me touching you," he said.

Malajia spun around and faced him, eyes blazing. "How do you *expect* me to react after what you did?"

Tyrone placed the roses on the step. "I didn't hit you again," he argued.

"No, but you still *hurt* me," she shot back. "Twisting my wrist is *still* assaulting me, something you said you wouldn't do anymore."

Tyrone ran a hand over his hair. "I know," he said. "I lost my temper and I'm sorry."

Malajia folded her arms again but didn't say anything.

"Look, my anger wasn't even about *you*. I had some other shit on my mind... I got kicked out of school."

Malajia's eyes widened. "You *what*?"

Tyrone nodded. "Yeah."

"What the hell *happened*?" she wondered. Malajia first met Tyrone a year ago, when he played football during homecoming for their rival school, Prime State University. Him being kicked out was the last thing that she expected to hear.

Tyrone rubbed his face. "A combination of shit... my grades, got in a few fights—"

"Why am I not surprised by that second part?" she sneered. Seeing the sullen look on his face, Malajia felt bad for her snide remark. Despite how he acted, she couldn't imagine being kicked out of school. "Look, I shouldn't have said that. Sorry."

"I know that I deserved it," Tyrone muttered. He took a step forward. "I messed up... I won't do it again."

"You said that *last* time," she reminded him.

"I *mean* it this time," he persisted. "I'm not perfect, but I care about you and...all I'm asking is for another chance, Malajia... I'm sorry."

Malajia held her gaze on him. Part of her wanted to tell him where to stick his apologies and promises, but the other part—the part that cared for him—wanted to give him another chance. "You can't hurt me anymore." Her tone was almost pleading, "Do you understand?"

"I understand," he assured, stepping closer.

Malajia closed her eyes as Tyrone gently took hold of her injured wrist and gave it a kiss. He then tried to wrap his arms around her, but Malajia pulled away from him. "I have to go."

Tyrone watched her walk inside. "Can I call you tomorrow?"

"Yeah," she answered after a moment.

"Don't forget your flowers," he said, picking the bouquet up and handing it to her.

Malajia reluctantly grabbed the flowers. "Thank you," she muttered, shutting the door behind her.

# Chapter 16

Emily grabbed several notebooks and a pack of ink pens off a shelf, and placed them in her shopping cart. "I can't believe how many notebooks I've gone through so far," she said. "These classes are brutal this semester."

"Welcome to junior year," Sidra chuckled, pushing the shopping cart through the Mega Mart aisle. "I am *not* looking forward to midterms."

"Don't remind me," Emily scoffed. "Luckily they aren't for a few weeks."

Sidra stopped in the middle of the air freshener aisle. "Ooh, I love scented candles," she declared, picking up a large yellow one. She opened the top.

Chasity approached, placing items in the cart. "Are y'all almost done?" she asked.

"Yeah, almost," Sidra answered. She held the candle near Chasity's nose. "Here smell this; do you think it'll be nice for the house?"

Turning her nose up, Chasity pushed Sidra's hand away. "Ugh, that shit stinks," she scoffed.

Sidra frowned in confusion as she sniffed the candle again. "It does *not*," she argued. "It smells like pineapples."

"A *rotten* ass one," Chasity grunted.

Sidra rolled her eyes, "You are so damn dramatic," she

murmured, putting the candle back on the shelf. She picked up another one. "What about this one?"

"Don't put that in my face, I smell that from here," Chasity replied, backing away from Sidra. "Don't get *any* of these, they *all* smell like trash."

Emily giggled as Sidra slammed the candle back on the shelf. "Let's just get one *without* a scent," Emily suggested.

"No, forget it. I don't want any now," Sidra huffed.

"Whatever. I'm tired, just come on," Chasity demanded.

"Yeah, yeah," Sidra fussed, counting the items in the cart.

Mark, seeing the girls walk out of the aisle, walked up to them, holding a food sample. Holding the item in Chasity's face, he said, "Hey Chaz, smell this and tell me what kind of meat this is."

"Boy move," Chasity spat, knocking his hand out of the way.

"So, this isn't chicken?" Mark jeered at Chasity's departing back.

Sidra giggled, halting her cart. "You here picking up food or supplies?" she asked Mark.

"Food," Mark answered, popping the sample into his mouth. "Damn this is good," he mused, eyeing the leftover toothpick. "Anyway, the guys are being stingy with their snacks so I'm being forced to buy my own."

"Well, good for them," Sidra teased. "It's about time they stopped supporting your freeloading ways."

"Funny," Mark replied, sarcastic. "Have you seen Malajia? She left her notebook in English earlier today. I was gonna give it back to her."

"I think she's in class, but I can take it and give it to her when I see her later," Sidra offered.

Mark thought for a moment. "Naw, it's cool. I have class in the same building with her in about a half hour. I can just give it to her then," he said finally.

Sidra shrugged then pushed her cart. Mark put his foot on the wheel, stopping her. "What are you doing?" she asked.

"How about you let me put a box of brownies and juice on your tab?" his face held a hopeful look.

Sidra rolled her eyes. "Mark, pay for your own stuff."

Mark looked at Emily as Sidra walked away. "Come on Em, help a brother out," he persisted.

"Emily, don't do it. Trust me," Sidra called to her.

Emily, trying not to laugh, just shook her head then took off to catch up to Sidra.

"Forget y'all then," Mark fussed, walking in the other direction.

Holding her cell phone discreetly under her desk, Malajia sent a text message. Looking up at her professor, she pretended to be interested in the lecture, hoping not to draw attention to herself. Her hope was shattered when her phone started making noise. *Shit!* She quickly turned it off.

"Malajia, I hope that was the sound of the answer to this question jumping into your brain," the professor jeered.

Malajia laughed nervously. "Sorry," she said, covering her face with her hand as her fellow classmates started snickering.

She was relieved when the professor announced that class was dismissed. Quickly grabbing her belongings, she headed for the door. "Malajia, can I speak to you for a moment?" the professor asked just as Malajia was about to walk out.

"Sorry, I'm in a hurry," Malajia quickly replied, opening the door.

"It will just take a second," he insisted.

Approaching the desk, Malajia rolled her eyes and sighed. "Yes?"

"I've noticed that you're distracted in class lately," he began.

Malajia looked down at the floor. "Sorry about my phone. I forgot to silence it," she muttered.

"It's not just *this* incident," he clarified. "Over the past week, you have not been participating like you *normally* do. You usually have some great input on our discussions, but not recently."

Malajia pushed some of her hair over her shoulder. She knew that he was right; she had begun to enjoy her business class, especially when they started discussing the different practices of various companies. However, her mind hadn't been on school lately. "I just have a lot on my mind right now. But next class I'll be sure to participate," she assured.

"Well I sure *hope* you'll participate next class," he replied, wiping the board clean with an eraser. "Otherwise, your team will be pretty upset... Your team presentation is due."

Malajia threw her head back. She had totally forgotten. "Crap," she mumbled.

"I'm sorry, what did you say?" he asked, not quite making out what she said.

"I said, great," she lied, glancing at her watch. "No disrespect, but I have to go."

"See you Monday," he dismissed.


Opening the door to the building, Malajia was ready to jump down the steps, but she was stopped by Mark, who grabbed her shoulder.

"Hold up," he said.

Turning to him, Malajia frowned. "What?" she bit out.

Mark sucked his teeth at her nasty tone. "Damn, hey to you *too*, jackass," he shot back. "I was just trying to give you your stupid notebook that you left in English this morning."

Feeling bad for her reaction, Malajia relaxed her face. "Oh, sorry," she said, then giggled. "Who knew you could be nice sometimes."

Mark made a face at her, then playfully tapped her on the arm. "See you later, ugly," he joked when they approached the bottom of the concrete steps.

"Later." Malajia again glanced at her watch. Looking up, she was caught off guard at the sight of Tyrone standing a few feet away. "Ty?" she questioned, frowning.

Mark, having heard Malajia mention Tyrone's name, stopped and looked over at them.

"What are you doing over here?" Malajia asked, approaching Tyrone. "And how did you know where I was? I said to wait for me back at the house."

Tyrone stared her down. He fixed the baseball cap on his head. "Your text said you were leaving your business class, so I asked someone where the business building was...and here I am," he finally answered with a deceptive calm.

Malajia shook her head. "This popping up thing that you do is really weird," she commented, adjusting the book bag on her shoulder. Noticing the stern look on Tyrone's face, she raised an eyebrow. "What's wrong with you?"

Tyrone reached for her arm. "We need to go," he urged.

Watching from a distance, Mark went into protective mode when he witnessed the tense exchange. He hurried over. "What's up Tyrone? You good man?" he said, standing in front of Malajia.

Tyrone frowned at Mark, then a smile crossed his face. "Yeah, everything is good," he replied, holding his hand out for Mark to shake.

The gesture took both Malajia and Mark by surprise. Mark stared at him skeptically, shaking his hand.

Malajia, on the other hand was pleasantly surprised; she never in a million years would have thought that Tyrone would be nice to Mark. She stood next to Tyrone, beaming. *Thank God, he's over that jealous nonsense.*

Tyrone held the same smile as he glanced at Malajia, putting his arm around her shoulder. "You ready to go?"

"Yeah, I just have to grab my overnight bag from the house," she answered.

"Cool, let's go get it," Tyrone said, nudging her along.

Mark watched their departure, frowning. He then shook

his head. "Dude is fuckin' weird," he said to himself.

The car ride to Tyrone's small apartment was a quiet one. But unlike the other quiet rides to his house, Malajia wasn't on edge. Sure, he hadn't said anything since they left campus, but at least they weren't arguing. He walked through his front door, with her following close behind. As soon as Malajia shut the door and sat her belongings on his couch, Tyrone turned around to face her. The calm face from earlier was masked with anger.

"What the hell did I tell you about hanging around that damn Mark?" he seethed.

Malajia looked at him with confusion written on her face. "What are you talking about?"

"Don't play with me!" he erupted, causing her to flinch. "I saw him put his hand on you when you were coming outside of the building."

Malajia thought for a moment, then realization hit. "What? You mean when he touched my shoulder to get my *attention* so he could give me my *notebook* back?" she threw back, loud.

"He shouldn't be putting his damn hands on you in the *first* place," Tyrone fumed.

Malajia threw her head back and groaned. "Oh my God, don't start this shit again," she hurled. "And if you were so damn mad about it when you saw it, why didn't you address it right then and there?"

"And what? Give that bastard the satisfaction of knowing that I feel threatened by him?"

Malajia rolled her eyes. "You know what Ty, if I would've known that you were going to act like this, I would have never gotten in your car." She turned to walk out of the room. "I don't feel like this mess today, I had a long week."

"Are you fucking him?" Tyrone barked.

That question, so disrespectful, caused Malajia to stop her departure and spin around to face him. Face masked with anger and hands on her hips, she stared him down. "What did you just ask me?"

"You heard what the hell I asked you. What are you, stupid?"

"I'm not stupid!" she yelled. "And how dare you ask me that? You know that you're the *only* one that I have *ever* been with."

"I don't know *shit* for sure. Malajia," he spat out. "You dress like a whore, so I wouldn't be surprised if you actually *were* one."

She felt tears well up in her eyes. "Oh, so you go *right* back to accusing me of being a whore?" her voice was filled with disdain. "Even though you *know* I'm *not*? ...What the hell is *wrong* with you?"

Tyrone rubbed his face; his temper was on high. "If I had known that you were gonna cause me this much fuckin' trouble, I would've *never* called your smut ass after you left my apartment that night... You already wasted my time by not putting out."

She couldn't believe what was coming out of his mouth. "So why *did* you call me again after that?" she challenged.

"'Cause I wanted to fuck you," he hissed.

Malajia's eyes widened. He'd gotten nasty with her in the past, but this was a new low. To insinuate that he only pursued her in order to fulfill his mission of sleeping with her and not because he actually *liked* her, was beyond hurtful. "And yet you're *still* with me, so I guess *you're* the stupid one," she sneered. "Screw you."

"Watch your damn mouth!" he hollered. "And if I have to tell your hard-headed ass *one* more time to stay away from Mark, you and me are going to have problems," he threatened.

"Don't tell me what to do!" she screamed. "I can't take this from you anymore. You're acting completely crazy and being totally disrespectful. Take me the fuck home!"

"Why? So you can go fuck Mark?" he barked. "I'm not taking you *nowhere*, bitch."

Malajia gasped. "Did you just call me a bitch?!"

"Sure *did*, bitch," Tyrone snarled.

Malajia shook her head as she fought the urge to bust out crying. "You know what, I don't need you to do *shit* for me," she declared, reaching for her bag. "Just like my *first* time here, I'll get home on my own."

"Don't walk away from me Malajia," Tyrone warned, pointing at her.

"Fuck you, you crazy bastard," she snapped, turning away. Tyrone walked up to her, grabbed her arm and yanked her. She snatched away from him and pushed him. "Keep your fuckin' hands off me!" she hollered.

When she turned away again, Tyrone lost all sense of sanity and control. Darting up to her, he grabbed her and pushed her with so much force that she went falling into a nearby end table. The table broke under her; she fell to the floor. Malajia cried out as she laid there, grabbing her side. Before she knew what was happening, Tyrone was standing over her and with his boot-covered foot, he repeatedly kicked her in her midsection.

Each kick that he delivered knocked more wind out of Malajia. She tried to scream, but nothing would come out. She tried grabbing his leg to stop him, but he just stomped on her hand. With one last kick, Tyrone stared down at her. Not knowing what else he was about to do to her, Malajia balled into the fetal position. She held her breath, closed her eyes, and prayed. It wasn't until she heard the front door slam shut that she breathed out. Barely able to move, she clutched her abdomen and cried out hysterically.

# Chapter 17

Malajia blinked several times before opening her eyes completely. Her body was stiff and sore. Pulling her covers up to her neck, she closed her eyes tight as she felt pain shoot through her ribs. She didn't remember what time she ended up making it back to her room the night before. After Tyrone assaulted her, she laid on the floor for what could have been hours. She was in so much pain that she could barely move. She would have laid there forever, but the realization set in that Tyrone was going to come back. Not knowing what he was going to do when he returned, she mustered up whatever strength she had to get up and leave.

She opened her eyes again when Sidra walked through the door. "Hey sleepy head," Sidra teased, tapping her nails on her dresser. "The drama club is putting on a play at the student theater in like ten minutes. I'm going with Alex and Mark. You want to go?"

"No," Malajia replied, voice barely audible. It hurt to breathe.

Sidra frowned slightly. "Ooh, you sound terrible," she pointed out, concerned. "Are you catching a cold or something?"

"Probably," Malajia lied.

Sidra grabbed her purse off her dresser. "Well, feel better soon sweetie," she responded. "Seriously, the sooner the better. I don't want to catch what you have." She walked out the room, shutting the door behind her.

Malajia laid in the bed for several more minutes before carefully pushing the covers off her. Slowly, she sat up. She had to coax herself to stand up and go to the bathroom.

Taking nearly a half hour to shower due to her injuries, she grabbed the first pair of jeans and tank top that she saw in her closet. She was in no mood and in too much pain to care about being her normal fashionable self. Catching a glimpse in her floor length mirror as she pulled her black tank top over her head, she finally saw the damage done to her by Tyrone. Her midsection was covered in large black and blue bruises. She looked at her hand, bruised and swollen from being stepped on repeatedly.

Tears filling her eyes, she pulled her shirt down, put on a long burgundy cardigan, and pulled part of her hair back with a clip.

After painstakingly making her way down the steps, Malajia let out a labored sigh. She walked over to Chasity's room door and tapped on it.

"It's open," Chasity called through the closed door.

Malajia opened it and walked in. "Hey, what are you doing?" she asked softly.

"Trying to update this website for my mom's company," Chasity replied, not taking her eyes off her laptop screen. "Why, what's up?"

Malajia closed the door and folded her arms across her chest. "Can I talk to you?" she asked.

"Can it *wait*?" Chasity asked, exasperated. "I told her I would have this done for her like *now*."

Malajia shook her head. "No, it *can't* wait," she persisted. "I really need to talk to you."

Annoyed by the interruption, Chasity closed her laptop and turned around in her seat. "What is it Malajia?"

Malajia looked at the floor. "Um… I want to talk to you

about Tyrone."

Chasity rolled her eyes as she stood from her seat. "No," she bluntly responded.

Malajia slowly ran her hand over her hair. "Just listen—"

"No, I'm *not* going to listen," Chasity interrupted. "We already talked about this. I don't want to hear about another one of your stupid ass arguments."

Malajia took several labored breaths. "Chaz, could you stop—"

"I *said* no," Chasity snapped. "Go take that shit to somebody else."

The more Chasity rejected her request, the more Malajia felt like she was about to have a nervous breakdown. She had to make her listen. "Will you shut the fuck up and listen to me?!" Malajia hollered with every bit of strength that she had.

Completely taken off guard by Malajia's shouting, Chasity frowned. "What Mel?!" she yelled back. "What the hell is so damn important?"

The words refused to form in her mouth; Malajia slowly lifted her tank top up.

Chasity stood there, stunned at the sight of Malajia's bruises. It took Chasity several tries to get any words out of her mouth. "What…What the fuck happened Malajia?" she asked, trying to control her rising temper.

Malajia pulled her shirt back down as tears flowed from her eyes. "Tyrone did this to me," she said, voice cracking. "You were right about him… He hit me."

Chasity put her hands over her mouth, unable to speak.

"I don't know what happened," Malajia said, trying to maintain her composure. "We were arguing and then he pushed me and then he—he kept kicking me and—he wouldn't stop. I thought he was gonna kill me."

Chasity walked over and gently wrapped her arms around Malajia as Malajia broke down and cried uncontrollably

"I can't believe he did that to me. I just…I can't believe

he did that to me." Malajia sobbed, grabbing on to Chasity tightly.

"Yo Alex, you never again get to pick activities for us to do," Mark complained, walking out of the student theater. "That play was wack as shit."

Alex shook her head. "It was *not*," she contradicted. "You're always exaggerating. I think they did a good job for creating their own play."

"You know you can't take Mark anywhere different," Sidra slid in. "If it doesn't involve, sports, food or games, it's not going to hold his attention."

"Exactly," Mark agreed, adjusting the sleeve on his sweatshirt. He stopped when he noticed a familiar figure across the path. "Yo, I *know* that's not Tyrone's dumb ass walking around our campus," he fumed, following Tyrone's progress with his eyes.

Sidra craned her neck to see. "Is he with Malajia?"

"No, he's by himself," Mark replied.

Alex frowned in confusion. "That's weird. Who just strolls around the campus of a school that he doesn't go to?" she wondered. "I thought Malajia was supposed to be spending the weekend at *his* place anyway."

Sidra shrugged. "She was *supposed* to, but she ended up coming back to the house last night sometime after I fell asleep," she informed. "It's probably because she isn't feeling well. She sounded like she was coming down with a cold earlier."

"Well, in that case, he may be on his way to the house to look for her," Alex figured.

"I don't care *what* the hell he's doing here," Mark seethed. "I hate that bastard."

Sidra looked at him. "*You too?*" she asked. "Damn, do *any* of us like him?" she chuckled.

"Fuck no," Mark said. "I don't think David or Jason have met him before, but I'm sure when they *do, they* won't like his punk ass *either*."

Alex shook her head. "A damn shame," she concluded.


Chasity tapped her fingers on the keyboard of her laptop. She had been staring at the screen for nearly an hour. Unable to concentrate on Trisha's webpage, she closed her laptop and ran her hands through her hair.

She'd held onto Malajia as she cried for nearly a half hour. She hadn't said a word, rather just let Malajia cry out her anger and pain. It wasn't until Malajia had fallen asleep on Chasity's bed did she try to finish her task.

Folding her arms to her chest, she took several deep breaths. The thought of what Tyrone had done to her best friend made Chasity sick to her stomach. A light knock on the door snapped her out of her thoughts. She opened the door slightly. Even though it was Jason, she was unable to smile.

"Hey babe, do you want to go see a movie?" Jason asked.

Glancing back at Malajia sleeping, she shook her head. "Not right now. I have to finish this website," she replied. It was the half-truth.

"Oh? For class?"

"No, it's for my mom. She wanted me to add some updates to her webpage for her," Chasity answered, running her hands on the back of her neck. "I was supposed to have it done earlier."

He studied the sick look on her face, frowning in concern. "Are you okay?"

"Uh, yeah I'm fine. I'm just tired, that's all," she replied.

"Okay," Jason said, gently touching her arm. "Well, go ahead and get back to work and I'll see you later. Tell Ms. Trisha I said hi when you talk to her."

Chasity nodded.

"Love you," he threw over his shoulder as he headed for the door.

Chasity slowly closed the door and leaned her forehead against it. "Love you too," she said quietly.

"You should've gone with him," Malajia said, startling Chasity who spun around.

"How long have you been up?" Chasity asked.

Malajia leaned her back against a few decorative pillows on Chasity's bed. "I've been up for like the past fifteen minutes. I just didn't want to disturb you."

Chasity sat on the bed next to her. "Dumb question... How are you feeling?"

"Um, I'm okay. The aspirin that you gave me helped some," Malajia responded, gently rubbing her side.

"Did it really?" Chasity asked, skeptical.

Malajia nodded, then managed a labored chuckle. "All that crying got me hungry," she said, examining her swollen hand. "*You* hungry?"

Chasity slowly shook her head as she stared at Malajia. "So, um...Tyrone needs his ass beat," she stated bluntly.

Malajia let out a sigh and closed her eyes. "Chaz don't—"

"No, don't 'Chaz don't' me okay," Chasity snapped. "He can*not* get away with what he did. Now either he needs to get beat the fuck up, or he needs to go to jail... I'm good with *both* actually."

"I don't want anyone else to get hurt," Malajia argued. "I just want to be done with this whole situation."

"Bullshit," Chasity fumed. "You have men in your life who would be happy to beat the living shit out of that punk ass bastard for you... Hell, we *girls* will jump his ass."

"No, nobody is jumping or beating *anybody*," Malajia fussed, slapping her hand on the bed.

"So, he gets *no* punishment for beating *you* huh?" Chasity snarled.

Malajia rolled her eyes. "Chaz, I just want to be done," she slowly stated. "Pressing charges will draw things out and I just want to walk away."

Chasity couldn't understand how Malajia was okay with

nothing being done to Tyrone in retaliation. Her nonchalance about the entire subject was making Chasity angry. "You *better* not go back to him," Chasity seethed, pointing at her.

"Don't worry, I *won't*," Malajia assured.

"You've said that *before*," Chasity reminded. "But… that was *before* he hit you, so maybe you'll do it for good this time."

Malajia looked down at her hands. She'd almost forgotten that Chasity had no idea that this wasn't the first time that Tyrone had struck her. If Chasity knew that Malajia went back to him after he hit her the first time, she would probably never speak to her again.

"Yeah," Malajia mumbled finally. She looked at Chasity as she pushed some of her hair behind her ear. "Can you do me a favor?"

"What's that?"

Malajia hesitated. "Um…don't tell anybody about this please," she requested, much to Chasity's annoyance.

Chasity slammed her hand on her bed. "Come on Malajia, don't put this on me," she fussed.

"Chaz, I'm sorry," Malajia pleaded. "I know this is a big secret for you to carry for me, but I don't want anybody else to know about this… If the guys found out about what he did to me, they'd kill him."

"*And*?" Chasity sneered. "It'll be one less woman beater walking around."

"I'm begging you…please just keep this between us… *Please*?"

Chasity could have shaken Malajia right then and there. How could she put the burden of keeping a secret so serious on her? Chasity fumed in silence for several seconds.

Malajia stared at her, afraid. "Chaz, say something please."

"Fine Mel, you want me to keep this a secret?" she asked, Malajia nodded. "You need to do something for *me*."

"Whatever you want," Malajia agreed.

"You need to take your ass to the hospital to get checked

out," Chasity stipulated.

Malajia frowned. "Girl, I'm not going to no damn hospital," she dismissed with a wave of her hand. "I'm fine."

Chasity narrowed her eyes before giving Malajia a sudden, soft poke on her rib. Malajia shrieked as she grabbed her side. "Why the fuck would you do that?!" she hollered.

"Why the fuck would you *lie*?" Chasity shot back. Malajia, shocked and in pain couldn't even get any words out. Chasity rose from the bed. "Get the hell up and come on," she demanded.

Malajia sighed loudly as she reluctantly got up from the bed.


After sitting in the emergency room of Paradise Valley Memorial Hospital for over two hours, Malajia was relieved when she and Chasity pulled into the cluster parking lot. "Thank God," Malajia groaned, gingerly removing her seat belt. "I freakin' hate the emergency room. People was coughing all hype and shit."

Chasity shook her head as she turned her car off. "What did they say?" She hadn't asked Malajia when they left the hospital because Malajia had fallen asleep as soon as they got in the car.

"Bruised ribs," Malajia informed. "I'll be okay in a few weeks. Just have to take it easy."

"And what bullshit excuse did you give them when they asked you what happened?"

"That I fell down the steps," Malajia replied.

Chasity rolled her eyes. "How original," she sneered, still upset at the fact that Malajia wouldn't press charges.

Malajia shot her a glare. "That's not funny," she chastised.

"I'm not *laughing*," Chasity shot back, opening the car door.

Rolling her eyes at Chasity's snide remark, Malajia slowly got out of the car.

"Where *were* you two?" Alex asked as the girls walked into the house. "And why didn't you answer your phones?"

"Shut up *Mom*," Chasity sneered, walking over to the dining room table.

"Whatever." Alex made a face at Chasity. "I was trying to decide what to make for dinner and I wanted to see what y'all wanted." Alex sat a bowl of prepared food on the table. "But since you didn't answer, I just made what *I* wanted."

Chasity put her hand over her mouth and nose. "What the hell *is* it?" she scoffed. "It smells like garbage."

Alex frowned in confusion. "It's spaghetti," she informed, showing Chasity the bowls' contents. "I made it with ground beef."

Unable to take the smell, Chasity stood from the table and headed for her room. "Was the beef *rotten*?"

Alex sucked her teeth. "No, it *wasn't*," she ground out. "You've had my spaghetti plenty of times already, so stop being a smart ass." She looked over at Malajia who was leaned over the chair with her hands gripping the fabric. "What's wrong with *you*?"

Standing up right, Malajia pulled her sweater closed. "I'm just tired," she lied. "I'll just take my food upstairs so I can lay down."

Alex fixed a plate and handed it to Malajia. "A few of us saw Tyrone walking around campus when we left the play earlier," she informed.

Malajia froze on the steps at the mention of his name. "Um...did he say anything?" she asked.

Alex shook her head. "We saw him across the path, so nobody actually talked to him," she replied. "He didn't come by here to see you? We thought that he was on his way over here."

Malajia looked down at her plate of food. "No, he didn't come over here and I hope he never does again," she mumbled, continuing her walk up the steps.

Setting her plate on the floor by her bed, Malajia sat down on her bed and grabbed her phone from the floor. She scrolled through all twenty of her missed calls and fifteen of her unanswered text messages. Seeing that all but two were from Tyrone, she turned her phone off and threw it on the bed. Glancing over at her nightstand, she eyed the mirror that Tyrone had given to her. Picking it up, she stared at her reflection. Tears glassed over her eyes. Feeling angry, hurt, humiliated and most of all stupid, she hurled the mirror to the floor, cracking the glass. "Fuck him," she sniffled.

"Mel," Alex called, opening her door.

Malajia quickly wiped her eyes. She glanced up at Alex, annoyed. She just wanted to lay down and sleep her pain and the rest of the day away. "What?"

"Tyrone is outside," Alex informed, scratching her head.

Malajia's eyes widened in fear. "Can you tell him that I'm not here?" she asked, voice trembling.

"He already said that he saw you come in here," Alex replied. "What's going on? Did he do something to you? You look scared."

Malajia shook her head. "No, it's nothing like that," she lied. "We had a little disagreement and I just need some time to cool off."

"Well okay—" Before Alex could finish, Chasity pushed past her to get into Malajia's room.

"Give us a minute," Chasity demanded, shutting the door on an astonished Alex. She turned to Malajia. "That bitch got five seconds to get from in front of this house or I'm gonna go out there *myself* and crack his fuckin' face open," she seethed.

"He might leave, just ignore him," Malajia said, putting her hand up.

Chasity narrowed her eyes and folded her arms. "Yeah, he doesn't seem like the 'go-away-without-causing-a-scene' type of person," she implored, before looking at her watch. "Oh, look at that, five seconds are up."

Ignoring her pain, Malajia jumped from the bed and grabbed Chasity's arm to stop her from heading out of the door.

"Don't. He might hurt you too, and that's the last thing I want," Malajia pleaded.

"I bet you I do damage to him before he does any to me," Chasity argued, reaching for the door knob.

Malajia grabbed the knob first. "Just stop. I'll get rid of him," she insisted.

"There is no way in hell I'm gonna let you go out there with him!" Chasity exclaimed, blocking her way.

"He's not gonna leave unless he sees me," Malajia resolved. "I'm not going to let him near me...I just want him to go... Come stand behind the door if it'll make you feel better. I don't want you outside with him; he's fuckin' crazy."

"Fine," Chasity relented through clenched teeth. Malajia opened the door and walked out, followed by Chasity.

"You know what Chasity, I don't appreciate you slamming the door in my face," Alex hurled, walking out of her bedroom.

"She's sorry," Malajia cut in, not wanting an argument to ensue. "She had to tell me something important."

"That's fine, but *damn*," Alex muttered, going back into her room.

Malajia opened the door to find Tyrone standing at the walkway. She closed the door just enough so he wouldn't see Chasity standing on the other side. Leaving it cracked would allow her to run inside if he tried to assault her again. Her jaw clenched as she saw him just standing there; at that point, she hated him.

"What the fuck are you doing here?" she hissed.

"I came to apologize."

She looked at him as if he had completely lost his mind. "Apologize?" she seethed. "You must have lost your damn mind to think that you can come here and—" She backed up against the door when he took a step towards her. "Don't come near me."

He put his hand out. "I'm not going to hurt you," he assured.

Shaking, she held her hand on the doorknob. "Why were you walking around campus all day?" she questioned, voice trembling. "My friends said they saw you."

"I was looking for you," he informed. "You weren't answering my calls or texts and nobody answered when I knocked earlier."

"You wasted your time," she ground out.

"I know that I messed up," Tyrone admitted. "I should have never—I'll make it up to you, I promise." He then smiled a hopeful smile at her.

She put her hand up as her eyes filled with tears. "I...am so done," she sniffled. "There is no way that I will ever take you back after what you did to me...*Ever.*"

Tyrone's smile faded as he looked at the ground. "I don't want to lose you," he pleaded.

"According to what you said to me last night, the *only* reason you wanted me was to fuck me anyway," she hissed. "So this should be easy for you."

Tyrone put his hands over his face; he'd come to the realization that he had gone too far. "It's not," he said. "I know that I have problems and I need to get help."

Malajia had no interest in hearing any more of the crap he was spewing. "Get the hell way from my house and don't contact me anymore... If you do, I'm calling the police," she threatened.

Tyrone rubbed his face. "Malajia I'm so sorry...I didn't mean—"

"Don't test me," Malajia snapped, walking into the house and slamming the door behind her.

Tyrone thought about knocking on the door, but decided against it. Feeling that she would make good on her threat, he just walked away. As far as he was concerned, this was over.

Shaking, Malajia sat down on the couch and let out a long sigh, then clutched her side. "I don't know how I didn't pass out just now," she said to Chasity, who had sat down on the arm of the couch. "This pain is so bad."

"Adrenaline, probably," Chasity concluded. "You

okay?" she asked.

Malajia nodded. "I *will* be," she responded, she sighed again. "I *have* to be."

# Chapter 18

Chasity awoke feeling worse than she had the night before. Head pounding and feeling nauseas, she rolled over and pulled the covers over her head. "Nasty ass cafeteria food," she scoffed to herself. Letting out a groan, she got out of bed to get herself together.

"Hey sicko," Malajia teased when Chasity emerged from her room thirty minutes later.

Chasity made a face at her.

Malajia giggled. "You done throwing up your insides?" she asked. "You sounded like you were losing a kidney last night."

"Malajia, leave me the hell alone, or I'm gonna throw up right on your weave," Chasity warned, putting her hand on her stomach. "I feel something coming up, come here."

Malajia put her hands on her head and moved out of the way. "Ewww, back up or I'll kick you right in the stomach." she threw back.

"That'll only make it come up faster," Chasity smirked.

Sidra, who'd been quietly fixing her breakfast, nudged Malajia. "Mel, leave the girl alone and get ready to leave," she cut in. "You know if you're late to Lit again, your professor will lock you out...just like he did the other day."

Malajia thought for a moment. "Shit!" she panicked,

grabbing her book bag and running out the door.

Sidra shook her head as Chasity leaned against her closed room door. "You want some breakfast, sweetie?" she asked. "I have some extra eggs and turkey bacon."

Chasity turned her lip up and put her hand up. "Hell no," she refused. "That food I ate last night is still messing with me."

Sidra frowned. "*What* food?" she asked. "You only had a salad last night, and you barely ate *that*."

"Well it was *something*," Chasity insisted. "I feel like shit. Been throwing up since last night."

"Might be a stomach virus," Sidra pondered. "I think I heard that a few people had gotten sick sometime last week."

"Maybe," Chasity shrugged, walking towards the door.

"Why don't you take the day and just rest?" Sidra suggested. "I don't see how you're going to make it through all your classes feeling like that."

Chasity put her hand on the doorknob. "If it wasn't for midterms being this week, I damn sure *would*."

Sidra held a sympathetic gaze on Chasity. "Poor baby," she said, opening a jar of instant coffee.

"Sidra, that coffee smells strong as shit," Chasity complained. "You're gonna be up for like three days straight."

Sidra looked down at the opened jar. "How did you smell that from all the way over there? *I* can barely smell it and I'm right in front of it."

"How the hell should *I* know?" Chasity replied. "I guess my nose is just sensitive."

"No, sensitive is *one* thing, completely *weird* is another," Sidra argued. "You have been smelling off the wall stuff for weeks... I wonder about you sometimes," she teased, removing a glass mug from the cabinet.

Chasity just rolled her eyes and walked out the door.


"God, these midterms are going to be the death of me,"

Emily complained, opening a small bag of chips. "I'm ready to scream already," she added, offering Alex a chip.

Taking a chip from the bag, Alex chuckled. "Yeah I know, but we'll get through them just like always," she assured. "Just need some study sessions."

"I guess I'm just really nervous," Emily admitted. "I mean, I've been doing pretty well in my classes so far but... I just don't want to throw all that away by messing up on midterms."

"Em, you'll be *fine*. If you need help, just ask any of us," Alex responded. She stopped and smiled at Eric as he passed by her. He returned her smile with one of his own.

Emily caught the exchange. "Alex, you can go catch up to him if you want," she said. "I can go to the library by myself."

Alex looked back at him as he continued his quick pace. Smiling, she did not hear Emily say anything.

"Alex," Emily called, this time louder, nudging her in the process.

"Huh?" Alex snapped out of her trance. "I'm sorry, what did you say?"

Emily giggled. "Go catch up to him."

Alex waved her hand dismissively. "No, he has a class now." She pushed hair out of her face. "I'll talk to him later."

"Have you hung out since...well you know?" Emily asked.

"Yes, we have... But we're still *just* friends," Alex replied, then smiled to herself. "*Really* good friends."

Emily studied Alex's dreamy expression for a moment. "Do I need to stay out of the room for a while today?" she chortled.

Alex playfully poked her on the arm. "No, you don't," she laughed. "I need to focus on these midterms. Come on, let's hit up this library."

"Ugh, my home for the next few days," Emily groaned, throwing her head back.

On their way to the library, they saw Chasity sitting on a

bench outside with her face in her hands.

"Chaz, what are you doing?" Emily asked, tapping her on the shoulder.

Chasity looked up, fatigue and annoyance written on her face. "I'm doing back flips," she hissed. "What the fuck does it *look* like I'm doing?"

Emily pushed some hair behind her ears as she looked down at the ground. Chasity still had the ability to shut her up with her harsh tone and words.

Noticing the look of embarrassment on Emily's face, Alex lightly rubbed her shoulder. "Are you okay?" Alex asked Chasity, not fazed by her attitude.

"I'm fine," she hissed, running her hand over her hair.

"I find that hard to believe," Alex threw back, ignoring Chasity's nasty tone. "You're leaned over like you don't feel good. So, what's up?"

Chasity rolled her eyes. Truth was, the walk from the science building to the clusters seemed much too long for her today. She needed a break. "I'm tired," she replied.

"You're *always* tired," Alex pointed out.

"So?" Chasity snarled.

"Well you can't sleep *here*, so you might as well come in the library with us and study for these midterms," Alex insisted, grabbing Chasity's book bag from the ground.

"Alex, I will literally punch you in the face if you don't leave me alone," Chasity threatened evenly.

"Oh, shut up girl, and come *on*," Alex urged, grabbing Chasity's arm and pulling her from the bench. Chasity, realizing that Alex wouldn't leave her alone, just groaned as she allowed herself to be pulled along.


Music blared through the stereo speakers and the smell of seasoned beef and chicken filled the house. Malajia danced and sang along to one of her favorite tracks as she diced up tomatoes, lettuce, and onions.

Bruises gone, ribs nearly healed and feeling back to her

old self for the first time in nearly a month, Malajia decided to celebrate by cooking dinner for her friends. She hadn't heard from Tyrone since their last encounter outside of the house the day after he had beaten her, and that was perfectly fine with her.

"Heeeeyyy," she sang as the girls walked through the door. "This is my song, come dance with me." She danced as she stirred the meat around in the pans.

"What's all this?" Alex asked, pleasantly surprised.

Malajia turned the burners off. "Well, I decided to make dinner for you guys tonight because A, I'm in a good mood. B, we got through our first day of midterms and C, because I love you heffas," she chortled.

Sidra walked over and lifted the lids off the pans. "Ooh, you're making tacos?" she asked, noticing the diced vegetables, packages of hard and soft taco shells and condiments.

"Sure am," Malajia smiled. "And I have cake... I didn't make *that* though, I bought it." She pointed to the sheet cake on the counter.

Sidra gave Malajia a playful nudge. "You're so sweet sometimes," she mused.

"Yeah, I know," Malajia agreed, turning the music down with a remote. "The guys are on their way over here to eat too."

Alex chuckled. "You're *voluntarily* feeding Mark?" she teased. "You *must* be in a good mood."

Malajia smiled and nodded. *I sure am.*

Chasity looked at the food and felt sick to her stomach; she turned to walk in her room and was stopped by Malajia.

"Where are you going?" Malajia asked. "We're about to eat dinner."

"I'm not hungry," Chasity replied, tone dry.

Malajia frowned. "Oh bitch you better *get* hungry," she snapped. "I went to that crowded ass grocery store on the shuttle *right* after my last class and spent all this time in here cooking and dicing shit...you better *eat*."

Chasity folded her arms and sighed. She felt bad because Malajia did seem to have gone through a lot of trouble. But her stomach couldn't take the greasy food. "I think I'm getting a stomach virus or something…I don't want to eat anything heavy," she explained. "I think I just want some cantaloupe."

Malajia held a blank stare. "Cantaloupe? You want *cantaloupe*? Of *all* things?" she ground out.

Chasity shrugged. "Do we have any?"

"No, we don't have no goddamn cantaloupe," Malajia fussed, stomping her foot on the floor. "Who the hell buys a cantaloupe for no damn reason? You don't even *like* the shit."

"Well I *want* some," Chasity threw back. "Is that okay with *you*? What, do you control what I eat now?"

"I could punch you in the throat right now," Malajia hissed, causing Chasity to snicker. "You're not getting no damn cantaloupe, so you better eat these tacos and this damn cake and shut up," she demanded, handing Chasity a plate.

"Malajia, I don't—"

"Eat it and throw up later," Malajia interrupted, walking away.

Chasity looked down at the food and turned her nose up. She figured that the cake wasn't that heavy and took a piece of it.

Mark busted through the door dancing, followed by the other guys. "Where's the food at?" he bellowed.

"Here on the table," Emily answered, sitting the last of the bowls on the dining room table.

"Yeeessss tacos," Mark mused, grabbing a large spoon. "Mel, any drinks?"

Malajia pointed to the kitchen. "There's coolers and some beers in the back of the fridge," she informed. "No hard liquor."

"That's fine with *me*," Josh slid in, grabbing a couple of beers from the fridge and tossing them to the guys.

Mark looked at Malajia as she sat down on a chair in the

living room. "Sooooo…you really ain't got no hard liquor?"

She squinted at him. "Boy you better drink what's in there and get out my damn face," she fussed.

Mark laughed. "I'm messing with you."

Jason walked over to Chasity, who was standing in the kitchen, still eating her piece of cake. "You feeling any better from yesterday?" he asked, moving some of her hair out of her face. He was with her most of the previous night while she felt the effects of whatever was bothering her stomach.

Chasity shook her head as she put the rest of her cake back on her plate. "No not really, and I don't want this food either."

"What do you think is wrong?" he asked, concerned.

"Somebody probably breathed on me and gave me their stomach flu," she scoffed. "That's why I don't like people in my face."

He felt her forehead with the back of his hand. "*Whatever* it is, you need to take care of yourself…eating cake isn't going to cut it," he chided, noticing that she hadn't touched her other food.

"I don't even want *that*…I want some damn cantaloupe," she pouted.

Jason frowned in confusion. "You don't even like—"

"I know I don't *like* it Jason, but I want some *anyway* alright?" Chasity snapped.

Jason put his hands up in surrender. "Okay, I will see what I can do about getting you some tomorrow."

She rolled her eyes and sighed. "Fine," she huffed. She handed him her plate. "You can have mine."

"Naw bitch, why does Jason have your plate?" Malajia charged as Jason and Chasity emerged from the kitchen.

Jason shook his head. "Chill out Mel, she doesn't feel good," he defended, sitting on the arm of the couch.

"I don't give a hot damn *how* she feels," Malajia argued. "She better eat a damn taco shell with lettuce in it if she don't want the meat. I'm not playing with her."

Chasity tried to suppress a laugh at Malajia's over the

top reaction. "Fine," she sighed. "I'll eat the vegetables," she stipulated.

"And a taco shell," Malajia insisted.

Chasity smiled a phony smile. "I can shove that taco shell up your *ass*, how's that?" she threatened.

Malajia flagged her with her hand. "Very well. Vegetables it is," she relented. "Ooh! Turn that song up," she exclaimed, hearing one of her favorite Baltimore club tracks come through the stereo.

Mark turned the sound up as he took a bite of his taco. Malajia jumped up and started dancing, urging her friends to do the same.

# Chapter 19

Sidra laid her head down on her desk. "I think I'm about to have a nervous breakdown," she complained into the phone.

James laughed. "Calm down honey, it's only midterms," he declared. "It's not like its finals yet."

"It's not funny," Sidra spat, sitting up right. "These classes are *killing* me this semester." She let down her ponytail and ran her hands through her hair. "Can't you come down here and lend me your brain so I can pass?"

"I'd love to, but I'm working on a big case right now," he said, apologetic. "But I *will* have some time off for Thanksgiving and I will be able to spend it with you…if that's what you want."

Sidra smiled at the thought of spending her first Thanksgiving with James as a couple. "Yes, that'll be nice," she gushed, then her smile faded. "But that's not helping me *now*; I'm about to throw something."

"Wow, you weren't kidding when you told me that your stress level goes through the roof during testing," James said.

"Nope, I *wasn't*," she scoffed. "And now you're stuck with me…crazy, stressed out *me*."

"And I am perfectly fine with that," James laughed. "But listen, I have to go into this meeting, so I'll call you later."

Sidra sighed. "Okay."

"Good luck…and breathe."

She rolled her eyes. "Yeah, right," she grumbled before hanging up the phone. Slamming her book closed, she rose from her seat, headed across the hall, and knocked on the door.

"It's open," Emily called.

Sidra opened the door to find Emily angrily tossing a balled-up piece of paper on the floor. "You making paper snowballs?" Sidra teased, seeing multiple paper balls littering the floor.

Emily looked up as she sighed. "No. I'm trying to concentrate on this paper for my Literature midterm," she informed. "I've been trying to write this since last weekend and nothing is coming out."

Sidra shot her a sympathetic look. "Sorry to hear that," she said. "What is it about? Do you want to bounce some ideas off of me?"

"I don't think that's going to help me, but thanks," Emily sulked, scratching her head. "I'm just irritated because I should've finished this a *week* ago."

"Emily, you can't beat yourself up," Sidra placated. "I *myself* have waited to the last minute to do a few papers. It happens."

"Sid, *you're* not on academic probation," Emily pointed out. "I can't afford to wait to the last minute to do *anything*… This thing is due tomorrow and its thirty percent of my grade."

Sidra winced. "Sheesh," she said. "Well maybe you need to step away from it for a minute. I need to do the same thing with this business class. You want to go for a walk or something?"

"What I *need* is a drink," Emily mumbled.

"Emily," Sidra warned.

"Don't worry, I'm not going to have one," she assured. "It's just the stress talking."

Sidra nodded. "I hear you...Well since we'll both be up all night, let's go get some coffee...and chocolate," she suggested.

Emily smiled slightly. She could use something to pick her mood up. "Okay," she agreed, rising from her seat. "Can we get hot chocolate instead of coffee?"

"Sure," Sidra chuckled as Emily grabbed her jacket.


Chasity let out a loud sigh as she stared at the problem on her paper. She knew she had to solve it, but she couldn't concentrate. She couldn't concentrate on much of anything lately.

"Chasity," Jason called sternly.

She shot him a cold stare. "What is it?" she hissed.

"You've been staring at the problem for the past fifteen minutes," he stated, pointing to her book. "Now I know you hate this, but you need to do it."

She slammed her notebook closed. She was grateful that Jason made time for her to come over to his room after his practice to help her work on her math problems, but she just wasn't in the mood for studying.

"I don't give a fuck about this stuff," she snapped, tossing the book to the floor. "I *hate* this shit."

Jason frowned at her outburst. "*Hating* it isn't going to change the fact that you have your midterm tomorrow," he scolded, picking her book up from the floor and handing it to her. "So get over it and work on your problems."

Chasity slapped the book out of his hand. "Fuck that midterm and fuck *you* for making me do these," she fumed.

Jason raised his eyebrow at her. "Um... Everything good with you Chasity?" he asked, voice not hiding his frustration. He was annoyed at her behavior.

"Obviously *not*," she sniped.

"*Clearly*," he shot back. "You've been snapping at me

all day. In fact not just *today*, for the past few weeks."

She rolled her eyes. He was right; she'd been taking all her frustrations out on him for no reason. She didn't know why, but her mood had been out of whack. Even more than usual.

"Now, normally when you get all extra evil, it's because it's that time of the month," he said.

Chasity rolled her eyes. "That's nice Jason. Go ahead and blame everything on my damn period," she sneered. "You're such a damn man."

"Well I *would*," Jason replied smartly. "But you haven't had your period in over a month, so I have no idea *what* it is."

She looked at him, frowning slightly. "What did you say?"

"That you haven't had your period in over a month." He looked down at his book. "Who knows, but it's been awhile. I wouldn't complain, but I'd take *that* over your damn attitude."

Chasity frowned as she tried to wrap her mind around what Jason just said. *My period is that late? When the fuck did I stop tracking the shit?* "I'm sorry okay," she said calmly. "I'm just stressed over these tests and you know I haven't been feeling that well."

"I *know* that, and that's why I have been trying to just deal with it," he said. "But you're getting ridiculous."

She looked down at the floor as she stood up from the bed. "I know Jase," she agreed. "I have to go."

He looked at her. "You really need to study babe," he urged.

"I know and I will," she assured. "I'll be back later."

Jason shook his head as she walked out of the door. "She's lucky I love her," he said to himself, then looked back at his book.

Chasity paced back and forth in her room, cussing at

herself. "Stupid," she hissed.

She'd checked her calendar when she returned from the store and realized that Jason was right; she'd missed a period, and was coming up on her next cycle. She stopped pacing to grab the pregnancy test box from her dresser. She'd read the time frame instructions three times already—she had a minute to go—but her patience was wearing thin.

Hearing a knock on the door, Chasity quickly threw the box in the trash and sat on her bed. "Come in," she called.

"Hey girl," Malajia said, walking in and shutting the door behind her.

"What do you want?" Chasity bit out.

Malajia made a face. "Eww, your attitude sucks more than usual."

Chasity glared at her. "What do you want?" she repeated the words slowly.

"I need to borrow your flat irons," Malajia informed, running her fingers through her hair.

"What's wrong with *yours*?"

"They broke," Malajia declared. "And Sidra is in class, so I can't ask her where hers are…Well, no I'm lying. I don't like hers so I want to use *yours*."

"You need to stop buying cheap shit," Chasity scolded.

Malajia sucked her teeth. "Can I borrow the damn thing or *not*?"

Chasity flagged her with her hand. She was in no mood to go back and forth with Malajia. "Whatever, just take it and get out," she said. She put her head in her hands as Malajia walked into the bathroom. She was so preoccupied with her thoughts that she forgot for a split second that her pregnancy test was sitting on the sink. *Shit!* she jumped up. "Mel—"

She didn't get a chance to say anything else because Malajia walked out of the bathroom and slowly folded her arms. "Shit," Chasity said, seeing the smirk on Malajia's face.

"Mmm, mmm, mmm," Malajia goaded. "Miss Parker, I do believe I saw a pregnancy test in there."

"Don't worry about it," Chasity spat.

"Oh no, I think I'll worry *plenty*," Malajia shot back. "You really think you're pregnant?"

"I highly doubt it, I just want to be a hundred percent sure," Chasity declared.

"Well it *would* make perfect sense," Malajia pointed out. "You've been a bigger bitch than normal. You've been sick to your stomach for weeks and your sense of smell has been ridiculous...it's like you're a damn wolf."

"Don't say that. I'm not pregnant *okay*," Chasity fussed.

"But you're taking a *test*," Malajia pointed out, skeptical.

"Like I *said*, I just want to be sure."

"Chaz come on, don't be naïve," Malajia chided. "How late is your period?"

Chasity closed her eyes. "Almost two months," she stated hesitantly.

Malajia's mouth dropped open. "Two months?!" she exclaimed. "How the hell can you not notice you were two months late?"

"I don't know, I had a lot on my mind," Chasity argued. "I just didn't notice."

"For *two* months?" Malajia repeated, still unable to fathom what Chasity said.

"I've been late before," Chasity argued.

"Before or *after* you started having sex?" Malajia shot back.

The look on Chasity's face gave the answer that Malajia suspected.

As Chasity sat back down, Malajia walked over to her. "So, what if you're *really* pregnant? What are you gonna do? What's going through your mind?"

"I don't know Malajia. I can't wrap my head around *any* of this right now," Chasity muttered.

"Oh," Malajia said quietly as she looked at her nails. "Well sweetie, you better wrap your head around it quick, because you're pregnant," she blurted out.

Chasity looked at Malajia and felt the blood rush from

her face. She could have passed out right then and there. "Um...what?"

"According to that plus sign on that stick in there, you're pregnant," Malajia informed.

Chasity jumped up and pushed past Malajia to get into the bathroom. She picked up the stick and looked for herself. There it was clear as day, a pink plus sign. Closing her eyes, she slammed the stick in the trash. "Shit!"

Malajia clapped her hands together as she stood in the doorway. "I'm going to be an auntie," she gushed, trying to touch Chasity's stomach.

"No, stop that," Chasity snapped, smacking her hand away. "This is *not* a good thing."

Malajia frowned as Chasity walked out of the bathroom. "What do you mean?" she asked. "A baby *is* a good thing."

"Not *now* it's not," Chasity argued.

"Girl you act like you're fifteen. You'll be twenty-one in a few months," Malajia pointed out. "You're *grown*, it's not a bad thing."

"I'm still in *college*, Malajia," Chasity ranted.

"*And*? It's not the end of the world to have a baby in college," Malajia threw back. "It's been done before."

"By anybody *you* know?" Chasity asked smartly.

Malajia thought. "Well no, but still...."

"I can't take care of a baby right now," Chasity fumed. "What am I gonna do?"

"Chaz, it's not like you're hurting for money. And you know that Ms. Trisha will be happy to take care of her grandchild while you finish college."

"It's not just about money, Malajia," Chasity pointed out. "I am not mentally ready to take care of a child. And I wouldn't want my mom to raise my child either."

"It won't be just you. *Jason* will be there too."

Chasity ran her hand through her hair as she sat back on her bed. She'd forgotten all about Jason in her reaction. "Damn it," she said.

Malajia frowned at Chasity's response. "It *is Jason's*,

right?" she asked.

Chasity nearly slapped her for asking such a stupid question. "Seriously bitch?"

Malajia put her hands up. "Just making sure," she teased. "But in all seriousness, you know that he'll be there for you every step. He is going to make a great father."

"If he finds out I'm pregnant, he'll quit football and get a job. That will ruin his scholarship," Chasity said. "I can't let him do that."

"If that's what he wants to do to support you guys, then you can't stop him," Malajia implored. "I mean, he doesn't seem like the type who would live off you, so he's definitely going to want to make his own money."

"Yes, I *know* that," Chasity sniped. "He's stressed out enough with trying to maintain his GPA *and* play football... He doesn't need the added pressure."

Malajia sat down on the bed next to Chasity. She could see that her friend was feeling tortured. "You need to tell him," Malajia said softly. "This way you can talk about a plan and you won't have to deal with these thoughts and feelings on your own. Unless..."

"Unless *what*?"

"*Unless* you're planning on getting rid of it and not telling him."

Chasity's eyes widened. "I would never do that!" she exclaimed. "God, you're just accusing me of all kinds of shit today, huh?"

"I'm just asking," Malajia placated. "I don't mean to come off a smartass."

"I'm not getting an abortion okay. I'm going to have it, I just...I just need time to think about the best way to tell him."

"How about 'hey baby I'm pregnant'," Malajia suggested.

"Shut up," Chasity bit out. "I'll tell him how and *when* I'm ready...and in the meantime, don't *you* say a damn word, you hear me?"

Malajia looked at her with shock. "Come on Chaz, I wouldn't say anything," she said, offended.

"For real?" Chasity asked sarcastically. "You run your fuckin' mouth more than a little bit. So for *once, don't* open it. I can't handle everybody knowing right now."

Malajia put her hands up. "Okay, okay you have my word. I won't tell anybody," she assured. She smiled. "You two are going to have such a pretty baby," she mused, clasping her hands together.

Chasity rolled her eyes. "Get out," she sneered.

# Chapter 20

"I can't believe it's been two weeks since midterms," Malajia said to Mark as they walked outside of the English building. "How do you think you did on that English midterm last week?"

Mark shook his head. "Man, I don't know," he grunted. "Fuck that midterm."

Malajia chuckled. "You are such a slacker," she teased, pushing hair behind her ear.

"Yeah sometimes," he agreed. "Are we planning any trips for the winter break this year? I'm not really tryna stay home the whole break."

Malajia nodded in agreement. "Shit, I'm with you on that," she said. "I'll think of something."

Mark adjusted his book bag on his shoulder. "You just had *better*," he joked. "And it better be good."

She sucked her teeth at him. "Boy shut up. Why don't *you* plan something?" she challenged, backhanding him in the abdomen.

"Not gonna happen," he refused, rubbing his stomach. "*Wherever* we go, I should bring a girl."

Malajia frowned slightly. "*What* girl? You *have* no girlfriend," she jeered. "And I know you're not gonna bring one of those raggedy trash bags that you bang, around us. *Nobody* wants to catch whatever disease they gave to *you*."

"Always hating on my chicks," Mark laughed. "They're ten times better than that punk ass dude of *yours*."

Malajia looked down at the ground, wincing slightly at the mention of Tyrone. She'd hope to never hear of him again. "Yeah well, I'm not with him anymore," she admitted. "It wasn't working out, so I ended it."

Mark looked at her, intrigued. "That may have been the smartest thing that you ever did," he said. "Anyway, I'm about to go play some ball, so I'll catch you later," he said before walking away.

"Later," she waved, keeping on her way. Seeing Jason in the distance, she smiled and walked towards him. "Jase!" she called.

Hearing his name, Jason stopped and turned around. "What's up?" he asked, adjusting his gym bag on his shoulder.

"Haven't seen you in a while. You on your way to practice?" Malajia asked, stopping in front of him.

"As always," he mumbled. Between keeping up with his studies and spending long hours at football practice, nobody had seen much of Jason lately.

Malajia stared at him, looking for some form of excitement in his eyes.

Noticing her stare, Jason shot her a confused look. "Uh...did you need something?" he asked.

"No, why?"

"Because you're giving me that look that you used to give me when you had a crush on me," Jason said.

Malajia sucked her teeth. She hoped that he would forget how desperate she seemed when they first met freshman year. Before she realized that he wanted Chasity, not her. "Yeah let's not bring that up anymore okay. Not one of my proudest moments," she grumbled, causing Jason to chuckle. She looked at him as if she was urging him to say something. "Anyway… So?"

If Jason wasn't confused before, he really was *now*. *What is wrong with her?* "So *what*, Mel? Is there something that you want to say?"

*Seriously, you're going to just act like you're not happy about becoming a dad?* she thought. "Are congratulations in order?" Malajia asked, smiling brightly.

"What are you *talking* about?" Jason asked, not masking his annoyance.

"Come on Jase, don't tell me that you and Chaz haven't talked," she chortled, tapping him on the arm.

Jason scratched his head. "I talk to her every day," he declared. "I *still* don't know what you're congratulating me for."

Malajia's smile faded as she came to a realization. *Shit! He doesn't know.* She let out a nervous laugh. "Um...I was uh...I was saying congrats on you winning the game last week," she sputtered.

"Oh...Well thanks," he responded. "Speaking of games, I have to get to practice. You know I have a game Saturday. You coming?"

"Wouldn't miss it," Malajia smiled. She then waved to Jason as he headed off to his destination. She stomped her foot on the ground. "Damn it Chasity," she said to herself as she hurried off back to the clusters.


Malajia walked into the house and headed straight for Chasity's room. Twisting the door knob, she pushed the door open.

Startled, Chasity spun around. "What the hell?" she fumed. "You know not to walk in my damn room without knocking."

Malajia tossed her book bag on the floor. "Sorry," she said with feigned remorse. She folded her arms. "So, I've been meaning to ask you...how did Jason react when you told him that you were pregnant?"

Chasity frowned slightly. "He took it fine," she

answered evenly.

"Oh? *That's* funny because I ran into him just now and he doesn't seem to know a goddamn thing," Malajia snapped.

Chasity's eyes widened as she leaned against her desk. "What the fuck did you say to him?"

"I just said 'are congrats in order?'—"

"Why would you say *anything*?" Chasity fumed.

"Hey, don't turn this around on me, okay," Malajia shot back, pointing to herself. "I thought that he'd know by now."

"Yeah well, I didn't get around to telling him," Chasity admitted, opening a pack of cookies.

Malajia shot her a glare. "Seriously?!" she exclaimed. "You've known that you're knocked up for *two* whole weeks and you still haven't told him? What the hell are you waiting for? To start showing?"

Chasity rolled her eyes. "No, I'm not," she ground out. "I'm going to tell him."

"Well, you better tell him *soon* because you're starting to show in your face," Malajia stated.

Chasity's eyes became slits. "You saying that my face is fat, you bitch?"

Malajia giggled. "I'm kidding. Your face isn't getting bigger," she amended. "But it *will* if you don't stop eating all these damn cookies," she said, snatching the pack from Chasity.

"I just want cookies," Chasity whined. "This damn baby is making me crazy."

"Yeah well that's *probably* because he or she knows that you haven't told their daddy yet," Malajia ground out, Chasity sucked her teeth "Stop stalling and do it."

Chasity sighed. "I am."

"When?"

"After his game on Saturday," Chasity stated. "He's really stressing out about it and I just want to wait until it's over before I drop this news on him."

Malajia stared at her for a few seconds. "Are you sure?"

"Yeah."

"Okay Chaz, I'll take your word," Malajia responded, putting her hands up. "But I *will* say this… Even though my loyalty is to you, it's also to my Godchild in there," she said, pointing to Chasity's stomach. "And what's best for him or her, is their father knowing. So, if you don't tell him Saturday, then I'm gonna write him a note."

Chasity stared at Malajia as if she was crazy. "You're going to write him a note?" she asked slowly.

Malajia nodded. "Yep, from the stork," she added much to Chasity's annoyance. "It's gonna say 'hey Jason, I left a gift for you in Chasity's uterus' and I'm gonna sign it with stork's feet."

Chasity shook her head as she tried to process the nonsense that Malajia was spewing. "You are one of the simplest people I have ever met."

"That may be true, but I can draw good bird feet, so don't test me," Malajia threw back.

"Whatever dumbass," Chasity sneered, flagging her with her hand. "And what makes you think that you're going to be my baby's God mother?"

Malajia shot her a knowing look. "Bitch please. You already know," she declared. Chasity just rolled her eyes and walked out of the room.


"So, what time is James coming to take you out tomorrow?" Emily asked, placing several perishable items in the refrigerator.

"Probably around three," Sidra replied, throwing a paper bag in the trash. The two girls had just returned from grocery shopping. "I'm so glad that he was able to get a day off sooner than he originally thought," she smiled. "It's funny Em…I missed him before we actually became a couple and now that we *are*, I miss him even *more*."

Emily returned Sidra's smile with one of her own. "I'm glad that you found someone. You two make a great couple," she gushed.

"Thanks sweetie," Sidra beamed, leaning up against the counter. "So, when are *you* going to start dating?"

Emily's eyes widened, then she waved her hand, "Oh please, no one is interested in dating me."

"How do you know? I'm sure there are plenty of guys who would *love* to go out with you," Sidra assured.

Emily shook her head as she opened a can of soda. "No, that's the farthest thing from my mind right now. I need to focus on my grades."

Sidra nodded in agreement. "I guess you have a point," she said. "How did you end up doing on your midterm paper?"

"I got a C. Not bad but not *good either*," Emily admitted, rubbing her arm. "I don't know. I started off so well when I first came back, but now I feel like my mind is beginning to get too preoccupied with other stuff."

"You can't let that happen. The last thing you want is to be academically dismissed," Sidra pointed out.

Emily sighed. "I know… This may sound stupid, but I think I need to talk to my mom," she said.

"Why would that sound stupid?" Sidra frowned.

"Maybe because I finally got her to leave me alone and now…"

"You just miss her, that's all," Sidra sympathized. "It's not stupid that you want to resolve things with her. She may have been all kinds of controlling crazy, but at the end of the day she is still your mother. So call her."

"She won't pick up," Emily solemnly replied. "I think she hates me."

"Sweetie, I promise you she doesn't hate you," Sidra said. "She's *mad*, that's all."

Emily looked at the floor as she pushed some of her hair behind her ear.

"At least you're trying," Sidra added.

"Yeah, I know," Emily replied as she went back to

putting away groceries.

"Chaz, I'm fine," Jason assured, slowly sitting on his bed.

"No, you're *not* fine!" Chasity yelled, pacing back and forth. "You almost passed out on the way back here."

Jason chuckled. "I just got light headed. It's not a big deal," he replied calmly, rubbing his head. Jason had been in practice since after his last class. He'd pushed himself to the limit, and as he walked back to his room with Chasity, he began to feel dizzy and had to sit down on the grass until the feeling subsided.

Chasity was furious at his nonchalance. She stopped pacing and glared at him for several seconds. "It's not fuckin' funny *dawg*," she snapped, causing him to shake his head. "You're pushing yourself too damn much."

Jason rubbed his face. "Baby, I promise you that I'm fine. If I just sleep for the rest of the day, I'll be good for tomorrow's game."

"No fuck that game tomorrow. You're not playing," she demanded.

"Chasity, I *have* to."

"No, you *don't*. Don't play," she persisted.

"I can't just *not* play," Jason argued. "My scholarship depends on me playing for this school," he barked. "I can't afford to lose it. With my dad's medical bills, my family doesn't have much money left over to pay my tuition. I don't have a choice Chaz and you *know* that."

"*I'll* just pay for your tuition," Chasity offered.

Jason frowned. "You know damn well I'm not going to let you pay for *anything* for me," he fumed. "I'm not living off my woman. I'm not that dude."

She ran her hands through her hair. She already knew how Jason would respond to her offer even before it came out of her mouth. *Damn his stupid man pride.* "Okay, I'm sorry. I shouldn't have offered that," she admitted.

"But…You're tired and I'm scared that something is going to happen to you… I won't be able to handle it if something bad happens. I need you to be here," she stammered.

Jason knew that Chasity was worried, and for that reason he was trying his best to reassure her. He stood up and walked towards her. "I'm not going anywhere," he replied softly as he touched her face. He frowned in concern as he noticed tears in her eyes. "You don't have to cry, I'm fine."

Chasity looked at him with confusion as she wiped her eyes with her hand. She didn't even realize there were tears forming. "What the fuck?" she spat, looking at the wetness on her fingers. *Damn kid got me crying and shit.*

"Are you okay?" Jason asked, confused.

"Um…yeah. I'm fine. I'm just worried about you that's all," she answered carefully.

Jason studied her for a moment. *She's acting really weird.* "Chasity are you pregnant?" he asked bluntly.

The question caught her off guard. "Say what?" she asked.

"Are you pregnant?" he repeated, this time slowly.

"What would make you ask me that?" she responded defensively.

"Well, for *one* your emotions are all over the place. You hardly ever cry…like ever. So to see you do that, unprovoked, is a little weird," he pointed out.

Chasity hoped that the look on her face didn't reveal how freaked out she was on the inside.

"You haven't been feeling all that great and then there is that issue of your period still not showing up…So? What is it? Am I about to be a dad?"

Chasity was struggling internally. She knew that she needed to tell him the truth, but she just didn't want to put more on him than what he was already dealing with. Seeing him almost pass out scared her; she wanted his mind to be clear for his game. "No," she answered after several seconds of silence. "I'm not pregnant," she lied.

"Are you sure?"

"Uh huh," she replied. "I'm just stressed out, that's all. It's no big deal."

"Okay then. I just figured I'd ask," Jason said, walking back to his bed. He had to admit that he was a little disappointed that she wasn't having his baby. Sure, it wouldn't be the ideal time for them, but he would have been happy nonetheless.

"I'm going to go and let you rest," Chasity said, heading to the door. "And you *better* rest."

"I will," he promised, laying down.

She smiled at him slightly, then shut the door behind her. She closed her eyes as she leaned the back of her head against the door. *Damn it*, she thought. She hated to lie to him, but it was the best thing for him she figured. *I'll tell you tomorrow.*

# Chapter 21

"We about to win this game bee," Mark beamed, taking a big bite out of his hotdog.

Malajia looked at him with disgust. "Why you eatin' those dirty ass hot dogs?" she scoffed. "You the *only* one eating them."

"Shut up," he shot back, grabbing his large cup of soda off the bleacher floor.

Malajia shook her head at Mark, before turning her attention to Chasity, who was sitting next to her with her head in her hands. "You okay?" she asked.

"Sure, why not," Chasity snarled, lifting her head up.

Malajia looked around to make sure no one was paying attention before leaning in closer to Chasity's ear. "Is it the b-a-b-y?" she whispered.

Chasity scowled at Malajia. "Yeah 'cause none of these college students know how to spell *baby*," she spat out.

Malajia giggled. "I'm just trying to be discrete," she joked. "No but seriously, *is* it?"

Chasity shook her head. "No. I'm just concerned about Jason," she admitted. "I can't wait for this damn game to be over."

"Me too," Malajia said. "Then I can finally say congrats to him and can celebrate my Godchild with everybody else. Because he'll finally know." She shot Chasity a stern look. "He *will* know after this game, right?"

Chasity let out a loud sigh. "Yes nosey, I'm going to tell him today."

"Well you just had better," Malajia replied, moving hair over her shoulder. "'Cause I have my stork letter all ready to go."

Chasity rolled her eyes and shook her head at Malajia.

"Aye Mel, you want the rest of this?" Mark asked, holding his half-eaten hotdog in Malajia's face. "This shit nasty."

"Boy, get that out my face," Malajia snapped, knocking it out of his hand. He laughed. "Play too damn much."

"I just saw Jason's dad," Alex informed as she and Emily sat in the row behind Chasity, Mark and Malajia. "I swear, those two have the best father-son relationship."

"Yeah, I know," Chasity responded in a low voice as she opened a pack of cookies.

"Stop eating so many damn cookies," Malajia whispered, snatching the pack away. "You're about to be a fat ass."

"Bitch if you don't give me my damn cookies back I promise you I will break your fuckin' fingers!" Chasity snapped.

Malajia was startled by Chasity's outburst. And was even more startled to see her eyes glistening. "Are you crying?!" she exclaimed.

Chasity wiped her eye and looked at her hand. "Damn it," she fussed. "Just give them here," she fumed, snatching the pack back from Malajia.

Malajia couldn't help but laugh. "You cryin' over cookies," she teased. "Poor hormonal baby."

Alex just shook her head at the byplay. "You two's constant arguing never ceases to amaze me," she declared, shoving popcorn into her mouth.

"That other team is tackling all hype for no damn
reason," Malajia seethed, pointing to the field.

"It's football. They're *supposed* to tackle," Mark pointed
out. "It's part of the game."

An hour into the game and the team was tied. Many of
the Paradise Valley students felt that the opposing team was
tackling harder than normal. Malajia was one of them.

"No fuck that shit. They're doing it too hard," Malajia
argued.

Mark threw his head back and groaned. "Yo, you need
to chill. You're getting everyone all worked up and shit," he
barked. "This is how the game is played. You've seen *plenty*
of them."

Malajia flagged Mark with her hand as she turned to
Chasity, who was sitting there quietly. "Do you see what I
see?" she asked her.

"Please stop talking to me," Chasity spat out.

Malajia frowned. "What's the damn attitude for?"

Chasity's head snapped towards her. "I don't want to
hear you run your mouth about how hard they're tackling. I
*know* that. I *see* that," she fumed. "I'm already nervous and
you're not helping."

"I get you're stressed out but snapping at me isn't going
to—" Malajia's rant was interrupted by a loud collective gasp
from the crowd.

"What the fuck!" Mark hollered, hopping out of his seat.

Chasity frowned as she and Malajia stood up, along
with the entire field. "What happened?" Chasity asked.

"Oh shit," Mark said as he ran his hands over his head.

"Oh shit? What do you mean 'oh shit'?" Malajia
panicked. "What's going on?"

"Two players from the other team tackled Jason and he
went falling pretty hard," Mark informed.

Chasity craned her neck to see. Her eyes widened when

she noticed Jason laying on the ground, surrounded by his teammates and coaches. "He's not moving," she observed quietly. "Why isn't he moving?"

"He took a pretty hard hit," Alex informed, putting her hand on Chasity's shoulder.

Chasity felt like she couldn't breathe as she watched the medical team rush to the field to tend to Jason. She watched as the team put Jason's unconscious body on a stretcher. She knew she had to get to him. Malajia grabbed her arm as she went to leave.

"No Chaz, you'll never get through that crowd," Malajia stated.

Chasity snatched away from her. "Get off me," she snapped, before she took off.

"Chaz, you have to be careful!" Malajia hollered after her. "Shit," she said when Chasity ignored her.

"Mel, go with her," Alex commanded. "I'll let the others know what happened and we'll see you at the hospital."

"Mark, come with us. She isn't in the right state of mind to drive her car," Malajia ordered, grabbing Mark's arm and pulling him along.

"You got it," Mark said, heading off with Malajia.

Alex ran her hands through her hair as Emily, tears in her eyes, held her hands over her mouth in horror. "Don't worry, he'll be okay," Alex reassured her. "Let's go call Sidra and the other guys."

Emily sniffled as she followed Alex out of the aisle.

Mark, Chasity, and Malajia hurried into the hospital emergency room. By the time they pushed their way through the concerned crowd to get to Chasity's car and made it to the hospital, Jason's ambulance had already arrived.

"Yo, I promise, we finding out who number five and fuckin' eight was who tackled Jase and we ridin' on those bastards," Mark fumed, pounding his fist into his hand. "I'm knocking both of them the fuck out."

Malajia rolled her eyes. "Boy, you ain't doing shit," she scoffed.

"You don't know *what* I'm gonna do," Mark shot back. "Always talking that bullshit."

Chasity's hands began to shake as she put them on her head. Mark and Malajia's pointless arguing wasn't helping the situation. "Just shut the fuck up!" she erupted.

"Okay, okay, calm down," Malajia responded softly. "Mark, can you please go see if you can find out anything? Jason's dad is probably already here."

"I'm on it," Mark said, taking off for the front desk.

Malajia directed Chasity to a spot near a wall away from the crowd. "You *really* need to calm down," she urged.

Chasity's eyes filled with tears. She had never been so worried in her life. "I don't know what's going on," she cried.

"Mark is going to find that out now," Malajia placated. "Jase is going to be okay. You have to believe that."

At that point, Chasity wasn't paying any attention to the comforting words that were coming out of Malajia's mouth. All she could see was Jason's lifeless body laying on the ground. "He wasn't moving... I don't know what to do... I can't do anything for him... I need to get to him."

Malajia's face didn't hide the concern that she was feeling. Chasity was crying and rambling. She was trying her best to get Chasity to calm down, but Malajia had to admit that she would be reacting the same way if the shoe was on the other foot. "Listen sweetie, you need to sit down," Malajia said, grabbing Chasity's arm. "I promise you, we *will* find out what's going on."

Chasity jerked away from Malajia. "I don't need to sit any-damn-where!" she yelled. "I need to find out what the fuck is going on—" She paused as she felt a sharp pain.

Noticing the pained look on Chasity's face and the way that she grabbed her stomach, Malajia's eyes widened. "What's wrong? What happened?"

Chasity couldn't speak because her cramping was

getting worse. She cried out in pain as Malajia tried to steady her.

"Chaz, say something. What's wrong?" Malajia panicked as Chasity fell out on the floor, clutching her stomach. "Shit! Somebody help!" Malajia called out as she held on to Chasity's hand while she cried hysterically.


Mark and Malajia paced up and down the emergency waiting room for over two hours. Malajia hadn't heard anything since she watched doctors put Chasity on a stretcher and wheel her into a room. Mark tried his best to get information on Jason's condition, but the only thing that he could get was that his friend was still unconscious.

"This is bullshit that they won't tell us anything," Mark fumed, flopping down on one of the empty seats. "Talking that 'you're not biological family' mess…We *are* family, fuckin' bastards."

Malajia took a seat next to Mark. She sighed and put her hand on his shoulder. "I know."

"Where's Chaz?" Mark asked, looking around. "I haven't seen her since you sent me to get information."

Malajia's eyes shifted. She didn't want to alarm him. "Um…I think she went to try to find Jason's father," she lied.

It was a lie that Mark seemed to have bought because he just said, "Oh." He leaned his back against the seat and pulled out his cell phone. "Let me call Alex and give her an update. I told her that it was no point in them coming down here since we don't know anything yet."

Malajia just nodded as she felt her cell phone vibrate. Her eyes widened when she saw that it was a text message from Chasity. Malajia stood up and hurried off as Mark talked on the phone.

She walked down the hall and looked for a certain room number. She knocked on the door, before slowly opening it to find Chasity laying on the bed. "Hey sweetie," Malajia said, walking over to her side. "You alright?"

Chasity didn't answer; she just slowly sat up and leaned her back against the pillows.

Malajia frowned. "Um…what happened? …Is the baby okay?"

Chasity's eyes filled with tears as she shook her head no.

Realizing what happened, Malajia closed her eyes. "Oh my God," she said.

"I miscarried," Chasity said, wiping her eyes.

Malajia put her hand on her chest, her heart was broken. "I'm so sorry, sis," she said softly. "You know that this isn't your fault, right?"

"That's what they say," Chasity sniffled.

"And they're *right*," Malajia assured. "These things happen. It…It just does. You have to know that."

"Okay," Chasity said as she looked at her shaking hands. "What's going on with Jason?"

Malajia didn't know what to say to her. They had no information. "Um…he's fine."

"Malajia, don't lie to me," Chasity hissed.

"Okay. I'm sorry," Malajia amended. "Truth is, we don't know much of anything. Other than the fact that he's still unconscious."

Chasity wiped her eyes again, then tried to get out of the bed. "I'm going to tear this fuckin' hospital apart if they don't tell me something."

Malajia put her hands on Chasity's shoulders to push her back down. "No, you don't need to go anywhere," she urged. "We'll find out something and I'll come in here and tell you."

"I'm not staying in this damn hospital bed," Chasity refused.

"You don't have a damn *choice*," Malajia argued. "Don't you need surgery or something?"

"No. I don't," Chasity sneered. "I wasn't far enough along."

Malajia sighed. "I'm sorry. I didn't mean to…I just think… I don't know what to say or do right now."

"You want to know what you can do?" Chasity asked, exasperated. Malajia nodded. "Go to my car and get my overnight bag out of my trunk. I have a change of clothes in there. My damn jeans I wore in here have blood all on them."

"Okay," Malajia nodded. She slowly walked out of the room.

Once the door closed, Chasity put her hands over her face as she tried to maintain her composure. It was so much going on at once and she didn't know how to deal with it all. Malajia returned several minutes later with Chasity's bag. Malajia sat in the room, while Chasity got herself together in the bathroom.

Malajia didn't leave Chasity's side as they went walking through the halls, trying to get back to the front desk at the emergency room.

"Shit," Chasity complained, stopping and grabbing her stomach.

"See, you're still cramping. You need to go back and lay down," Malajia advised. "I'll go find Jason's father."

"Shut up," Chasity spat. She felt relieved as she saw Jason's father sitting on a chair outside of one of the hospital rooms. Both girls hurried over to him. He stood up when he saw them approach.

Mr. Adams smiled slightly. "I was wondering when I would see you, Chasity." He gave her a hug.

"I'm sorry, I was um…is Jason okay?" Chasity asked, pushing some hair behind her ears.

Mr. Adams ran his hand over his head as he sighed. "The blow that he took knocked him unconscious. They ran scans on him, and luckily there is no permanent damage as far as they can see."

"Thank God," Malajia breathed, putting her hand on her chest.

"Jason has a concussion," he informed. "They're keeping him for another day or so just for observation. It was his *head* after all. But they're pretty sure that he will be just fine."

"Okay… Did he wake up at all?" Chasity asked.

"Briefly," Mr. Adams answered. "He asked for you."

Chasity looked at the floor. She was so angry that she wasn't there when he woke up. "Can I go in?"

"Sure," Mr. Adams smiled.

Without another word, Chasity opened the door and walked in. Malajia peeked through the door as she watched Chasity walk over to Jason's bed and climb in to lay next to him. Malajia figured that she was okay to go back to the waiting room as Chasity was now where she wanted to be.

Mark stood up when he saw Malajia approach. He held a hopeful look on his face as he waited for her to give him some news…any news.

She walked up and stood within several inches of him. "He'll be fine," she said.

Mark let out a sigh of relief, smiling slightly. Malajia, feeling completely overwhelmed with the day's events, put her hands over her face and leaned into Mark's chest as she began to cry silently. She couldn't believe what had happened all in one day. One of her friends got hurt and the other lost their baby. All she felt was sadness. Mark, not saying a word, just wrapped his arms around her.

# Chapter 22

"I'm really glad that you're feeling better, Jase," Sidra said, stirring some food around in a pot. "I'm so pissed that you got hurt," she fumed, slamming the lid back on the pot.

Sitting on the couch in his house, Jason ran his hand over the back of his neck. "Thanks Sid. I'm fine though."

Sidra was furious. She wasn't at the game when Jason had gotten hurt three days ago because she was on a date with James. But as soon as she got the phone call, she went into worried sister mode. Knowing that someone that she loved like one of her brothers was in the hospital made her stress level spike. "Stupid, rough football players," she seethed. "I bet you they tried to take you out on purpose. They knew you could beat all of them hands down."

Alex walked over to Sidra as she began slamming the spoon on the side of the counter. "Alright sweetie, give me the spoon," Alex teased, taking the spoon. She directed Sidra away from the kitchen.

"I appreciate you ladies coming over to cook and everything, but I really *am* fine," Jason assured.

"No matter how many times you say that, it's not going to make us leave," Alex said.

Jason shook his head. He was appreciative of the girls

doting on him, but he didn't really want all the attention. He had just gotten his mother to leave earlier that morning. His father had to practically drag her to the car.

"Ladies, have you seen Chaz today?" Jason asked, looking at his phone.

Alex grabbed some plates from the cabinet. "She was in her room when I left… I think," she answered. "Why, everything okay?"

"Yeah, I'm sure it is, I just haven't spoken to her all day," Jason said. Chasity spent as much time in the hospital with Jason the first night, but once his mother arrived, she left. When he got back from the hospital earlier that morning, he'd tried to call Chasity, but his calls went unanswered.

"I'm sure she'll be over later," Sidra said. "She might be still asleep."

Jason just nodded as he put his phone on the coffee table.

"Jase, you want a drink or something?" Mark asked, searching in the cabinet for a bottle.

"Thanks man, but I can't drink alcohol while I'm taking these pain meds," Jason said, rubbing his shoulder. Not only did he suffer a concussion, but his shoulder was badly bruised in the fall.

"Oh yeah. Sorry man, I forgot," Mark grimaced.

Jason chuckled. "Don't worry about it. You guys don't have to walk on egg shells. I'm good."

"We know," Josh slid in from the dining room table. "Can't blame us for worrying though."

"I don't," Jason replied.

"No, but you can blame those stupid ugly bastards for doing what they did," Sidra fumed, slamming her hands on the table. "I better not see any of them on the street."

Her friends looked at her. "Um Sid, I think you need to calm down just a bit," Josh suggested, trying to suppress a laugh.

"Don't try to pacify me, Josh!" Sidra snapped, causing

Josh to shake his head.


Walking down the steps, Malajia clutched her stomach. She lightly tapped on the door, then twisted the knob. She was surprised that it wasn't locked. "Left your door unlocked again, huh?" she asked, walking in. "You must want company."

Chasity was laying in the bed, with her arm thrown over her face. "I forgot to lock it. A decision that I am now regretting," she grunted.

Malajia rolled her eyes.

"What do you want?" Chasity hissed, moving her arm from her face.

"I have cramps," Malajia groaned, hand still covering her mid-section.

"Join the club," Chasity snarled.

"Yeah well, I'm *seriously* regretting getting off that damn birth control pill right about now," Malajia ground out. "I never had to deal with them before."

"And you did that *for?*" Chasity's tone was condescending.

"I got tired of taking them," Malajia shrugged. "Anyway, I came to get some of your aspirin, 'cause I *know* you got some more," she added. "*That*…and I came to check on you. Three days locked in here by yourself is enough."

Chasity let out a loud sigh as Malajia went into her bathroom to retrieve the bottle of aspirin.

"I can huff *too*," Malajia replied, unfazed by Chasity's attitude. She opened the bottle and popped two pills without water, nearly choking on them in the process.

Chasity just stared as Malajia began coughing. "Dumbass."

Malajia flipped her off as she patted her chest. "Damn bitch, I was really choking!" she exclaimed. Chasity held her stare, unfazed. Malajia shook her head as she dug into her jeans pocket. "You left your phone on the counter," she informed, retrieving Chasity's phone. "You got like four missed calls from Jason."

Chasity didn't say anything, she just held her hand out for her phone. She looked at it and there were indeed four missed calls from him. She knew that Jason was coming home that morning, she just couldn't face him.

Malajia let out a huff at Chasity's silence; she walked over to her bed and nudged her over. "Move."

"Get the fuck outta here," Chasity barked.

"Look girl, I'm dying right now and I don't feel like walking my ass back upstairs," Malajia snapped, leaning over the bed. "So move over so I can lay down."

Chasity reluctantly moved closer to the wall, sucking her teeth in the process.

Malajia got comfortable before gathering her thoughts. "So...why haven't you talked to Jason today?" she asked. "I know he hasn't seen you since you left the hospital."

"I stayed as long as I could. I didn't feel like dealing with his mother," Chasity bit out.

"I understand that," Malajia said. She laid there for a moment while she patiently waited for the medicine to kick in. "I'm sure he's wondering if you're okay, though," she continued. "Especially after what happened with the baby."

Chasity's eyes shifted.

Malajia, picking up on the silence turned on her side and looked at Chasity. "He *does* know, doesn't he?"

Chasity took a deep breath. "No...I didn't tell him."

"What?!" Malajia exclaimed. "Girl, are you crazy?"

Chasity didn't say anything.

Malajia could not believe what she'd just heard. "How could you not tell him?"

"Tell him for *what*?" Chasity sneered. "There's no baby anymore."

"You *tell* him because he has a right to *know*," Malajia argued.

"Drop it, Malajia."

Malajia let out a sigh. "I'm just going to say this..."

"Please don't," Chasity groaned.

"Oh, I'm gonna say it *anyway*," Malajia persisted. "You're wrong for keeping this from him. He has a right to know what happened. This way you two can mourn together. You can't go through this by yourself."

"I'm fine," Chasity insisted.

"That's straight bullshit and you *know* it," Malajia contradicted. "If you were fine like you *say*, then why have you been held up in your room all this time?"

"*God*," Chasity groaned. The sound of Malajia's voice was like nails on a chalkboard at that point.

"You need to talk to someone and that someone needs to be Jason," Malajia harped. "Tell him, Chasity. Because if you *don't* and he finds out, he's gonna be pissed at you."

"And how the hell is he going to find out?" Chasity asked, tone filled with disdain. "What? Are *you* gonna tell him?"

"No, I wouldn't do that," Malajia said. "I told you that you have my word. But I really think that—"

"Are you done?" Chasity barked, interrupting Malajia. "Either drop it like I said, or get the fuck out my room."

Malajia rolled her eyes. Chasity was so damn stubborn, she didn't know what to do with her. "Do you at *least* wanna talk to *me* about how you're feeling?"

"No," Chasity's answer was instantaneous.

Malajia sighed. "Fine," she mumbled, folding her arms.


For twenty minutes, Chasity laid in her bed, wide awake. With so much on her mind, sleep wasn't happening. Leaving snoring Malajia in her bed, she got up and walked over to Jason's house.

"Hey sis, long time no see," Mark greeted from the kitchen when Chasity entered the house.

"It's only been three days," Chasity said, folding her arms.

"Well, to me, that's a long time," Mark shrugged, putting the finishing touches on his sandwich.

Chasity shook her head. "Jason in there?" she asked, gesturing to the room door.

"Yep," Mark answered, putting the top back on a jar of mayonnaise. He followed Chasity's progress as she made a beeline for the room. "Yo, I got a test tomorrow so I have to go to bed early," he said.

Chasity turned around, shooting him a confused look. "So?"

"So, I'm not sleeping on this couch tonight. If y'all wanna get it in, go to *your* room."

"Shut up," Chasity spat, walking in the room.

Jason smiled at her from his bed. "I've been calling you," he said, reaching out for a hug.

"I know," she replied, closing the door. She walked over to him and laid down next to him. "You okay?" she asked, as she hugged him.

He nodded. "Yeah…feeling a lot better." He moved some hair out of her face. "You look sad," he observed. "Are *you* okay?"

Chasity contemplated taking Malajia's advice and just telling him the truth. But knowing what he had already been through, she didn't want to cause him any more pain. *There's no point,* she thought. "Yeah, I'm fine. Just tired," she answered, laying her head on his chest.

# Chapter 23

"How the hell did I accumulate more crap?" Sidra complained, forcing one of her suitcases closed.

Alex leaned against the wall and folded her arms. "Easy. You have a shopping problem," she teased.

Proceeding to zip the massive suitcase, Sidra rolled eyes. Packing for school breaks always stressed Sidra out. This Thanksgiving break was no different.

Malajia groaned as several of her sweaters tumbled out of the top of the closet, while trying to reach for one. "Damn it!" she yelped, kicking one across the floor.

Alex laughed, causing Malajia to shoot her a glare.

"Why are you over here anyway?" Malajia sneered. "Don't you have shit to pack in your *own* raggedy ass room?"

"I'm finished actually," Alex proudly declared.

Malajia looked at Sidra. "She threw all her cheap shit in that dirty ass duffle bag," Malajia teased, pointing at Alex.

Alex's eyes became slits as Sidra snickered. "Really Sidra?" Alex ground out.

Sidra put her hand up as she tried to stop laughing. "I'm sorry, Alex," she defended. "You know Malajia is a fool."

Alex shook her head. "Yes, unfortunately I *do*," she scoffed. "Anyway, I don't have much, so it doesn't take long for me to pack. I'm a minimalist."

"That's code for poor," Malajia mumbled, picking up her sweaters from the floor.

Alex stomped her foot on the floor. "Shut the hell up," Alex fumed. Malajia laughed, relishing the fact that she could get under Alex's skin.

Alex pointed a warning finger at Malajia as Emily walked into the room. "Do any of you have any extra trash bags?" Emily asked. "Packing has revealed that I am a hoarder of papers."

"Check under the bathroom sink," Sidra directed.

"Em, what are your plans for Thanksgiving?" Alex asked.

"Um, nothing much really," Emily answered from the bathroom. "My dad will be traveling for business this week, so I'll be in the house by myself."

Alex frowned. "Well that's no fun," she pouted as Emily walked back into the room, box of bags in hand.

"Hell yes it *is*," Malajia disagreed, tossing some clothes in her suitcase. "I would *love* to have the house to myself."

Alex rolled her eyes. "Mel, you haven't seen your family in months. Suck it up and spend time with them." She turned her attention back to Emily. "Listen Em, you're more than welcome to come home with *me* for Thanksgiving," Alex offered. "Do you think your dad will mind?"

Emily smiled. "No, I'm sure he'll be fine with it," she stated. "But you don't have to do that. I'll be okay."

Alex put a hand up as she reached for her cell phone in her jeans pocket. "No arguments. I'm calling my parents right now."

"You better hope that flip got minutes," Malajia jeered.

"You got one more damn time to make a smart comment, Malajia," Alex snapped.

"Hey, whoever's leftovers are still in the fridge, you need to throw them out," Chasity demanded, walking in the room. "That crap will go bad while we're gone."

"It's mine. I'll get it," Alex said, holding the phone to her ear.

Malajia smirked. "Hey Chaz, guess who else is riding in your car with you back to PA?"

Chasity raised her eyebrow. "Who?"

Malajia pointed to Emily, who stood there staring back at her. Chasity looked at the smile plastered on Emily's face and narrowed her eyes.

"Yep. Alex invited Emily home with her for the holiday," Malajia informed. "You gotta deal with Alex *and* Emily for *four hours...five* with that traffic. They gonna bore up your car and shit."

Chasity then frowned at Alex, who in turn smiled. Completely annoyed, Chasity stomped her foot on the floor. "Fuck my life," she huffed, storming out the room.

"Mel, you're such an asshole. You didn't give me a chance to break the news," Alex complained.

"Break the news? You should've *asked* first," Malajia shot back, she then laughed. "Chaz is gonna cuss you a new ass the whole way there."

Alex flagged Malajia with her hand. "Shut up." She nudged Emily. "Don't worry about Chaz, I'll deal with her. Let's just make sure you're finished packing because she *will* leave without us. That, I *do* know."

Sidra chuckled as Alex and Emily walked out the room. "You're always starting trouble," she said to Malajia.

"It's a gift," Malajia agreed, tossing her hair over her shoulder.


Chasity slammed another item into her suitcase. With her room door open, she saw Jason walk in the house. "Hey babe," she said.

"Hey," he smiled, approaching. "You still packing?"

"As always," she grunted. "What time are your parents coming?"

"They'll be here in a few minutes," he answered. "I told my dad that I could just catch a ride with *you* but—"

"Yeah, I don't know why you *don't*," Chasity pouted. "*You* could drive and I wouldn't have to be stuck alone in the car with freakin' Alex and Emily."

Jason laughed. "Be nice."

She rolled her eyes. "I don't want to."

He shook his head. "Anyway, my mom started complaining to my dad, saying that they should come and get me because she wanted to make sure I got home safe... Like I'm not a grown man," he complained.

Chasity folded her arms. "She's still trippin' huh?"

"Yeah. I mean I get that I scared her when I got hurt, but that was a month ago," he said. He ran his hand over his hair. "Anyway, my dad asked me if I could just take the ride with them because she was getting on his nerves about it."

"Well, I guess I'll see you after Thanksgiving then," Chasity assumed.

Jason smiled at her. "*About* that," he began, putting his arm around her waist. "I was thinking that I would spend Thanksgiving with *you* this year."

"You already know your mother is *not* gonna go for that," Chasity said.

Jason frowned. "She'll get over it," he said, tone stern. "If she doesn't want you at her house, then I'll be at *yours*. Simple as that... Unless you and your mom already have plans to do something else."

"Nothing that my mother *ever* plans on Thanksgiving works out well for me, so she's banned from planning *anything*," Chasity replied. "So yes, you're welcome to come."

"Cool. I'll see you tomorrow then." Jason gave her a hug. "I better get out of here, they're probably at my house by now."

Chasity waved to him as he walked out of the door. She smiled to herself, then was interrupted by loud noise from upstairs.

"Chaz! Alex's ugly ass duffle bag ripped and she said she was gonna throw her stuff in the trunk without a bag!" Malajia hollered down the stairs.

"What?!" Alex yelled. "My bag didn't even *rip* and you're not even in my room to see anything."

Chasity rolled her eyes. "Hey, kill the bullshit Alex, or I'll leave without you!" she hollered up the steps.

"I didn't even *do* anything!" Alex exclaimed, making Chasity snicker.

"Em, I hope you don't mind sleeping on an air mattress," Alex said, pulling a large plastic, deflated mattress into her room.

Emily held her phone to her ear as she gave the thumbs up sign. "Hey Mommy, it's Emily...*again*," she spoke. "I wanted to call you to wish you a happy Thanksgiving early, since I know you'll be busy cooking tomorrow...So um, I hope that you have a good one and I'll talk to you... whenever."

Watching Emily hang up the phone, Alex shot her a sympathetic look. "Answering machine again, huh?"

"Yep," Emily mumbled, tossing the phone on Alex's bed. "But to answer your question, no I don't mind sleeping on the mattress. And thanks again for inviting me to spend the break with you and your family. My dad was just saying that he would've felt bad if I stayed home alone."

"Of course," Alex said, with a wave of her hand. "There was no way I'd let you spend Thanksgiving alone. We may not have much here, but we always have room for family."

Emily managed a smile, but it quickly faded. Although she was happy to have freedom, she still couldn't get over the fact that her mother refused to talk to her, "I'm sorry Alex, I don't mean to keep bringing up my mother but... I hate that she's mad at me and was just hoping that the holiday would make her want to talk to me."

Alex sat on the floor. "Sweetie, if your mom can't put her own feelings aside to see that you did what was best for *you*, then...that's on *her*," she consoled. "You can't allow her to steal the happiness that you *finally* got."

Emily just sighed, then flopped down on the flat mattress. "Oww," she whined, rubbing her behind.

Alex giggled. "Hey, do you want to go to the Thanksgiving parade tomorrow?" she asked, handing Emily a towel and washcloth that was on her bed. "I think it'll be fun. Which is what you need right about now."

"I think I need a *butt donut* right about now," Emily jeered, wincing. "But yeah, I'm game."


"Hey, I have a suggestion for Thanksgiving this year," Trisha blurted out, picking up her glass of wine.

Chasity rolled her eyes. Not even home four hours, and Trisha was already starting with her forced holiday plans. "I promise you that I'm not going to do whatever you're suggesting," she refused. "You always have these stupid plans for me to spend Thanksgiving with family. And every year since I've been in college, it's been crap."

Trisha let out a quick sigh as she took a sip of her wine.

"*Freshman year*, I got into a fight with your sister. *Last* year, I got in a fight with *you*. Who's it gonna be *this* year? Melina? Oh, I know, Uncle John's ratchet girlfriend."

Trisha held a stern gaze on Chasity across the dining room table. "Are you finished?" she spat out. Excited to have her daughter home, and eager to spend time with her, Trisha had prepared a small dinner for her and Chasity.

Sitting back in her seat, Chasity let out a sigh, "Yeah."

"Now, I wasn't going to make you spend the holiday with the family," Trisha assured. "I was thinking that maybe you can invite your friends over."

Chasity frowned. "Why?"

"Unfortunately, I have to leave for a business trip early tomorrow morning and won't be back until Saturday," Trisha informed. "I don't want you to spend Thanksgiving alone. And I already know that there is *no way* that you are going to your grandmother's house."

"Nope," Chasity agreed. "I won't be alone. Jason is coming over tomorrow, so I'll be fine."

Trisha placed her hand on her chest, beaming. "That is so sweet," she gushed. "But as much as I love Jason and can't wait until he is officially my son-in-law—"

Chasity rolled her eyes.

"You two will *not* be in here alone, getting busy all up and through this house, you hear?" Trisha chided.

Chasity smirked. "Well um…Where do you think our first time happened?"

Trisha narrowed her eyes at her smart-mouthed daughter. "For real? You're just gonna say that to me? Right in my face?" she barked.

Chasity put her hands up. "Chill out, okay. I'm just joking," she laughed.

"You're full of it," Trisha hissed, pointing her fork in Chasity's direction.

"I *was*," Chasity mumbled.

"Excuse me?" Trisha challenged, eyes flashing.

"Nothing," Chasity replied innocently, playing in her food with her fork. "So um, what were you saying about your trip?"

"Mmm hmm," Trisha grumbled. "Anyway, like I was saying. I think it'll be nice for them to come over and you can all spend the day together. I'll have a caterer come out and cook for you guys and everything."

"I just left them *today*, why are you forcing them on me *again*?" Chasity whined.

"Stop acting mean," Trisha scolded.

"*Acting*?" Chasity joked. "Look, everybody spends Thanksgiving with their own families. Who's to say that they want to spend it *here*?"

Trisha grabbed her cell phone from the table. "Chasity, I have *four* voicemail messages from Malajia complaining that she is bored already with her family and wishes that she was here with *us*," she said, trying to suppress a laugh.

"Seriously?" Chasity fussed. "That idiot called you?"

"Yes, she did," Trisha chuckled. "She said that she tried calling *you*, but your phone went straight to voicemail."

"That's because I blocked her ass," Chasity sneered. "I knew she was going to start that mess as soon as she got home."

Trisha shook her head. "Well, you know I love Malajia, and she is welcome here any time. So that just goes to show that your friends wouldn't mind coming…So do you want to call them or should *I*?"

Chasity let out a loud sigh. "Damn it," she mumbled, grabbing her phone. As soon as she unblocked Malajia's phone number, a call came in. She stomped her foot on the floor as she answered. "What Malajia? …Wait *what*? … When? …Are you serious?!"

Trisha frowned as Chasity hung up her phone and slid it across the table. "What's wrong?"

Chasity rested her elbows on the table and put her head in her hands. "Malajia is on her way here," she answered with a deceptive calm. "Her damn train will be in Philly in twenty minutes."

Trisha busted out laughing. "My girl, she plays no games," she mused.

Chasity slowly stood from the table. "Well Mom, have fun driving to the train station in holiday traffic to pick up *your girl*."

Trisha's laughter subsided. "No girl, I *can't* go pick her up. I have to pack," she protested.

"I care not," Chasity threw back, walking out of the dining room.

"Chasity! I'm not playing, come back here," Trisha called after her.

"You're not the boss of me!" Chasity shouted from the other room.

Trisha rolled her eyes. "Shit," she huffed.


Sidra flopped down on her bed, relishing the softness. She had to admit, compared to her queen-sized pillow top mattress at home, those college beds felt like bricks.

"God, I wish I could take this whole mattress with me," she muttered to herself, closing her eyes. Sidra was exhausted. She'd been on the road for hours, maneuvering through holiday traffic. She was relieved when she pulled into the driveway of her house ten minutes ago.

Hearing a light tap on her bedroom door, she jerked her eyes open. "Come in," she called, sitting up.

"Princess, I'm about to make dinner, do you want anything special?" Mrs. Howard asked.

Sidra shook her head. "Whatever you make, I'll eat."

"Okay, well I'm making baked chicken, macaroni and cheese, potato salad, green beans and corn bread."

Sidra giggled. "All that?" she teased. "*And* you have to cook tomorrow?"

Mrs. Howard shook her head. "I'm actually *not* cooking tomorrow," she revealed. "Which is why I'm making a big dinner tonight... I feel cheated."

Sidra looked confused, "What do you mean? Is *Daddy* cooking this year?"

"No. Aunt Diana asked everyone to come to *her* house for Thanksgiving dinner this year."

Sidra couldn't conceal her look of disappointment. "Mama, no offense, but Aunt Diana irritates me," she declared bluntly. "Every time I see her, she messes with my hair, criticizes my outfits and she keeps asking me when I'm going to get married."

Mrs. Howard chuckled. "Yes, I know that sweetie, but she *is* your great aunt, so just tolerate her for a day, okay?" she ordered. "That is unless you have something *else* planned."

Sidra sighed. "If I do, I'll let you know," she replied

solemnly. Then she flopped back down on the bed as her mother closed the door. She groaned when she heard her phone beep. Sidra looked at it, then popped up as she read the text message. "Thank God," she breathed out loud.


"Sidra said she's down for spending Thanksgiving with us tomorrow," Malajia informed, looking at her text message. "And she's gonna spend the night too."

"Fine," Chasity replied, clicking through the channels on the television in her living room.

"Um, she wants to know if it's okay if James comes over on Friday," Malajia added, looking at her phone. "He's going to be in town."

"I really don't care," Chasity answered evenly.

Malajia shot her a glare. "The hell is *your* problem?" she sneered. She felt that Chasity's attitude was uncalled for at that moment.

Chasity turned the television down, shooting Malajia a glare in the process. "Why are you here tonight?" she bit out. "Thanksgiving is *tomorrow*."

"Oh, for real? It's like *that* now?" Malajia grunted.

"What do you mean *now*?" Chasity hissed. "You know I get irritated *every time* you come over here. I just saw your ass earlier today."

Malajia sucked her teeth. "And you're seeing me again *now,* so get the hell over it," she bit back. "I didn't come all the way over here to hear you bitch."

"Simple fuckin' solution. Go home."

Malajia flagged Chasity with her hand. "Nah, I have my own room in here and *everything*," she mocked. "This is *my* house now."

Chasity just shook her head, then started flipping through channels again.

Malajia sighed after several moments of texting on her phone. "You want to know the real reason why I'm here tonight?" she asked.

"What? You mean it's not to piss me off?" Chasity jeered.

"Well yeah there's *that*," Malajia teased. "But no. As *soon* as I stepped foot in my house my parents started in on my clothes, and my grades, and my sisters kept asking 'where's Tyrone?' 'When are we going to meet him?' 'Is he still coming to dinner?'" Malajia put her hand up. "I *had* to get the hell out of there."

Chasity glared at Malajia. "You were going to take that bastard to your *house*?" she snarled.

"I was *thinking* about it," Malajia admitted. "But that was *way* before...well you know."

"Before he beat you up?"

Malajia let out a loud sigh. "Thanks for the reminder Chasity," she scoffed. "But yes, before he beat my ass... I just couldn't deal with all of their prying. Hell, I didn't even think they remembered that I was *seeing* him... They seem to never pay attention to anything I do unless it's bad."

"Yeah well, you probably ran your mouth about his stupid ass so damn much—"

"That they figured I'd bring him around, yeah, yeah, I *get* it," Malajia ground out, rolling her eyes.

"Uh huh," Chasity muttered, "He still needs his ass beat."

"So you've said, over and over again," Malajia huffed, taking the remote from Chasity. "Anyway, you got any more of that—" her eyes widened, then she quickly turned the television off.

Chasity looked at her with confusion. "What the hell did you do that for?"

"No reason," Malajia lied, looking away.

Chasity folded her arms, staring at her. "You think I didn't see that diaper commercial just now?"

Malajia ran her hand over her hair. "What are you talking about? I didn't see any such commercial."

Chasity smirked. "You are *so* not the subtle type," she pointed out. "I'm not going to fall apart over a commercial that has to do with—"

"No don't even say it," Malajia interrupted, putting her finger up.

"Don't say what? *Baby*?" Chasity frowned.

"Shhhhh!" Malajia exclaimed, waving her hands wildly in the air.

Chasity put her hand up. "There is nobody else the fuck *here*, why are you shushing me?"

"I'm just looking out for you," Malajia comforted. "Did you or did you *not* bust out crying while we were in the store looking at baby items for Sidra's cousin?"

"That was like a week after it happened, what did you expect?" Chasity threw back.

"I didn't expect to have to lie and tell the other girls that you were crying happy tears because you passed your midterms," Malajia shot back.

"Yeah, that was a weird lie," Chasity admitted. "Look, it's been a month now. I'm fine."

Malajia eyed her skeptically. "Are you sure?"

"Yes," Chasity answered slowly. "I mean, I still think about it, but I don't cry anymore."

Malajia sighed. "Still not gonna tell Jason, huh?"

"Still not gonna tell anybody about what Tyrone did, huh?" Chasity shot back.

"Touché." Malajia muttered, turning the television back on. "I still think you're wrong though."

"The feeling is mutual," Chasity threw back. Malajia rolled her eyes.

# Chapter 24

"You know Jason, I still say that you should be spending Thanksgiving with your family." Mrs. Adams fumed, chopped vegetables on her cutting board early the next morning.

Jason rolled his eyes behind his mother's back. *Here she goes.* "Mom, you know that I had my heart set on spending Thanksgiving with Chasity. It's not *my* fault that you won't welcome her *here*," Jason hissed. "So, since you can't respect me enough to put aside your ridiculous issue you have with her and let her come over here, then *I'm* going to *her*. Simple as that."

Mrs. Adams stopped chopping vegetables and spun around to face her son. "Oh, it's like *that*? You're really going to forget about your family and spend the day with some girl?"

Jason narrowed his eyes at his mother. It was taking everything in him not to snap. At the end of the day, she was still his mother and he was going to respect her, but not without making his point. "You already know that Chasity isn't just 'some girl'. So cut it out," he ground out. "You're acting ridiculous."

"Get mad at me all you want, but I don't think it's a good idea to be away from family. Especially with your injury and all," Mrs. Adams persisted.

Jason raised his eyebrow at her. "Really Mom? Is this what you're going to do now? Bring up my injury *every* time you want to get me to do something?" he asked. "I'm good now, and I'm still going."

Mrs. Adams watched with sadness as her eldest son walked out of the kitchen.


Jason said goodbye to his family, before hopping into his father's car and speeding off. It took him less than fifteen minutes to reach Chasity's house.

Chasity opened the door when Jason knocked. It was clear by the look on her face that she was annoyed.

Hearing bickering coming from inside the house, Jason frowned in concern. "What's going on?"

Chasity shook her head as she moved aside to let him in. "Don't even ask," she grumbled.

"Yo Jase, can you *please* tell Alex that nobody wants to go to this damn Thanksgiving parade?" Mark charged, pointing to Alex. "She always tryna get us to do happy-go-lucky group shit."

Mark, along with most of the gang, arrived early that morning after Trisha had left for the airport.

Jason chuckled. "It's freezing out there," he pointed out, taking off his coat. "I don't think anybody wants to stand around just to look at floats."

Alex sucked her teeth. "Come on guys. It'll be *fun*," she insisted. "This is the first Thanksgiving that we're all spending together, and I think going to the parade will make for some great memories."

Malajia sucked her teeth. "Alex, screw you and your wack ass memories," she jeered. "Did you *not* see that penguin sitting outside when you left your house to come over here this morning? It's too damn cold."

Alex tossed her arms up. "You guys act like it's never been cold before," she belted out.

"That don't mean we wanna be standing *outside* in it," Malajia shot back, taking a bite of a piece of bacon that was in her hand.

"Ooh, can I have a piece?" Emily asked, reaching for Malajia's bacon.

"Girl no," Malajia scoffed, moving her hand away. "Breakfast was for the people who live here. *You don't.*"

"Neither do *you*," Chasity slid in, frowning at Malajia.

Malajia pointed her half-eaten bacon strip at Chasity. "Oh, I *do*...You just don't know it. Ms. Trisha and I worked it all out," she teased, much to Chasity's annoyance.

"Anyway, like I said. I really think it'll be fun," Alex put in, bringing the focus back to the subject at hand. "Besides, Emily and I were going to go *anyway* before we were invited here."

"Then *go*. Nobody's stopping you," Chasity sneered.

Alex made a face at Chasity before running her hands through her hair. "I want us to all go *together*...so we're *going*. It's only downtown."

Chasity shot a skeptical glance Alex's way. "Downtown Philly?" she asked.

"Yes."

"Yeah, I don't think that's where it is," Chasity contradicted.

Alex put her hand up. "Chasity, I watch the thing every year and I *live* in Philly. I think *I* would know where the parade is, more than *your* suburban behind," she argued.

Chasity narrowed her eyes at Alex. She looked as if she was about to spew off one of her profanity laced rants, but completely shocked everyone when she just put her hands up. "If you say so," she relented, before folding her arms.

Malajia sucked her teeth as the others groaned and complained. "We might as well figure out whose riding in what car," she said.

"Why don't we take the train?" Alex suggested.

"Girl, you lost your goddamn mind," Chasity snapped. "I'm not taking no damn train in the city."

"Chasity, are you really that stuck up?" Alex quibbled, putting her hands on her hips.

"Yes," Chasity bluntly admitted.

Jason chuckled. "Alright, let's just chill out," he slid in. "The train actually isn't a bad idea. It's going to be hell trying to drive through the city. Especially since today *is* Thanksgiving."

"Thank you, Jason," Alex said, pointing to him. "At least *one* of you is on my side."

A half hour and countless complaints later, the gang finally made it outside in route to their destination.

Bundling her coat collar to her neck, Chasity let out a loud sigh. "This is some bullshit," she huffed.

Mark laughed. "I know right? It *is* cold as a brick out here," he agreed, pulling his knit cap over his head.

Alex sucked her teeth as they ambled out of Chasity's neighborhood. "It's really not that bad," she said, fixing the ear muffs on her ears.

"That's because your broke ass is *used* to walking in the cold," Malajia snarled, resulting in a backhand from Alex on her arm.

"Maybe one of us should've stayed with the caterers," Josh suggested, blowing in his glove covered hands.

"Nah, they're fine in there without us," Chasity assured. "They've been catering my mom's shit for years."

"Josh just wanna breathe on the turkey and shit," Mark goaded. Josh just shook his head.

"How far is this train anyway?" Emily asked after taking a few more steps. "Your neighborhood doesn't look like the type to have a train station around the corner, Chaz."

"Oh, it *doesn't*," Chasity confirmed. "Alex played the shit out of *everybody* because it's a twenty-minute walk to a station,"

"Oh come on!" Mark exclaimed, while Alex avoided the gazes of her annoyed friends.

"I hate public transportation," Sidra complained, hurrying up the subway stairs to center city Philadelphia with the rest of the group. "There are some crazy people that ride the train."

Malajia laughed, placing her hands in her pockets. "Yeah, that man was serenading the shit out of you on there, Sid," she recalled. "He was hitting high notes and *everything.*"

Sidra rolled her eyes. "I know!" she exclaimed. "Even after the guys stood in front of me to block me, he was *still* singing...all off key and he smelled like trash."

Alex looked around. She saw people milling around the sidewalks, trying to get last minute items before many of the stores were to close for the rest of the day. But the crowd wasn't big enough for an actual parade. "Um... I don't get it. Where are all the floats?" she asked, holding her arms out. "Where's the parade?"

Chasity moved some of her windblown hair out of her face. "Probably at the Art museum where it is *every* year," she answered, nonchalant.

Everyone stopped walking and looked at Alex. "Alex, why do you have us the *fuck* out here in this arctic blast, and you don't even know where you're going?" Malajia charged.

"I thought it was down here," Alex explained. "Chasity, why didn't you say anything?" she hurled, shooting Chasity a glare.

"Oh no the hell you *won't* blame this on me," Chasity shot back, putting her hand up. "I tried to tell you, but you basically told me to shut my mouth."

"Yeah, you watch the parade every year, right? You live in Philly, right?" Jason mocked, voice not hiding his agitation.

Alex's eyes widened as she heard her words thrown

back at her. "Well, I guess I was wrong," she muttered.

"Yeah no shit, Sherlock," Mark sneered. "Nobody listen to Alex for the rest of the weekend."

"Gladly," Malajia hissed. "Stupid mop," she mumbled, adjusting the scarf on her neck.

Alex flagged them with her hand. "It's no big deal, we can always get on the bus and head to the museum," she suggested.

"No, *you* can go to the museum and the *rest* of us can go back to that big ass, warm house and wait for the food to get done," Mark said.

Josh sighed. "The food won't be done for hours, so since we're already out, we might as well just go," he put in. "No need in wasting a trip."

As the group made it to the nearest bus that would take them to their destination, Malajia looked at Chasity. "If you have us all over again next year, don't invite Alex," she grumbled.

Chasity snickered as Alex shot Malajia a glare. "I'm walking right next to you, Malajia," Alex hissed. "I can *hear* you."

"Good. Then you won't be surprised when you don't get an invite next year," Malajia retorted.


"Never again will I go to a parade," Malajia complained, flopping down on the couch. "All that standing in the cold for some dumb ass floats."

Sidra laughed. "You are so full of it. You were hype to see the Santa Clause come out at the end of it." She ran her hand through her ponytail.

After a long day out at the parade, the gang finally made it back to Chasity's house and were patiently waiting for the Thanksgiving dinner to be finished.

"I know, she started jumping up and down and shit," Mark added. "Stepping all on my foot."

"Look, I was just excited because I know that Christmas

is around the corner," Malajia stated defensively. "That means winter break and presents."

"How long until the food is done?" Mark asked, rubbing his stomach. "I'm hungry bee."

Chasity slapped her hand on the arm of the chair. "I will give you the same answer that I gave you the *last* five times that you asked me... I don't fuckin' know," she snapped. "You can always take your ass home and eat *there*."

"How you don't know bee? Don't those cooks work for you? Go ask them," Mark persisted, taking a sip of his juice.

Chasity pointed at him, shooting daggers with her eyes. "Call me bee one more time, hear?" Mark spat out his drink, trying to hold in his laugh.

"I was just in there and they said it won't be too much longer," Alex informed. "They're just setting the table and putting the stuff out."

"Of course *your* fat ass was just in there," Malajia mumbled, examining her nails. "Probably sneaking food and shit."

Mark's head snapped towards Alex. "You snuck some food and you ain't bring us none? ...You not looking out, bee," he said.

Alex let out a loud sigh. "Who is bee?!" she snapped. "I *hate* when you say that shit."

Malajia threw her head back and groaned, when she heard her phone ring. "Oh my Goooooodddd," she complained.

Sidra giggled. "Your mom again?"

"Yes! This is the fourth time that she's called me today," Malajia growled. "I already told her, I'm not coming the hell home." She sucked her teeth as she answered the phone. "Yes Mom...I'm *not*...Yes, I know that having dinner at home is a tradition...I'm grown Mom......Why would I care about Uncle Gary being there? I don't even like him...Why do you always have to threaten to slap me? ...Well then, it's a good thing I'm not home then, huh?" Malajia laughed as she removed the phone from her ear. "She hung up on me."

"Girl, you better stop talking to your parents like you're crazy," Sidra advised, amused. "You know you're not too old to get smacked."

"Oh yes the hell I *am*," Malajia contradicted, tossing her phone at the other end of the couch.

Sidra shook her head and was about to say something, when one of the chefs came out of the dining room and announced that dinner was ready.

"Yeesssss!" Mark hollered, jumping up from the floor. He almost tripped over David while trying to run for the dining room.

"Come on man!" David complained, backhanding Mark on the leg.

Mark, with a big smile on his face, did a dance as he grabbed a plate off the table. He began piling his plate high with turkey, baked macaroni and cheese, candied yams, potato salad, macaroni salad, collard greens, cornbread, and mashed potatoes. "I'm gonna tear this food up," he sang, sitting down.

Malajia stared at his plate, disgusted. "Why do you always have to go overboard?" she snarled, unfolding a cloth napkin. Mark ignored her while he began to stuff his face. Malajia shook her head, then turned her attention to Chasity. "Shouldn't they be serving us?"

Chasity frowned at her as she sat down. "Is there something wrong with your hands?" she hissed. "That's what I thought," she said when Malajia didn't respond. "I sent them home; they did what they were supposed to do."

Sidra broke off a piece of her cornbread. "So, I know—"

"Oh my God this is sooooo good," Mark rejoiced, throwing his head back.

Sidra frowned slightly at the interruption. "Anyway, I know why Malajia and *I* are away from our families for Thanksgiving this year. What made the *rest* of you come?"

"My dad still can't cook," David joked.

Josh laughed. "He's gotten better."

"No, he *hasn't*," David insisted, taking a bite out of a

piece of turkey. "I usually spend the holiday with you guys anyway, so wherever you all were going, I was *too*."

"Mom damn near pushed me out of the door when I said I was invited out," Mark slid in, once he swallowed some of his food.

"Well, *I* thought that it would be fun for us to spend the day together," Alex added, spreading some butter on her cornbread. "It's just like being back at school."

"Messing around with Alex and that parade made me miss the football game," Mark grumbled, taking a sip of juice. "Jase, speaking of football, when is the school gonna let you play again?"

Jason took a sip of water from his glass. Ever since his injury, the coaches had him sitting on the bench during games. Surprisingly, he was not opposed to it. "I was told that I probably won't play for the rest of the season," he revealed. "I guess they just want to make sure I have all the rest that I need."

Mark tossed his hands up in the air. "Aww man. They're gonna *lose* without you playing," he complained. "Fuck it, I'm not going to any more games."

Jason chuckled. "Naw, still come to the games. It's *still* my team."

"Wait a minute; if you're not playing, does that affect your scholarship?" Sidra wondered.

Jason shook his head. "No," he answered. "I'm still on the team, so my scholarship is good. I just don't play for now. But I'll be back in action next season." He took a bite of his food. "To be honest, I'm a little relieved. It was beginning to be too much with all of the extra practices and trying to keep my B average. I'm glad for the break."

Alex shook her head. "Well, although it seems to have worked out for you, I wish you didn't have to get hurt for that to happen," she said. "I mean that day was the worst. The whole campus was in an uproar."

Malajia glanced over at Chasity, who was slightly stabbing her food with her fork. Malajia guessed that bringing up that day was striking a nerve.

"We wanted to come to the hospital, but we were told that the doctors wouldn't—"

"Alex, let's talk about something else," Chasity quickly interrupted. "He's fine now. No need in reliving that day, okay?"

Alex shrugged. "Okay."

Malajia texted a message on her cell phone, then poured herself a glass of wine. "So anyway, did everyone figure out where they're sleeping?" she asked, changing the subject.

Chasity noticed that her phone lit up. She looked at the text message from Malajia '*I thought you said you were fine*' it read. Shooting Malajia a glare, she turned her phone off and put it back on the table.

"All I know is, I'm sleeping in a bed," Mark declared. "I'm not getting stuck sleeping on the floor like I did in that hotel freshman year."

"Alright, shut up," Chasity spat. "Trisha's room is off limits, but there are two extra bedrooms. There is a sofa bed in the den and there are like two couches in the living room, so just figure it out."

Malajia slammed her fork down. "Hey, one of those extra bedrooms is *mine*, I'm not sharing," she protested.

"You do *not* live here," Chasity barked, slamming her hand on the table "You're not getting a damn room to yourself."

Malajia took a sip from her glass. "Oh that *is* my room," she mumbled. "Sidra, you already know you're my roommate."

"Yes, I know," Sidra giggled.

"I'm on that sofa bed," Mark said. "And I'm *not* sharing."

Josh frowned. "Nobody *asked* you to," he sneered. "I'm cool with the couch. It's comfortable anyway. Probably cost more than my entire bedroom set."

"It *does*," Malajia teased. "And Alex's entire wardrobe."

Alex slammed her hand on the table. "You know

what—"

"I'm joking," Malajia laughed, putting her hands up. "You know I love your cheap ass." Alex made a face at her.

# Chapter 25

"Whose damn idea was it for us to ice skate?" Chasity sneered, staring at the skating rink downtown.

"Josh's," Sidra admonished, shivering.

"Oh okay," Chasity said. "Remind me to slap him later."

After awaking early the next morning and spending the better part of the morning at the mall, Josh suggested that they go ice skating. His suggestion was naturally met with some complaints.

"Y'all need to stop girlin'," Mark taunted, inching up in line for his ice skates. "Always complaining."

"Um *first* of all, we're *girls*. So saying that we are girlin' is redundant," Sidra ground out. "*Second*, its freezing and the last thing that I want to do is be on this ice."

"Come on Sid, it'll be fun," Josh mused. "You can always hold on to me if you don't feel steady."

Mark sucked his teeth. "You *still* trying to get her to touch you, huh?" he teased.

"Mark!" Sidra exclaimed as Josh shot him a glare. The last thing that the two of them wanted was to bring up any old awkward feelings due to Josh revealing how he felt about Sidra. "Why do you always have to start?"

"I'm just playing," Mark explained. "Geez, I thought y'all were over that."

"We *are*. But that still doesn't give you the right to be a jackass about it," Josh scoffed.

Mark just flagged them with his hand, turning around in line.

Chasity mumbled several curse words as she tied her ice skates. "I don't feel like doing this bullshit," she complained.

Jason laughed. "Stop being a baby," he teased. "You act like you've never done this before."

"That's because I *haven't*," she admitted, trying to stand up.

Jason grabbed her arm as she wobbled. "Really? You've never ice skated?"

"No," she sniped. "And don't you start laughing at me either."

"You think so little of me," he said, feigning hurt. Stepping onto the ice, he reached for her hand. "Come on, it's not as hard as it looks."

"You're full of shit and you know it," she bit out, reluctantly grabbing his hand. She tensed up as Jason guided her onto the ice. "Shit, shit," she panicked, feeling herself wobble. Jason laughed when she gripped his arm. "Stop laughing!" she snapped.

Alex held on to the rail. "Emily, when did you learn to ice skate?" Alex asked, watching Emily skate.

Emily did several effortless twirls around Alex before stopping in front of her. "My dad used to take me when I was younger," she answered. "I've always enjoyed it."

"I'm impressed," Alex smiled. Her smile faded as she wobbled. "*And* I'm about to fall," she said while trying to steady herself. Emily giggled, and grabbed Alex's arm to keep her from falling.

"Josh! Don't let me fall!" Sidra screamed, clutching Josh's hand while taking baby steps on the ice. "I swear to God, I hate you for making me do this."

"If you would just *relax* and let me show you what to do, you'll see that it isn't so bad," Josh calmly stated.

"Okay, okay," Sidra whined, trying to steady herself. "Just...don't go so fast."

"Don't worry," he assured her. "Now, I'm just going to pull you a little so we can get some momentum going."

Sidra began screaming as Josh slowly pulled her forward. "No, I don't want any momentum! Noooooo."

"Ahhhh, you can't outskate me. I'm a beast at this," Mark boasted, skating circles around Malajia. "I can be a professional, dawg."

Malajia glared at him while skating a few circles of her own. "Yeah, a professional asshole," she jeered.

Mark sucked his teeth. "Boooo," he jeered of Malajia's lackluster comeback. "Let's race," he suggested.

"Um, how about naw," Malajia refused, moving some hair over her shoulders. "You can go flying down this rink like a fool if you *want* to."

"You corny man," he complained. "Fine, I'll go myself." He bent down like he was about to start running track. Just as he rose and took a glide forward, he was bumped by David, causing him to slip and fall on the ice. "Goddamn it David!" Mark hollered, sliding a few inches on his back.

Malajia and David busted out laughing. "My fault," David apologized, trying to regain his composure.

Malajia then skated over and stopped right in front of Mark, sending ice shavings from her skates flying at him.

"Damn Mel, that almost got in my eye and shit," Mark

admonished, rubbing his face with his glove-covered hands.


Chasity held on to the railing, watching Jason skate around the rink. After fifteen minutes of him trying to teach her how to skate, she became frustrated and told him to skate without her. "Never again," she promised herself.

Malajia skated over to Chasity. "Girl, why are you hanging on the damn wall?" she wondered. "You better get out here and act like you know how to skate."

Chasity rolled her eyes at her. "Get away from me."

Malajia was about to fire off a smart retort, when a child, who was skating fast, bumped into her in passing. The impact caused Malajia to stumble into Chasity. Malajia, who was used to the skates could keep herself from falling, but Chasity wasn't so lucky; she went falling on the ice.

"Oh shit," Malajia laughed. "It wasn't my fault! That kid came out of nowhere."

Chasity was too angry to even say anything. She just let out a loud groan as she laid on the ice. She did however slap Malajia's hand away when she tried to help her up.

Jason, who had witnessed what happened from the other side of the rink, skated over. "See, if you would have come with *me* then you wouldn't be down there," he teased, helping Chasity up from the ice.

"Shut up," Chasity spat, holding on to hm.

Malajia giggled as Jason slowly skated away with Chasity on his arm. Turning to head off in another direction, she heard Alex yell. "Crap, crap! Mel move."

"The hell?" Malajia said, spinning around. She ended up colliding with Alex, who was wobbling towards her. Both girls went falling to the ice. "Why is your big ass over here near me?!" Malajia yelled, nudging Alex off her.

"I *told* you to move!" Alex shouted back, struggling to get up.

Before Malajia could say another word, Mark skated

over, stopping several inches from her, sending ice shavings flying. He laughed as he skated off. "You fuckin' jackass!" Malajia hollered after him.


Lounging back at the house later that evening, Alex put her hand up. "Ooh I have an idea!" she exclaimed.

Mark quickly pointed at her. "No, we already told you we're not listening to you for the rest of the weekend," he reminded.

"Boy shut up," Alex dismissed. "This is a good idea... How about we have a pie baking contest?"

Everyone stared at her for several seconds. "On what planet is that a good idea?" Chasity quibbled, lighting the fire place.

"*Where* do you come *up* with this corny shit?" Malajia added. "And completely out of nowhere too. Like, nobody was even *talking* about pies."

Alex chuckled. "There's no more pie from last night, so I was thinking instead of us going out to *buy* one, we can all *make* one." She smiled brightly.

She was once again met with confused stares. "I just *said* that nobody said anything *about* pies," Malajia snapped, slapping her hand on the floor. "You are the *only* one in here thinking about some goddamn pies."

"You know what? I agree with Alex on this," Emily slid in, voice filled with amusement. "I think it'll be pretty cool."

"Ain't shit cool about baking no pies," Malajia grumbled.

Sidra snickered as Alex made a face at Malajia.

"Just quit the whining for once and participate," Alex commanded. "How about girls versus guys?"

Jason put his hand up. "How about no," he jeered.

"Yeah man, I'm not kneading no dough near Josh and shit," Mark joked.

"Okay fine, we'll do boy/girl teams," Alex amended,

looking around the room. "So, we know that's Jase and Chaz, Mark and Mel—"

"Who said I wanted to be on Malajia's damn team?" Mark loudly interrupted.

"You act like I want to be on *yours*," Malajia shot back, tossing a throw pillow at him. "You can't even *spell* pie."

Alex rolled her eyes at the interruption. "Anyway," she continued. "Josh and Sid and that leaves David with me and Em."

"How David got two girls, yo?" Mark complained.

Alex pulled her hands down her face. She was annoyed with the interruptions. "We are uneven, man. What do you *want* from me?" she said, exasperated. "Do you want to take one of us on *your* team?"

"Hell no," Malajia quickly declared.

Sidra, noticing that Alex was two seconds from cursing Malajia out, decided to offer a distraction. "Um, it won't be uneven because...James is coming over in a few minutes," she slid in, hesitantly. "So, I can be on *his* team. I'm sure he'll participate. "

Everyone slowly turned and looked at Josh, who was sitting on one of the accent chairs. He met their gazes with a slight frown. "What?" he asked. He rolled his eyes when realization set in. "Come on y'all. I'm good. There are no hard feelings," he assured. "I have nothing against the man. Sid is happy with him, so everything is cool."

"You sure man?" Mark asked, eyeing him skeptically.

"Yes."

Mark put his hands up. "Okay, we'll take your word for it," he said. "But I *will* say this to you. If you decide to get all swole in the chest and test James and he knocks you out...well then, you'll just be knocked out 'cause I ain't fighting no lawyer."

Sidra rolled her eyes as Josh shook his head.

Alex grabbed a piece of paper and tore it into five pieces. "I'm writing out five different pies and putting them in a bag, and we'll pick from it," she announced.


Staring at a recipe book, Mark frowned. "Mel, what pie did we pick out the bag again?"

"Lemon meringue pie," Malajia replied, lacking enthusiasm.

Mark slammed the book closed. "Man, how we gonna make a dancing pie?" he snapped.

Malajia shot him a confused look. "What the hell do you mean by a dancing pie?" she questioned. "What are you talking about?"

"Isn't meringue that dance?" Mark asked. She frowned with even more confusion. "That dance," he persisted. "That Latin dance. Come on, you know what I'm talking about."

Malajia stared at him for several seconds. Sighing, she pinched the bridge of her nose with two fingers. She was completely outdone. "You mean *merengue*?!" she erupted. She slapped her hand on the counter when Mark stared at her with a stupid look. "Oh my God! I can't. Please somebody switch with me," she exclaimed. "He is the dumbest—A dancing pie dawg? *Really*?"

Mark just shrugged, much to her annoyance.

Alex giggled. "Mark, you're a fool," she joked, stirring the filling for her pie. "Josh, we lucked up and got an easy pie."

Josh shot her a skeptical glance. "You think that pecan pie is easy?"

"Sure. I watch my mom make it all the time," Alex assured. "How hard can it be?"

"Alex, what the fuck is a rhubarb?" Chasity spat out, slamming her spoon on the counter. "Why would you put a damn strawberry rhubarb pie in the bag? Nobody knows what the hell that is."

"Come on Chasity, you really don't know what a rhubarb is?" Alex frowned.

Chasity tossed her spoon on the counter and folded her

arms. "Do *you* even know what it is?"

Alex thought for a moment. "I think it's a type of plant that you eat."

Chasity glowered at Alex for several seconds. "Did it *look* like I had any fuckin' plants in my fridge?" she sniped.

Alex laughed. "Okay sorry. Just make a sweet potato pie."

"Why wouldn't you put that in the bag in the *first* place?" Chasity complained, picking her spoon back up. "Fuckin' rhubarb...You're about to get put out."

Alex shook her head. She didn't care how much complaining her friends were doing; she was proud of her idea and knew that each pie would turn out good.


A half hour later, Alex began to doubt her decision. There was entirely too much arguing going on.

"Why is the damn meringue all runny?" Malajia barked, tossing her flour covered dish towel on the counter. "Mark, what the hell did you do?"

"Aye, stop yelling at me alright," Mark shot back, pointing at her. "I put the damn cornstarch in there like the recipe said."

Malajia looked at the box he was pointing to. She gritted her teeth then grabbed it and put it in his face. "You mean *this*?" she charged. He nodded and she nearly lost it. "This is sugar! It's not even the same damn *texture*," she yelled. "I just hate you with every fiber of my soul!"

"Jason, I swear to God—stop eating the damn pie filling," Chasity demanded. "We're going to have a shallow ass pie."

Jason shrugged as he dug his spoon into the bowl for the fourth time. "It's good."

"Yes, I *know* that and it will be even *better* in the damn pie crust," Chasity fumed.

"You need to chill," Jason advised, taking another spoon. Frustrated, Chasity tossed her hands up in the air and walked out the kitchen, inciting a laugh from him. "Come back," he called after her.

"You're on my damn nerves!" she yelled back into the kitchen.

"Emily, I don't think we should fill the pie crust all the way to the top," David suggested, pushing his glasses up on his nose. "We don't want it to bubble over in the oven."

"Yeah, that makes sense," Emily agreed. She took her spoon and removed some of the apple pie filling from the pie crust and put it back in the mixing bowl. As she turned to put the bowl in the sink, her waist brushed up against the pie pan, which was on the edge of the counter.

"Em, grab the pie!" David exclaimed, but he was too late. He put his hands over his head as he watched their pie fall to the floor.

Emily winced. "Sorry," she said softly.

"Ahhhh haaaa, y'all pie on the floor and shit," Mark teased, wiping flour off his shirt.

"Shut up, at least they actually *made* theirs right," Malajia scoffed, still upset about her pie's outcome.

Sidra repeatedly banged her spoon on the side of the mixing bowl. "This looks like shit," she grunted of her and James's coconut cream pie filling.

James gently grabbed her hand and removed the spoon. "Honey, don't worry about it. It doesn't look bad," he assured, amused.

James was excited when Sidra had invited him over. He wanted to spend time with her, and if it meant sharing her with her friends, then he was for it. He even agreed to the pie baking contest, but he didn't expect it to be so tense.

"Sure, we added too many coconut flakes, but it'll still be fine," he placated.

Sidra frowned at him. "No, it *won't*," she contradicted. "There is entirely *too* much coconut in there. Would *you* want to eat a pie that's mostly dry ass coconut flakes and hardly any custard?"

James looked at her, pondering what to say. Sidra

seemed like she was about to fly off the handle at any given moment. Who knew that making a pie would stress her out? "Um…You look really pretty," he smiled.

Not amused, Sidra rolled her eyes and walked out of the kitchen, leaving him astonished.

"Okay, you guys are around her more than *I* am," he said to the others. "Does she get like this a lot?"

"You mean a neurotic, dramatic stress ball?" Malajia asked.

"Ummm, I wouldn't say *that* exactly," James slowly put out.

"You *can*, 'cause it's *true*," Malajia chuckled. "Welcome to *our* world."

"I'm just gonna go check on her," James said, walking out of the kitchen.

"She's *his* problem now," Mark joked, stirring his failed filling with a spoon.

"She's not a *problem*," Josh spat at Mark.

Mark raised an eyebrow at Josh's tone. "Bruh, don't get this runny ass pie filling thrown on you," he threw back.

Alex removed her apron. "Okay *maybe* this *wasn't* such a good idea," she admitted, tossing the apron on the counter.

"You think?" Malajia sarcastically asked, taking a spoon of Chasity and Jason's sweet potato filling out of the bowl. She turned her nose up. "What smells like burnt sugar?"

Alex lowered her head as Josh's head snapped towards the oven.

"Damn," Josh admonished, walking over to it. "Hey Alex, our pie is burning."

"Yeah, I know," Alex sighed.

# Chapter 26

"Yo Chaz, we're gonna kill this history test tomorrow," Mark boasted, taking a tortilla chip from a bag while sitting at the girls' dining room table.

Chasity looked up from her book, rolling her eyes in the process. "I'm going to kill *you* if you don't get the fuck out this damn house," she fumed. Mark had been in the girls' house for over two hours, and he had been working her nerves the moment he stepped foot in there.

"Why you so mad, beautiful?" he teased. "You suggested that we study for this test together."

Chasity frowned in confusion. "No the hell I *didn't*," she contradicted. "You walked in here and asked where Malajia was, and when I told you she wasn't here, you asked me what I was studying and I said history. Then you said that you had the class after me, sat your black ass down, and started eating my damn chips."

He chuckled. *Chasity has the memory of a damn elephant*, he thought. "Didn't nobody ask you for the full recap," he jeered, removing another chip and dipping it in some salsa.

Chasity stared at him, gritting her teeth. She was about to fire off a remark, when Malajia walked through the door.

"Thank God," Chasity grumbled. "Mel, come walk your damn dog. He's been shitting in the house for two hours."

Malajia laughed as Mark made a face at Chasity. "What are you doing here, Mark?" Malajia asked.

"I'm bored and the drama club is putting on a rendition of the horror movie that we saw last week. You wanna go?" Mark asked.

Malajia sucked her teeth. "Boy, don't nobody wanna see that bullshit," she scoffed. "They always tryna do some shit. They can't even *act*."

"*Exactly*," Mark agreed. "Which is why I figured we could sneak in some drinks and laugh at them."

Chasity shot Mark a puzzled look. "Seriously?" she barked. "You irked my soul for *two hours* just to tell her *that*?" Mark squinted his eyes at Chasity. "You could have taken your ass home and *called* her."

Mark pointed his finger at Chasity. "Hey, hey... shut up," he shot back, prompting a middle finger from Chasity and a snicker from Malajia. "Anyway, what do you say? Wanna go?" he asked Malajia.

Removing her cell phone from her purse, Malajia giggled. "As much as I would love to laugh my ass off..." her words trailed off as she stared at her phone screen.

"You cool?" Mark asked, noticing the troubled look on Malajia's face.

"Um..." Malajia quickly put the phone back into her purse. "Yeah I'm good. But no, I don't wanna go see that mess...I *do* want to go eat though."

Mark rose from his seat. "Cool, that works for me. I'm starving."

"What *else* is new?" Malajia giggled. "Chaz, you wanna come with us?"

"I'm not hungry," Chasity bit out, turning the page in her text book. She looked up from her book when the door opened.

"Hey guys," Alex said, stepping inside the house with Eric following close behind. Grinning, Malajia shot a knowing look Alex's way. "Stop it," Alex mouthed to Malajia.

"Hey, what's up Alex's F.B.?" Chasity smirked, earning a loud snicker from Malajia.

Alex glared at Chasity. "That's real cute, heffa," she hissed, sitting her books on the coffee table.

"What are y'all about to do?" Malajia asked both Eric and Alex. "Y'all want to come eat with us?"

"Thanks, but I ate not too long ago," Eric smiled, rubbing his stomach.

"I'm sure you *did*," Chasity teased.

Malajia clapped her hands as she busted out laughing. "Yeeesss! I was thinking the same thing," she howled.

Eric shot Alex a baffled look. She returned his look with a wave of her hand. "Don't mind my friends. They're ignorant," she spat. "Just so you know," she pointed to Chasity and Malajia. "I hate you *both* right now."

As Alex headed for the kitchen, Chasity closed her book and stood from her seat. "On second thought, I'll come with y'all," she declared. "Her room is right above mine."

Alex slammed a cabinet door shut. "Chasity!" she hollered from the kitchen.

"Yes?" Chasity laughed.

"Zip your damn mouth," Alex scolded. "You're being disrespectful."

"So?" Chasity's voice was full of amusement.

Mark shook his head. "Eric man, don't mind these girls, they *all* crazy," he joked. "Hang out with us more and you'll see what I mean."

Eric chuckled while Alex rolled her eyes.

"Yo Chaz, why you call him F.B.?" Mark whispered as the three of them walked out the door.

"'Cause he's a fuck buddy," Chasity whispered back.

"So, you're saying that Eric is Alex's fuck buddy?" Mark blurted out, intentionally loud, much to Alex's embarrassment.

"Why would you do that, you ass?!" Malajia exclaimed,

slapping Mark on the arm. "We can't tell you *nothing*," she scolded, shutting the door behind them.

Alex shook her head. "I apologize for that," she said to Eric. "I love my friends to death, but sometimes they are just too much."

"Don't worry about it," he placated, walking into the kitchen. "I think they're funny."

"Yeah well, *I don't*," she grunted, grabbing a bottle of water from the refrigerator.

Eric studied Alex as she opened her water and began to drink. "So, I've been meaning to ask you something," he began.

"What's that?" Alex wondered, drinking her water.

Eric leaned against the counter. "I want to know if you would go on a date with me?"

Alex nearly choked on her water. *Crap!* As much as she liked hanging out with Eric, she wasn't interested in dating him. "Um... Listen Eric, I *love* spending time with you, *trust* me I do," she began, sitting her water bottle on the counter. "But...I just don't want to date right now."

Eric frowned slightly. "You don't want to *date* me, but you're okay with *sleeping* with me?" he questioned, bite in his voice.

Alex was taken back by his tone and question. It showed on her face. "It's not like I wasn't honest with you from the beginning about what I didn't want," she threw back, folding her arms. "You know what happened in my *last* relationship."

"I know that your boyfriend cheated on you," Eric sympathized. "And while I'm sorry that that happened to you, it happened over two years ago. It's time to move on."

Alex rolled her eyes. *He has some nerve telling me to get over it.* "Whatever. I'm enjoying being single," she huffed. "I don't need to answer to anybody. Or wonder what anybody is doing...or who they're doing it *with*...."

Eric thought for a moment, then nodded. "Okay, so since we're not exclusive and you have no *desire* to be...you won't be mad if I start seeing other women?"

Alex stared blankly. "Nope. Do what you want," she ordered, teeth clenched. "And while you're doing *that*. *I'll* be seeing other *men*."

"Yeah, I don't think you will," Eric contradicted. "You don't seem like the type to sleep around. Even though you *did* sleep with *me* pretty fast."

Alex nudged him. "Hey, no need to throw that in my face," she scolded, causing him to chuckle.

"Okay look, I don't mind chillin' with you. If sex and friendship is all that you want right now, I'm good with that," he declared. "But if I happen to meet someone else who I'm interested in and who actually *wants* to be in a relationship, you'll be the first to know."

"That's fine with me," she returned. Eric stared at her longingly. Catching his stare, she quickly shook her head. "Naw buddy, not today," she said. "It's that time of the month."

"Aww man," Eric teased. "You're messing up, Alex."

"Oh shut up," she laughed. "You can rub my back though."

"Sorry, that's boyfriend stuff," he joked, grabbing the bottle of water from the counter and taking a sip.

Alex made a face at him before playfully slapping him on the arm. "Very funny."


"Stupid Legal Studies paper, having me up until one in the damn morning," Sidra grumbled to herself. She placed a lid onto her travel coffee mug. "Thank God it's Friday." Taking a quick sip of her coffee, she adjusted the scarf around her neck and headed for the front door. Upon opening it, Sidra let out a loud groan. "Craaaap!"

"Girl what's your problem?" Malajia asked, hurrying down the steps. Without saying a word, Sidra pointed outside. Malajia sucked her teeth at the sight of thick snowflakes falling from the sky. Malajia unzipped her coat.

"I'm not dealing with that bullshit today," she refused, heading back upstairs.

"Wait a minute. You're not going to go to class?" Sidra asked, following Malajia's progress up the steps.

"Fuck class," Malajia hurled down the steps.

Shaking her head, Sidra walked out of the house, closing the door behind her. She frowned when she saw Chasity walking back to the house. "Don't you have a nine o'clock class too?" she asked. "What are you doing back here?"

"My class was cancelled, *Alex*," Chasity jeered.

Sidra made a face at her. "I'm *not* that nosey."

"Yeah a'ight," Chasity returned, heading in the house.

Sidra let out a loud sigh, then headed for the cluster gates. Each time her boot covered foot touched down on the inches of snow, she became even more agitated. Her foot sank in a snow pile; Sidra let out a scream as she tried to keep her balance. Feeling someone grab her arm, she glanced up. "Thanks Josh."

Josh let out a laugh. "You might want to change into a shoe without a heel," he teased, observing her high-heeled boots.

She stuck her tongue out at him. "Whatever." She dusted the snow from her pant leg. "If I go back in that house, I'm not coming back out."

"In that case, we should probably get a move on," Josh suggested, giving her a soft nudge.

Sidra nodded in agreement as the two of them began their journey to class. "First week of December and we're greeted with a damn snowstorm," Sidra ground out, after moments of walking.

"Well... Yeah," Josh returned, voice laced with amusement. "You said it yourself, it's *December*. What did you expect?" He adjusted his book bag on his shoulder. "Did you ever finish your paper?"

"Yeah, I finished it like one this morning," she groaned. "I'll be glad when this semester is over."

"I hear you," he agreed. "We only have a few weeks left."

Sidra smiled slightly. "You know, it's been a while since we walked to class together," she said, pushing her bangs out of her face.

Josh glanced at the ground. "I know."

Sidra looked at him. Almost as if she was waiting on him to say something else. "We can still walk together, you know," she said. Although she and Josh were on good terms, she could feel the differences in their relationship, and she hated it. "I miss your company when we walk together."

Josh let out a sigh. "Sid, I've told you before that I'm just giving you some space."

Sidra rolled her eyes. "*Still?*" she bit out. "It's been *three months.*"

Josh stopped walking and shot her a glare. He didn't appreciate the disregard that she was showing for his feelings. "Don't do that," he spat.

"I'm sorry," Sidra muttered. "I understand why you're still doing it... But that doesn't mean that I *like* it."

"I'm still around, Sidra," he pointed out. "We're still friends."

"I know, I know," Sidra huffed, clutching her coffee cup in her hand. She sighed. "Josh—do you think it would help if you started dating?" she hesitantly asked.

"Help with what?" Josh wondered, adjusting the hat on his head.

Sidra wanted to be careful in what she said. She didn't want to rub salt in his wounds. "I mean, if you started seeing someone, then maybe you would..."

"Maybe I wouldn't be in love with you anymore?" he asked, point blank.

Sidra looked at the ground. *Nice going, idiot,* she chided herself.

"If I start dating now, then I'd just compare every girl to you, and that wouldn't be fair," he replied. "I just can't erase my feelings that fast... I've had a crush on you from the first day I met you…been in love with you since we were in high school."

Sidra was almost speechless. She had no idea how long he'd been feeling this way. She could only imagine what it felt like, keeping feelings that strong to himself for so long. "Josh…I—I don't know—"

Josh smiled. "You don't need to find the words to say…I told you, I'm fine," he replied.

Sidra opened her mouth to speak, but her phone ringing halted her response. She retrieved her phone from her purse and looked at it.

Josh gave her a light pat on the arm. "Tell James I said hi." He adjusted the book bag on his shoulder, once again. "I gotta go."

Sidra watched Josh walk away. Then glancing at the caller ID, she smirked when she saw James's name on her screen, then placed the phone to her ear.


Emily trudged through the snow later that afternoon to get to the front door of her house. Sighing loudly, she pushed the door open and stepped inside. "That snow is covering my ankles and it's *still* falling," she complained to Malajia, who was watching TV on the couch under a blanket.

"I know. That's why my ass has been in this house all day," Malajia declared, flipping through the channels.

Emily let out a laugh. "You really didn't go to *all three* of your classes today?"

"Hell no," Malajia confirmed. "I wasn't trying to go out in that mess. It's supposed to be like eight inches before it's all said and done."

Emily put her book bag on the chair and removed her coat. "I don't blame you. It's a mess out there," she said. "At least it's Friday, so we won't have to worry about missing any classes after today."

"Hell, if this shit doesn't melt by Monday, I'm not going to class *then either*," Malajia ground out. Her cell phone made a noise. Picking it up, she checked the text message, frowning. "What the hell?" she mumbled, turning the phone off.

"Something wrong?" Emily asked, removing her boots.

"No, everything's fine," Malajia muttered.

Emily studied her; Malajia's face had a blank look, completely different than when she was speaking to her before she looked at her phone. "Are you sure? I mean—"

"Yes Emily, I'm fine," Malajia interrupted, exasperated. "What are we eating for dinner?" she asked, quickly changing the subject.

Emily shrugged, before rubbing her shoulders with her hands. "It's cold in here. Is the heat on?"

"I *thought* it was," Malajia said. "I turned it up high this morning."

Emily walked over to the heating vent and put her hand in front of it. "Um, there's no heat coming out," she declared. "I think it's broken."

Frustrated, Malajia tossed her hands in the air. "That's just freakin' great," she fussed. "It's cold as shit outside. What are we gonna do with no damn heat?"

Emily again shrugged, but didn't get any words out because the front door flung open. Both girls turned to see Chasity running into the house laughing, with a snow-covered Alex stumbling in the house after her.

"What the hell happened to *you*?" Malajia asked Alex, tossing the cover off.

Alex slammed the door and snatched her knit hat off her head. "Your fuckin' bitch of a friend pushed me and I fell in the snow," she seethed, pointing to Chasity.

"Chasity, that's terrible," Emily chided, voice laced with amusement.

Chasity could barely get her room door open, she was laughing so hard. "I didn't push her," she denied. "I *bumped into* her by accident and her goofy ass fell," she laughed, much to Alex's annoyance. "Then her big ass couldn't get up 'cause the snow is so deep."

Fuming, Alex took off one of her boots and hurled it at Chasity, who quickly ducked, causing the shoe to hit her door.

"Missed bitch," Chasity hissed, then was hit on the arm with Alex's other boot. "Ouch!" she yelped, grabbing her arm. "The fuck is wrong with you?"

"Damn Alex, why you gotta throw shoes at my girl?" Malajia exclaimed, jumping up from the couch.

Alex pointed at Malajia. "Sit your hype ass back down before I throw one at *you*," she ordered. "I'm in no mood for *your* bullshit *either*."

Seeing that Alex wasn't playing, Malajia slowly sat back down. "You ain't gotta cuss at me," she mumbled. "I didn't even do nothing."

Emily watched as Alex kicked her book bag to the steps and flopped on the chair. "Alex, are you okay?" she asked. "You seem like something else is bothering you."

"I'm fine Emily," Alex grumbled, running her hands through her wild hair.

Malajia folded her arms. "Naw, you called Chaz a bitch. You hardly *ever* use that word," she mentioned. "Not to mention that you threw not one but *both* of your ugly ass, man boots." Alex shot Malajia a death stare. "Something ain't right."

Sitting up in her seat, Alex tried to calm her rising temper. "Malajia…I swear I'm not in the mood for your mouth," she slowly ground out. "Stop talking before I slap the shit out of you."

Malajia was taken back and it showed on her face. "The hell? I wish you *would* slap me," she challenged. "I'll perm your damn hair in your sleep. And I'll leave it on extra-long so it burns your hair out."

Chasity walked over to the couch. "She's just salty because she saw her fuck buddy talking to some girl outside the library," she revealed, rubbing her arm.

Between hearing the words "fuck buddy" come from Chasity, when she'd asked her repeatedly to stop saying it, and being reminded of what she witnessed Eric doing while she was coming back from class, Alex snapped.

Alex jumped up from her seat, darted over to Chasity and grabbed the back of her hair, taking Chasity completely by surprise. Alex didn't pull it, just grabbed a handful of it and held it. "I told you to shut your damn mouth about that!" Alex wailed.

Malajia jumped up from her seat; Emily put her hands over her mouth from shock. They knew that this could get ugly.

Chasity reached around and grabbed a handful of Alex's hair, then pulled it. "Bitch, get the fuck off me or I swear I'll rip this shit out," she fumed.

"Alex, you trippin'!" Malajia exclaimed, trying to remove Alex's hand from Chasity's hair.

Alex released Chasity's hair; Chasity didn't. Still furious, Chasity gave a hard tug and Alex's head yanked, causing her to yell out. "Let go! Mel, can you get her off my hair please?" She let out a scream when she felt Chasity pull her hair harder.

"Chaz, come on, let go," Malajia calmly said, untangling Alex's locks from Chasity's grip. "You'll ruin your manicure on those naps."

"That's not funny!" Alex yelped. "She's pulling hair out."

"Let go, Chasity," Malajia ordered, tone stern.

Chasity finally released Alex's hair, then pushed her. "Don't ever put your fuckin' hands on me."

Malajia quickly stood in between the two girls as Chasity took another step towards Alex. "Nah, go chill out," she urged, giving Chasity a soft nudge in the direction of her room. "Y'all are not gonna be fighting."

Alex rubbed her head as she watched Chasity storm to her room. She flinched when the door slammed shut.

"That was uncalled for, Alex," Malajia chastised. "I should've let her beat your ass."

Alex rubbed her head again, then flopped back down on

the couch. "Whatever." Realizing her error, she put her head in her hands and sighed. "Shit," she mumbled. "Chaz, I'm sorry!" she yelled at the closed door.

"Fuck you!" Chasity shouted through the door.

Malajia shook her head. "Damn girl, you did all that because you saw Eric with a girl?" she questioned. "You're not even *dating*, why do you care?"

"I *don't*," Alex grunted.

"If you *didn't*, then you wouldn't be acting like this," Emily slid in, folding her arms. "You put your hands on your friend; that's not right."

Alex threw her hands up. "I know, I screwed up just now," she admitted. "And yeah, maybe I feel some kind of way about seeing Eric with some girl…who wasn't even *cute* by the way."

"Now, now, petty," Malajia scolded.

Alex let out a huff. "Yeah, I know… Can't even lie, she was pretty." She ran her hand through her hair, pulling out a loose strand. "He told me that if he met someone else that he would do me the courtesy of telling me… He lied to me."

Malajia shot a puzzled look Alex's way. "Huh?" she sneered. "*First* off, that man don't owe you shit. You are *not* his girlfriend. You made that perfectly clear."

"But—"

"Naw, no buts," Malajia interrupted, putting her hand up. "*Second*, you don't even know what he was talking to her *about*. And even if you *did*, so what? He. Is. Not. Your. Man. I don't care if you *are* screwing him," she bluntly added. "You in here acting all crazy, throwing shoes, grabbing people's hair and shit. You almost got your ass beat."

Alex narrowed her eyes. "I can fight *too*, you know."

"I don't know about all that, I've *seen* you in action," Malajia mocked. Alex flagged Malajia with her hand. "And, I've seen *her*…just ask Emily's face."

Emily let out a gasp. "Seriously Malajia?!" she exclaimed.

Malajia busted out laughing. "My bad Em, was that too

soon too?"

"Yes!" Emily folded her arms in a huff. She didn't need to be reminded of the fact that Chasity tapped her face last semester in an effort to force Emily to stand up for herself. Sure, Chasity apologized, but that didn't mean that Emily wanted to relive the embarrassment.

Alex put her hands up. "Look...I'm sorry for snapping," she cut in.

"I don't want your funky ass apology," Malajia said, hiding a smile.

Shaking her head, Alex stood up and walked over to Chasity's door. Knocking, she sighed.

"What?!" Chasity snapped through the door.

"I'm sorry Chaz," Alex said, remorseful. "I was way out of line."

"Get away from my damn door Alex," Chasity barked.

"Come on, you got me back." Alex stomped her foot on the floor. "You pulled some strands out my hair. Can you just come out please?"

"Alex, I'm warning you," Chasity maintained. "Leave me alone." Chasity was desperately trying to maintain the space between her and Alex because she was trying to calm herself down. She didn't really want to hurt Alex any further.

Alex sighed. "We're both adults here, Chasity," she persisted. "Just come out so we can get past this please? I don't want to fight with you."

Malajia chuckled. "I suggest you move from that door."

"Alex, just give her a minute," Emily suggested, signaling for Alex to move. "She'll come out when she's ready."

"Either when she's ready, or when she realizes that heat in her room ain't working," Malajia chortled.

# Chapter 27

"Can you please just deal the damn cards, Jase?!" Mark yelled, slamming his hand on the dining room table.

Jason paused his shuffling of the cards and stared daggers at Mark. "Why are you hollering at me?" he asked, his voice deceptively calm.

"'Cause man, you all slow, shuffling the cards and shit. We tryna play," Mark shot back, grabbing a handful of chips from a large bowl on the table.

"Well this is a new deck of cards, so we're not playing *anything* until I shuffle them thoroughly," Jason maintained, shuffling the deck again.

Patience gone, Mark slammed his hand on the table and pointed his finger at Jason. "Look muthafucka, I already *told* you—" Mark's profanity laced rant was interrupted when the entire deck of cards was hurled at him. "Ow! Those hit me in the face!" he exclaimed, rubbing his face.

"I told your dumb ass to stop talking to me all crazy," Jason fumed.

Josh and David doubled over with laughter. "Mark, you stay getting in trouble," Josh mused, taking a sip of his soda.

Mark picked up his glass of rum and coke. "He always gotta go overboard," he fussed. "A card could've poked my eye out."

Jason rolled his eyes, then took a chip from the bowl.

A knock at the door startled Mark. "Shit, it's campus security," he panicked, trying to hide his drink. "Hide the drinks. Hide the drinks!" Mark went to snatch Josh's cup, but Josh moved it out of his reach.

"Man this is soda, chill out," Josh ground out, smacking Mark's hand away.

David went to answer the door. "Ladies, what brings you here?" he smiled, stepping aside to let the girls in.

"Our heater is broke and won't be fixed until tomorrow," Malajia said, removing her coat. "So we're sleeping here tonight."

"Sleeping *where*?" Mark frowned, gathering the cards into a pile. "Ain't nobody sleeping in my damn bed."

Malajia flopped on the couch. "Trust me, nobody *wants* to," she shot back.

"Of course, you're welcome to stay over. But we should probably check with our other two housemates," David stated.

"Are they here?" Malajia asked, David nodded. "Oh, I got this...Westley!" she hollered.

The dark-skinned guy hurried down the steps. "What's up Malajia?" he smiled.

"You and your roommate don't mind if me and my girls chill in your house overnight while our heater is being fixed, do you?" Malajia smiled back.

"Hell *no* we don't mind," Westley beamed. "Anybody want to share a bed with *me*?"

"No," the girls flatly responded in unison.

Mark sucked his teeth. "You always tryna get a chick to sleep in that nasty room of yours," he teased. Westley flipped Mark off, then headed back up to his room.

"Thanks guys," Alex gratefully slid in. "I brought a few extra blankets."

"So y'all just *assumed* that we were gonna agree to this?" Mark scoffed.

"Of course," Malajia boasted. "Who would turn down a

chance to spend the night with us?"

"Any man with some sense," Mark joked.

"It's a good thing you have none, huh?" Malajia countered.

Mark chuckled, giving her a nod, *good one*, he thought.

"I'll sleep on the floor. You ladies can have my bed," David offered, sitting on the couch next to Sidra.

"Aww David, that's sweet, but you don't have to do that," Alex said with a wave of her hand. "We can bunk on the floor."

"No the hell *we can't*," Malajia contradicted. "*I'll* take the bed David. Appreciate you homie."

David chuckled. "No problem, Mel."

Malajia looked at Alex and Emily. "Where *y'all* gonna sleep? 'Cause I'm not sharing," she teased. "And Josh will probably let Sid have *his* bed, so you two are about to be on that hard ass floor."

"Wait a minute. How are you just going to take the man's bed and not share?" Alex quibbled; Malajia shrugged. "Just for that, I'm gonna make *sure* I share that bed with you. My feet will be all in your face tonight."

Malajia turned her nose up. "Eww, those feet been in those boots all damn day," she realized. "Naw I'm cool. Mark, I'm bunking with *you*. Head to foot dawg."

"Naw, if you're in *my* bed it's gonna be dick to ass," Mark joked. "No chick gets in my bed unless I'm about to bang her."

The girls complained as Malajia dry heaved. "Ugh, I'm about to throw up," she complained.

Mark sucked his teeth, grabbing a chip. He turned his attention to Jason and Chasity. "Hey you two," he called, grabbing their attention. "I'm not playing with y'all tonight."

Jason looked perplexed. "What are you talking about?" he asked as Chasity sat on his lap.

"If y'all are gonna bang each other, then take that to Chasity's cold ass room," Mark commanded.

Chasity sucked her teeth. "You must not be getting any

because you keep bringing up somebody getting banged," she mocked, pushing hair over her shoulder.

Mark made a face at her. "You heard what I *said*, damn it," he reiterated. "Either *that* or wait 'till I'm sleep...or at least 'till I *pretend* to be sleep, like *last* time," he mumbled.

Both Chasity and Jason's head snapped towards him. "What?" Jason barked.

"The fuck you *mean* 'like last time'?" Chasity snapped. "What are you talking about?"

Stuffing another chip in his mouth, Mark smiled slyly. "The other night," he chortled, much to their embarrassment.

Jason put his hand over his face as Chasity's eyes widened. "What?!" she exclaimed. "You heard that?" she turned to Jason, "He heard us?"

"Mark, chill man," Jason warned.

"Did you know he was awake?" Chasity barked at Jason, much to his surprise.

"Baby come *on*, how would I have known?" Jason replied, trying his best to stifle a laugh. "That would be really weird if I did. I thought he was sleep. He was snoring and everything, *you* heard him."

Chasity was both furious and embarrassed. Jumping up from Jason's lap. "I *knew* I shouldn't have stayed. Listening to *your* horny ass," she hurled at Jason.

Jason couldn't help but find the situation amusing. "But...you know how I get when you wear tights," he teased. Mark snickered, loud.

Chasity rolled her eyes at Jason, then pointed at Mark. "Why the hell didn't you say anything, you nasty prick?" she shot at him.

"Hey, I didn't want to disturb y'all," Mark shrugged. "Plus...I was getting off on it," he joked, prompting disgusted complaints from the room.

"Dawg!" Jason snapped, slamming his hand on the table.

"Eww!" Chasity exclaimed.

"You're so damn gross," Malajia scoffed.

Laughing, Mark quickly put his hands up. "I'm joking,

I'm joking," he assured. "I wasn't doing anything but listening."

Chasity started making her way to the door. "You know what? I'd rather freeze in my *own* damn room than sleep in the same room with that pervert," she hissed.

"Chaz, it feels like ten below out there," Jason stated. "Don't leave. Mark won't mess with you anymore."

Mark smiled wide while eyeing the fuming Chasity. "Hey Chaz," he called. She glared at him. "You sound sexy as hell, even when you try to be quiet," he teased.

"Fuck you Mark," Chasity barked, flipping him off.

Jason rose from his seat as Chasity stormed out. Picking up a handful of chips from the bowl, he threw them at Mark. "Shut the fuck up sometimes," he fussed. "You play to goddamn much."

"Salt got in my eye!" Mark howled, rubbing his eyes frantically.

Ignoring Mark, Jason hurried after Chasity. "Baby! Come back, you know he's a jackass," he called after her, shutting the door.

Alex glared at Mark while he continued to rub his eyes. "You're so inappropriate," she scolded. "*And* disrespectful."

Mark looked at her. "Wow. That sounds like misguided anger to me," he perceived.

"What are you talking about *now*?" Alex frowned.

Sitting back in his seat, Mark folded his arms. "Are you sure you're mad at *me*?" he probed. "You sure you're not really mad at Eric 'cause you saw him talking to another girl earlier today?"

Alex quickly turned in her seat to face Malajia, who was sitting there with her mouth open. "Malajia, what the hell?!" she yelled.

Malajia looked at her with shock. "How do you know it was *me* who told?" she exclaimed, pointing to herself.

Alex stared at Malajia with a knowing look. She could have strangled her.

Malajia looked around. "Well... Damn it." She glowered

at Mark. "Boy, you keep ratting me out."

"To hell with you *and* your secrets," Mark dismissed
with a wave of his hand. "I'm starting shit all night long," he
promised.

"Don't be juvenile, Mark," Sidra chided.

Mark stared at her. "All…night…long," he repeated,
pausing briefly between each word.


"I can't believe you got me doing this," Malajia
complained, grabbing snow off the front step.

"Hey, you didn't want to do the *other* thing I suggested,"
Mark argued, scooping snow into a large bucket. "So now
we're doing *this*."

Malajia sucked her teeth. "You suggested that we have
sex!" she bellowed. "Don't nobody wanna have sex with
your dog ass." She wiped her hand on her pajama pants. "No
matter *how* horny I am."

"Come on Mel, we could've turned all the lights off and
I could've put a pillow case over your face," he joked.

Malajia rolled her eyes and flagged him with her hand.
"Whatever fool," she sneered, provoking a chuckle from him.

Grabbing a handful of snow, Mark signaled for Malajia
to bring the snow-filled bucket, upstairs.

Tip toeing through the hall, they slowly opened the door
to Josh and David's bedroom.

"It's hot as shit in here," Mark whispered, looking at his
sleeping friends. David and Josh, who had given their beds
up to Emily and Alex, were sprawled on the floor. The two
girls, with covers pulled up to their faces, slept soundly.

"They're gonna kill us," Malajia whispered as Mark
crept closer.

"Stop bitchin'," he shot back. He leaned close to David,
raised his snow-filled hand and slapped him in the face,
jerking him out of his sleep and leaving snow on his face.

"What the hell?" David barked. He jumped up and
lunged at Mark, who took off running out of the room.

Running from David, Mark shouted, "Now Mel!"

Doubling over with laughter, Malajia raised the bucket and hurled snow onto Josh and Alex, who was on the bottom bunk.

"What's going on?!" Alex hollered, sitting up. She jumped out of bed when she saw Malajia run. Alex chased her down the steps. "You play too damn much!"

Mark opened the front door, grabbed David—who was right on his heels—and shoved him outside, sending him falling into a pile of heavy snow.

"Come on man! I don't have any shoes on," David wailed, struggling to get up.

Josh jogged downstairs. "I swear, next semester I'm getting my house switched," he complained, helping David up.

"What is *wrong* with you two?" Alex fumed, brushing snow from her hair. "You're always doing stupid shit."

Grabbing a handful of snow from outside, Malajia watched Emily, who was awakened by the commotion, walk downstairs.

"What's going on?" Emily yawned.

"You're not exempt," Malajia laughed, throwing the snow at her face. Emily let out a scream as she stumbled back on the steps. She wiped her face with her pajama sleeve.

Watching Malajia fall to the floor laughing, Alex gritted her teeth. Alex grabbed snow from the step, walked over to Malajia, and smashed it in her mouth. "How do *you* like it?" she mocked, backing away.

Malajia quickly spat the snow out. "Oh my God! Don't ever put your hands on my mouth," she squealed, rubbing her mouth with the back of her hands. "You know you like to play with yourself."

"Seriously Malajia?!" Alex wailed, embarrassed. She turned and met the wide smiles from the three guys. "Oh grow up," she bit out.

The door to Mark and Jason's room opened and Sidra stuck her head out. With Jason spending the night in

Chasity's room, Sidra took full advantage of his empty bed. "What is all the noise about?" she tiredly asked. "It's like one thirty in the morning." She screamed when snow hit her face. "Mark, what the hell?!"

"You not exempt," Mark goaded, pointing at her.

Suddenly the group darted for their shoes, then to the front step to gather snow to throw at each other. They gathered anything they could to fill with snow.

In the middle of the commotion, Westley, still half asleep, stumbled down stairs. "What the hell are y'all down here doing?" he barked.

"Shut up," Mark hurled, throwing snow at his bare chest. As Westley stumbled back on the steps, Josh followed up with a snowball to his head. Both guys took off running outside as their angry housemate chased them.


Laying on Jason's chest, Chasity had just closed her eyes after trying to fall back to sleep for the past half hour. Hearing her cell phone ring, she let out a loud groan. Not looking at the caller ID, she answered. "What?"

"Whatcha doin'?" Malajia sang.

Chasity squinted, pulling the phone from her ear. She looked at the time. "Bitch it's two in the morning, what the hell do you *think* I was doing?"

"Probably what I *wish I* was doing right now," Malajia teased.

Chasity rolled her eyes. "What do you want Malajia?"

"You should come out and play in the snow with us."

Chasity stared at the phone blankly for several seconds, then hung up. "Dumbass," she mumbled, tossing the phone on the side of her. She barely had a chance to lay back down when the phone rang again.

"What does she *want*?" Jason complained, throwing his arm over his face.

"Stupid shit, as usual," Chasity replied, turning her ringer off. "Talking about playing in the damn snow."

Jason shook his head, then closed his eyes. He opened them back up when his phone rang. Knowing exactly who it was, he let out a loud sigh before answering. "Mark, I'm not coming outside," he stated evenly.

"Come on dawg, we havin' fun," Mark laughed.

"Bye Mark," Jason spat, hanging up. "I knew it. When Malajia gets stupid ideas like this, Mark isn't far behind," he said to Chasity.

Chasity didn't get a chance to respond because she was startled by a loud bang on her door. "Are they fuckin' serious?" she barked, jumping out of bed. Snatching the door open, she gave a piercing look to Malajia, who was standing there smiling.

"Heeeyyy pretty," Malajia teased, reaching out to touch some of Chasity's disheveled hair.

Chasity smacked her hand away. "I should choke the shit out of you."

"Now why would you do that?" Malajia grinned. "I'm just trying to get you to join in the fun."

"Nobody wants to play in the damn snow," Chasity bit out, folding her arms.

"Come on, everybody *else* is out there," Malajia persisted. "Hell, half the damn clusters are out there."

"Malajia, tell Mark to stop calling my damn phone," Jason called from the bed.

Hearing commotion from inside, Malajia tried to poke her head in the room, but was blocked by Chasity's arm. "Stop being a bitch and let me in," Malajia then smiled when Chasity wouldn't budge. "Is he naked? Can I see?"

"Move, move!" Chasity snapped, nudging the laughing Malajia away from her door.

Before Malajia could say anything else, Jason, fully dressed, opened the door fully and walked out. "I'm gonna bury Mark in that fuckin' snow," he fumed.

"What's the matter with you?" Chasity frowned, folding her arms across her chest.

"He sent me a picture of my towels being buried in the

snow," Jason said, opening the front door. "He plays too much and I'm gonna kill him."

Chasity shook her head. "Damn it," she admonished. "Now I *have* to go out there to stop him from killing that jackass."

Malajia nodded happily. "Yep, sure do. Come on, throw your boots and coat on," she urged. "No need to put on real clothes, everybody is out in their pajamas anyway."

"Whatever," Chasity grumbled, turning back into her room.

After ten minutes of stalling, Chasity finally emerged from the house with Malajia. Bundling her coat up to her neck, she shook her head seeing many of her cluster mates, including her friends, playing in the snow. Some students were making makeshift sleds out of garbage can lids, some built snowmen, and others participated in the most common activity—snow ball fights.

"How in the hell did this happen?" Chasity asked, shivering slightly.

Malajia giggled. "Mark started running into people's houses and throwing snow on them," she recalled. "He's a whole fool. Luckily, he knows almost everybody in these damn clusters."

"They should've smacked him," Chasity scoffed. She let out a sigh when she saw Jason chase and tackle Mark into a pile of snow. "God," she groaned.

"Mark's face is gonna get frost bite," Malajia laughed, watching Jason scoop snow in Mark's face.

"Jason knows his hands are cold as shit with no damn gloves on," Chasity said in an aside to Malajia. Malajia snickered.

"Jase chill, this snow is cold dawg!" Mark shouted, trying to shield his face. "Cut it out."

"I already told you to stop touching my shit," Jason seethed, stumbling back in the snow.

"*I* didn't even throw the towels outside," Mark argued, wiping the snow from his face. "*Josh* did."

Before Jason could react, Josh ran past and smacked Mark with one of the snow-covered towels, causing Jason to bust out laughing at the look on Mark's face. "Josh! What the hell was *that* for?"

"Stop lying," Josh scolded, tossing the towel on the ground. "You know good and damn well *you* were the one who grabbed all of his towels out of his closet," he added. "Talking about 'I bet you he comes out *now*'."

Mark's eyes widened as he looked at Jason, who was glaring at him. Mark laughed nervously. "Um... See what happened was..." he stammered.

Jason held his angered stare, he was not in the laughing mood.

"Fine, I did it," Mark admitted.

"Yeah, no shit," Jason hissed.

"I'll wash the towels tomorrow, damn," Mark promised.

"No, you'll buy me *new* ones tomorrow," Jason demanded, pointing at him.

"Fine," Mark mumbled.

Satisfied, Jason walked away; but not before he hit Mark with a snow ball. "Damn Jase!" Mark hollered.


"Sidra, where are you going?" Emily called, laughing.

Sidra stomped her way back to the guys' front door. Her coat was covered in snow. "I'm sick of this shit. I don't even know why I came out here," she fumed. "That was the fourth time I fell in that mess."

Emily wiped her snow-covered gloved hands on her coat, removing some of the snow. Although she would much rather be sleeping after midnight, she was enjoying playing outside with her friends and classmates. Being a part of the fun was something that she avoided while living with her mother, and although Emily missed her, she didn't miss the hold that her mother had had on her.

Chasity and Malajia approached Emily, snapping her out of her mental trance. Emily quickly picked up snow and backed away. "Don't try it you two," she cautioned. "I have snow and I'm not afraid to use it."

Holding a hand behind her back, Chasity rolled her eyes. "Emily, I'm not even playing in this shit," she huffed. "I'm about to go back in the house."

"Yeah and I've had *enough* of playing," Malajia added, holding a hand behind her back as well. "I already got my ass bombed with snow."

Emily lowered her defenses and her hand, dropping the snow on the ground. "Oh," she said. "Yeah, I'm about to go back inside—"

"Now Chaz!" Malajia shouted, interrupting Emily's train of thought.

Emily was stunned when Chasity and Malajia pulled their snowball filled hands from behind their backs and threw them at her. Emily tried to run, but ended up stumbling and falling.

Chasity shook her head as she laughed. "Still naïve," she teased.

"Still *mean*," Emily retorted, somewhat amused.

Out of the corner of her eye, Chasity saw Alex approaching her quickly. Moving aside, Alex stumbled past her and bumped into Malajia, who nudged Alex with her shoulder, causing Alex to fall in the snow next to Emily.

"Alex, what was your slow ass tryna do?" Malajia asked, voice laced with laughter.

Struggling to sit up, Alex brushed snow out of her hair. "I saw y'all bomb Em with snowballs, so I was trying to come help."

"Nice try," Malajia mocked, folding her arms.

"I appreciate the gesture," Emily giggled, standing up. She reached her hand out to help Alex up.

Alex smiled gratefully at Emily. She brushed the snow

from her pajama pants, then turned to Chasity. "I'm surprised you didn't kick snow in my face while I was on the ground," she said.

"Trust me, I was tempted," Chasity bit out.

"You ready to accept my apology now?" Alex wondered, hopeful.

"Hell *no* she's not," Malajia cut in. "How you gonna grab somebody's hair 'cause *you* mad and expect everything to be cool?"

Alex sighed heavily. "You may not accept it, but I'm sorry," she directed at Chasity. "For the shoe throwing, the hair grab... I was wrong on *so* many levels."

Chasity folded her arms. She didn't say anything, she just held an icy gaze.

"I know that I get on you girls all the time for childish behavior, and then *I* turn around and do the same thing," Alex continued, shameful.

"Yeah," Malajia agreed "You *have* been acting like a big hippopotamus lately." Her response was met with perplexity.

"You mean hypocrite?" Alex corrected.

Malajia shook her head. "No, I meant *hippopotamus*," she repeated. "I know what I said, fat ass."

Emily put her hands over her face, trying to hide the fact that she was laughing.

Chasity couldn't help but laugh. Leave it to Malajia to cut the tension by saying something silly.

Malajia too broke into laughter. "That was a good one, you can't even lie," she said to Alex.

Alex put her hand up. "Fine Malajia, you got it," she agreed. "So?" she pressed to Chasity. "Can we *please* put this behind us? I feel terrible."

Chasity pondered Alex's plea. "Let me think about it," she said finally.

Alex closed her eyes and sighed. "I guess, I—" She shrieked when snow hit her face. Opening her eyes, Alex brushed the snow from her face. "Oh my God Chasity!" she screamed when Chasity threw another snowball at her, hitting her and sending her stumbling back into the snow.

"Alex, why you always falling?!" Malajia barked at her. "Goofy ass."

Alex sat in the snow, cold and defeated. "Really? That was you *thinking* about it?" she spat at Chasity.

"A much better alternative to me cracking your face, huh?" Chasity goaded, brushing snow from her glove-covered hands.

Alex sucked her teeth. "Whatever."

# Chapter 28

"If I have to write another damn paper. I'm gonna slap somebody," Chasity groaned, putting her head in her hands.

"Well, as long as it's not *me*, knock yourself out baby," Jason joked, eyes not leaving his textbook. The semester was nearing its end, and that meant finals. Jason and Chasity, trying to take advantage of the quiet in the girls' house, were working at the dining room table.

Raising her head, Chasity angrily tapped the keys of her laptop. "This is the seventh paper that I had to write for this dumbass class," she fumed.

"Well it *is* English Lit," Jason reminded, writing in his notebook. "That class is nothing *but* papers."

"Yes, I know that Jason," Chasity barked, running her hands through her hair.

Jason looked up from his book. Knowing that her attitude was more than likely just stress over finals, he wasn't surprised or angry. He frowned with concern when she closed her eyes and pinched the bridge of her nose. "You okay?" he asked.

"No, I have a headache," she huffed, rubbing her forehead. "I swear to God, I'd rather deal with cramps over this bullshit."

"You should probably go lay down."

"I will when I finish this draft," she promised, typing once again.

Jason looked back down at his book. "Well, it seems that things are back to normal with you now," he chuckled after a moment of quiet.

"Meaning what?" Chasity wondered.

"You're no longer missing periods," he replied. "Don't get me wrong, I hate that you feel terrible, but still."

Chasity felt a chill run through her. That was the last thing that she wanted to be reminded of. "Yeah," she mumbled.

"It's weird though. You've been stressed out plenty of times since we've been together, and that hasn't happened before," he continued.

*Fuckin' drop it!* Chasity fumed, staring at her screen.

"I mean, it's been late before but you haven't missed one."

"I thought you came over to study, not talk about my goddamn cycles," Chasity fussed, shooting him a glare.

Jason sighed. "Fine, I'll drop it," he said.

As Jason focused back on his studies, Chasity glanced up at him. She felt bad. Jason was just concerned about her, and she was giving him attitude in return. The guilt of her secret was eating at her, and because of it, she was lashing out.

Chasity stood from her seat. "You know what, I think I *am* going to lay down," she announced.

Jason began gathering his books. "Okay, I'll leave."

"No, you don't have to go," she protested. "Stay and finish studying."

Not really wanting to pack up and leave, when he was already in the groove of studying, Jason smiled gratefully.

Chasity closed her laptop and went into her room

without saying another word.

Sitting in the cafeteria, Malajia squirted ketchup on her cheese burger, while gesturing to her friends. "I know what we can do for winter break this year," she said, then took a bite of the burger. "For a *week*, anyway."

"What would *that* be?" Sidra asked, cutting her lasagna. "And don't let this be like *last* winter break, where you booked that ski trip at the raggedy motel."

Malajia cut her eye at Sidra. "You ain't even have to bring that up," she sneered. "Anyway, *no* it's not a ski trip. I was thinking that we can just stay here in Virginia."

Mark picked up a french fry and sucked his teeth. "Man, ain't nobody trying to stay on this dry ass campus for winter break."

Malajia giggled. "No fool. I don't mean on campus," she clarified. "I was thinking we can rent a lodge near the river."

Josh shot her a confused look. "But…it's *winter* time," he complained, sitting his cup of juice down. "Why would we want to stay near a river?"

"Yeah, it's not like we can get in the water or anything," David chimed in.

Mark curled his lip up. "Why would you get in that dirty ass river, even if it *wasn't* cold?" he scoffed. "It's probably dead fish in there and shit."

David rolled his eyes. "I wasn't really—never mind," he dismissed.

"Fine, if not the river, we can stay by the mountains," Malajia suggested, bringing the focus back.

"It's even *colder* up *there*," Sidra criticized.

Frustrated with the complaints, Malajia slapped her hand on the table. "You're missing the point," she snarled, voice raised.

Mark laughed at her reaction.

"What *is* your point then, Malajia?" Sidra spat.

"The point is, that we get to spend some of the winter

break *together*," Malajia proposed. "I looked up some lodges about an hour or so from here...they're pretty big."

"Which also means, *expensive*," Josh put in.

"Split between *nine* of us won't be that bad," Malajia pointed out. She picked up her phone and frowned at it.

"*I* actually don't have a problem with the plan," Mark stated. "It'll be no different than staying on a ski resort. It was cold *then* too." He took a sip of his soda. "It beats sitting at home hearing my mom bitch at me all day."

Sidra chuckled. "If you would stop irritating her, then she wouldn't *need* to bitch at you."

Mark pointed a warning finger at Sidra. "Hey...hush," he demanded. He then turned his attention to Malajia. "What website can we go on to check out those houses?"

Malajia, who was vigorously texting on her phone, did not respond.

Mark balled up his napkin and tossed it at her, hitting her on the chest with it. "Hey!" he called.

Startled, Malajia smacked the tissue off her. "Boy that had mustard on it," she snapped, examining the stain on her sweater. "You play too much."

"I was trying to get your damn attention," Mark bit back. "You always on that phone. Who you texting anyway?" he asked, curious.

"None of your damn business," Malajia sneered, standing from the table. "I'll send you guys the link later. I have to go."

"You're not even finished your food," Sidra pointed out, gesturing to Malajia's half-eaten burger and fries. "You seem antsy, are you okay?"

"Y'all are asking me too many damn questions," Malajia bit out, slinging her purse on her shoulder. "I'm cool, see you later."

The remaining group looked at each other once Malajia departed. They were confused about Malajia's shift in mood. Mark put his hands up. "Hey, that wasn't my fault," he threw out. "Her face got all sour when she picked up that phone."

"Nobody is blaming you sweetie," Sidra assured, scooping up some of her food. "For *once*."


Irritated, Malajia hurried down the steps of the cafeteria. Feeling like her legs were going to give way, she made a beeline for a large tree. Leaning her back against it and looking around to make sure no one was in ear shot, she dialed a number on her phone and put it to her ear. She ran a hand through her hair as she waited for the person to pick up.

"I thought I told you to stop texting me," she barked once they answered. "No, I told you that I was done... Do you want me to call the police? Is that what you want? Because you're driving me to that... Leave me alone.... What?... No, I don't think that—" Malajia closed her eyes. Placing a hand on the top of her head while listening. "Look...I'll think ab—I gotta go."

She hung up the phone and stared at it. Sighing, Malajia dropped her arm to her side and slowly walked off.


Pulling her hair up into a ponytail, Alex let out a groan. She'd been in the library for hours trying to retain information for her upcoming finals. However, her thoughts were elsewhere, and it was frustrating her.

"I can't wait until this damn semester is over," she mumbled to herself, highlighting lines in her book.

"Is this seat taken?" a deep voice asked, snapping her out of her trance.

She looked up, face void of any smile. "Nope, all yours," she said, pointing to the seat. She looked back down at her book as Eric sat in the seat across from her.

Setting his books on the table, Eric stared at her. "Why haven't you returned any of my phone calls?" he asked.

Looking up again, Alex rubbed her head with her hand. "I've been busy Eric," she ground out. "Sex has been the *furthest* thing from my mind."

Eric frowned, he was clearly insulted. "That *wasn't* why I was calling you," he hissed. "I wanted to hang out. I thought that we were at least friends."

"Yeah, I thought so *too*," she mumbled.

"Are you upset with me or something?"

Clearly Alex wasn't going to get any studying done with Eric there. She closed her book, sat back in her seat and folded her arms. "Why didn't you tell me that you were talking to someone else?"

Eric looked puzzled. "What are you talking about?"

"Don't play stupid," Alex snarled. "I thought we agreed that if we met someone else while we were messing with *each other* that we would have the courtesy to let the other person know."

"Yes, we did agree to that."

"*Obviously* you forgot," Alex sniped.

"I haven't forgotten *anything*," Eric shot back. "If I met someone, I'd tell you."

"Stop lying Eric," Alex snapped, slamming her hand on the table, much to the annoyance of library attendees.

"Shhhh," several students hissed.

"You need to calm down," Eric advised, putting his hands up.

"And *you* need to stop acting like a little boy and tell the truth," she countered. "I saw you talking to some girl."

"*What* girl?"

Alex rolled her eyes. *He's really going to play stupid.* "A week ago, I saw you talking to some girl outside the library."

Eric looked confused.

"The day that we had that big snow storm," she reminded.

Eric stared at her, his memory jogging. "Alex…she was just a classmate," he claimed, tone calm.

"Oh please," Alex scoffed.

"No, I'm serious," he insisted. "She's in my marketing class and she was in my project group."

Alex unfolded her arms and looked down at her hands. She was embarrassed by her mistake *and* her reaction.

"We had just wrapped up a group meeting and were just talking about some extra details... That was all."

"Oh my God," Alex groaned, putting her face in her hands. "I feel so stupid."

"Well...you *should*," Eric agreed.

"I deserved that." she looked at him. "I'm sorry for acting like that."

"You should've said something to me *that day* and this could have been cleared up," he chastised.

"You're right...I just... I got jealous." She sighed. "Even though I really have no *right* to."

"You do."

"No, I *don't* actually," Alex contradicted. "You're not my boyfriend and I made it clear that you were free to do what you wanted."

"Even if I *was* dating her and told you from the beginning, would you still have been mad?" Eric asked, already feeling like he knew the answer to that question.

Alex was silent for a moment. She had to think about that question, and in doing so, she came to a realization about her feelings. No matter what Eric would have said to her, she still would have been upset because she not only liked him, but she cared for him.

"Yes, I would've," she answered finally. "I don't think we can sleep together anymore."

"Um...Okay."

"Not that I don't *want* to," she quickly amended. "It's because I *can't*. I thought that I was built to do this casual sex thing, but I'm not," she admitted. "I caught feelings and it's making me crazy... I'm not acting like myself and I don't like it."

"If you caught feelings Alex, then just date me," Eric suggested. "You know I want us to date *anyway*."

"I *can't*, Eric. I do like you but I meant what I said; I don't want to be in a relationship," she responded.

"Relationships are distracting and I can't afford to be distracted right now. School is my priority and I need to focus... I'm sorry."

Eric sighed. "Fair enough...can't say that I'm not disappointed."

Alex looked down at the table.

"But...I do understand," he added.

Alex smiled, grateful. "Thank you."

Eric nodded. "So... does this *at least* leave us as friends?"

"Of course it does," Alex beamed. "Just without the *benefits*."

"Okay then," Eric said, standing from his seat. "I'll see you later."

Alex waved, watching him walk away. *God, I hope I don't regret that decision.*

Malajia nervously tapped her foot, staring at the glass of water in front of her. She'd been waiting at the bistro in center city Paradise Valley for fifteen minutes.

"What the hell am I doing?" she asked herself. That question she had been asking herself ever since she made the decision to call Tyrone back a day ago, agreeing to meet with him. Now waiting, fear was taking over.

Malajia fidgeted in her seat as she ran her hands over her hair. "Forget this," she muttered, rising from her seat. She didn't get a chance to leave, because Tyrone walked over to her table.

"Hey," Tyrone greeted, hands in his pockets.

Malajia slowly sat back down. She glanced away when he sat in the seat across from her.

"Thank you for meeting with me," Tyrone said, removing the knit cap from his head. "You look pretty, as always."

"Why did you ask me here Tyrone?" Malajia spat out. She was in no mood for his compliments or small talk.

"I wanted to see you," he replied softly. "To um...talk to you...I need—"

"I thought I told you not to contact me anymore," Malajia hissed. "From the time that you started texting me *last* week, I told you that."

Tyrone looked down at his hands. "Baby, I know—"

"You don't get to call me 'baby'," she snapped, folding her arms. "You lost that privilege when you damn near broke my ribs."

"I know what I did to you was wrong," Tyrone said, nervously rubbing his hand on his head. "I'm not in a good space."

"You could've *killed* me, do you understand that?" Malajia barked. She felt tears fill her eyes. She was so angry, at him and at herself for even allowing him in her presence again. "I still can't wrap my head around what you did to me."

Tyrone looked like he could break down at any given moment. "If I could take back everything, I swear to God I would," he sputtered. "Every disrespectful thing that I said, the things that I *did*... I will apologize a million times if you need me to."

Malajia rolled her eyes as a few tears spilled. Tyrone was spewing the same garbage that he always did when he wanted her to take him back. "Save the bullshit, Tyrone," she sneered, rising from her seat.

Tyrone stared as Malajia grabbed her purse. Feeling desperate, he tried to reach for her hand, but she jerked away from him.

"I swear, I'll scream," she threatened.

"I'm not trying to hurt you," Tyrone assured, putting his hands up in surrender. "Please don't leave... I need someone to talk to, things are fucked up in my life right now."

"Yeah? I don't give a fuck," Malajia threw back.

"Malajia...I love you and I miss you," Tyrone blurted out, tears filling his eyes.

Malajia halted her departure. Hearing "I love you" come

from Tyrone's mouth was something that Malajia had wanted to hear ever since first meeting him. But after what happened, the words didn't mean anything to her…at least she thought they didn't.

"I don't know what to say to that," Malajia said, looking at him. "I don't know how to *believe* that, coming from you."

"I don't blame you," he replied. "But…I'm willing to prove it… I'm getting myself some help. For my temper, my jealously, my violence…I'm actually starting therapy."

Malajia narrowed her eyes at him. "You don't strike me as the therapy type," she ground out.

"I'm *not*, but I'm willing to do it for *you*…for *us*," he replied, removing a card from his jeans pocket. "I have an appointment tomorrow at three." He handed Malajia the card. "I would like for you to go with me."

Staring at the appointment card, Malajia didn't know what to feel. "I can't. I have class."

Tyrone didn't mask his disappointment. "Oh," he sulked. "I just thought that you being there will show you that I really *am* making an effort to change."

Handing him back the card, Malajia adjusted the purse strap on her shoulder. "I'll think about it," she stated flatly. "I have to go."

Tyrone just sat there as Malajia walked out of the restaurant.

Malajia let out a long breath once she got outside. She looked down at her hands; they were shaking. So many emotions were going through her; anger, sympathy, confusion—shaking her head, she made a beeline for the bus stop.


The twenty-minute ride back to campus failed to put Malajia's mind at ease. All she could see was Tyrone's sad face and hear his somber voice. She felt bad for the mental space that he was in, but still couldn't forget what he had done to her.

Sighing as she approached her front door, she stuck her key in and turned the knob. Her thoughts were overtaken by the sound of her friends.

"Yo, I swear I'm switching roommates next semester," Jason complained, picking up a slice of pizza. "I'm so sick of your freeloading ass."

"What did I do *now*?" Mark exclaimed, picking up a pack of cookies from the kitchen counter.

Alex shot Mark a puzzled look. "Seriously? You really don't know what you did?"

Mark shook his head as Malajia sat her purse on the couch. "What is all the noise about?" Malajia asked, sitting on the arm of the couch.

Josh gestured to Mark. "Mark is pissing everyone off again," he chortled.

"I'm not surprised," Malajia sighed, examining her nails. She was in no mood for petty arguments. She had way too much on her mind.

Mark slammed the cookie pack back on the counter. "Mel, we looked at the lodge that you want us to rent over break," he informed, putting his hand up. "And all I did was make one little suggestion, then everybody got all hype and shit."

"You suggested that the *girls* pay most of the fee for the house," Sidra chimed in, breaking her pizza into small pieces.

Malajia scrunched her face up at Sidra. "Why do you do that to your damn pizza?" she griped. "Just pick the shit up and *bite* it."

Sidra scowled. "Leave me alone about how I eat my damn food," she demanded. "Did you hear what I just said?"

"Yeah, I heard that bullshit and Mark, you're out of your damn mind if you think that's gonna happen," Malajia replied.

"Why should the guys split the cost evenly, when we never get to sleep in any beds anyway?" Mark argued. "You girls *always* take the damn beds."

"Man up and pay up," Jason ground out.

Mark cut his eye at Jason. "Says the guy who is *guaranteed* to sleep in a damn bed," he jeered, pointing to Chasity who, suffering with another headache, sat in one of the accent chairs with her head leaned back.

"Leave me out of this please," Chasity responded dryly.

"Lunar Lodge has *plenty* of space and huge beds," Alex said. "I'm sure we can come to an agreement on who can share a bed with who."

"*I'm* not sharing *shit*. This was my idea," Malajia protested. "*Y'all* better figure that out. Nobody's feet is gonna be in my damn face all week."

Alex flagged Malajia with her hand. "We'll work it out somehow," she resolved. "Just know that everybody is putting in the same amount of money. Nobody is getting over."

Mark made a face at Alex. "You just hype 'cause your broke ass *finally* got some money to contribute," he snapped, incited snickers from the room. "Coming up in here smelling like cheese, tryna put your foot down and shit."

"Damn!" Malajia erupted with laughter. Leave it to her friends to bring her out of her bad mood.

Furious, Alex flipped Mark the finger. "Shut up," she barked, then sniffed her uniform shirt. "I don't even *smell* like cheese," she grunted. Hearing her friends laugh around her, Alex stomped her foot on the floor. "It wasn't that damn funny!"

# Chapter 29

Emily rubbed her temples with the tips of her fingers. "Come on girl, stay focused," she encouraged herself. She sipped her hot chocolate then took a bite of pretzel, as she highlighted some notes in her notebook. Her first final was a week away, and she was determined to do her best.

Her cell phone rang while she was highlighting. She picked up the phone without looking at it. "Hello?"

"How's it going sweetie?" A deep voice responded.

Emily smiled at the sound of her father's voice. "Hi Daddy. How was your business trip?"

"It was the same as all of the others. Boring work," Mr. Harris sighed. "I have another one the week after Christmas. That one will have me gone for two weeks."

"Oh," Emily replied, tone dry.

"I hate that I won't be able to be here for your whole winter break."

"Daddy, I told you before that you don't have to feel guilty about leaving for work," Emily assured. "That may have bothered everybody else, but it never bothered *me*."

Emily remembered the many times that her father had to travel for work when she was younger. Being a sought-after architect, her father traveled often. Emily recalled how her mother would complain and drag her and her siblings into the drama and arguments. She couldn't help but be relieved when her parents divorced.

"I appreciate that honey," Mr. Harris replied.

"Besides, I wanted to ask you something anyway," Emily alluded, running her hand over her hair. "My friends are planning on renting a lodge here in Virginia the week after Christmas...I was wondering if I could go."

"Sure, I don't have a problem with that. How much do you need?"

Emily smiled, *that was easy.* "Thanks. I have to check the prices again, but the cost isn't bad since it'll be split between nine of us."

"Okay, just let me know." There was a long pause on Mr. Harris's end. "Em, I thought I should tell you that your mother called me the other day."

Emily stiffened. "Um...what did she say?"

"She found a few of your things that you left at her house and wanted to know when she could mail them to me."

Emily frowned. "So...did she ask about *me*?"

"No sweetie, she didn't," Mr. Harris admitted. "I tried filling her in on how you were doing and she rushed me off the phone. I was debating on if I should tell you that, but I know that you've been wondering if she was okay, so I wanted you to know that I heard from her."

Emily was too angry and hurt to care how her mother was feeling. "I can't believe she's really acting like that," Emily fumed. "Like I don't even exist...all because I grew up." Emily tossed her highlighter on her desk. "I've been sitting here stressing myself out over her and she doesn't even *care*."

"I'm sorry Emily. I love your mother, but she has always been dramatic," Mr. Harris stated bluntly. "I'm sure she'll come around one of these days."

"At this point, I don't even care," Emily hissed.

"I know you don't mean that. It's not in your nature not to care," he contradicted. "But please, try not to let it stress you out too much."

Rubbing the bridge of her nose with her finger tips, Emily let out a long sigh. "Okay," she mumbled. "I have to get back to studying, so can I just call you back later?"

"Sure."

Emily hung up her phone and sat it back on her desk. She was hurt, angry; she wanted to cry, but wouldn't allow herself to do it. "No, study Emily...just study," she sadly coaxed herself, picking her highlighter back up.


Malajia zipped up her black high-heeled boots in a hurry, then grabbed her scarf and quickly wrapped it around her neck. "God, I am so late," she complained to herself, glancing at her watch.

"Malajia, can I use your laptop?" Alex asked, sticking her head in the room.

Startled, Malajia spun around. "Girl, why don't you knock?" she spat, pulling her coat from the closet.

Alex sucked her teeth. "I know *you're* not talking," she shot back. "*Nobody* in this house has *any* privacy with you around, barging in whenever you feel like it."

"Yeah, yeah," Malajia muttered, putting her coat on.

"So, can I borrow your laptop?" Alex pressed. "I need to finish my paper, and I kinda don't want to walk across campus to the computer lab."

"My laptop is broke," Malajia informed, touching up her lipstick in the mirror.

"Damn it," Alex grumbled, running her hand through her hair. "Why does your stuff always break?"

"'Cause I buy cheap shit," Malajia admitted.

Alex sighed. "Sid and Chaz are the only other ones who have laptops, and they're in class."

"I know where Sid's laptop is, I'm sure she wouldn't mind you using it," Malajia said.

Alex shook her head. "That may be true, but I'd rather ask her first."

"Shit you better than *me*," Malajia joked. "I use her stuff all the time without asking."

"Which would explain why she's always cursing you out," Alex laughed.

"I pay that no mind. She already knows the deal," Malajia countered. "Go use David's laptop. I'm sure he's home, Hell if not his, use *Jason's*. Those guys are always over here eating up our food; you better go over there and use something of *theirs*."

Alex shook her head in amusement. "True." She stared as Malajia gave herself a once over in the mirror. "Where are you going, all dolled up?" she asked.

"None of your business mother," Malajia jeered.

"You've been sneaking off quite a bit lately," Alex pointed out. "Like you're going on dates or something."

Paying Alex's pestering no mind, Malajia walked out of her room. "Go write your paper," she suggested, walking down the steps.

Malajia stepped off the bus. Bundling her coat to her neck, she trotted up the steps of the building that she had visited the previous week. Walking through the door, she smiled when she saw Tyrone sitting on a couch, flipping through a magazine.

He looked up and caught her stare. Smiling back, he rose from his seat as she walked over. "I didn't think you would make this session," he said, hugging her.

"Why would you think that?" she wondered, removing her coat and taking a seat.

Tyrone sat back down. "I don't know. I just didn't know what to think after the *first* one," he admitted. "I thought you would've gotten scared off."

Malajia picked up a magazine. "It's not like I haven't seen you after that session," she reminded. "So obviously I'm not scared."

Alex was right; Malajia was in fact sneaking off lately,

to hang out with Tyrone. After accompanying him to his first therapy session a week ago, and seeing the changes that he was trying to make, Malajia met with him a few more times after. Even though it was only for the occasional cup of coffee or a quick bite to eat, she had no intention of letting any of her friends know...especially Chasity.

"I know, but—" Before Tyrone could say another word, the receptionist informed them that the therapist was ready to see them. Holding his hand out for Malajia, he took a deep breath. "You ready?"

Setting the magazine down, Malajia placed her hand in his, and they walked into the room.


Emerging from the building once the hour-long session was over, Malajia looked at her watch. "I need to hurry if I'm going to make this next bus," she said.

"Do you *have* to go now?" Tyrone asked, shoving his hands in his coat pockets.

"I kinda do," she replied. "Finals are next week so I really have to study." Malajia then chuckled to herself. "Wow, what a difference two years makes. Freshman year I couldn't care less about studying."

Tyrone forced a smile as he looked at her. He really wasn't in the best of moods. He felt that this therapy session was a bit too intense for him. "Um okay," he mumbled.

"Speaking of finals, I may not be able to come with you to your session next week," Malajia informed, pushing some hair behind her ears.

"That's fine," Tyrone replied with a shrug. "Will I be able to see you before you leave campus, at least? I know after finals are over everyone will be leaving."

"Maybe we can meet for lunch or something before I leave," she proposed. She was trying to keep Tyrone at a distance while he went through therapy. Meeting him here and there was okay. But deep down, and as crazy as she felt that she was, Malajia wanted to spend more time with him.

Tyrone gently adjusted the red scarf around Malajia's neck. "That'll work," he crooned. "I'll call you later." Malajia nodded, then hurried off.

Sitting on a cold bench outside of the History and Culture building, Mark stared blankly into space. He was mentally drained from taking his history final; he didn't even notice Chasity stopping in front of him.

"Why are you sitting there looking like an entire idiot?" Chasity asked, clutching her books to her chest.

Mark slowly directed his gaze to her, blinking slowly. "Yo...I just spent an hour in that damn classroom failing my history final," he slurred.

Chasity frowned. "Boy, are you drunk?" she sneered. "You look crazy."

"I wish I *was* drunk," he snarled, rubbing his face with his hands. "At least I wouldn't feel so bad." He shook his head. "Chaz, why you ain't tell me that the test was so damn hard?"

"Was I *supposed* to?" she shot back smartly.

"Hell yeah. You're supposed to look out for the cookout," he argued. "You took that test *yesterday*. You let me walk in there unprepared."

Chasity stared at Mark; she wondered why she wasted her time talking to him. "I swear, every minute I talk to you I lose a brain cell," she jeered.

Mark sucked his teeth, flagging her with his hand. "Maybe if you looked out, you wouldn't be *losing* brain cells with this conversation," he mumbled.

Chasity's retort was interrupted when Alex trotted over to them.

"I just finished my statistics final and I *know* I aced it," Alex gushed.

"Good for you," Chasity replied flatly.

"I practiced those formulas all last week. I don't even think I got one answer wrong," Alex boasted, clasping her hands together. "Come to think of it, I think I aced *all* of my finals. How great—"

"Oh my God, will you shut your big ass *up*?" Mark snapped, taking Alex by surprise and making Chasity snicker.

"What the hell is *your* damn problem?!" Alex hollered.

"Nobody wants to hear about you passing your dumb ass finals," Mark shot back. "You all loud and shit."

Alex narrowed her eyes at him. "Spoken like someone who probably *failed* every damn final," she sniped, folding her arms.

Mark hopped up from his seat. "You know what…I probably *did*," he admitted. "But you don't hear me bragging all loud about it."

"Why would you brag—I can't. Mark, you make my head hurt," Chasity ground out before walking away.

Alex shook her head at Mark, who was staring at her with a stupid look. "Come on fool," she urged. "Let's get out of this cold."

Mark sighed as he solemnly walked along side of her.


"Two more finals to go and this damn semester is over," Sidra mused, stretching out on the couch.

"This semester went so fast," Alex slid in, putting her hair into a high ponytail. "Before you know it, we'll be seniors."

After a long day of tests, Alex and Sidra walked over to the guys' house to wait while dinner was being prepared.

"Man, fuck this semester," Mark scoffed, grabbing a bottle of juice from the refrigerator. "I'm just looking forward to going to that lodge over winter break."

Alex chuckled. "You still bitter about failing that history final, huh?"

"Fuck that final," Mark hissed, leaning against the counter.

Jason glared at Mark while flipping a piece of fried fish

in a large skillet. "Mark, can you stop standing around and help with this dinner?"

"What am I supposed to do?" Mark asked. "Y'all know I can't cook."

"Chop up the stuff for the salad at least," Josh commanded, pouring cake batter into a bunt cake pan. "You're standing around doing nothing, but will be the first one to grab a plate."

"So!" Mark bellowed. "Why are we even cooking anyway?"

"Because *we* are always cooking for *you* guys and now it's *your* turn," Alex informed from the living room.

Mark threw his head back and groaned loudly. "Why am I *not* surprised that Alex was the one to say something," he huffed, grabbing a head of lettuce off of the counter.

"Shut up and wash that damn lettuce," Alex teased.

As Mark washed the head of lettuce in the sink, he mumbled, "I'll spit on this damn lettuce, how about that?"

"If you do that I will punch you in the back of the head," Jason calmly threatened, placing a perfectly fried piece of fish on to a paper towel covered plate.

"Oh shit, you heard that?" Mark laughed.

"I'm standing right behind you," Jason stated flatly.

The door opened and Chasity walked in, with Emily following close behind.

"Hey everybody," Emily greeted, removing her coat. "It smells good in here."

"It sure does," Alex agreed, flipping through the channels on the television with the remote.

Chasity walked into the kitchen and placed a bag down on the counter. "Here is y'all stupid liquor," she spat, removing her coat. "Don't ever send me to find anything that Malajia hides again."

Jason chuckled. "That bad, huh?"

"Yes!" Chasity exclaimed. "The bitch told me that she bought a bottle and put it in her closet. What she *didn't* tell me was that it was in the closet, hidden in a suitcase, wrapped in two big ass towels, with a bunch of sheets covering it."

Josh busted out laughing. "Damn, what was she hiding it from?"

"Oh, she's paranoid that an RA is gonna do room checks when she's not there and find it," Sidra said with a wave of her hand. "The girl is nuts."

"You should've heard Chaz. She was cussing out Malajia like she was standing right there," Emily added, amused. "I swear the profanity combinations that you come up with are classic."

Chasity rolled her eyes as Mark removed the bottle from the bag. "Don't nobody want this nasty ass vodka," he barked, turning his nose up. "I told her to get *tequila.* Where's the damn tequila?"

Chasity looked at Mark as if she was about to choke him. "You better *drink* that shit!" she snapped, pointing to the bottle.

Jason tried to suppress a laugh at Chasity's outburst; he was unsuccessful. "Go sit down and relax babe," he insisted. "Don't let his stupid self stress you out."

"I was just talking about tequila," Mark mumbled.

"Shut the fuck up, Mark," Chasity sneered, walking to the couch.

Mark chuckled, relishing Chasity's annoyance. "Where *is* Mel anyway?" he asked, grabbing a large bowl from one of the overhead cabinets. "I need to tell her off for getting this cheap ass vodka."

"I haven't seen her since she left for class earlier," Sidra answered, examining her nails. "It's weird; she's been disappearing a *lot* lately."

"I've noticed that *too,*" Alex added. "Chaz, do you know where she's been?"

Chasity shot Alex a puzzled look. "I'm sorry, I didn't know that I was her mother."

Alex rolled her eyes at Chasity's smart tone. "I figured if *anybody* would know, *you* would," she said. "She's always calling you her best friend. I figured she would tell you."

"She *didn't*," Chasity bit out.

Sidra looked over at Chasity. "I always wondered how you got the title of best friend *anyway*, Chasity," she commented, voice laced with amusement, "*I* knew her *first*."

"You sound jealous," Chasity declared flatly.

"Not hardly," Sidra dismissed. "I was just joking."

"No, you *weren't*," Chasity shot back with the same flat tone.

Sidra rolled her eyes and sat back in her seat, crossing her legs.

"Guys, is the food ready yet?" Alex asked, trying to diffuse the tension between Chasity and Sidra.

"No!" Mark hollered. "Stop asking. *Shit*."

Alex looked at him with shock. "This is the first time I asked!" she barked back.

"So what? Just shut up anyway," Mark shot back.

# Chapter 30

Malajia glanced at Tyrone once he sat in the driver seat of his car. "Thanks for dinner," she said. "It was good."

"No problem," Tyrone returned, closing the door. "Glad that you came out."

"Me too," Malajia returned, moving hair from her face.

Despite the studying that she needed to do for her business final tomorrow, Malajia didn't hesitate to take Tyrone up on his offer for a dinner date. Despite all that had happened, Malajia was getting to a place where she was starting to enjoy his presence again.

"Though I'm gonna pay for it later with an all-night cram session," she chortled.

"Yeah, I remember those," Tyrone sulked.

Malajia shot him a sympathetic look. "Sorry...I didn't mean to bring up school," she apologized. "I know you're still upset over having to leave."

Tyrone gave a quick shrug. "It is what it is," he resolved. He turned in his seat to face her. "What are your plans for winter break?"

Malajia glanced at her watch. "We're really gonna sit here in the parking lot?" she wondered, amusement in her voice.

"I don't mind," Tyrone replied.

"Okay then." she took a deep breath. "Well, I'll mostly be home except for the week after Christmas…that's when I'll be at a lodge here in Virginia with my friends."

Tyrone held a blank gaze. "You're spending a week at a house with your friends?" he repeated, calm. "As in *all* of your friends?"

Malajia felt a chill, glancing down at her nails. "Yes…all of them," she clarified.

She knew that Tyrone was more concerned with the fact that Mark would be in the house with her. She knew that he would be upset, but she didn't want to lie to him. *God, things have been good so far. Please don't act crazy now.* When Tyrone didn't respond, Malajia looked at him. He was staring at her, face void of expression.

"You okay?" she slowly put out.

Tyrone's jaw clenched. He then cleared his throat. "Yep, fine," he grumbled.

Malajia's eyes never left him as he fidgeted in his seat. She cautiously placed her hand on the door handle. Despite what his mouth said, she knew otherwise.

"I'm gonna miss you when you're gone," Tyrone said.

Pleasantly surprised by his lack of a jealous outburst, Malajia let go of the door handle. "Same here," she returned, smiling.

He reached over and gently caressed her cheek. "Four whole weeks."

Malajia touched his hand. "I know, they'll fly by," she promised. "We can talk, though."

Tyrone moved his hand from her cheek to her slender neck. "Not good enough," he crooned.

Before Malajia could respond, Tyrone leaned over and kissed her. It'd been a long time since she felt his passionate kiss, and though her body was reacting, her mind wasn't ready for something so intense. When she felt his hand touch her between her legs, she gasped. "Okay, stop please," she muttered against his lips.

Tyrone, though he was turned on, complied. "Sorry,

you're just so—"

"I'm not ready for that again, yet," Malajia interrupted, shifting in her seat. "But I'm flattered."

Tyrone nodded, touching his mouth with his hand. He could taste her cherry-flavored lip gloss.

"Listen, before I get you back to campus, I want to run something by you," he proposed.

Malajia held her hands on her neck, she felt hot. "Okay."

"How about instead of you spending the week at that lodge…you spend it with *me*?"

Malajia shot him a stunned look. "You want to spend a whole *week* with me?" she asked. He smiled and nodded. "Ty—I—I can't. My plans are set."

"So, break them."

"I can't *just break* them," she argued. "This trip was *my* idea. I can't just back out… I'm looking forward to—"

"So, what you're saying is that you'd rather spend time with *them*, over *me*," Tyrone spat. He made no efforts in hiding his true emotions this time. "*They* get *all* your damn time, I guess *I'm* not worth any."

Malajia was taken back. "That's not what I said or meant," she assured him. "You know I want to spend more time with you—"

"Then *do* it," Tyrone barked. "Words don't mean shit if your actions don't match."

Malajia sighed in frustration. "That's not fair," she hissed. "I think my actions have spoken *volumes*… I'm here with you *now* after everything, aren't I?"

Seeing the agitation on Malajia's face, Tyrone relaxed his frown. Taking a deep breath, he reached for her hand. "I just—I think it'll be good for us, being alone for a few days…" he smiled. "We can really start to feel like we're back together."

Malajia looked perplexed. "We're back together?" She didn't recall confirming that they were back in a relationship.

"Well…I *want* to be," he admitted, caressing her hand. "Don't *you*?"

Malajia hesitated. "I—I guess, but—"

"Look, just spend the week with me and we'll take it from there," Tyrone persisted. "Please."

*I can't take it when he gives me those begging eyes*, she thought. Running her hand through her hair, Malajia let out a long sigh. "Okay Tyrone," she agreed after a long pause. "I'll spend the week with you."

Tyrone smiled. "Yeah?"

She offered a slight smile back. "Yeah."

While Tyrone rejoiced, Malajia was silent. *What am I gonna tell the others?* Malajia racked her brain with what she would say to her friends. How could she tell them that not only was she backing out of a trip that *she* planned, but that she was doing so to be with the man who they deemed unworthy of her—and with good reason. Malajia kept her silence as a satisfied Tyrone finally pulled out of the parking lot.


Malajia walked into her house and went upstairs to her room. She stopped short of entering her room and removed her stiletto heels. "Why I walked in these things is beyond me," she fussed to herself. Her feet were killing her. Having made Tyrone drop her off in front of campus to avoid any chances of her friends seeing her with him, Malajia made the long walk back to the clusters and her feet were paying the price.

"Hey girlie," Sidra smiled, when Malajia walked into their room. "Where have you been?"

"Out," Malajia muttered, tossing her shoes near her closet.

Sidra shook her head at Malajia's short answer. "Yes, I know that smart ass," she shot back.

Malajia chuckled. "How was dinner at the guys' house?" she asked, sitting on her bed. "What did they make?"

Sidra closed the textbook that was in her hand. "Dinner was good. They made fried fish, rice, salad and biscuits," she replied. "I brought you some leftovers. It's in the fridge."

"Yeeeesssss," Malajia rejoiced, rubbing her hands together. "I'm gonna tear that up for breakfast tomorrow."

"Oh, and Mark told me to tell you never to buy that cheap vodka again," Sidra relayed, laughter filling her voice.

Malajia sucked her teeth. "He always complaining about shit that he don't pay for."

"Yeah well, you know he drank almost all of it anyway," Sidra said. "Then tripped over his own foot and fell on his behind when he got drunk."

Malajia shook her head as she grabbed a textbook from the floor. "I'm not surprised," she muttered.

Both girls sat in silence for several moments. Sidra looked over at Malajia. "Malajia, is everything okay with you?" she asked.

Malajia glanced at her, baffled. "Yeah, why?"

"You're quiet."

Malajia frowned. "I'm studying," she spat. "And what, I'm supposed to be loud at *every* given moment?"

Sidra was taken back by her tone. "Come on Malajia, any other time you call yourself studying, you still talk," she pointed out.

"Sidra…you're being weird," Malajia threw back. "Where is this coming from?"

"Honestly, you've been distracted, disappearing, and depressed quite often lately," she pointed out. "I just wanted to know if there was something that you needed to talk about."

Until now, Malajia thought that she was doing a good job of hiding her stress. Clearly, she was mistaken. "Everything is fine, Sidra," she answered, tone dry.

"Are you *sure*?" Sidra pressed. "I mean, if you need to talk…I'm here."

"Unless you're willing to talk about taking this business final for me tomorrow, there isn't anything I need to say right now," Malajia replied. "I'm good."

"Okay Malajia," Sidra relented, putting her hand up.

"And no, I'm not taking your final for you."
"Didn't think so," Malajia chuckled.

# Chapter 31

"I'm mentally drained," Emily stated, placing toiletries into a duffle bag. "I hope I did well enough on my finals. If I don't get off academic probation, I'm going to scream."

"I'm sure you did just fine," Alex assured her, taking a sip of water from a glass. "You studied your butt off."

Finals week now over, the students were now packing up to go home for winter break. Emily smiled. "Yeah," she agreed.

"Chasity, how do you deal with packing all this stuff?" Sidra wondered, folding Chasity's comforter.

Chasity looked up from putting items into a suitcase. "Just fine without y'all down here bothering me," she spat.

Alex giggled. "What, you don't appreciate us helping you pack?"

"I didn't *ask* you to help me," Chasity threw back. "And *you* ain't doing shit but taking up space." Chasity was enjoying her music while packing up to leave, until she was bombarded by Alex, Sidra and Emily, who felt the need to join in on the packing.

"Well, I'm finished packing *finally*, so I figured I'd lend my services to *you*," Sidra chimed in.

Chasity shook her head. "This whole conversation is pointless."

Malajia barged in. "Do any of you have any extra laundry detergent?" she asked. "I ran out."

"You mean *I* ran out," Sidra hissed. "I *knew* you were gonna use all my detergent."

"Okay, *you* ran out. I still need some," Malajia huffed.

Alex chuckled. "I think I might have some left," she offered. "Just check in my—"

"No offense Alex, but I ain't tryna break out from your cheap ass, watery, generic detergent," Malajia jeered, putting her hand up.

Alex stared at Malajia, eyes blazing. "You know what, screw your ungrateful behind," she sneered. Malajia laughed. "Good luck with your dirty draws."

Sidra shook her head. "Girl, go finish packing," she directed to Malajia. "You already know you're just gonna take those clothes home."

"Yeah, I don't know what I was thinking," Malajia chortled. "Those draws are my *mom's* problem now."

"So, because you waited until the last minute to do your laundry, you're going to make your mother suffer?" Alex grunted. "Selfish."

"Sure *am*. Just like *you* make *us* suffer by shaking the house every time you walk, fat ass," Malajia threw back.

Annoyed, Alex picked up one of Chasity's folded washcloths and threw it at the laughing Malajia, hitting her in the face with it.

"Bitch, you better pick that up and re-fold it," Chasity snapped at Alex, pointing to the fallen item.

"Did you *have* to call me a bitch?" Alex grunted, picking up the washcloth from the floor.

"Did you *have* to throw my shit?" Chasity retorted.

Emily laughed at the byplay. "I'm happy to get back home for a bit, but I can't *wait* to get to that lodge," she mused. "When is the reservation again? We'll have it for a week, right?"

"The week after Christmas," Sidra answered. "Right Malajia?"

Malajia looked down at her hands. *Shit.* "Yeah," she
mumbled.

"And don't worry; this won't be another blind purchase
like that *ski trip* was." Sidra added. "I actually went up to
Lunar Lodge *with* Malajia last week, to see it… It's
beautiful."

Sidra almost cringed, remembering the ski trip that
Malajia planned over winter break sophomore year. Malajia
made a reservation and pre-paid for a motel in New York,
sight unseen. When the group arrived, they were horrified by
the conditions. Luckily Chasity, who was staying at a luxury
ski resort with Trisha at the same time, got her father to put
the group up in some rooms free of charge where she was
staying.

"I know everybody will like it," Sidra added.

"Cool. I'm looking forward to it," Alex chimed in,
leaning back in her seat.

"Mel, you can take the train to my house and we can
follow the guys in my car," Sidra suggested, folding a shirt.

"Um…" Malajia hesitated, rubbing her forehead. "You
can just drive up without me."

Sidra frowned. "How are you going to get there then?"
she pressed. "Were you going to take the train to Chasity's
and ride with *her*? You live closer to *me*."

"Malajia has been banned from my house this break,"
Chasity cut it, pushing hair out of her face. "So, she'll be
taking that lonely train ride to *your* house, Sid."

"You might as *well,* Malajia," Sidra insisted. She then
giggled. "I promise, I won't criticize your choice in music."

Malajia vigorously rubbed her face with her hands.
Although she had anxiety about breaking her news, she knew
that she had to. "Look…I'm not going to the lodge," Malajia
blurted out. She braced herself for reactions. And like she
expected, her friends didn't disappoint.

"What do you *mean* you're not going?!" Alex
exclaimed, jumped out of her seat.

"What *else* do you have to do?" Chasity sneered.

"Why aren't you going?" Emily asked, clearly disappointed.

"This was *your* idea, and now you're just going to back out on us?" Sidra fumed, folding her arms.

Malajia took a deep breath as she took the questions and attitudes that were being thrown at her. "I actually made plans to do something else," she vaguely put out.

"To do *what*?" Alex sked, not masking her impatience.

"Yeah, what could be more fun than hanging out with *us*?" Emily smiled.

*Come on, just say it!* "I can't go because I um—I'm spending that week with…" Malajia swallowed hard. "Tyrone."

Chasity's head immediately snapped towards Malajia, her eyes held a fiery gaze.

"Tyrone?" Alex asked, scratching her head. "I haven't heard his name come out of your mouth in *months*."

"Yeah, I thought you two broke up," Sidra added, surprise in her voice.

"Well, we *did*. But we kinda just got back together," Malajia slowly revealed, her eyes locked with Chasity's.

Chasity was so furious, she couldn't speak.

Emily tossed her arms up. "Well… we'll miss you, but as long as you're happy, then I'm happy *for* you," she sincerely said.

Malajia found it hard to speak as she tried to avoid Chasity's continuous glare. The girl barely blinked. It was almost like Chasity's eyes were cutting through her like a knife.

"Thanks, Em," Malajia finally replied.

Chasity glanced at the other girls. "You three, do me a favor," she said.

"What's that, Chaz?" Alex asked.

"Get out," Chasity demanded.

"Well damn, what did we do to you?" Sidra chuckled. That type of tone and behavior from Chasity no longer shocked her.

Chasity took a deep breath, trying to control her rising temper. "I need to talk to Malajia about something private... *now*," she hissed.

"No, she doesn't," Malajia quickly contradicted. "Stay."

The three girls looked back and forth between Chasity's angry face, and Malajia's hopeful face. They decided to do as the angry face asked.

"Come on girls, let's go to the cafeteria," Alex suggested, heading for the door. "I hope everything isn't picked over."

"Damn, I wish we didn't throw out those leftovers," Sidra huffed, following Alex out the door with Emily in tow.

Chasity slowly folded her arms as the door closed.

Malajia sighed loudly. "I already know what you're gonna say," she huffed.

"Oh, I don't think you do," Chasity hissed, holding her gaze.

"*Try* me," Malajia challenged.

"Fine." Chasity tapped her foot on the floor. "You are the *dumbest* fuckin' person that I have *ever* met," she snapped.

Malajia rolled her eyes. "Thanks for that, Chasity," she sniped sarcastically. "I truly appreciate you calling me dumb."

"What the hell *else* am I supposed to think when I hear that you are back with him?" Chasity argued.

"You're *supposed* to be supportive," Malajia shot back.

"*Supportive*?!" Chasity erupted. "Girl, are you—do you *not* remember two months ago, standing in this *same* fuckin' room showing me the bruises he gave you?"

"Chaz—"

"Malajia, he *beat* you and you're back with him!" Chasity hollered. She couldn't understand how Malajia could be so stupid and blinded by whatever feelings that she had for Tyrone.

"He's different now," Malajia claimed. "He knows what he did was wrong and he's been going to therapy...he's better."

Chasity put her hands on her head. "Are you *serious* right now?" she exclaimed.

"Oh, I am *very* serious," Malajia threw back, temper rising. "And I don't need this attitude from you. That's why I didn't tell you that I started seeing him again."

"You didn't *tell* me because you know how *stupid* it is."

"No, because I wanted to avoid this self-righteous tirade that you're on right now," Malajia barked, folding her arms.

Chasity shook her head. "So, you think by some *miracle* he won't put his hands on you again?" she wondered. "You really think that one time was *it* for him?"

Malajia looked down at the floor, not bothering to answer.

"Guys like him don't stop. *Especially* when they know that they can get away with it," Chasity ranted. "Malajia," she barked when Malajia remained silent.

Malajia looked up at her. "I gotta go," she grunted, heading for the door.

Having a thought, Chasity grabbed her arm, stopping her. "That wasn't the first time that he hit you, *was* it?" Chasity fumed.

Malajia jerked her arm from Chasity's grip. "I don't want to talk to your ass anymore," she bit out.

"Answer the fuckin' question!"

Malajia spun around. "Fine!" she screamed, fed up. "No, that wasn't the first time, okay!"

Chasity's face showed just how shocked she was.

Malajia rubbed her face with her hand, taking a deep breath. "...he slapped me once before and bruised my wrist another time," she revealed, voice lowered.

Chasity shook her head, astonished. "I guess you *can't* slap sense into people," she snarled.

Malajia glared at Chasity, flipping her off. "Fuck you, Chasity," she raged, then stormed out the room.

"No. You're not doing that," Chasity fumed, following Malajia into the living room. "You're not brushing this off."

Malajia spun around to face Chasity. "I don't need no fuckin' lecture from you!" she yelled, then put her hand up. "You know what, this is my own damn fault," she realized. "I should've *never* told you what happened in the first place."

Chasity folded her arms, staring at Malajia.

"I should've stuck with our pact," Malajia ranted. "So, my bad for breaking that. I promise you this will be the *last* thing that I tell you about Tyrone, or *anything else*...now you don't have to pretend to care about poor little Malajia's problems, and *I* don't have to hear you bitch about how stupid you think I am."

"Are you fuckin' finished?" Chasity spat out

Malajia rolled her eyes.

"That whole speech was cute," Chasity continued, tone sarcastic. "For the record, I don't *pretend* to care Malajia, I *do* care. I wouldn't be standing here *yelling* at you if I *didn't*."

"What do you want me to *say*, Chasity?" Malajia huffed, tossing her hands up in frustration. "What do you think *you* can say?" She put her hand up when Chasity opened her mouth. "I'll answer *for* you, nothing...there is nothing you can say to change my mind. I'm back with him, I'm spending the week with him and I'm happy about it."

Chasity felt like pulling her hair out she was so frustrated. "God, this is the whole 'virginity loss' thing all over again."

Malajia's eyes widened. "*Excuse* me?"

"You lied to yourself *then*, and you're doing it again *now*," Chasity argued. "Your transparent ass is *not* happy. You never *were* with him. I don't know who you're pretending for, but you need to stop."

"Bitch *you* would know *all about* pretending," Malajia snapped. "You're an expert at it. The way you walk around *pretending* not to give a fuck that you lost your baby. How about instead of trying to tell me about *my* feelings, you deal with *yours*."

Malajia's words hit Chasity like a ton of bricks. It took

everything in Chasity not to punch Malajia dead in her mouth. "You really just said that to me?" she spat, fighting to keep her tears in.

Malajia looked at the floor. She felt that she went too far. "I shouldn't have brought that up. Sorry," she stated flatly. "I need to go."

"Keep your sorry," Chasity fumed. She wasn't interested in Malajia's apology, nor was she interested in harping on her own feelings. Despite her anger with Malajia, she still wanted to get through to her. "You want to go? You want me to leave you alone?"

"That would be nice," Malajia grunted, examining her nails.

"Give me *one* good reason why you're back with him," Chasity challenged, putting a finger up.

Malajia's face showed that she was struggling with finding an answer. "Because...he loves me," she answered finally.

"No, the fuck he *doesn't*," Chasity rebutted.

"He *does*," Malajia insisted. "He told me."

"Men who love you don't *hit* you, Malajia," Chasity argued. "You're smarter than that."

"Oh *now* you think I'm smart, huh?" Malajia spat out. "Just a minute ago, you were calling me dumb."

"Yeah, keep fuckin' deflecting," Chasity threw back.

Malajia let out a huff then tossed her hands up. "Yes, he hit me! That's been established," Malajia yelled. "He made mistakes, *nobody* is perfect. But he's changing and I'm not going to turn my back on him."

"Malajia, you *have* to know that this type of relationship isn't normal," Chasity fumed. "You've been in relationships before him, so why are you settling for this bullshit?"

Malajia looked away. "You don't know as much as you *think* you do," she seethed. "For your information, this is the *first* relationship that I've been in."

Malajia's revelation took Chasity by surprise. "What?" she replied, confused. She never would've imagined that the loud, flirty, party girl in front of her had never been in a relationship prior to Tyrone.

"You heard me," Malajia bit out. "Tyrone is my first boyfriend. So, I don't know what's *normal*. Maybe *this* is my normal."

"You can't seriously believe that," Chasity said. "You can do so much better. You *deserve* so much better."

"Maybe I *can't* do better!" Malajia yelled, tears filling her eyes. "Maybe this is as good as it gets for me."

"What are you talking about?"

"The *good* men don't want me…no guy worth *anything* wants to be in a relationship with *me*," Malajia vented. "All I attract are guys who just want to fuck. And when I let them know that I'm not like that, they lose interest." Malajia ran her hands over her face. "It's been that way since I was in high school. Yeah, I was popular, I still *am*. But that's because of what people *think* I am. I'm just the simple girl that guys want to party with, to drink with, to *chill* with, as long as they think they can get something from me."

Chasity stood there listening, face void of emotion.

"Tyrone…after he got over the fact that I wasn't going to give him what he initially wanted…he still wanted to date me…to get to know me," Malajia continued. "And yeah, things—things in this relationship didn't go how I thought they would, but…despite everything, I know that he's a good person and I still held his interest enough for him to fall in love with me so...why would I give up being loved because things aren't easy?"

Malajia took a deep breath. Revealing feelings of rejection from men that she harbored for years was something that she thought she would never do. Her confidence and ego never let her, but now that she had done it, she had to admit that she felt like some of the weight had been lifted from her shoulders. Malajia searched Chasity's face for understanding and sympathy. But couldn't find a sign of either.

"Well maybe if you acted like you have some fuckin' sense and not bounce around like some fast ass idiot all the time, then *maybe* you would stop attracting garbage," Chasity spat out, much to Malajia's disappointment.

Tears spilled down Malajia's face. "Wow," she admonished, sniffling.

"I'm not gonna pacify you," Chasity bit out. "You dress trashy, act dumb and do dumb *shit* for *attention*. Then you wanna cry about getting the wrong kind. You do this shit even with your own *family*."

Malajia put her hands over her face and sobbed as Chasity ripped into her. She couldn't believe how cold Chasity was being.

"I'm not saying this to hurt you," Chasity assured.

"Oh, you're *not*?" Malajia shot back sarcastically. "Could've fooled me."

Chasity shook her head. "Malajia, if you want to attract better attention, *act* better."

Malajia wiped the tears from her face. She had had enough; her feelings and pride were hurt and she wanted to get away as quick as possible. "I'm done with this conversation." Turning to walk out, Malajia flipped hair over her shoulders. "My man loves who I am…so I'm gonna be with hm."

"Malajia, if you stay with him, he's eventually gonna kill you," Chasity hurled at Malajia's departing back.

Malajia halted her progress. Those words roared in her head; they scared her. But she didn't want to give Chasity the satisfaction of knowing that.

"Well, if that happens, then you should be relieved," Malajia ground out. "You'll no longer have to put up with such a *dumb* person."

Chasity frowned at Malajia's flippant response.

"Have a nice break," Malajia threw over her shoulder, walking out. Slamming the door behind her.

Mentally exhausted, angry and worried, Chasity slowly sat down on an accent chair. Staring out in front her, she felt tears build up. She put her face in her hands as they spilled over.

# Chapter 32

Malajia poked her blueberry pancakes with her fork, letting out a long sigh in the process; she had no appetite whatsoever. "Mom, can I just eat this later?" she asked, interrupting her parents' conversation.

Mrs. Simmons shot her a stern look. "I would appreciate it if you would eat that *now*. I *did* get up early to make them for you guys." Noticing the somber look on Malajia's face, she frowned in concern. "What's wrong? I thought you liked my homemade blueberry pancakes. You always said that was the only good thing that I made," she added, voice laced with amusement.

"No, I do like them. It's just…" Malajia sighed again; she didn't have the mental energy to go back and forth with her mother over something as simple as pancakes. "Never mind, I'll eat them now."

Geri reached over and grabbed one of Malajia's pancakes off her plate. "Girl you've been moping around this house ever since you got back from school," she pointed out, drizzling maple syrup on the pancake. "What's up?"

Malajia rolled her eyes. *Oh please, y'all don't really care how I feel*, she thought. "I guess I'm still drained from the semester," she answered.

Maria chuckled. "Girl please, like *you* actually worked hard," she teased, reaching for her cup of orange juice. "Besides, even if that were true, you've been home on break for almost a week. That's more than enough time to rejuvenate that brain that you never use anyway."

Malajia narrowed her eyes at her sister. She was in no mood for the snide remarks. Her mind was preoccupied with more important things. She hadn't spoken to Chasity since their argument. Even though she'd been speaking to Tyrone and knew that he was looking forward to her spending the week with him after Christmas, she was beginning to regret backing out of the trip with her friends.

"Whatever Maria, keep those snide comments to yourself," Malajia sneered. "I'm sick and tired of you talking trash about me."

Maria looked stunned. "Why are you being so defensive?" she wondered. "We *always* joke like this with you."

"That doesn't mean I like it—you know what, I'm done eating." Malajia pushed herself back from the table. "I'm going to check on Melissa."

"Wow, you're actually volunteering to check on your baby sister?" Mr. Simmons joked. "Yeah, something is *definitely* wrong with you, Buttons." His teasing incited snickers and giggles from his wife and daughters.

Malajia resisted the urge to snap at her father for calling her by her hated childhood nickname. Instead, she just rolled her eyes and walked out of the kitchen.

"While you're up there, can you check on Dana and Tiana too?" Mrs. Simmons asked. "I'm sure those two are up and terrorizing each other by now."

"Sure, why not?" Malajia mumbled, heading for the stairs.


Emily stared at the cell phone in her hand, contemplating whether to dial the number on the screen or not. She felt tortured. Here it was, Christmas Eve, and she couldn't even call her mother to talk to her. Sucking her teeth, she cleared her mother's phone number from the screen and tossed the device on the couch cushion next to her.

"Em, we'll be leaving in about ten minutes," Mr. Harris said, walking into the living room.

Emily forced a smile. "Okay," she replied. "I haven't seen the other side of my family in a long time...I hope it's not going to be awkward." Ever since her parents divorced, Emily hadn't seen very much of her father's side of the family.

"It won't be. Your aunt has been begging me to bring you around ever since you moved down here," Mr. Harris revealed. "She insisted on us coming over for Christmas Eve dinner."

Emily smiled, rising from the couch. "I'll go grab the cake from the kitchen."

"Okay. I'll go warm the car up," he returned, grabbing his coat off the coat rack.

Emily opened the white bakery box to peek at the strawberry shortcake that her father purchased. Dismissing the thought of cutting a small piece to sample, she closed the box and carefully placed it into a gift bag. As she grabbed the bag by the handle, she heard her cell phone ring. *Maybe that's Mommy!* Darting to the couch where she left it, she grabbed the phone and put it to her ear without looking at the caller ID. "Hello?" she answered, the sound of hope filling her voice.

"Hey Em," the female voice answered.

Recognizing Alex's voice, Emily sighed. "Oh, hey Alex."

Alex chuckled. "Wow, you seem disappointed that it's me," she observed.

Emily sat down on the couch. "I'm sorry Alex. I'm glad to hear from you," she assured. "I just thought that... Never mind. How's your break so far?"

"Girl, I've been working at the damn diner since I've been home," Alex said. "I'm so glad to be off tomorrow for Christmas."

"And don't forget next week too, when we go back to Virginia," Emily reminded her, pushing hair behind her ear.

"Trust me, I didn't forget," Alex chortled. "How's it going? I know this is the first Christmas you're spending with your dad in a long time. Does it feel weird?"

"Not at all," Emily replied. "I've always had a relationship with him, even though I didn't get to see him all the time. I'm enjoying being here."

"I'm glad. And I'm sorry Em, I didn't mean to imply that things were weird between you and your dad," Alex said.

Coming from a family where the parents were no longer together was foreign to Alex. Her parents were still together and still happy after twenty-five years of marriage. She couldn't imagine not being able to see either one of her parents regularly.

Emily shook her head, even though Alex couldn't see her. "I didn't take it that way," she assured. "Another good thing is that I get to see the other side of my family. I have a ton of aunts, uncles, and cousins that I haven't seen in *years*." Emily's mouth dropped open; she just remembered that her father was sitting in the car. "Oh man! I'm supposed to be in the car right now," she giggled, jumping from the couch.

Alex's laughter came through the phone. "Well, you have fun, and if I don't talk to you tomorrow, Merry Christmas and I'll see you next week."

"Same to you." Emily hung up the phone and darted out the door. "Sorry Daddy!"


Chasity rolled her eyes and let out a loud sigh as Trisha rambled. "Can you stop now?" she asked tiredly, unfastening her seat belt.

"No, I'm not going to stop until I know that you heard

what I said," Trisha persisted, turning the engine of her silver Mercedes Benz off. "Your grandmother is really looking forward to you being here with her and the rest of the family."

Chasity once again rolled her eyes. She wasn't sure how her mother was able to drag her to Christmas dinner at her grandmother's house, but somehow, she had managed to do so. Chasity dreaded spending any time with her family outside of Trisha for any reason, let alone the holiday. "Mom, you've been running your mouth ever since we left the house," she hissed. "Trust me, I heard you."

Trisha glared at her daughter; she could've slapped her. "Hey girl, kill that damn attitude, you hear?" she scolded. "Now like I told you all the way here, be nice."

"Whatever," Chasity mumbled, opening the car door and stepping out.

Trisha hopped out of the car and met Chasity at the beginning of the lit path leading towards her mother's massive home.

As the two women walked up the path, Trisha adjusted a large gift bag on her arm. "You know, despite how you feel, the family will be glad to see you," she said, sensing Chasity's feelings. "They ask me about you all the time."

"I promise I don't care," Chasity sneered, earning herself a pinch on her arm. "Ow," she whined, grabbing her arm.

"I said kill the attitude," Trisha scolded.

Chasity resisted the urge to say something else smart as they stood in front of the door. Trisha rang the doorbell before looking over at Chasity, who looked as if she was entering a funeral. "God girl, fix your face, will you?"

Fed up with Trisha bothering her, Chasity plastered the biggest, fakest smile on her face and held it as the door opened. "Hi Grandmom, Merry Christmas!" Chasity exclaimed in her best "nice" voice, the smile still plastered to her face.

Trisha shot Chasity a sideways glance. Although

irritated with her daughter's behavior, she couldn't help but chuckle at her. *Ugh, my child is so much like me it's scary,* she thought, amused. She could remember behaving the same way at her age, and although she changed a lot over the years, Trisha still tended to let her attitude seep through on occasions.

Grandmother Duvall smiled brightly, welcoming her daughter and granddaughter into her home. "I'm so glad you both came," she gushed, giving both women hugs.

Removing her coat, Trisha handed her mother the gift bag. "It smells good in here, Mom," she complimented.

"Thank you darling," Grandmother Duvall replied. "I've been cooking all day; I hope everyone enjoys it."

"Oh, I'm sure they will. Everybody always *does,*" Trisha assured. She looked around; her mother certainly did not skimp on the Christmas decorations. From the colorfully decorated tree, to the flickering lights and garland, the house truly was festive. "Where is everybody?"

"The dining room. We were waiting on you two."

Smiling, Trisha made a beeline for the dining room. Grandmother Duvall stared at Chasity, who was slowly hanging her coat up on the coat rack. "You know, you get prettier every time I see you," she mused.

Chasity gave a slight smile. "Thank you."

"Are you okay, sweetie?" Grandmother Duvall asked. She wasn't fooled by Chasity's fake happiness. "You would rather be home, huh?"

Chasity wanted so bad to be honest and tell her "yes", but looking at her elderly grandmother standing in front of her holding a somber look on her face, made Chasity feel bad. She never had an issue with her grandmother; the woman always made Chasity feel loved, even when others didn't.

Chasity smiled sincerely as she looped her arm through her grandmother's. "No Grandmom, I'm good."

Grandmother Duvall gave Chasity's hand a soft pat,

smiling back. "Glad to hear it. Now come on, let's go eat."

Trisha glanced over at Chasity, a proud look on her face. Despite her reservations with attending the dinner, Chasity seemed to leave her bad attitude at the door. The girl was *actually* participating in conversation during their hour and a half at the dinner table.

Trisha leaned over to Chasity while the others conversed. "Are you being nice just so you don't have to hear my mouth later?" she whispered jokingly.

"Absolutely," Chasity joked in return, rising from her seat.

Reaching for her drink, Trisha shook her head and giggled as Chasity walked away.

On her way to the kitchen to get something to drink, Chasity heard her cell phone ring. Removing the phone from her jeans pocket. She made her way upstairs in an effort to get away from all of the noise. "Hello?" she answered.

"Hey beautiful, how's your dinner going?" Jason replied. Chasity had ranted to him earlier when she initially found out that she had to attend, so he figured he'd check on her.

"It's fine I guess," she said, sitting on a chair in her grandmother's bedroom. "Nobody's killed anybody yet," she joked.

"See, I told you it wouldn't be so bad," Jason chuckled. "Time heals things. You needed to give your family another chance."

Jason had been at that same house for Thanksgiving freshman year, when Chasity had the big fall out with Brenda Parker, which had led to a fist fight along with the revelation of her adoption. He knew firsthand the feelings that Chasity had about going to any more family functions. And although he understood, Jason didn't want her to continue to harbor those feelings. Not for them, but for her.

"Yeah, I guess," Chasity sighed. "Honestly, it's not so bad. My family actually act like they like me now," she joked.

"Even Melina?" Jason asked, surprised.

"Nah, fuck that bitch," Chasity spat, of her cousin and former childhood bully. "She knows not to talk to me."

"Well, as long as you're not getting into any fights, I'm satisfied," Jason replied.

"The night isn't over," Chasity muttered.

"Stop it," Jason chortled. "Anyway, I gotta get back to my own dinner...God forbid I disappear for more than ten minutes."

"You wanna come over later?"

"Yeah," Jason answered. "Love you."

"Love you too." Chasity ended the call and rose from the chair. She headed back down stairs. Reaching the bottom step, Chasity spotted a familiar face walking out of the dining room.

Recognizing Brenda, Chasity tensed up. She'd heard someone come in the house while she was on the phone with Jason. Now she knew who that person was. Chasity hadn't seen the woman since their falling out; she had hoped to never see her again.

At that moment, Chasity regretted coming to dinner. Brenda locked eyes on her from across the room. They stared at each other, almost a room between them. Neither woman said anything.

Chasity felt her breath shorten. What was Brenda there for? Was she going to attack her again? Was she drunk? Did she still blame Chasity for her sister's actions? Although she joked about it, Chasity didn't want to fight. And she certainly wasn't going to stick around.

Chasity turned to leave, but bumped into Trisha, who had walked up behind her. "What the hell?" Chasity admonished. "Why are you walking up on me like that?"

"I came to find you," Trisha replied, tone calm. "I just saw her come in a few minutes ago."

Chasity shook her head. "What is Brenda *doing* here?" she hissed.

"I guess Mom invited her," Trisha figured. "I swear, I
had no idea she was going to be here. If I did, I would've
never made you come. I wouldn't put you through that." She
ran a hand along the back of her neck. "Hell, *I* wouldn't have
even come."

Chasity put her hands up. "It doesn't even matter. I
can't stay here now."

"I understand," Trisha said. "You want me to drive you
home?"

"No, I'll walk," Chasity huffed, walking pass Trisha,
heading for the door.

Trisha watched Chasity walk out, letting out a long sigh.
Hesitantly, Trisha glanced at her older sister. The woman
whom she held a pact of secrecy with, regarding her child.
The woman whom she despised for the treatment of her
child... The woman whom she had hurt and betrayed at a
young age. The woman whom she hadn't spoken to in over
two years.

Both women gazed at one other for what seemed like an
eternity. Trisha was nervous, but unlike her daughter, she
wasn't leaving. Now that Chasity knew the truth about
everything, Trisha figured it was time to talk to Brenda.
Taking a deep breath, she made a beeline for her.

# Chapter 33

"I swear Mark, I'm *never* following you again," Sidra fussed, stepping out of her blue Mazda, slamming the door.

"Whatchu mean?" Mark asked, shutting his car door. "We got here, didn't we?"

"Yeah, after getting lost!" Sidra exclaimed. "We could've been here an *hour* ago." Christmas had come and gone, and it was now time for the gang to start their weeklong stay at Lunar Lodge. Sidra, wanting to drive her own car, agreed to follow Mark for the drive from Delaware. She'd forgotten how much sense of direction Mark *didn't* have.

"Yeah well, you should've turned on your GPS," Mark shot back, grabbing his bags from the trunk of his car. "You know mine is broken."

"It's *not* broken," Josh contradicted, grabbed his own bags out of Mark's trunk. "You just refuse to *use* the damn thing. I told you, you have no sense of direction."

"Shut the hell up Josh," Mark barked. "I didn't see *you* offering to drive."

David—who had been riding with Sidra—grabbed both of their bags from her trunk. "Guys, chill with the arguing," he cut in. "We're here now, so let's go in and take a look around."

"Agreed," Sidra said, removing the house key from her purse. Since Malajia backed out of the trip, Sidra ended up being the one to finalize everything; that included picking up the keys. The four friends walked up the snow-covered walkway and into the house.

"Wow," David gasped at the first glance of the fully-furnished house. "Look at this place. It's huge!"

Mark dropped his bags on one of the accent chairs in the living room, then headed for the kitchen. "Yo, this place got a full kitchen," he mused, touching the grey marble counter tops. "That means y'all ladies are gonna be cooking. Right Sid?"

"*Wrong* Mark," Sidra sneered, hanging her coat on the coat rack near the door. She grabbed the remote to the gas fireplace and turned it on. "I didn't come here to be your maid *or* your cook. We're *sharing* those duties brotha."

Mark flagged her with his hand. "Yeah whatever," he dismissed, grabbing a can of soda from the stocked chrome refrigerator. "I don't like your attitude right now."

Sidra frowned in confusion. "Why? 'Cause I said I wasn't going to be cleaning up and cooking for you?"

"You've been girlin' since we left Delaware," Mark argued. "All calling my phone every five minutes while I was tryna drive and shit."

"That's because you were taking us to *Baltimore*," Sidra threw back. "I was trying to tell you not to get off at that exit."

Mark sucked his teeth. "I should've *kept* on to Baltimore and picked Malajia up," he mumbled.

"I already told you, she's not coming," Sidra said, sitting on the couch.

"Yes, I know that," Mark bit out. "She's with that bum ass dude of hers...I could've sworn she was done with his ass."

"I guess she changed her mind," Josh shrugged, flopping

down on the love seat. "Ahhh, this is so comfortable," he sighed, leaning back and closing his eyes.

"Josh about to jizz on the love seat and shit," Mark joked, earning a snicker from David and a pillow being thrown at him by Josh.

"You're so gross," Sidra scoffed at Mark's lewd comment. The sound of the doorknob turning put a smile on her face. She jumped up when she saw Alex, Chasity and Jason walk in. "My girls are here!" Sidra exclaimed, bouncing over to them.

Chasity looked at her like she was crazy. "Sid, you're acting weird."

"I've been around boys all damn day. Trust me, I'm happy to see you two," Sidra replied, giving hugs. "Where's Emily?"

"She's on her way," Alex informed, taking her coat off. "Her father is bringing her; they should be here in another hour or so."

Jason sat his bags down. "You can see the mountains really well from here," he said, gazing out a window.

"I think we should take a drive up there," David suggested.

"Count me out," Mark said from the kitchen. "Ain't nobody tryna drive up no cold ass mountains. It's probably billy goats up there and shit. I don't want to be near those."

"Why not? Aren't they your family members?" Chasity jeered, provoking snickers from the group.

Mark gave Chasity a long glare before turning to Jason. "Jase, get your girl man," he commanded. Jason chuckled.


Sitting on Tyrone's couch, Malajia played a game on her cell phone. *I wonder what the others are doing.* She figured that her friends had probably arrived at the lodge hours ago. "Damn it," she mumbled to herself when she lost her game.

Tyrone flopped on the couch next to Malajia. "I don't

have much food, so we're having grilled cheese," he said, grabbing the TV remote from his end table.

Malajia glanced at the table; it was the same table that she had fallen on the night that he beat her. She wondered how he fixed it. "That's fine," she responded flatly. She placed her phone on the arm of the chair. "Do you have anything to drink?"

Tyrone glanced at Malajia's phone. "Water and orange juice," he answered. "Who was on the phone?"

"What phone? Mine?" Malajia asked, confused.

"Yeah," he said, flipping through channels.

"Nobody. I was playing a game." Malajia didn't know why Tyrone was asking about her phone again; that was one of the things that they had discussed in a therapy session several weeks ago. He promised the therapist that he was working on his trust issues, and wasn't going to hound Malajia about the phone every time he saw her on it. "So um, maybe instead of grilled cheese, we can grab something else to eat on our way back from your therapy session," she suggested.

"One, I have no money and two, I'm not going to therapy today," Tyrone replied, nonchalant.

Malajia frowned. "Why not?"

"Because I stopped going," he informed.

This news shocked Malajia. She agreed to get back together with Tyrone only because he was getting the help that he needed. "What do you mean, you stopped going?" she made no attempt to hide her frustration. "Why would you do that?"

"Because I didn't want to *go* anymore."

Malajia stood from the couch. "Is this because I stopped going *with* you?" she asked.

"No, that's not why I stopped going," he replied, cutting the TV off.

Malajia stood there perplexed. "But...I don't get it Tyrone. Your therapy was helping you...helping *us*."

"No, it *wasn't*," he argued. "To have to sit there for an hour and have someone judge me is not my idea of help." "She wasn't judging you. It's her job to ask questions. She was trying to find out where your issues came from," Malajia shot back, frustrated. "I don't think you should've quit."

"So, what are you saying? You want to leave now?" Tyrone's tone was nasty. "Because I'm not doing what you *want* me to do?"

"I didn't say I wanted to leave," Malajia declared, even though she was thinking about it. "I said I would spend the week with you and that's what I'm gonna do. Okay?"

Seeing the sincerity on Malajia's face, Tyrone softened his hard expression. "Okay." he rose from the couch. "I'm gonna go make those grilled cheeses," he smiled, then headed for the kitchen.

With Tyrone out of sight, worry fell on Malajia, and it showed on her face. With him out of therapy, his rage could resurface, and that terrified her. Shaking the thoughts free from her head, she took a deep breath. *It'll be fine, we'll be okay.*

Mark stood close to Chasity as she sprinkled mozzarella cheese on top of the lasagna that she was preparing.

"Yo, hurry up with that food bee," Mark said, rubbing his stomach.

Chasity glared at him. "You wanna stop breathing on my damn neck?" she scoffed, nudging him with her arm.

"Mark, get your greedy behind out the kitchen," Alex said, pouring brownie mix into a glass pan. "Go play in the snow with the guys."

"Y'all taking forever with the food. I'm starving," Mark complained, grabbing the empty brownie bowl. "We got here hours ago, why is dinner just *now* being started?" He put the bowl close to his face to avoid the glares that the girls were giving him.

"You've got some damn nerve," Sidra seethed, furiously chopping vegetables for a tossed salad. "*You* could've come in here earlier and started dinner."

"Y'all know I can't cook," Mark argued, licking chocolate from his fingers. He sat the bowl down and walked back over to Chasity. "Yo, can you not put so much cheese on that lasagna?"

Chasity slammed the empty cheese bag on the counter. "If you don't get away from me!" she snapped.

"No listen," Mark protested, putting his hands up. "Too much cheese is gonna mess with my stomach and shit. I think I'm lactose intolerant."

"*Or* your stomach is gonna be messed up because you drank all that hot chocolate with *Kahlua* mixed in, earlier," Alex contradicted, placing the brownie pan in the oven. "It would serve your greedy behind right."

Ignoring Alex's comments, Mark focused his attention on Chasity. "Seriously, can you take some of that cheese off?" he pleaded. "I really want some of that food, but my stomach though."

Chasity stared at him. "Is there something on my face that indicates that I give a fuck about you *or* your nasty stomach?" she hissed, earning laughter from the girls.

Mark narrowed his eyes at her.

"No seriously. Because if there is, then I'm slipping with my facial expressions," Chasity continued.

"I love your smart mouth sometimes, Chaz," Alex laughed.

Embarrassed, Mark pointed at Chasity, "You are a vile, nasty woman," he jeered, she shrugged, unfazed. Heading out of the kitchen, he directed his focus on Alex. "You wanna be loving people's ignorant remarks. How about you love my farts on your pillow later," he taunted, much to Alex's disgust.

Alex frowned "Boy I wish you *would*," she challenged, folding her arms.

"Oh don't worry, I *will*," Mark assured, leaving the kitchen.

"He is so gross," Sidra chortled, putting the salad fixings into a large glass bowl.

"He better *not* fart on my damn pillow," Alex mumbled. Chasity laughed as she placed the heavy pan of lasagna into the oven. "Shut up Chaz," Alex hissed.

Emily walked into the kitchen with a smile on her face. "Hey girls," she greeted.

"Emily!" Alex exclaimed, hugging her. "We didn't even hear the door open. We expected you hours ago."

Sitting down at the large kitchen table, Emily pushed hair behind her ears. "I know. My dad wanted to drive up to the mountains for a bit before he dropped me off," she replied. "He said the scenery was good for calming his mood... He's on his way to the airport to go out of town for a business trip."

"Well, we're glad you made it," Alex smiled.

"You're just in time. Dinner will be ready soon," Sidra informed, washing her hands in the sink. "Did you see the guys out front?"

"Yeah, they threw snowballs at Mark when he walked outside," Emily giggled. "Mark said something about his stomach hurting."

"There's nothing wrong with that boy," Alex dismissed.

Emily played with a faux flower from the table centerpiece. "So...still no Malajia, huh?" she asked, somber.

"Nope," Sidra answered. "She went to Tyrone's, just like she said she would."

Alex tossed her hands up. "I just don't get what she sees in that boy," she huffed. "That girl can get any guy she wants, and she's wasting her time with some standoffish... nut."

"Well, maybe she sees something in him that no one else does," Emily put in, folding her arms on the table top. "There must be *something* special about him for her to be with him."

"There's nothing special about him...*nothing*," Chasity snarled, wiping the counter clean with a dish rag.

"Yeah, I think I agree with you Chaz," Sidra added. "I don't like him."

"It's like she's a different person when she's with him," Alex said. "Chaz, have you talked to her since we went on break?"

"Nope," Chasity replied. She had no interest in speaking to Malajia after their blow up. She couldn't allow herself to be stressed over Malajia's situation, especially when the girl refused to listen to reason.

Alex didn't get a chance to ask another question, because the guys walked into the kitchen. "What are y'all blabbing about?" Mark asked, wrapping his arms around Emily, hugging her.

"Tyrone," Sidra replied.

"Fuck that dude," Mark blurted out. "He's a clown."

"From what I've heard about him, I don't understand why Mel is with him," Jason said. He didn't know Tyrone personally, but from all the complaining Mark did about him, Jason formed his own not so good opinion of him.

"She's blinded by whatever bullshit he's telling her," Chasity spat out. "Can we not talk about this anymore? It's making me lose my appetite."

"Did you take some of that cheese off the lasagna like I asked you to?" Mark asked, hopeful.

"Fuck you and no," Chasity shot back, inciting laughs from everyone but Mark.

Light peeked through the blinds, shining right in Malajia's face, pulling her out of her deep sleep. Groggy, she sat up in bed. She glanced over at Tyrone, who was still asleep next to her. Not wanting to wake him, she crept out of bed and tiptoed out of the room into the bathroom down the hall.

Turning the water on, she looked at herself in the mirror. After being at his house for two days, against her better judgment, Malajia slept with Tyrone again.

Malajia ran the water in the sink, holding her hand under the cool stream. She remembered trying to talk herself into enjoying sex with him. But she couldn't; she only did it to calm him down.

Tyrone had gotten upset with her the night before, over her lack of enthusiasm for the movie that he chose. He accused her of being ungrateful. When he threw his glass of juice against the wall, shattering the glass, Malajia contemplated leaving. But just like her judgment when it came to all things Tyrone, she went against it and stayed. She never thought that she would be the type of woman who would offer up her body as a solution to a problem.

Mentally drained, Malajia let out a heavy sigh. After washing her face and brushing her teeth, she went back to the room. Seeing Tyrone sitting up in bed, she forced a smile.

"Did I wake you?" she asked, running her hands through her disheveled hair.

Standing up, Tyrone shook his head 'no'. "Last night was amazing," he gushed.

"*Was* it?" she mumbled

Tyrone frowned. "You don't think so?"

Malajia's eyes shifted. She didn't think that he heard her. "I didn't say—look, I'm gonna go make us some breakfast," she sputtered.

Tyrone walked over as Malajia went to walk out. "Malajia," he called.

Malajia slowly turned around, locking eyes with him.

"You cool?" he asked, noticing the sadness on her face. "I know I got mad—"

"It's fine, I'm gonna go get breakfast started," she quickly cut in. Not wanting to give Tyrone the opportunity to say another word, Malajia left the room with haste.

Walking down the hall, tears filled her eyes. Angry, she

wiped them with her hand. *I'm getting the fuck out of here today*, she promised herself.

"Chaz, are you seriously not coming hiking with us?" Josh asked, zipping his coat up to his neck.

"You already knew I wasn't going. I don't even know why you asked me," Chasity answered, sitting on the couch. "Y'all can go get lost if you want to, I'm good right here."

"You're so dramatic," Jason teased, adjusting his black scarf around his neck.

"Look, if *I'm* going, then *you* should come too," Sidra persisted.

Chasity shot her a glance. "How did they even talk *you* into it?" she asked, tone laced with amusement.

"They guilted me into it," Sidra admitted, giggling. "They said I was complaining too much and was ruining the trip."

"Yeah, they tried that bullshit with me too," Chasity confessed. "It didn't work."

"I swear, if I see a billy goat up there, I'm leaving y'all asses," Mark promised, putting his gloves on. "It'll be like I don't know you."

"Well, at least we know who to push in front of us if we *do* have to run from one," Alex jeered. Mark made a face at her in retaliation.

"Let's get going, guys," David urged, opening the front door. "We don't want to be out there when it gets dark."

"Later babe," Jason said to Chasity.

"Yeah, later babe," Mark joked, earning a smack to the back of the head from Jason. Mark laughed as they headed out.

Enjoying the peace and quiet, Chasity flipped through the electronic pages of her e-reader. The R&B music playlist blared from her cell phone. The group had been gone for hours. She glanced out of the window, darkness had fallen. "They better get their asses back here soon," she said to herself.

Not a moment later, her phone rang, interrupting the music. Not checking the caller ID, Chasity answered the phone.

"Let me guess, you guys are lost and you want me to come find you," she chuckled.

"Chasity, it's me. Can you come get me?" the desperate female voice on the other end blurted out.

Recognizing the voice, Chasity frowned in concern. "Malajia?" she replied. "What's wrong?"

"Tyrone is fuckin' crazy. I'm really scared, please come and get me," Malajia begged.

Hearing the desperation and fear in Malajia's voice, all the frustration that Chasity held flew out the window. "Where are you?" she asked, darting over to the coat rack.

"I'm still at his apartment. I locked myself in his bathroom." Malajia's voice was trembling. "He's banging on the door—Tyrone I'm on the phone with the police!"

"Did you *actually* call them?" Chasity barked, jerking her coat on.

"Not yet, I thought that maybe he—I *will*," Malajia informed. "Hurry please."

Chasity let out a huff. "Text me the address. I'm on my way," she promised. Hearing the phone go dead, Chasity clutched the phone in her hand. "Goddamn it, Malajia," Chasity fumed, snatching open the door and hurrying out.

# Chapter 34

The drive to Tyrone's apartment from rural Virginia took way too long as far as Chasity was concerned. She'd driven as fast as she could without completely disregarding the speed limit. She figured that getting stopped by the police for speeding would only delay the trip further.

Chasity came to a quick stop when she approached the apartment complex. Turning the car off, she jumped out and ran up the steps to the front door.

Chasity banged on the door to Tyrone's apartment. When she didn't hear an answer, she twisted the doorknob and was relieved to find it unlocked. Slowly pushing the door open, Chasity's eyes widened at the scene in front of her. All lights were off. The only illumination came from the moonlight, which peered through the broken blinds. Although minimal, the light allowed her to see the toppled over furniture, broken lamps, and shattered mirror that littered the floor.

Chasity carefully stepped over the mess. "Malajia," she called, looking around. "Malajia!" she called again after hearing no answer.

Fear filled Chasity as she wondered where her friend was and what had happened to her. Her fear became reality

when Chasity stepped around the toppled couch to find
Malajia laying on the floor, on her stomach, unconscious.

"Shit," Chasity panicked, kneeling next to her.
"Malajia." She shook her. "Mel." *Please don't be dead.*
Chasity grabbed Malajia's limp body and carefully turned her
over. "Malajia, get up," Chasity pleaded, shaking her again.
Chasity was relieved when Malajia began to stir. "Come on,
I'm gonna get you out of here."

Chasity tried to help Malajia to her feet, but her progress
was short lived when she felt someone grab the back of her
hair, pulling her to her feet.

"What are you doing here bitch?!" Tyrone yelled,
slamming her against the wall. The force of Chasity's
collision with the wall knocked a shelf to the floor.

Chasity spun around, but before she could react, the
enraged Tyrone attacked her. Fearing for her life, she fought
back with everything that she had.

In their tussle, he punched her in her stomach and chest.
Despite her efforts in blocking her face, Tyrone managed to
get a hit in. Chasity delivered several punches to his face,
body, and even managed to kick him in his groin. Although
Chasity put up a good fight, Tyrone still overpowered her. He
grabbed her and pushed her to the floor. Before she could get
back up, he was standing over her and kicking her in the ribs.
Chasity felt the wind being kicked out of her as she tried to
shield herself.

Tyrone's attack was halted when a glass vase broke
over his head, knocking him unconscious. As he fell to the
floor, Chasity, delirious and in pain, looked up to see Malajia
standing there.

Malajia bent down and grabbed Chasity's arm to help
her up from the floor. "I'm so sorry," Malajia sputtered, as
both girls struggled to stand up. "Are you okay?"

"Not really," Chasity groaned, grabbing her side.

Malajia placed Chasity's arm around her shoulder to
help her walk. "Let's get the hell out of here," she urged,

heading for the door.


The front door to the lodge opened and Malajia and Chasity slowly made their way inside. Malajia closed the door and leaned against it. "Where is everybody?" she wondered. "Nobody's car is here."

Chasity slowly and painstakingly removed her coat and dropped it to the floor. "Probably still out hiking," she said, making her way to the kitchen with Malajia following close behind.

As Chasity sat down at the table and put her head in her shaking hands, Malajia grabbed some towels and ice from the freezer. She wrapped ice in the towels and walked over to Chasity, handing her one. "Here, this might help," she suggested. Malajia placed one of the towels to her chest, wincing.

Chasity looked up at her. She was furious; she'd gone to Malajia's aid and got beaten up in the process. Tossing the towel that Malajia gave her on the floor, Chasity jumped from her seat. "I *told* you!" she yelled, pointing at Malajia.

"I know you did," Malajia admitted, putting her towel on the counter. "You told me that he would do this again and you were right. You were right about *everything*," Malajia touched her own bruised cheek. Tears filling her eyes at both the pain and the memory of Tyrone punching her there. She then looked down at the blood on her arm. "I thought he was changing— that he was getting help... He quit therapy." she revealed.

Chasity was fighting the urge to cry; her body hurt so badly.

"I'm so sorry," Malajia apologized. "I wish I hadn't—I should've left yesterday when he started going off on me but...I thought that sleeping with him—"

"You *what*?!" Chasity exclaimed.

Malajia wiped the tears from her face. "I didn't *want* to," she confessed. "I just thought it would calm him down...

I woke up today feeling like shit over it. I avoided him most of the day 'cause I knew I planned on leaving. When I was packing, he started apologizing." Malajia sniffled. "When he saw that I wasn't falling for it, he got pissed and started screaming, saying that I was screwing with his head and that I'd much rather be here with you guys and—he started knocking shit over—I tried to get to the door, but he blocked me and punched me in my face... That's when I ran into the bathroom and called you."

"Did you call the fuckin' police after you hung up with me?" Chasity questioned, angry.

Malajia looked at the floor. "I didn't get a chance to," she confessed. "He kicked the door down and started attacking me...I managed to get to the living room, but he just wouldn't stop—I got cut the fuck up on broken glass... He slammed my head against the wall and that's when I passed out."

Chasity put her hand over her head. "You better put him the *fuck* in jail," she seethed. "I swear to God Malajia—"

"I *am*," Malajia promised.

Chasity glared at her; she didn't believe Malajia, not for a second. She didn't get to respond, because she and Malajia heard cars pulling in front of the house. Malajia panicked. "Chaz, where is your room? I need to get out of these bloody clothes," she said. "Can I borrow something to put on?"

Chasity nodded. "Up the steps. First door on the left."

Malajia grabbed her towel in a hurry. Before heading out of the kitchen, she turned to Chasity. "I know you're going to think I'm out of my mind to ask you this but, can you not tell anybody?"

Chasity's eyes widened; she was seething. "Are you fuckin' crazy?!"

Malajia put her hand up. "Please sis, I just need a few days to get myself together and I *promise* I'll tell the others myself."

"What the fuck am I supposed to tell Jason when he sees my damn bruises that *your* boyfriend put on me?" Chasity raged.

"I don't know sweetie, just *please* think of something," Malajia begged. "I just need a few days... Please."

Chasity shook her head. She was in too much pain to argue any further. "Fine Malajia," she relented.

"Thank you," Malajia said, grateful. "Please don't let anybody come in your room, I'll be down once I clean myself up."

"Fine Malajia," Chasity repeated. She sat down on the chair as Malajia darted up the steps. Chasity looked in the living room as her friends entered the house.

"Chaz, you wouldn't believe what Mark did," Alex laughed from the living room.

"What's that?" Chasity managed to say.

Walking into the kitchen, Jason laughed. "This fool stepped on a branch and thought it was something behind us," he said.

Chasity sat at the table staring at Jason, trying to keep her face from reflecting her pain.

"He took off running and ended up getting lost," Jason added. "We spent all that time trying to find his simple ass."

"Y'all can't tell me it wasn't a billy goat out there!" Mark hollered from the living room.

Jason shook his head as loud talking filled the other room. He walked over to Chasity and touched her shoulder. "You okay?" he asked, noticing the sick look on her face.

"Uh huh," she mumbled.

Jason grabbed her and tried to pull her to her feet. "Come on, give me a hug," he smiled.

The tugging wasn't helping Chasity's ribs. "Jason, wait," she pleaded.

He wrapped his strong arms around her waist and she cried out. Jason was startled. Chasity put her hand on his chest and pushed him back.

He frowned. "What's wrong with you?" he asked, confused and concerned.

Placing her hands on the table, Chasity didn't answer.

"You look like you're in pain. What's wrong?" he persisted. When she failed to respond yet again, Jason reached out and tried to touch her side.

Chasity pushed his hand away. "Don't," she fumed, glaring at him.

Jason wasn't backing down. "What happened between the time that I left and now?" he asked, not hiding his anger. "What? Did you fall or something? Why are you hurt?"

Chasity looked at him; she was trying to think of a lie, any lie. But she couldn't. She was tired of lying for Malajia. She looked at the floor. "I got in a fight," she confessed.

"A fight with *who*?" Jason fumed.

"Malajia's boyfriend," she clarified. "Tyrone…he um… He attacked me."

The look on Jason's face went from concerned to pure rage. "Where the fuck is he?" he raged, heading for the kitchen exit.

Chasity grabbed his arm. "Jason wait," she pleaded.

"No, don't 'Jason wait' me," he snapped, spinning around to face her. "He put his hands on you and he's a dead man because of it." Chasity watched as Jason paced back and forth. "Where is he Chasity?"

"Probably still on the floor at his apartment," she answered. "Malajia knocked him out while he was kicking me."

The more Chasity revealed about what happened, the angrier Jason became. "You better tell me the whole story and you better start talking *now*," he demanded.

Chasity slowly sat back down in her seat. She took a deep breath, then began to reveal everything that happened. She not only told Jason about all that took place at Tyrone's apartment that night, but she also told him about what he did to Malajia months ago.

Jason was in total disbelief. "How could you not say anything to any of us?" he fumed, placing his hands on the table in front of her.

"I don't know," Chasity muttered.

"And what were you thinking even going *over* there by yourself?" he seethed. "You should've called the fuckin' police and let *them* handle it. Why did you do that?"

"She was in trouble and I just wanted to get to her… She's my friend Jason," Chasity said, voice low.

"Your *friend* almost got you killed tonight," he ranted. Chasity couldn't say anything; she knew that he was right. "This secret shit ends tonight," Jason demanded.

Chasity jumped up as Jason turned to walk away. "Just wait," she said. "I'll do it. I'll get it out." Jason held her arm to help her walk out of the kitchen.

Chasity saw that the others were engaged in conversation. She walked over and tapped Emily on the shoulder, then signaled for her to come with her.

Emily hopped off the arm of the couch and followed Chasity off to a corner, as Jason looked on. "What's up Chasity?" Emily asked.

"Can you do me a favor?" Chasity requested.

"Sure," Emily smiled.

"I need you to go in my room and get um…one of my sweaters out of my closet."

Emily looked perplexed at first. "Um…okay," she said, then headed up the stairs. Jason walked over to Chasity and stood next to her as they waited.

Emily opened the door to Chasity's room and was horrified to see Malajia standing there holding a bloody towel to her arm. "Malajia?!" Emily exclaimed.

Malajia looked up, shocked. "What the fuck!"

"Are you okay?" Emily stammered.

"Get out Emily!" Malajia yelled.

Emily quickly backed out of the room and shut the door. Worry written on her face, she hurried down the steps. "Guys, Malajia's hurt," she blurted out, halting the conversation in the living room.

"What do you mean?" Sidra asked, confused.

"I just went in Chaz's room and she had this towel on her arm and it was covered in blood," Emily revealed.

"What?" Alex charged.

"Wait, when did she get here?" Mark asked, stunned.

Before Emily could get another word out, Malajia stormed downstairs. Everyone stood from their seats.

"Chasity!" Malajia hurled. "You sent Emily up there, *didn't* you?"

"I did," Chasity admitted, taking a step forward.

"I asked you to keep people *out* of there," Malajia fumed. "Why would you send her in when you knew I was cleaning myself up?"

"I'm sorry, I had to," Chasity said.

"Wait a minute, what's going on?" Alex interrupted, putting her hands up. "Malajia, when did you get here? And why are you bleeding?"

"You're all bruised up, did you get in a fight?" Sidra added, upset. "Did you get jumped? What *happened*?"

"Tyrone beat her," Jason blurted out, not wanting to prolong this any longer.

"He did *WHAT*?!" Mark hollered, furious.

"Yeah, and he beat up Chasity too," Jason revealed. The group was horrified. "Chaz went to his house to get Malajia because Malajia called her. And when she got there, the son of a bitch attacked her. He had attacked Malajia earlier."

"Oh my God!" Sidra exclaimed, putting her hands over her mouth.

"Hold up, so he actually put his fuckin' hands on *our* girls?" Mark seethed. "I knew I didn't like that punk bitch. I'm whooping his ass *tonight*!"

"You already know I'm about to head to his place right the fuck now," Jason approved.

Anger registered on Malajia's face. "I can't believe you told him, Chasity," she fumed.

"I *had* to," Chasity shot back. "This shit had to stop."

"I trusted you!" Malajia shouted.

"You keep going back to him!" Chasity yelled back. "He fucks you up and you go *back*. You got *me* dragged into your bullshit."

"Malajia, I can't believe that you actually stayed in an abusive relationship," Alex cut in. "Then you forced Chasity to keep that secret for you. Why would you burden her with that?"

"I'm not trying to hear that bullshit, Alex!" Malajia shouted. "I didn't *force* her fake ass to do *shit*."

"Wait, did you just call me fake?" Chasity barked.

"You damn right I did, you phony bitch," Malajia ranted.

"Now hold on Malajia, you don't get to catch attitude with her for this," Jason chided furiously. "She's *far* from fake, and less you forget she got beat up trying to help *you*," he reminded. "So kill that nonsense."

"What made you think that this was something that should remain a secret?" Sidra charged, folding her arms. "What's *wrong* with you Malajia?"

Malajia shot Sidra a glance then looked back at Chasity. "You think *I'm* the only one keeping secrets in this room?"

"Obviously you *are*," Sidra shot back. "Nobody *else* is that damn foolish."

"Oh no?" Malajia challenged, fixing her eyes on Chasity, who was staring at her confused. "Chasity, since you decided to free your burden of *my* secret. Why don't I return the favor?"

Realizing what Malajia was implying, Chasity slowly shook her head no. "Malajia don't," she pleaded.

"Oh no, we're *both* gonna be secret free, tonight," Malajia taunted, then looked at Jason. "Hey Jase, since you have so much to say about your girlfriend keeping my secret for *me*, did she ever tell you the one I'm keeping for *her*?"

"I don't have time for your games, Malajia," Jason bit out.

"This is no game sweetie, your girlfriend was pregnant with your baby," Malajia blurted out.

The room fell silent. Horrified, Chasity's eyes shifted from one person to another as they all stared at her with wide eyes and open mouths. The one person she couldn't bring herself to look at was standing right next to her.

Jason shook his head. "That's not funny, Malajia," he fumed.

"I'm not joking *Jason*," Malajia shot back. "She was pregnant and now she's not. Take that how you want it."

"Chasity, you were pregnant?!" Alex belted out. "What the hell is going on?"

"Is that true Chasity?" Jason asked, looking at her. When she didn't answer or look at him he became angry. "Chasity!" he barked. She slowly and hesitantly looked at him. "Is what Malajia said true?" he repeated.

Chasity could barely speak. "Jason I—I'm sorry—I…" Chasity wished that she could block out the look on Jason's face. He looked like she had stabbed him in the heart.

"So how does it feel to have *your* secret out in the open, bitch?" Malajia taunted.

Chasity's head snapped towards Malajia as she began breathing heavily. The smug look on Malajia's face and the hurt look on Jason's made her snap. Forgetting about any physical pain she felt, she grabbed the nearest item that she could throw—a large glass vase—and hurled it in Malajia's direction.

Shocked, Malajia quickly ducked, sending the object flying at the wall behind her, shattering it. Malajia looked down at the broken vase, then back at Chasity; who was charging towards her. Her own self-control now gone, Malajia charged Chasity head on.

The group was stunned as Chasity grabbed Malajia and both girls went to the ground. Chasity pinned Malajia to the ground by straddling her; Malajia tried to shield her face as best she could as Chasity began wailing on her with her fists. Malajia, after taking several of Chasity's hard punches to her face and body, managed to reach up and grab a handful of Chasity's long hair, yanking it, sending Chasity to the floor. Taking her opportunity, Malajia then straddled Chasity and began raining punches down on her.

Their friends were shocked and horrified by the vicious fight that was taking place in front of them.

"You two stop that fighting!" Alex hollered as she and Sidra took a step forward in the direction of the tussle. Mark and Josh stopped them by grabbing them and pulling them back.

"What are you doing?!" Alex yelled as Mark held on to her. "We need to stop this!"

"They will tear you apart if you try to get in the middle of that," Mark predicted, much to Alex's fury.

Chasity delivered a punch to Malajia's chest, sending her falling back off her. Chasity then jumped up, grabbed Malajia, and slammed her into a wall, knocking several pictures to the floor. Both girls continued to beat on each other as if they were mortal enemies.

Sidra, furious and close to tears, jerked Josh's arms off her. "I'm not gonna stand here and watch them kill each other!" she hollered, before she took off running up the steps.

"You don't want *us* to jump in, then *you* guys stop this shit!" Alex wailed.

Jason was too much in a daze to care about what was going on in the room with him. He stood with his back leaned up against the wall, staring into space.

Malajia grabbed Chasity and tried to push her, but Chasity had no intention of letting Malajia go. Both girls went falling onto a nearby end table, breaking it. Landing on one of the table legs further injured Chasity's bruised ribs; she grabbed her side as she laid on the floor. Malajia took advantage of Chasity's incapacity and hopped to her feet. Blinded by pure anger, she kicked the girl in the stomach twice. Chasity reached out and grabbed Malajia's leg when she went to deliver a third kick, and pulled her leg out from under her, sending Malajia falling back. Malajia hit her back on a nearby chair before falling flat on the floor. Chasity jumped on top of Malajia, placing her hands around her neck, choking her.

Hearing Malajia gasp for air while she unsuccessfully tried to pry Chasity's hands from her neck, Mark darted over and grabbed Chasity around her waist, pulling her as Josh tried to pry her hands from around Malajia's neck himself.

"Jason, come get Chaz, man!" Mark yelled, while Chasity, still straddling Malajia, struggled to get out of his grasp. "Jason!" Mark hollered when Jason didn't answer him.

Jason snapped out of his trance. He walked over, grabbed Chasity and pulled her up off of Malajia.

Mark turned Malajia over on her side as Jason pulled Chasity outside. "Malajia. Baby are you okay?" Mark asked, concerned as Malajia coughed and tried to catch her breath.

Malajia couldn't speak, she just started whimpering. Mark carefully helped Malajia to her feet. He then picked her up in his arms and carried her upstairs, leaving the rest of the group downstairs, reflecting on what had just taken place as well as surveying the damages.

"I can't believe this shit just happened," Alex seethed, running her hands through her hair. "What the hell? Abused?—Pregnant? What is going *on* with those two?"

Josh and David shook their heads as Emily ran her hands over her neck, letting out a long sigh.

# Chapter 35

Jason stood and looked at Chasity while she tried to catch her breath. She wiped the blood from her nose and mouth with her hand and stared at it.

"Chasity," Jason called sternly. "You need to start talking."

In a trance, Chasity continued to stare at her bloodied hand while trying to keep herself from hyperventilating. The events of the evening were too much for her to handle.

As much as Jason wanted to tend to Chasity's injuries, he was frustrated. He needed answers.

"Hey, hey calm down," he ordered, then walked over and wiped the blood from her hand with his shirt. "Calm down and start talking. Now." He backed away.

Chasity looked down at the ground as her breathing steadied.

"Were you really pregnant?" Jason asked point blank. When she didn't answer, he raised his voice. "Chasity, I swear to God, don't do this shut down bullshit! Were. You. Pregnant?"

"Yes," Chasity answered.

Jason glared at her, folding his arms. He was trying to keep his rising temper in control. "When?" he asked.

Chasity hesitated as she felt tears well up in her eyes. "Two months ago," she finally answered.

"Two!—Two months ago?!" he yelled, startling her. "And you kept this from me all this time? How could you not tell me?"

"I don't know," she said.

"Don't fuckin' play stupid Chasity," he fumed, pointing at her. "What happened huh? Did you get rid of it behind my back or something?"

Chasity looked at him with hurt in her eyes. "No!" she exclaimed. "I had a miscarriage. How could you say that? I would never do something like that."

"And I'm supposed to believe that?" Jason sneered.

"Yes, you *are*," Chasity argued. "You should know me better than that."

Jason's face took on an expression telling Chasity that he remembered something. "Wait a minute," he said, putting his hand up. "You said two months ago... This wouldn't be around the time when I flat out *asked* you if you were pregnant, was it?"

Chasity looked down at the ground. "Yes...it was."

Jason put his hands on his head. "You told me that you *weren't*!" he yelled. "Did you know when I *asked* you?"

"Yes," Chasity answered, tears falling down her face.

"So basically, you're a liar," he fumed.

"Jason—"

"No, you straight up lied to my damn face," he fumed. "How could you do that to me?!"

"I was going to tell you, I swear I was," she sniffled.

"Why *didn't* you?"

"I don't know—I saw that you were stressed out over everything and I was trying—I didn't want to burden you."

Jason frowned in confusion. "Burden me with *what*? My *child*? Does that really make sense to you?!"

It didn't make sense, and Chasity knew it. But she didn't know what to say; she'd never seen Jason so angry and so hurt, and it was killing her that she was the cause of it. She put her hand over her face as Jason ranted on.

"So, you didn't tell me when you first found out, you *lied* about it when I asked you, and you kept the miscarriage from me," he ran down, counting on his fingers. "Did you even think about how I would feel when I found this out? Or were you planning on keeping this from me forever? Are you *that* fuckin' selfish?" Jason stood there and waited for Chasity to say something; anything. When she didn't, he shook his head and proceeded to walk away. "Fuck this."

"Jason, I love you!" Chasity blurted out, stopping Jason dead in his tracks. She looked at him with a tear-streaked face. "I'm sorry okay? I'm so sorry."

Jason turned and stared at her, not saying a word.

"I'm sorry that I didn't tell you. I'm sorry that I lied to you and I'm sorry that I lost our baby," she cried. "If I could take it all back, I would, but I *can't.*"

"I can't trust you," he bluntly stated. "If you can keep something like this from me, what *else* are you keeping?... Was it even *mine?*"

Chasity felt like he'd stabbed her in the heart. First, he accused her of having an abortion behind his back, now he was accusing her of cheating on him. "Whose *else* would it be?" she asked. "Don't hurt me like that."

"Why not?" he spat. "You hurt *me*. What, you think *you're* exempt from it?" He took a step forward, putting his hand on his chest. "You robbed me of the opportunity to be excited about our child, then you took away my opportunity to mourn the loss of it with you."

"I was trying to *protect* you."

"It's not your damn job to protect me! It's your job to be *honest* with me!" he yelled. "You didn't consider my feelings at all on *any* of this." He shook his head as he looked at the woman that he loved. The woman he fought hard to be with, and now, at this moment, she was the last thing that he wanted to see. "I can't even look at you right now," he seethed, turning to leave.

"Please don't leave me," she begged. "Tell me what to

do. Tell me how to fix it."

Not turning back around, Jason sighed. "You can't...I'm done."

Out of all the blows that Chasity took that evening, watching Jason walk away and disappear into the night was a blow to her heart that she couldn't take. She meant it when she said she loved him; he was the best thing that happened to her and the thought of him not wanting her anymore was too much for her to handle. Her hands began to tremble as she ran them through her hair.

The door opened and Alex stepped outside, shutting the door behind her. "Chasity, you need to come inside, it's freezing out here," Alex urged, folding her arms to her chest. She looked around. "Where's Jason?"

Chasity looked dazed. "I—I don't know...he left...he left me."

Alex frowned in concern as Chasity broke down crying.

"He's gone, he left me," Chasity cried. Alex wrapped her arms around Chasity as she began sobbing out loud. Alex tried to steady Chasity when she proceeded to go limp in her arms.

"I'm so sorry sweetie," Alex sympathized, sitting down on the step, holding the crying Chasity in her arms. "It'll be okay." Even though she said the words, Alex had no idea if those words would ring true.


Emily gently rubbed Malajia's back as she sat on the floor with her head in her arms, crying hysterically. Adjusting a bloody towel on Malajia's arm, Emily moved hair out of Malajia's face.

The events from the past few months had come to a head. All the fighting that she'd done with Tyrone, the arguing that she did with Chasity over it, her feelings of being stupid for continuing to go back to him, she couldn't do anything else but cry it out. Malajia was furious with herself. Not only did she put herself in a position for Tyrone to hurt her again, she got her friend hurt in the process. Then Malajia hurt her even more by spilling a secret that she had no right to, and fighting the one person that was trying to help her.

Sidra stood off to the side, staring at Malajia. Although Emily felt for Malajia, Sidra's feelings were different. She was angry, angry that this girl that she thought she knew would put herself in a position like that. "Malajia what the hell is wrong with you?" Sidra spat out. "How could you do this to yourself?"

Emily rolled her eyes as she continued to rub Malajia's back. "Sidra," she warned. "Not now."

Sidra unfolded her arms and took a step forward. "I'm not trying to hear that shit, Emily," she seethed, holding her gaze on Malajia. "What were you *thinking* staying with a woman beater? How could you think that was okay? You *never* saw anything like that growing up. Your father never laid a hand on your mother *or* his daughters," she hissed. "What? Did you need attention *that* badly?"

Malajia continued to cry as Sidra ripped into her. She couldn't say anything; she felt that Sidra was right.

"Then you go drag someone *else* into your bullshit. You got your friend hurt as well. You're selfish, do you know that?"

Emily's head snapped towards Sidra. "Sidra, that's enough!" she yelled, shocking Sidra.

"Excuse me, Emily?" Sidra snarled.

"Yeah, you need to excuse yourself out this room," Emily shot back. "Look, I know you're angry about what happened. We *all* are. But this is not the time to attack Malajia. She doesn't need that right now," Emily argued as Sidra rolled her eyes and folded her arms. "What she *needs* is our love and support. What she *needs* is our sympathy and what she *needs* is to go to the hospital."

Sidra had no desire to offer any sympathy. As far as she was concerned, Malajia brought this on herself. Furious, Sidra could do nothing but walk out of the room in silence.

Emily shook her head as Malajia calmed her crying. Lifting her head from her arms, Malajia rubbed her eyes. "Thank you," she sniffled.

"No problem. I know you feel bad enough already," Emily said. "She shouldn't be attacking you."

"She's right though," Malajia admitted, slowly sitting on the bed with Emily's assistance. Malajia put her face in her hands.

Mark walked into the room and stood against the wall. "Emily, can you excuse us for a minute?" he requested.

Emily looked at him. "You're not going to do anything to upset her, are you?" she asked sternly, knowing Mark's ability to act a fool in any situation, whether it was warranted or not.

"Absolutely not," Mark promised, tone serious.

Emily rose from the bed and walked out, shutting the door behind her.

Mark stared at Malajia as she continued to hold her head in her hands. "What's Tyrone's address?" he asked, deceptively calm.

Malajia looked up at him. "What?" She was unsure if she heard him correctly.

Mark looked at his hands as he slowly rubbed them together. "Tyrone is gonna get his ass beat tonight," he promised. "He has that coming and whether *you* give me the address or Jason gets it from Chasity; either way, I'm *gonna* find him. I promise you that."

Malajia grabbed her cell phone, which was sitting next to her on the bed, and tossed it on the floor at Mark's feet. "The address is in my phone," she said, voice low. "Do what you want to him, I don't care."

Mark picked up the phone and had every intention of leaving right then. But seeing Malajia sitting there looking and feeling broken, he knew he couldn't leave right away. Placing the phone in his pocket, he walked over and sat down next to her.

She looked up at him as he moved hair from her face and

stared at her. "What smart thing do you have to say about all of this?" she hissed.

He frowned slightly. "Trust me when I say that none of this is funny to me," he assured, touching her face.

Relieved, Malajia let out a long sigh as she looked away. Mark watched as tears welled up in her eyes again. He felt helpless; as her friend, he wished he could take away the pain that she was feeling. He wished that he would have tried harder to persuade her to get rid of Tyrone sooner. He wrapped his arms around Malajia as she started balling again. Malajia, needing the hug, wrapped her arms around him as she continued to cry.

Mark returned downstairs fifteen minutes later to find Josh and David trying to clean up the mess. "Guys, I need you to do something for me," Mark said, approaching.

"Sure. Just let us know when you're rolling out to Tyrone's," Josh seethed, tossing a pillow on the couch. "I'm coming with you."

Mark put his hand up. "No, I need you two to stay here," he protested much to Josh and David's confusion. "David, I need you to take Sidra's car and take Mel to the hospital to get checked out."

"You got it," David said, taking off up the steps to retrieve Malajia.

"Josh, you need to stay here and look after the other girls," Mark ordered. "We're in the middle of nowhere, and they're upset."

Josh nodded in agreement. "So where are *you* going?" he asked.

Mark looked at Malajia's phone. "I'm going to deliver on a promise," he said before walking out the house.

Mark arrived at his destination quickly. Following the GPS instructions to a tee and blowing past the speed limit, he cut out several minutes of driving time. Walking up to the apartment door, he looked through the damaged blinds and saw a light on. He put his ear at the door in hopes of hearing his target inside. Not sure if he heard anything or not, Mark banged on the door as hard as he could.

"Who is it?" Tyrone boomed from the other side.

Mark stood there silent and fuming, waiting for his opportunity. He finally got it when Tyrone snatched open the front door. Tyrone was startled to see Mark standing there.

"What the fuck are *you* doing here?" he scoffed.

"Take a wild guess," Mark seethed before lunging forward, pushing Tyrone back into the living room. He pushed the door shut then tackled Tyrone to the floor. Enraged, Mark rained punches down on Tyrone, who was desperately trying to get away. Tyrone managed to crawl away as Mark stood up. "Where're you going, you punk bitch?!" Mark hollered as Tyrone stumbled to his feet. "Now you running?" he taunted as he stalked the terrified Tyrone around the couch. "What? You can only fight *women*?"

Just thinking about how he beat up Malajia and Chasity had Mark's temper on one hundred. He jumped over the couch, grabbed Tyrone, and threw him into the wall, following up with several hard punches. With each punch that he delivered to Tyrone's face, Mark felt his anger intensify. If he could've punched Tyrone's face clear through the wall, he would've.

Tyrone, desperate to escape his beating, grabbed a nearby bottle on a table and hit Mark over the head with it. The crash from the bottle on his head sent Mark stumbling back; he grabbed his head in the process.

Seizing the opportunity, Tyrone made a dash for the front door. Hoping to escape further harm, he snatched the door open. His relief was short lived as he saw the angered face of Jason standing there. "Oh shit," Tyrone panicked.

Jason, coming face to face with the guy who put his hands on the women he loved, punched Tyrone square in his face, then tackled him as he stumbled back into the house.

Mark, recovering from the blow to his head, darted over to the door and shut it again. He then stood back and folded his arms, allowing Jason to get his hits in. He watched with satisfaction as Jason let all his anger out on Tyrone's face with his powerful punches.

After letting Jason go long enough, Mark walked over and grabbed his arm. Tyrone laid there dazed, but still alive. "Jase, let's get out of here," Mark urged, pulling Jason off of him.

As Jason jerked open the door and stormed out the apartment, Mark turned to the bruised and bloodied Tyrone who was lying flat on his back. "If you so much as *look* at Malajia again, I swear to God you won't survive the next beating," he threatened before walking out, slamming the door behind him.

# Chapter 36

Chasity slowly placed some of her belongings in her suitcase. After Alex brought her back from the emergency room several hours ago, she laid in her bed, wide awake until the sun peering through the curtains made her get up. She decided that this trip was over for her.

Although she didn't have much packing to do, the task was taking longer than normal. Trying to maneuver with a stiff body, bruised ribs, sprained wrist and sprained ankle was nearly impossible. She limped over to her bed to grab one last item and tossed it in her bag before zipping it. She slowly headed over to the dresser to examine herself in her mirror. She sucked her teeth seeing the bruise on her cheek and her swollen nose. She couldn't remember if it was Tyrone's hit to her face or Malajia's that caused it.

Her thoughts were interrupted when Emily walked into the room and stood at the door. "You getting ready to leave?" she asked, looking around.

"Yeah," Chasity answered, not taking her eyes off the mirror.

Staring at Chasity, Emily tilted her head; she'd never seen Chasity look so broken before. "Are you okay?" she asked, although she was pretty sure what the answer was going to be.

"No, not really," Chasity answered honestly, rubbing her wrist, which was wrapped in an ace bandage.

"Where do you hurt?" Emily asked.

"Everywhere," Chasity answered. It was the truth; it included her heart.

"Jason didn't come back last night," Emily informed. She figured that Chasity would want to know, since she was held up in the emergency room.

Chasity sighed. "I didn't expect him to."

Emily looked at the floor as she pushed some hair behind her ears. She struggled with what to say to Chasity. She wasn't sure if Chasity wanted sympathy, or to be left alone. Emily decided to just go with her gut. "Chasity before you leave, I just want to say something to you," she began.

Chasity looked at Emily, bracing herself for whatever lecture Emily was planning on giving. She had argued with Malajia, with Jason, and had to listen to a lecture from Alex on the way back from the emergency room. She was sure that Sidra would give her one too, whenever she decided to talk to Chasity again. She figured Emily would have one as well.

"I'm sorry about what happened to your baby," Emily said, causing Chasity to soften her angry expression. "And I'm sorry that you and Jason had a fight, as well as everything else that happened last night...I um...hope that you two can work things out."

Chasity took a deep breath. "Thank you," she replied, gratefully.

Without warning, Emily walked over and wrapped her arms around Chasity. Much to Emily's surprise, Chasity hugged her back. Chasity's eyes became teary as Emily embraced her.

Out of all the girls, Emily was the only one who wasn't judging her or offering her opinions on what she had done. She figured that Emily took enough criticism from other people that she didn't want to do that to anyone else.

Although Emily wasn't aware, Chasity really appreciated her for it.

Once the girls parted, Chasity wiped her eyes. "I need to go," she said, reaching for her bag.

Emily grabbed it for her and gently put her arm around Chasity's waist to help her walk. Chasity, accepting the aid, put her arm around Emily's shoulder as she limped out the room and to the stairs. "Let's see if we can get you down these steps without falling," Emily said.

"That might not be possible. But I can use you to break my fall," Chasity replied, grabbing on the banister as she limped down a few steps.

"Please don't," Emily chuckled.

"I'm joking," Chasity replied.


Malajia threw her arm over her face as she tried to block out the bright sun. She'd returned from the emergency room with David an hour ago and laid down to try to get some sleep. But sleep wasn't happening, not with so many things on her mind. She arrived right after Chasity left, which she figured was for the best. She didn't think that either of them could deal with seeing one another at that point.

Hearing the room door open, she slowly and painstakingly sat up. Every part of her body hurt. She was annoyed by the bandages that she had on her arm and leg, and even more annoyed that she had to get stitches on both.

Mark walked in, closing the door behind him. He stood there, holding a duffle bag, satisfaction written on his face.

Malajia glanced up at him. "Well? Did you do it?" she asked.

"You better believe it," Mark boasted. "Tyrone got a major, well deserved beat down...by me *and* Jase."

Malajia nodded. "Good," she fumed. "You should've killed him."

"He's not worth spending life in prison for," Mark pointed out.

"I know," Malajia said, rubbing her arm. "I didn't mean it."

Mark tossed the bag on the floor and sat next to her. "Sure, you did," he contradicted. "And it's okay to feel that way. He's a fuckin' punk... What kind of man beats a woman?"

Malajia shrugged, shaking her head. "Did anybody else besides Chasity leave?" she asked.

"Jason did. I took him to the train station at like two this morning," Mark informed.

Malajia let out a sigh; she felt so guilty.

"He couldn't even bring himself to come back here. I ended up coming back after we left Tyrone's to pack up his stuff for him."

"I have to talk to him," Malajia insisted. "I have to make it clear to him that Chasity wasn't being malicious when she kept that from him. I didn't mean to make it seem that way... I was just mad at her."

"I think this is something that you have to stay out of," Mark stated. "They have to work this out themselves. I don't think any talking from us is gonna fix anything."

Malajia sighed again. Mark had a point, but that didn't ease her conscious. "What's in the bag?" she asked, pointing to it, changing the subject in the process.

"Oh. I got your stuff from his apartment," Mark informed, proudly. "I just grabbed anything that looked like it belonged to a female. I figured you'd want it." He didn't want Malajia to feel the need to contact Tyrone for any reason, and that included getting her belongings back.

"I did, thank you," Malajia returned, grateful.

Mark dug his hand in his jeans pocket and pulled out an expensive looking watch. "Oh, I grabbed this off that bastards' dresser," he said, handing it to her. "I figured you'd want *that too*."

Malajia managed a laugh. "You damn right," she agreed. "I'm pawning this bitch to pay my medical bills."

"That's the spirit," Mark chuckled, rubbing his hand.

Malajia looked down at Mark's hand, which was clearly swollen. She grabbed it and examined it. "Damn Mark, are you alright?" she asked.

"I'm cool," Mark assured. "It's not broken... Apparently his face was harder than I thought."

Malajia put his hand on her lap as she looked at him. "I'm sorry that I dragged you into my mess," she apologized sincerely.

Mark stared at her, full of sympathy. "I'm sorry that *you* had to go through that," he said.

Letting out a sigh, Malajia leaned her head on Mark's shoulder, while still holding his hand.

# Chapter 37

Alex walked through the door of her home and removed her coat. She let out a long sigh as she placed her coat on the coat rack. She removed her boots and socks, before walking barefoot across the carpeted living room. She'd had a long day at work and was relieved to be home. She flopped down on the couch and leaned her head back on the cushy pillows.

"How was work?" Mrs. Chisolm asked, walking down the stairs.

"Tiring," Alex replied, letting her ponytail down. "The colder it gets, the more people migrate to the diner it seems like."

Mrs. Chisolm chuckled as she sat down on the couch next to her daughter. "Well, you have only a year and a half to go before you graduate college," she said, patting Alex's knee. "Once you have your degree, you won't have to waitress anymore."

"Here's hoping," Alex said. She took a deep breath, staring out in front of her.

Noticing the troubled look on Alex's face, Mrs. Chisolm shot her a concerned look. "What's wrong baby?"

"I don't know, Ma," Alex answered. "Actually, I *do* know… I'm worried about my friends."

"Still haven't spoken to Chasity or Malajia, huh?" her mother assumed.

Alex had filled her mother in on everything that happened during their short trip to the lodge the evening that she returned home. After Chasity and Jason left, the rest of the gang decided to cut the rest of the trip short as well and headed back home.

"No. And it's been a week," Alex revealed.

"Well, why *haven't* you?"

"Because I don't know what to *say* to either of them." Alex's tone was somber.

She'd pondered calling both girls the minute that she returned home, but like she told her mother, Alex had no idea what to say. She was both sad for them and angry at them for keeping those secrets from the rest of the group.

"I mean…what do I say to someone who had a miscarriage? What do I say to someone who was abused by her boyfriend?" Alex questioned, hoping her mother had the answers that she needed. "How can I try to talk to them and be there for them, when it was *clear* that they didn't want me to know about it in the first place?"

"You just have to be there," Mrs. Chisolm stated. "There is no right or wrong way to go about this. It's simple, your friends are hurting and you just have to be there for them. Don't lecture them, don't offer your opinion without asking if it's needed… Don't judge them. Just *be* there."

Alex sighed. "I know you're right Ma." She looked at her hands. "I know I have to talk to them… You're right; they need to know that I'm here."

Mrs. Chisolm put her arm around her troubled daughter and pulled her close. "That's my girl," she gushed, hugging her.


Emily sat at the kitchen table in her father's house, staring at an envelope that she'd retrieved from the mailbox over an hour ago. She knew what was inside that envelope; it was something that she was hoping for and dreading at the same time.

Picking it up for the fourth time in the last twenty minutes, she gave the top a little tear before putting it back down. *Come on Emily, just open the damn thing.* She groaned out loud and lowered her head on to the table.

Mr. Harris walked into the kitchen and chuckled at the sight. "What are you doing, silly?" he asked, going into the refrigerator and retrieving a bottle of juice.

Emily lifted her head and smoothed her hair back. "I've been trying to open this letter from my school for the past hour," she informed. "I just can't bring myself to do it."

"Nervous?" he asked, taking a seat in the chair across from her.

"That is a total understatement," Emily stated, folded her arms on the table. "I just don't want to open this just to see that I failed...*again.*"

"Emily, you shouldn't doubt yourself," her father said. "I know how hard you've been working this semester to turn your GPA around and get off academic probation. I'm sure all of your hard work paid off."

Emily looked down at the table as she played with a piece of paper that she had torn from the envelope. "I hear what you're saying Daddy, but you have no idea the anxiety I'm feeling right now."

Opening his juice, Mr. Harris leaned back in his chair. "Actually, baby girl, I *do*," he admitted.

She looked up at him, curious. "What do you mean?"

"I was on academic probation in college too," he confessed.

Emily's mouth dropped open in amazement. "You *were?*"

"Yep... *Twice*," he laughed. "Freshman year *and* sophomore year...Yeah, I played around a *lot*." Emily laughed along with her father; she was both amused and shocked. He was the smartest, most driven man that she knew. And to know that even he went through what she was going through as a college student, made her feel a lot better. She could never have had a conversation like this with her mother. "So, if *I* could turn things around, *you* definitely can," he assured.

Reaching back for the envelope, Emily smiled. Taking a deep breath, she ripped the top off and pulled the letter from the envelope. Mr. Harris sat there in anticipation as he watched for a reaction from his youngest daughter.

She jumped up, knocking the chair she was sitting in over, and started dancing around. "I passed, I passed!" she exclaimed, showing her father the letter. "I am officially off academic probation."

"See, I told you, you could do it," Mr. Harris gushed, giving the happy Emily a hug. "I'm so proud of you."

"I'm proud of me, too," Emily beamed, clasping her hands together.

"How about we celebrate?" Mr. Harris suggested, placing the letter neatly on the table. "Let me take you out to dinner, and then we can go ice skating. We haven't been since you were little."

"I'd like that," Emily confirmed, sending her smiling father heading upstairs to change. Emily sat at the table and looked at the letter again. She spent all that time feeling guilty for moving in with her father, and her letter just proved to her that she made the right decision. For once, Emily had done something for herself, and it worked out for the best.


Alex took a sip from her glass of water, while tapping her fingers from her free hand on the table. She'd arrived at the quiet restaurant in down town Philadelphia nearly fifteen minutes ago. She craned her neck to see if her invited guest was making her way inside. Alex smiled slightly when she saw her.

"Hey Chasity," she greeted as Chasity approached the table, slowly removing her coat in the process.

"Hey," Chasity responded, sitting down.

Alex shuffled in her seat as Chasity examined a menu. She didn't know why she was feeling nervous. After talking with her mother, Alex called Chasity and asked her to meet her for lunch a few days later so they could talk. She didn't know if Chasity would accept or not, and was relieved when she in fact did. "Thank you for coming," Alex said finally.

Chasity simply nodded as she looked at Alex, putting the menu back on the table.

"I didn't think you'd show up," Alex admitted.

"Why would you think that?" Chasity frowned.

Alex shrugged. "I don't know." She ran her hands through her hair as she searched for a way to start her impending conversation. *We've been friends for over two years, why is this so awkward?* "So um...I see the swelling in your nose is gone."

Chasity shot her a confused look. *Really? Of all things to say?* "Thanks Alex," she hissed.

Alex put her hand up. "I wasn't being a smart ass, I swear," she assured. "I just didn't know how to start off the conversation."

"Try thinking of a topic *other* than my damn nose," Chasity sneered, rolling her eyes.

"I'm sorry," Alex replied.

"My ribs still hurt in case you were about to bring *that* up too," Chasity spat out. "So don't try to hug me."

Alex took a deep breath. "Okay, okay," she placated, putting her hands up in surrender. "Let me just tell you why I invited you here in the first place." She leaned forward.

"That would make sense," Chasity sneered.

Alex ignored Chasity's smart tone as she formed her thoughts. "First off, I want to say that I'm sorry about what happened," she began. "That *includes* your miscarriage."

Chasity just stared at Alex as she continued to talk.

"Even though I'm sad for you, I have to admit that I feel some kind of way towards you."

"Why is that?" Chasity wondered.

"I just don't understand why you wouldn't tell any of us

about what you were going through, Chasity," Alex replied. "I mean, we're all friends... At least I *thought* we were."

"We *are*," Chasity assured.

"Then why didn't you feel that you could trust us enough to tell us? I mean, I know Malajia knew but... What is it about the *rest* of us that kept you from sharing it? Not just *you,* but Malajia too. You two are walking around keeping secrets about serious things... I just thought that we were *all* close."

Chasity leaned forward in her seat after she finished listening to Alex's concerns. "Look, I can't speak for Malajia, but I can speak for me," she began. "The reason that I didn't tell you guys about my miscarriage wasn't because I didn't trust you, it was because..." Chasity paused as she tried to find the right words to say. "I didn't want to face everybody's constant sympathetic looks or comments. I just wanted to deal with it on my own and *in* my own *way.*"

"But why *wouldn't* we express sympathy or concern for you?" Alex argued. "That's what friends *do.* They support each other in their time of need."

"Alex, have you ever lost a baby?" Chasity asked point blank. Alex rolled her eyes and let out a loud sigh at Chasity's attitude. "No, I'm not being a smart ass, I'm really asking you," she clarified.

Alex looked at her. "No... No, I haven't," she answered.

"Then you have *no* idea the thoughts and emotions that go along with something like that," Chasity said. "I thought that it was my fault. No matter how many times the doctors told me that it wasn't, I thought it *was.*"

Alex resisted the urge to hug Chasity as she shared her feelings; she was right, Alex had no idea how it felt to go through what Chasity had gone through.

"I thought it was punishment for me not telling Jason when I first found out. I thought it was because I was stressing and freaking out when he got hurt... All kinds of things were going through my head. And the last thing that I wanted was for everyone around me to be in my face telling me 'these things just happen'. I just…I just needed to deal with my feelings and my loss."

"Sweetie, I get what you're saying, but if you didn't want *anyone* knowing, why would you tell Malajia, of *all* people?" Alex persisted.

Chasity frowned. *Are you seriously still on this 'why didn't you tell me' bullshit?* "What's that supposed to mean?" Chasity asked defensively.

"Look, I'm not bad mouthing Malajia," Alex amended, putting her hands up. "I was just curious, that's all."

"The girl walked in my damn bathroom and saw my pregnancy test," Chasity explained. "*She's* the one who told me what the thing said… *She* was there when I had the miscarriage." Alex ran her hands through her hair. "I really don't know what else you want me to say about this, Alex," Chasity said, shrugging. "I'm not gonna sit here and continue to explain and defend the reason why I chose not to tell everybody my business… I'm sorry your feelings and the other girls' feelings got hurt. But at the end of the day, this situation is not about *any of you*."

Alex took in everything that Chasity said to her and she felt terrible. "You're right Chaz," she admitted. "I'm sorry. I was making this about me and the other girls and you're right, it never was about us… It was your business and you had every right to share or *not* share it with whoever you wanted."

Chasity just sat there in silence as she examined her nails. She was glad that Alex had finally gotten the point.

Alex grabbed a dinner roll that the waiter sat on the table, breaking it in half. "Have you talked to any of the other girls since the trip?"

"No."

"Well, I know Emily is spending a lot of time hanging out with her father right now, and Sidra… Well Sidra is pretty pissed at both you and Malajia," Alex revealed.

Chasity shook her head. "I'll talk to Sidra eventually. I just can't deal with her dramatics right now," she said.

"And Malajia? Have you talked to *her*?"

"Nope," Chasity answered.

"*Will* you?" Alex persisted, buttering her bread.

"Eventually," Chasity replied, looking at Alex defiantly.

Alex nodded. "Fair enough," she said. "I guess it's time for the big question... Have you talked to Jason?"

Chasity looked down at the table sadly as she spun a butter knife around on the table top. "No, I haven't."

Alex shot her a sympathetic look. "Really? Not *once* since your blow up?"

Chasity shook her head.

Alex sat her bread on a small plate. Taking the advice from her mother, she decided not to just blurt out her opinion, instead she would try a different approach. "Would you like my advice on what to do about Jason?" she asked.

"Sure," Chasity solemnly replied, shocking Alex.

"Really?" Alex asked, voice full of amusement. "You actually *want* to hear my advice?" If Chasity's acceptance of her offer didn't surprise Alex enough, seeing Chasity suddenly put her hands over her face and break down crying certainly did. "Oh my God, I'm sorry Chaz," Alex panicked, reaching out and placing her hand on one of Chasity's. "I didn't mean to joke around. I was just surprised because you *never* want advice from me."

Chasity removed her hands from her face and proceeded to wipe her eyes. "I'm dying here, Alex," she sobbed. "He won't talk to me. I've been calling him and he won't pick up. He's avoiding me. So, *any* advice that can get him to talk to me again, I'll take."

Alex looked at her. "Do you love him?"

"Yes," Chasity sniffled.

"Are you *seriously* sorry for lying to him?"

"Yes."

"Then you need to go to him and make that known," Alex insisted.

"I don't know what else to *do* Alex," Chasity snapped. "I've been *trying* to call him. He doesn't want to talk to me."

"I said *go to* him," Alex clarified. "Meaning physically go and stand in front of him so he can *see* you being sincere... Of *course* he's not answering your phone calls. He's pissed at you and in all honesty, he has every right to be, Chasity," Alex bluntly stated. "You kept secrets from him and you lied. And I know that you know that you were dead wrong for that."

Chasity leaned back in her seat and put her hand over her face as Alex continued.

"Trust me when I say that relationships don't work when secrets are kept and lying is done," Alex continued. "Jason was the *one* person that you should've told. Forget about the *rest* of us. You should've told *him*... So yeah, he's mad and he's ignoring you and that is the very reason why you need to stop being afraid and go face him. It's easy to ignore someone when they're not standing in front of you, looking you in your eyes."

Chasity sighed. "I miss him."

"I know you do," Alex sympathized. "So, be a big girl and go get your man back."

"Okay," Chasity replied.

"So, you're going to go see him?" Alex asked.

Chasity nodded.

"Good," Alex said, satisfied. She then picked up the menu and looked at it; she'd built up a serious appetite. "Well I *was* going to guilt you into paying for lunch, but since you started crying and all, I figure I would just treat *you* for once," Alex teased, causing Chasity to laugh a little.

"Yeah, well thanks," Chasity jeered, picking up her menu.

Alex smiled at her.

# Chapter 38

Malajia slowly paced back and forth in her living room, holding her cell phone to her ear. "Since you're not answering your cell phone, I'm calling your house phone... Sidra pick up the damn phone... Come on ponytail, you *know* you're sitting right next to it... You're really not gonna talk to me?... Fine, I'm not calling you anymore." She punctuated her last words to Sidra's bedroom answering machine by disconnecting the phone call and tossing the phone on the couch. "Stubborn heffa," she mumbled to herself, folding her arms across her chest.

A knock on the front door snapped her out of her thoughts. Malajia walked to the door, opened it and frowned in surprise at the guest. "Alex? What the hell are *you* doing here?"

"Well hello to you *too,* ignorant ass," Alex chuckled.

"Sorry, hi," Malajia smiled, giving Alex a hug before gesturing for her to come inside. As Alex removed her coat, Malajia stared at her skeptically. "So back to what I was saying...What are you doing here?"

"I came to visit you," Alex answered, handing her coat to Malajia who in turn hung the coat on a hook by the door.

"You rode the train all the way down here to B-more to see me?" Malajia laughed.

"Girl no, that damn train would've cost *way* too much," Alex clarified. "My penny pinching butt got on that bus."

Malajia cringed as she remembered having to ride that bus from college; she hated it. "Damn, well don't *I* feel special," she mused.

"As you should," Alex chortled, sitting on the couch. She looked around; the house was quiet. "Where is your family?"

"They went ice skating," Malajia informed, sitting on the couch next to her.

"Didn't want to spend quality family time with them, huh?" Alex assumed, rubbing her cold hands together.

"Well *that*, and skating requires me to use my legs, which still hurt," she said, rubbing the leg that she had to get stitches in.

Alex studied her; like Chasity, all the bruises on Malajia's face were now gone. "Did you tell your family about what went on with Tyrone?" she charged.

Malajia shot her a glance. "Just jumping right in, aren't you?" she asked snidely. "Is that why you came here?"

"I came here because I wanted to talk to you and check up on you," Alex said.

"You could've just *called* me," Malajia replied.

"I wanted to talk to you face to face," Alex said. "I sat down with Chaz a few days ago, and I wanted to do the same with *you*."

Malajia leaned her arm on the top of the couch as she turned herself to face Alex. "How *is* Chasity doing?" she wondered.

Alex shrugged. "She's…okay," she vaguely put out. "Actually, she's really going through it with Jason right now."

Malajia looked down at her hands; she still felt guilty about telling Jason Chasity's secret in the first place.

Sensing Malajia's feelings, Alex looked at her. "You should talk to her."

"I wouldn't know what to say," Malajia admitted. "What

do you say after a fight like that? Hell, after *everything?*"

"I really don't have an answer to that question, Mel," Alex said. "But, I think she feels the same way. She doesn't know what to say to *you either*... So maybe you can just meet and figure it out *together.*"

Malajia pondered Alex's suggestion as she ran her hands through her hair. "Yeah, you're right," she agreed solemnly.

"So...did you tell your family about your abuse?" Alex asked, going back to her original question.

"No," Malajia answered, shaking her head.

"Seriously?" Alex pressed. "They didn't notice the bruises when you got home?"

"Hiding my body was easy. It's winter time," Malajia explained. "And my *face*? ...I'm really good with makeup."

Alex sighed. "Covering up aside...why *didn't* you tell them?"

"I don't need them looking at me like I'm even more stupid than they think I already am," Malajia answered honestly. "I don't even think they'll believe me... They already think I lie all the time anyway."

Alex just shook her head as she listened to Malajia's reasons for not telling her family about what she'd been through. "Okay that's your decision, and I guess I have to respect that... Even though I don't agree with it."

Malajia rolled her eyes. "It is what it is," she stated flatly.

"So..." Alex hesitated. "Why didn't you tell *us*?"

Malajia looked at the ceiling, pondering her response. Taking a deep breath, she faced forward. "In all honesty...I was embarrassed," she revealed. "Who wants to tell her friends 'hey guys. You know that guy that I'm dating that you all hate? Well guess what, he hits me and I'm gonna keep on dating him even though I know he's gonna do it again'," she said, mocking herself with a phony smile on her face before putting up the thumbs up sign.

Alex resisted the urge to giggle at Malajia's silly antics.

She also resisted the urge to say anything while Malajia was still trying to get her feelings out.

"I just didn't want to hear everybody tell me how stupid I was being or 'I told you so'," Malajia continued. "I didn't want everyone in my business, with their judgments and opinions about my feelings, while I was still trying to figure them out."

"You told Chaz though," Alex pointed out. "Why not the rest of us?"

"She was my roommate when I started dating him. So, I started talking to her about stuff and…she was there when a lot of the signs started showing and I just—" Malajia let out a huff. "I'm just closer with her than I am with the rest of you," she bluntly stated. "There's no other way to put it." Malajia began to re-think her words at the sight of the hurt look on Alex's face "No, don't get me wrong Alex, I love every one of you. *Seriously*, I do. But I'm just closer with Chaz. Which is really weird because we butt heads like every damn day."

"Yes, I know. I live with you two," Alex said.

It was becoming more and more clear to Alex just how close Chasity and Malajia actually were. People who didn't know them personally would have no idea based on how they treated each other. It was a strange friendship, but a real friendship nonetheless.

"Come on, you know that even though you're friends with all four of us girls, you know that you feel closer to one, more than the rest of us," Malajia said. "Like Emily—you seem to be closer with *her*."

Alex shook her head. "No, that's not true," she protested.

Malajia frowned, that was a shock to her. "Oh…Sidra?" she asked. Alex once again shook her head. "David?" she asked, causing Alex to laugh.

"No, I'm close with *all* of you. I don't feel connected to one more than the other," Alex said. "But I get what you mean and I'm not offended," she assured, playfully nudging Malajia with her hand. "Speaking of Sidra, I talked to her the other day and she's still pretty upset with you."

"Yeah that would explain why she's not returning any of my phone calls," Malajia chuckled. "Sidra is just being dramatic."

Alex giggled. "No, I think she just feels some kind of way about being kept in the dark,"

"No, trust me she's being dramatic," Malajia insisted. "Everybody thinks I'm the drama queen, but it's really *her*."

"You're a mess," Alex laughed.

"No, I'm *right*," Malajia said. "I grew up with her, I should know. That chick can hold a grudge like no other… You see how crazy she can get with her multiple personalities."

Alex shook her head at Malajia's silliness. "So…are you gonna show me around your city?" Alex asked after several moments of silence.

"I'm not gonna show you around nowhere but this *house,* which you've already been to," Malajia replied. "It's cold as shit outside."

"You don't have to tell me, I was out there," Alex chuckled.

"Uh huh, you would've been a salty ass if you came all the way down here and I wasn't home."

"I knew you weren't going to be anywhere else *but* home. You have no life outside of school," Alex teased.

Malajia sucked her teeth. "That's a shame, 'cause you're right," she agreed.


After Alex left Malajia's house later that evening, Malajia figured that since her family was still out that she could enjoy the peace and quiet. Settling down on the couch and pulling a throw blanket up around her neck, she grabbed the remote to the DVD player and pressed play on a movie. Just as the film started playing, she heard a knock at her door,

"*Everybody* is visiting today, huh?" she said to herself, pushing herself up from the couch. She headed for the door and opened it. "Mark?" she blurted out, surprised.

"What's up with you?" Mark returned, trying to step inside the house. But Malajia, who was still shocked, was blocking his path. "Yo move, its brick out here," he jeered, of the cold.

"Boy, shut up and come on," Malajia shot back, gesturing for him to come inside. As she closed the door behind him, she stood there and folded her arms, watching him take his coat and hat off. "So…what are you doing here?"

"I'm here because I want that twenty dollars back that you owe me," he joked, holding his hand out.

Narrowing her eyes at him, she smacked his hand down. "Never in my life have I borrowed any money from you, fool," she sneered. "It's not like you *have* any anyway."

He chuckled. "Naw, I'm playing," he admitted. "I'm on my way to a basketball game in the city, so I figured I would stop by real quick."

Malajia looked perplexed. "There's no damn basketball game today."

Mark let out a frustrated sigh. "Fine, damn. I came to check on your ass, okay?" he confessed, exasperated. Mark hated to admit it, but Malajia had been on his mind since he dropped her off at home after they left Virginia. After everything that she had been though, Mark wanted to see for himself that she was okay.

Malajia resisted the urge to smile. *Awww, he cares.* "That's all you had to say in the *first* damn place," she shot back. "So damn extra," she admonished, smacking him on the back of his head.

"You play too much," Mark replied, rubbing the place where he had been smacked. "Don't make me go back home," he threatened.

Malajia sucked her teeth. "Bye," she challenged. "Go head and take that long ass drive back to Delaware after only being here five minutes," she continued, making her way to the kitchen.

"Stop playing...You got any food?" Mark replied, following her.

# Chapter 39

Chasity swiped the screen of her e-book reader to reveal another page of the book that she was reading as she propped herself up on a throw pillow. Lying on the carpeted floor by the fire place, she savored the quiet. That which was short lived once Trisha walked into the room. "Sweetie do you want to go to lunch with me?" she asked, hopeful.

"No thanks," Chasity responded blandly, continuing to stare at her device.

Trisha's face showed her disappointment. She'd noticed that Chasity had been moping around the house ever since Trisha had returned from her business trip a few days ago. She'd left the same day that Chasity left for Virginia, and had been traveling to different cities throughout that week and a few days after. She didn't know what had happened between the time that she had left and the time that she returned, but Trisha noticed a change in Chasity's mood.

"Are you sure? I was thinking that we could try that new restaurant that just opened in Delaware."

Chasity glanced at her skeptically. "You want to drive to Delaware just to go to a restaurant?"

"It's not like we haven't taken trips to other cities to do that before," Trisha reminded. "I'm just trying to get you to cheer up. You seem like something is wrong."

"I'm fine," Chasity replied, looking back at her device. Trisha put her hands on her hips. "I don't believe you."

"Sounds like a personal problem," Chasity replied nonchalantly. She was in no mood for her mother's prodding.

Annoyed by Chasity's attitude, Trisha walked over, kneeled beside her and snatched the e-reader from Chasity. Her daughter let out a loud groan and smashed her face down in her pillow. "What's going on with you?" Trisha asked, stern.

Lifting her head up from her pillow, Chasity rolled her eyes. "I don't feel like this right now."

"Well, I'm not leaving until you tell me something... *anything*." Trisha persisted.

Knowing that Trisha would make good on her promise and sit right in her face until she revealed something to explain her mood, Chasity let out a sigh. "Fine...I got in a fight," she answered reluctantly.

"An argument or a fist fight?"

Chasity hesitated. "Argument," she half-told.

"You wanna tell me with whom?" Trisha asked, trying to pull more information out of the vague Chasity.

"Jason."

"Oh..." Trisha's face took on a sympathetic look. She hated to hear of those two arguing; she thought that they were the perfect couple. "How bad was it?"

"Pretty damn bad," Chasity admitted.

"Who was at fault?"

"Me."

"Oh...well what—"

"Can we just not?" Chasity interrupted, trying to remain calm. "I gave you something, now you know why I'm not in a good mood. Can we just leave it at that?"

Trisha rolled her eyes. She wanted the whole story; maybe she could help. But not wanting this exchange between Chasity and herself to end up being an argument, she decided to let it go. "Very well," Trisha relented, standing up. "I'll just go check out the restaurant by myself," she said before walking out of the family room.

Relieved that the interruption was gone, Chasity picked her device back up. But before she could escape into the words on the screen, she heard her cell phone ring. Looking at the caller ID, she frowned before putting the phone to her ear. "Yeah?...Nothing...Um okay...That's fine." Hanging up the phone, she stood from the floor and headed for the steps.

Chasity sat on a bench in a small park directly across the street from a quiet restaurant. She'd been there for all of ten minutes. She was annoyed at having to sit outside, being the dead of winter after all. But fortunately, the weather was milder than normal for January. She looked up just as someone sat down on the bench next to her.

"Hi," Malajia smiled, removing her purse from her shoulder and placing it next to her.

Chasity glanced at her. "Why are we sitting outside, when we could've met inside the restaurant?" she asked, confused.

"Our meeting is more dramatic this way," Malajia shrugged.

Chasity held her confused look for several seconds before turning away. "That's weird, but okay."

Malajia chuckled. "No, I made us reservations, but it's not for like another half hour," she said. "I wanted us to meet up before we go in with all the noise."

"Alright," Chasity responded flatly.

Malajia adjusted the gloves on her hands as silence fell between the two girls. She was trying to figure out how to start this inevitable conversation. She'd driven her family's van to West Chester in hopes of resolving the issues with Chasity once and for all. Malajia was tired of the tension; she missed her friend.

"Malajia, why am I here?" Chasity asked bluntly, interrupting Malajia's pondering.

Malajia looked at her. "Damn, just starting off with

attitude, huh?" she teased.

Chasity wasn't amused, and it showed on her face as she stared at Malajia.

Malajia cleared her throat as the humor left her own face. It was time to be serious. "Okay, I just want to start off by apologizing to you," she began. "I know throughout my relationship with Tyrone I accused you many times of not being a friend to me... Truth is, I wasn't being a friend to *you*."

Chasity focused on the nature in front of her as Malajia continued.

"You were only trying to help me by telling me the truth about myself, and all I did was lash out at you...I insulted you, I um... I threw what happened to you in your face and that was just low, and I regret that." Malajia put her hand on her chest as she looked at Chasity, who still wasn't making eye contact with her. "I'm *so* sorry for all of that, for real sis. I am."

Chasity pushed some hair behind her ear. "I appreciate that," she replied in a low voice. "Just um...don't ever use my miscarriage against me. You got that?"

"I swear to God, I won't," Malajia promised. "And I didn't mean for you to get hurt by Tyrone because I didn't listen. I dragged you into my mess... I'm also sorry for telling Jason about the baby. Even though I was pissed at you, I shouldn't have done that." Malajia looked down at her hands. "And now he's mad at you and it's my fault."

"Jason is mad at me because of *me*, not you," Chasity corrected, shocking Malajia. "*I* should've been the one to tell him. And even though it was fucked up how it came out...it shouldn't have been a secret in the first place. So, you can stop feeling guilty about *that* part."

"Okay," Malajia answered after trying to find another response to say.

"And *I'm* sorry for not doing what I should've done when I first found out about Tyrone hitting you," Chasity began.

"What do you mean?" Malajia asked.

"I should've told someone sooner," Chasity declared. "That wasn't a secret that I should've kept for you. Things could have turned out a lot worse."

"Yeah, I know. You're right," Malajia replied. "I want you to know that I went to the police and filed a report on Tyrone."

Chasity looked at her. "Oh *really?*" she queried. Malajia nodded. "I never thought that you would go through with it."

"Yeah well, enough is enough with that son of a bitch," Malajia said. "Mark took me to the station before we left Virginia. I told them what happened and gave them his address. I don't know if they were able to pick him up or not... Well, I'm sure he didn't go anywhere after Jason and Mark beat the living shit out of him."

"He had that coming," Chasity declared.

"He sure did," Malajia agreed. "But when I say that I am *never* going back to him again, I mean it. I promise."

"Make that promise to your*self.* Not to me," Chasity replied, moving some of her blowing hair away from her face.

"I did," Malajia said. "I'm done."

"Good," Chasity replied.

Both girls sat in silence for moments before Malajia decided to bring up the other elephant in the room.

"Listen...about the fight—"

Chasity sighed. "Can we not talk about that?" she protested. Truth be told, out of all the fist fights that Chasity had been in, the one with Malajia was the only one that she regretted.

"We *so* need to," Malajia insisted. "...I know that I talk a lot of mess and joke a lot about it but...I never wanted to actually fight you. I'm not that girl who fights her friends."

"And *I am?*" Chasity asked, not sure what Malajia was insinuating.

"I didn't say that you *were*, but you *did* throw a vase at me first," Malajia shot back.

Chasity rolled her eyes. "Whatever Malajia," she sneered.

"Bottom line is, I didn't want to do it, but I *had* to...You were coming at me like a damn possessed demon."

Chasity managed a slight laugh. "Yeah, I do have that crazy, angry thing going on," she admitted, amused.

Malajia too laughed. "Girl, I was fighting for my damn life."

"Yeah well, it *showed*," Chasity admitted. "I actually had to put in some real effort... Did you *have* to kick me while I was on the floor though? You knew my damn ribs were already hurt."

Malajia looked at her with shock. "Bitch did you *not* try to punch my damn face inside out? *And* you tried to choke the life out of me!" she exclaimed, amusement filling her voice.

Chasity shook her head.

"I still got my ass whipped though," Malajia concluded after a few seconds, inciting laughter from Chasity. She herself, laughed again. "So did *you*."

"Whatever bitch," Chasity threw back.

"Yeah, I tagged that nose real good," Malajia continued, trying to poke Chasity in her nose.

Chasity quickly smacked her hand down from her face. "You irk my nerves," she said, laughter subsiding. She then took a deep breath. "I'm sorry about the fight."

Malajia smiled at her. "Me too." She held her arms out. "Now hug me, and no, you don't have a choice."

Chasity shook her head. "Fine," she huffed, allowing Malajia to embrace her.

"Girl, you would not believe who came to visit me," Malajia said, after parting from Chasity.

"Alex?" Chasity guessed.

"Yeah *her*," Malajia confirmed. "But Mark came too...trying to front at first," she mused, smiling. "He finally admitted that he wanted to check on me." Malajia continued to sit there smiling, staring out in front of her.

Chasity looked at Malajia and narrowed her eyes as she pointed to her cheek. "What's that?" she questioned.

Malajia put her hand on her cheek. "What? Is there something on my face?" she panicked, frantically wiping her face with her gloved hand.

"Yeah, a hype ass smile when you brought up Mark," Chasity teased.

Malajia smacked her hand away. "Whatever heffa," she sneered, rising from the bench. "Our table is probably ready now."

Chasity followed her. "Let me find out you like Mark, and shit," she teased.

"Shut up, I will *never* like him that way," Malajia promised. "He's just been…a little less irritating lately."

"Yeah okay," Chasity replied, not believing a word that was coming out of Malajia's mouth.

# Chapter 40

Jason flipped his younger brother Kyle's bike over to examine it. "What did you say happened to it?" he asked, surveying the red and silver mountain bike.

"I was riding the bike down the steps of the museum and the chain popped," Kyle informed, holding a towel to his leg. "Then the breaks gave out...and that's when I fell off."

Jason stared at his little brother as if he had lost his mind. "What did I tell you about doing all that crazy shit?" he scolded. "You're not a damn dare devil."

"Well, I saw some other people doing it and I wanted to try it," Kyle justified, shrugging.

Jason picked up a nearby tool kit from the basement floor as he pointed to Kyle. "You know Mom and Dad are gonna kill you," he warned. "They just got you this bike for Christmas and you already broke it."

"That's why I really need you to try to fix it for me, Jase," Kyle pleaded. "If they find out about this, they'll never buy me anything else."

Jason sighed as he opened the tool kit. "I'll see what I can do," he promised.

Kyle smiled gratefully. Jason laid the bike on its side and began tinkering with it. He stopped when he noticed Kyle standing over his shoulder watching.

"Yeah, I can't do this with you hovering," he said, nudging Kyle away. "Go play your game or something."

"You're the best big brother ever," Kyle beamed, scurrying out of the basement. Jason just shook his head as he went back to tinkering with the bike.

Fifteen minutes had passed before he heard the basement door open, followed by the sound of someone walking down the stairs. "Kyle, if you come back down here while I'm working on this thing, I'll step on it," Jason warned.

"That would be a shame since your mother and I paid so much money for it."

Jason was startled by the sound of his father's voice and it showed on his face as he jumped up and faced him. "Dad, what's up?" he said nervously, trying to kick the toolbox out of his father's sight with his foot.

"What are you doing down here?" Mr. Adams asked skeptical, folding his arms across his chest.

"Um…" Jason hesitated spilling the beans. He had always tried to protect his little brother from getting in trouble. "I'm just checking out Kyle's bike to make sure the store put it together properly." He lied. "Wouldn't want it to break or anything."

Mr. Adams nodded. "Oh okay… That would be a good answer if I didn't already know that Kyle broke his bike and you were down here trying to fix it," he revealed, amusement in his voice.

Jason shook his head. "How did you find out?" he chuckled.

"Kyle had no choice but to tell me what happened when I asked about those scrapes and bruises on his leg," Mr. Adams said, walking over to the overturned bike. "That boy is going to run up more medical bills than *I* did," he joked.

Jason forced a small laugh as he kneeled back down on the floor. Truth was, he didn't mind fixing the bike. Anything that would take his mind off what he was thinking and feeling was welcomed.

Mr. Adams watched as Jason solemnly began rummaging through the toolbox for another item. "Jason, have you spoken to Chasity yet?" he asked.

Jason paused; he remembered that the morning he returned home from the lodge, he was so enraged, his father became concerned. At that point, feeling the need to talk to someone before he exploded, Jason broke down and told his father about the details of the argument between Chasity and himself.

"No, I have not," Jason answered, not hiding the frustration in his voice.

Mr. Adams sighed as he patted Jason on his shoulder. "You may not want to hear this again because I know that I've been saying this since you told me what happened…but you two really need to talk this out."

"Dad," Jason warned.

"All I'm saying is that two weeks is long enough to go without speaking," Mr. Adams argued. "Actually, its *way* too long to go without speaking to someone you're in a relationship with… How are you ever going to get past this if you don't talk and hash things out?"

"Dad, like I told you the *other* times that you said this…I have nothing to say to her so could you just drop it?" Jason sneered.

Shaking his head at his stubborn son, Mr. Adams decided not to press the issue any further. He gave Jason another pat on his shoulder before heading out of the basement, leaving Jason alone with his project and his thoughts.

Mr. Adams settled down on his favorite chair in the living room and prepared for an afternoon with a football game on the big screen TV. With his wife out spending time with her friends, he could enjoy the game in peace. He reached for the remote on the coffee table, but a soft knock at the door made him get up from his seat.

Opening the door, he was surprised to see who was

standing there. "Hi Chasity," he warmly greeted her.

Chasity looked nervous. She'd talked herself into coming over to face Jason, but was having second thoughts once the door opened. "Hi," she returned.

"What brings you by?" Mr. Adams asked, feeling the frigid air.

"Um, I don't know exactly," she answered honestly "...Is Jason here?" she asked after a slight pause.

"Yes, he is."

Chasity fidgeted with her hands. "Um...can you tell him I'm here please?"

Mr. Adams hesitated. He knew that Jason wasn't interested in talking to Chasity, let alone seeing her face to face. "Well... Honestly I'm not sure that's a good idea," he answered sorrowfully. "I don't think he's ready to see you yet."

Chasity's face showed that she just came to a realization. "He told you, didn't he?" she assumed.

Mr. Adams nodded. "Just me, not his mother."

Chasity became horrified. "I'm gonna leave now. Sorry I bothered you," she stammered, before turning to make a quick getaway.

"No Chasity, wait," he called after her, standing outside and shutting the door behind him. "You don't have to leave."

"Yeah, I think I do," she insisted, turning to face him. "I made a mistake by coming."

"No, you didn't," he assured. "He may feel like he doesn't want to resolve things, but he *needs* to. So, this one time, I'm butting in," he smiled as he opened the door and gestured for Chasity to come inside.

After hesitating for a few seconds, she finally walked inside.


Jason was in the process of putting the chain back on the bike when he heard the basement door open again, followed by the sound of footsteps approaching. "Someone is here to see you, Jase," Mr. Adams notified.

"Dad, I'm really not in the mood for any guests right now," Jason said, not looking up. "Can you ask them to come back another time?"

"Um... No, I can't," his father refused, causing Jason to look up at him frowning.

He held the frown on his face as he rose to his feet, coming face to face with Chasity. They stared at each other as Mr. Adams looked back and forth between the two.

"So, I'm gonna take Kyle out for a bite to eat Jase," Mr. Adams informed. "I'll bring you something."

Jason didn't respond and his eyes never left Chasity's as his father hurried out of the basement. "You shouldn't have come here," Jason spat once he heard the door shut.

"Yes, I *should've*," Chasity shot back. "We need to talk."

"I have nothing else to say to you," he insisted, trying to keep his cool. "You need to leave."

"I'm not gonna do that," she persisted.

"Go home Chasity!" he yelled, calm now gone.

"No!" she yelled back. "I'm not leaving until we resolve this,"

He flagged her with his hand as he turned away from her.

"You can't tell me that you're okay with things being this strained between us," she said, taking a step closer.

Jason spun around and held his hands up. "Oh, I'm *perfectly* fine with it," he snarled.

"You're lying and you know it," Chasity sneered, folding her arms.

"You *would* know I was lying, wouldn't you?" Jason hissed. Chasity narrowed her eyes at him. "I guess I should expect that from a liar."

"Look," Chasity began, taking a deep breath. "I know you have a lot of animosity towards me right now, and I don't blame you."

Jason frantically rubbed his face with his hands before

kneeling back in front of the bike and picking up a wrench.

"I know I messed things up with you and I want to fix it... But I *can't* if you won't talk to me... Jason you *have* to talk to me."

Jason held a mask of anger on his face as he began tinkering with the bike again.

The blatant way that he was ignoring Chasity was driving her crazy. "You can't keep ignoring me!" she yelled.

"I can if you get the fuck out my house," Jason snapped, still maneuvering his wrench around the bike.

Chasity could have walked over and tore that bike apart with her bare hands. She was so frustrated with him. She understood that he was upset, but Jason was being just plain nasty when she was really trying. She pondered on whether she should turn and walk out. But instead, she started pacing back and forth, seething. She then walked over to a wall, and leaned against it.

"When did it happen?" Jason asked, stopping what he was doing.

Chasity looked at him. "What?" she asked, unsure if he really was speaking to her.

"When did you lose our baby?"

Chasity took a deep breath. "The day that you got hurt at your game," she revealed. "You were taken to the hospital and I went there to find you and when I couldn't... Nobody would tell me anything and I just...I lost it in the hospital."

Jason shook his head. "So that time you were avoiding me when I first got out of the hospital... It was because you were dealing with that," he concluded, sounding hurt.

"Yes," she answered after a few seconds.

"And all those times *after* that...when you avoided me, or when you had gotten sad out of nowhere...you were dealing with that." He put his hand over his face as he felt his temper rise. "You made me feel like I was *wrong* for saying that I thought something was different about you... Like I was out of line to find it weird that you missed your damn period."

"Jason—"

"You made me feel like I was going crazy," he snapped. "I can't believe you! I can't—we're in a fuckin' relationship! You can't keep shit like that to yourself! I should've *known*, I should've *been* there for you! You took that away from me."

"I *know* that!" she yelled back. "I'm sorry! I can say it over and over again but it won't change anything."

"So, what? Am I supposed to just get over it?!"

"I'm not saying that! I just—" She paused as she put her hands on her head. "What can I do? ...Just *tell* me what I can do to make things right with you," she pleaded.

"Nothing," he bit out. "Just leave."

Chasity sighed as she stared at him. She pondered his words, shaking her head. "Are we over?" she asked, point blank after moments of silence.

Jason avoided looking at her, not responding.

Chasity frowned. "Can you at least *look* at me, please?" She felt her own temper rise when he wouldn't comply. "Jason!" she yelled.

Throwing the wrench across the room, Jason jumped to his feet. "Goddamn it Chasity!" he shouted, "Why the fuck are you still here?!"

"I want you to be honest with me!" she hollered.

"Oh, you're demanding honesty from *me*?" Jason laughed. "I don't owe you shit."

"You owe me *that*," she argued.

Jason put his hands on his head. He was at his breaking point. His emotions were all over the place; this was too much for him to handle right now. Not wanting to risk Chasity seeing him break down, he went to walk out. "I'm done with you," he hissed.

Chasity watched as he tried to make his way pass her. Not wanting to end the conversation, she grabbed his arm and heard herself yell something that she'd heard Brenda yell to her too many times in the past. "Don't walk away from me!"

Jason jerked his arm from her grasp as he turned to face her, bringing him within several inches of her face. "What! What do you want from me?!" he fumed, piercing her with his angry gaze.

She stared at him as she calmed herself down. "I want to know if I'm wasting my time," she revealed after a long pause.

"What are you talking about?" he asked nastily.

She shook her head. "I love you...I really do. And I meant what I said when I told you that I was sorry and that I know I messed up," she said sincerely. "I want more than anything for you to forgive me and for us to move past this... I want to make this right...but, I don't want to waste my time hoping that we can move past this enough to be in a relationship, if that isn't something that you want anymore."

He looked at the floor as he pinched the bridge of his nose with two fingers.

"So, what is it Jason?" she pressed. "Am I wasting my time?"

Jason felt his hands tremble as he struggled to keep his emotions contained. The woman that he loved was standing in front of him, asking him if he wanted to continue a relationship with her. He knew what his heart wanted, but he was still hurt. He felt betrayed. Not knowing what to do, he raised his hand and slammed it against the wall behind her.

Chasity didn't flinch. She knew that no matter how angry Jason was at her, he would never lay a hand on her. She just looked at him, watching as he struggled to keep tears from falling. Feeling the need to comfort him, she slowly reached out to touch his face, causing him to flinch as if she'd burned him. Between Jason's reaction and his silence, Chasity felt that she had her answer. Sadly, she moved around him and headed for the staircase.

Jason turned around and watched as she departed. He knew he didn't want to lose her, no matter how he felt. "Chasity," he called, stopping her in her tracks.

Not turning around, Chasity stood there waiting to see if

he would say something else.

"You're not wasting your time," Jason said after a few seconds. He took a deep breath. "I still love you and I don't want to lose you, but I just...I need some time."

Still not turning around, Chasity felt tears well up in her eyes.

"Can you do that? ...Can you just give me some time?" he asked.

So many questions swirled in Chasity's head. How much time did he need? Would she ever earn back his trust? Would things ever be the same between them? Despite all the questions that she had, she could only respond with one word.

"Okay," Chasity answered, then headed up the stairs and out of the basement, leaving Jason standing there alone.

The cold air that hit Chasity's tear-streaked face as she walked out of the house didn't faze her. She felt like she was having an out of body experience as she made her way to her car. She got in and started it up in record time. She knew that if she stopped moving for even a second, everything that just happened, every word that was just said would all come flooding back to her at once, and she didn't know if she would ever stop crying.

In her haste, she didn't notice that Jason, who was feeling just as tortured, was watching her from the living room window. He'd followed her up the steps and watched her walk out of his home, resisting the urge to call for her to come back. Watching her black car make a U-turn and speed out of the cul-de-sac, he only hoped that the time that he had asked her for would be enough to mend his heart.

*J.B. Vample*

# *College life 302;*

## *Advanced Placement*

Book six

The College life series

**Coming soon!**

Made in the USA
Las Vegas, NV
15 June 2023